To Aunt

Love,

The PATCH
of GREEN

Greg Kaup

GREG KAUP

This is a work of fiction. Any resemblance to actual persons, living or dead, events, or locales is entirely coincidental.

DEDICATION

This book is dedicated to my wife Linda, my sons Dan and Jack, my sister Chris, my brother Jerry, and my parents Mary and Jack. With your love and support throughout my life I've been able to climb mountains and swim oceans. I love and thank you all.

CONTENTS

ACKNOWLEDGEMENTS

I would like to extend a special thanks to my Kickstarter Backers listed below. Without your support I would not have been able to make this dream a reality. Thank you very much.

Andy & Adrienne Torre
Bob Gomez
Carey Ann Lee Bianchi &
Jim Bianchi
Christine Madhani
Claudia Muskat-Weimann
Colleen Reppen Shiel
Connie Martin
Dan Kaup
Dave Lockhart
Debbie Rogers
Deven Madhani
Ed Gilliland
Finnegan Family
Ian & Catrina Moore

Jeremy Kaup
Jim Russell, Patch '67
Jo Ann Begrowicz
John Joyce
Kathleen & Guy Matthews
Lynn D. Ward
Melva Olsen
Mike
Nick & Peggy Ostojic
Rita Moore
Steve Lamont
Tim Kascher & Adriana Valencia-Kascher
Unknown Backer #1
Unknown Backer #2

I would also like to thank Robin Schoettle for creating the interior book illustrations and my wife Linda, for creating and allowing me to use her original artwork for the book's cover.

"So I've started out for God knows where
I guess I'll know when I get there…"

ACT I

1 FIRE, FIRE

.

"Oh, shit!" Those were the first words I ever remember my mother saying.
I awoke to them while lying in my crib. I pulled myself up and looked in the
direction of my bedroom door, which was about one foot ajar. I could
make out a set of shadows that seemed to be dancing like a rabid
marionette on the twelve inches of exposed hallway wall that I could see
from my crib perch.

Later in life, I learned that my father, a chain smoker and alcoholic, had
gone to bed that evening and very nonchalantly told my mother that he
thought the couch was on fire. Entering the living room and seeing, in fact,
the couch on fire, my mother let go her "Oh, shit!" comment that left a
rather indelible impression on my young mind.

At the time, being all of three years old, I didn't comprehend the sound
I heard after the "Oh, shit!" It was a sound I had not heard before. It was
not human, but mechanical, rhythmic, almost soothing. As the mysterious
sound droned on, the shadows that had been doing their odd dance on the
wall seemed to grow larger and larger. Then I heard my mother speaking to
someone in an excited voice, in words I really couldn't understand. She
yelled something out, again just a jumble of words I couldn't make out and
in a tone I don't think I had ever previously heard from her.

I fell back into the warmth and comfort that only a baby's crib can
provide and closed my eyes. As I was just about to fall off to sleep again, a
loud noise shook me back to consciousness. It grew louder and louder like
my mother's vacuum did on cleaning day as it advanced from room to
room growing ever closer to my quiet bedroom. Several minutes passed
when finally the noise, which seemed by now to be howling just outside my
bedroom door, stopped. I pulled myself up again and stood, shaking, at the
edge of my crib. I heard a commotion at the front of our three-bedroom
apartment. It startled me, and I let out a scream for help, feeling that
something was amiss but not knowing what nor why.

My mother entered my room, picked me up, and tried to comfort me as
best as she could. She walked with me to just outside my bedroom door. I
lifted my head from her bosom and peered down the hall to see three

1

firemen surrounding our couch in the living room. One fireman was busy moving the source of the mysterious noise I had heard away from the couch. It was our household fan that, I later learned, my mother tried to employ to "blow out" the couch fire. Instead, of course, it literally fanned the fire, causing it to spread from the couch to the wall of our living room and that compelled my mother to call in the professional fire fighters.

The other two fire fighters were busy dousing the couch with some type of white substance, and when they were done, they put down their canisters and went to our front window. As the couch smoldered and oozed thick, black smoke, they opened our window wide and proceeded back to the smoldering couch, like pallbearers making their way to a resting casket. The third fire fighter joined them as they raised the couch, unceremoniously carried it to the window, and shoved it out onto the waiting street, three floors below.

This was the Baby Boomer world I was born into in 1960. I was a member of the last wave of babies born to couples who had weathered World War II and who would enjoy the great prosperity in the U.S. that followed.

My mother was a good, simple Catholic woman who attended mass each Sunday and who stayed with my father out of a sense of duty. My father, a man whose own mother and father died while he was young, battled alcoholism and a severe nicotine addiction his entire life. Though blessed with a high intelligence, his vices would prevent him from ever "making it" in life. They were both good people in many ways, and their shortcomings really wouldn't come into focus until I was near adulthood.

My brother, Jerry, was older by eleven years, which I later considered evidence that, at one point, my mother did seriously consider leaving my father. My sister, Maureen, was younger than me by three years. Although at times she and I fought like cats and dogs, we later grew quite close, and this bond remained intact throughout our adult lives.

We Garritys were a working-class family living in an apartment in Rogers Park, the northeastern-most neighborhood in the great city of Chicago. We lived primarily among our own kind, so I never really noticed our material shortcomings until high school. There was a lot of hope and optimism as I grew up in the second half of the twentieth century. We were told at an early age that, if we put our minds to it, we could be anything that we wanted to be. Not only did we buy into this notion, but for many of those who were telling us this, the credo rang true.

The 1960s were an exciting time to be growing up. Television was bringing us up close and personal to the tragedies of the Kennedys and King assassinations along with the death and destruction that was Vietnam. However to balance the awful, we also had the wonderful: the Beatles, the moon landing, and Woodstock.

My life, particularly my adolescence and early adulthood, was shaped by Catholicism, my neighborhood, and the people I hung out with, not necessarily in that order.

I had a Catholic mother who made me go to church each Sunday up until I turned eighteen and attend eight years of Catholic grade school and two years of Catholic high school.

Rogers Park was a neighborhood that was eclectic in every way imaginable. Its southern boundary was Devon Avenue, a two-lane street that catered to many small storefronts and bars. Its western boundary was Ridge Avenue, a literal ridge that at one point in history was where Lake Michigan met the land. The boundary to the north was the suburban town of Evanston, Illinois, home of Northwestern University. The boundary to the east was a natural one, Lake Michigan. Sheridan Road, Ridge Avenue's counterpart on the east side of the neighborhood, was the busy, four-lane street that ran north/south through the neighborhood, a block west of the lakefront.

Tucked in the southeast corner of the neighborhood, between the lakefront and Sheridan Road, was Loyola University, a Jesuit school of higher education. The elevated, commuter train line, known as the "L" also ran north/south through the neighborhood, parallel to Sheridan Road.

The city blocks that comprised Rogers Park were bisected by narrow avenues, with names like Ashland, Loyola, North Shore, Albion, and Pratt. Along its tree-lined avenues, a hodge-podge of single-family homes, two-flat, three-flat, and courtyard-sized apartment buildings could be found arranged haphazardly throughout the neighborhood.

The section of Rogers Park I grew up in was referred to as the "Patch." This term was a holdover from when the Parish of St. Ignatius Church, at the beginning of the century, was primarily Irish and referred to as the "Patch of Green." Therefore, if you were a kid from the Parish, you were referred to as a "Patcher."

In the early sixties, Rogers Park was heavily Jewish, but as I witnessed during my time growing up there, the population shifted as Jews migrated to the suburbs during the 1970s and '80s while an influx of Hispanics, blacks, and Indians moved into the neighborhood.

My peers who helped shape my life were many, but none closer to me than Billy Smith and Will Striker. Billy and Will go so far back I don't remember when I first met them. It must have been in first or second grade as it seems as though these two guys had always been a part of my life.

My mother, God bless her, kept a baby book for me that contained a note that Billy wrote to me in second grade. The note read, "Greg tanks fur bragin me too da ofic ha ha youre freind Billy." Good old Billy boy was referring to all of the times the good sisters chose me to escort him down to see our school's principal, Mother Superior.

Exasperated by his in-class behavior, which included sudden outbursts and general acting up, our teacher decided to let Mother Superior have a whack at him, no pun intended. They chose me to be his escort because I was the only kid in class who was big and beefy like Billy and therefore physically could get him to the office if he didn't want to go. There were a couple of times I had to drag him down there, but most times he went willingly.

After handing Billy over to Mother Superior, I would linger just outside her closed door and hear poor Billy get the snot beat out of him by the paddle she had perpetually hanging behind her desk, as a hunter might display a prized rifle above a fireplace mantle. Billy would eventually emerge from her office in tears. I felt bad for him and often tried to console him on our way back to class.

"Billy, if you didn't act up so much in class, the teacher wouldn't send you down here for these beatings."

"I know, Greg, but sometimes I just can't help it, can't keep my mouth shut or my feet still," Billy replied through his tears.

"I know, Billy," I said not really understanding why he couldn't sit still but knowing it would just be a matter of time before I would be escorting him down for another beating at the hands of Mother Superior.

On days he was really upset, I'd throw my arm around his shoulder and tell him, "It's OK, Billy, this won't last forever."

Billy and I developed a special relationship because of these grade-school "death marches," and our special relationship lasted our lifetime together.

Will Striker, on the other hand, didn't need any help from little old me. Will was born a golden boy with a double dose of good looks who could do no wrong and who was perpetually popular with the girls. Although he was one of my best friends, I could never quite comprehend how easy everything was for Will and how much good luck seemed to come his way.

I spent my youth growing up with these two guys and continued to have them as good friends into adulthood, through the good, the bad, and the insane times. this tender age.

2 TOM SAWYER N HUCK FINN

Much of our early, shared journey through life revolved around the schoolyard of St. Ignatius grade school, the school we attended. During the school year, the schoolyard was where we had our recess and would stay briefly after school to talk about how mean the nuns were or to flirt with the cute Catholic girls we went to school with who were dressed in their plaid, Catholic-girl skirts and virgin-white blouses. As we grew older, the schoolyard became our meeting place where we either began or spent our nights of debauchery, but more about that later.

Our elementary school careers were fairly subdued, tempered by the good Sisters of the BVM, which stood for the religious order of the Blessed Virgin Mary but interpreted by us to mean Black Veiled Monsters. The nuns, dressed in starched black habits and flowing black robes, kept us in line for the most part. The guiding hands of the nuns coupled with our youthful interests in sports, especially basketball, kept us on the straight and narrow, up till about the summer between our seventh and eighth grade years, when things started to get a little more interesting.

Late that summer, Billy, Will, and I met on the black top of the schoolyard around ten in the morning and decided to hike the three odd blocks to Albion Beach. Leaving the schoolyard, we started out heading east and made our way around our school. We then made a left turn and walked a block to Albion Avenue. Once we reached Albion, we turned right, toward the lake, making our way under the viaduct, which supported the L trains that ran north from Howard Street to the south side of Chicago. As we walked down the tree-lined street, we passed an assortment of apartment buildings, mostly three flats and six flats on the block that led to Sheridan Road. Once safely across the four-lane road, we walked one more long block to the lake.

Once at the beach, we sat on steel benches, which had been painted bright green by the Chicago Park District. The benches, which faced the beach, were located on a walkway that ran parallel with the lake front. We stared out at the calm blue waters of Lake Michigan and tossed around ideas on what we could do on this boring, hot, summer day. A while had passed when we spotted a sailboat out on the lake, a good mile or so off shore, just sailing along majestically on the tranquil blue waters.

I mentioned to nobody in particular how much fun it would be to be in a boat, on the lake, on a beautiful day like today. My buddies agreed, and then Will made the announcement of the summer.

"Boys, we are going to be in a boat, on the lake, on a beautiful day like today!"

Billy and I answered Will's announcement with bewildered looks on our faces.

"How we gonna get a fuckin' boat!?" Billy demanded.

"We gonna build one or steal one?" I added as I shot Will a shit-eating grin.

"No, Double G, my dad has a fishing boat moored down at Belmont Harbor. All we have to do is to get down to the harbor, make our way to the boat, and the lake is ours for the taking. Are you guys in?" Will asked as he stood up from the metal bench and extended his right, tanned arm toward Billy and me.

"Fuck yeah!" Billy shouted as he jumped up, reached out his right arm, and placed his palm on top of Will's.

"Me too, captain," I said as I stood up, reached out, and placed my right palm on top of the back of Billy's hand.

"LET"S DO IT!" Will shouted, and off we went.

We began our walk up Albion Avenue heading west toward the Loyola elevated train station, past the upscale, single-family homes, which lined the street, excitedly chirping like a flock of birds on the first day of spring. We turned left when we got to Sheridan Road and made our way south toward the L station passing by the storefronts of Albion Liquors, My Pi Pizza, Bruno's Lounge, Round Records, Papa Dees and Cindy Sues. We entered the v-shaped elevated train station on the Sheridan Road side and made our way out the entrance on the Loyola Avenue side. We never paid to ride the elevated trains, opting to instead "hop" the L. We accomplished this by walking about two-hundred feet down Loyola Avenue, toward the schoolyard, which was located just two blocks away.

When we reached our train-hopping spot, we looked up and down the street to make sure the coast was clear. When it was, we climbed the six-foot-high chain link fence and came down on the other side. Once on the ground, we walked forward about twenty feet and began to climb a series of cement blocks that jutted out from the main support walls of the train tracks above, an almost-natural staircase to the two-story station we were about to invade.

The tricky and most dangerous part of our illegal maneuver was the last one, which required us to wiggle our youthful bodies between the last cement block that we had climbed onto and the wooden trusses that made up the bottom support beams of the train station platform. Once we wiggled ourselves through this narrow passage, we were literally lying on the train tracks, carefully avoiding any contact with the electrified third rail that powered the trains and which was about four feet beyond where we now lay. One accidental touch of the third rail and you would be electrified to a crispy remnant of your former self.

Once we had reached this position, we carefully got up and ran quickly down the tracks to the far end of the station were we climbed up a small ladder to reach the station's platform. The key to success when hopping the L was to listen very carefully for an approaching train. If you didn't hear any sound, you would then reach out your hand from underneath the platform and touch the rail nearest you, feeling for any rumbling from a train that might be too distant to be heard but may, in fact, be approaching quickly. This was a technique Billy taught me the first time I hopped the L with him. By then, Billy had done it many times already, having been shown the ropes by his older brother Sam. Some of the older guys in the neighborhood used the L to go to high school and hopped it every morning so they could pocket their train fare and spend it on beer during the weekend.

We each took our turn scrambling up the cement, wiggling onto the tracks, and then scrambling onto the station platform. Several minutes passed before a train came and stopped, ready to take us south toward Belmont Harbor and Mr. Striker's boat. The train car's doors slid open, inviting us in, and we promptly entered and sat down on the brown, plastic seats and began gazing out the windows.

The elevated train slowly pulled away from the station and creaked along at a two-story vantage point through the neighborhoods of the far north side of Chicago. Views of alley ways, rooftops, apartment buildings, and busy intersections made up a montage of sights for our inquisitive young eyes. Whenever I rode the L, I marveled at how close the train cars got to the sides of some of the buildings. At times it appeared that only a couple of inches separated the train from the brick and mortar. Often when the steel wheels of the L cars grinded and whined against the steel rails they rode on, I imagined that the inevitable finally had happened, a train car had finally tilted too far and was scraping up against one of the too-close buildings. As our train slowed down to stop at the Belmont Station, we each shot a smile to one another that exclaimed, "We're here!"

As the doors of the train car slid open, we let out a collective cheer and skipped out into the heat of the day and made our way down the stairs to the busy street below. We had a mile walk ahead of us to the lake, but it didn't matter as our anticipation of the fun ahead was enough to carry us there. As we walked, we discussed where we wanted to cruise to. Navy pier, back to our neighborhood, and the state of Michigan were some of the places that were bandied about.

Once we got to the harbor, we quietly made our way to the docks. The docks were lined with every kind of boat imaginable, sleek speed boats, cabin cruisers, sailboats, and even a couple of yachts.

"My dad's boat is at the very end of this dock," Will told Billy and me as we marveled at the beauty of the harbor.

Blue-green water, white hulled boats, and a powder-blue sky spackled with puffy, white clouds made for a smorgasbord for our young eyes. Seagulls shrieking in the distance completed the assault on our senses. As we arrived at the end of the dock, Will made his proud announcement, "Here she is!"

Compared to the sleek, expensive watercrafts that surrounded her, "she" wasn't much. Basically a fifteen-foot, aluminum, V-hulled row boat with a gas motor mounted on her bow. But we were thrilled none the less!

We scrambled onto the boat, and Will untied her moorings. He pushed her away from the dock, and we began to drift toward the open water of the harbor. We made no attempt at a pre-cruise equipment check, had no idea where we were heading, and had no way of contacting anyone should we get our young asses into serious trouble. Combined, we were looking at a very serious recipe for disaster, one that never entered our thirteen-year-old minds. Will primed the engine and then after three or four exhausting tugs on its pull cord, got it to cough black smoke, turn over, and then finally start.

"YEAH!" we all cheered as we got under power and headed for the mouth of the harbor, toward the treacherous open waters of Lake Michigan. Billy sat at the front of the boat, I was in the middle, and Will was in the rear, steering us ahead, playing skipper. We were in our glory, cruising out into the great unknown. Bright, angelic sunshine, cool blue waters and all framed by the skyscraper horizon that is the city of Chicago skyline.

We decided to head north and cruise along the shoreline toward our home turf of Rogers Park. We wondered what our neighborhood looked like from a boat two football fields off shore. We followed the shoreline for miles looking for familiar landmarks along the way. When we finally saw the Madonna Della Strada Chapel at Loyola University, the one that faces the lake, we knew we had reached home.

The chapel, built many years ago, faced the lake allegedly because at the time it was built, the plan was to have Lake Shore Drive extend all the way from downtown Chicago to the exclusive north shore suburbs where the high rollers of business and industry lived. However, it was a plan that never came to fruition, so instead the chapel peered out on an empty stretch of lakefront, appearing quite alone in its solitude.

We continued on and finally reached Albion Beach, where in essence our journey had begun. We dropped the small, metal anchor and decided to cool ourselves off by diving into the refreshing, spelled C-O-L-D, waters of Lake Michigan. We took our shoes, socks, and shirts off and one by one jumped overboard. Having cruised the lakefront in the late-summer heat, we had become very hot so the cold lake water was a much-appreciated blessing. After a while, one by one we clamored back on board and sat in the boat drying off under the gorgeous sunshine, talking about the future.

"I want to move away and be either a famous actor or a famous basketball player and have lots of money to buy things," Will announced.

No surprise there. He was the best basketball player in school and as a fifth grader had been recruited by high schools to play basketball for them. As if his athleticism wasn't enough, Will was also a natural actor who had starred in the past two year's spring play productions at our school. Will was movie-star thin with dirty-blond hair and bright hazel eyes. He skin tone, inherited from his mother, looked perpetually tanned even in the dead of the worst Midwestern winter. He was an all-American kid, a natural, and as everyone in the neighborhood agreed, his future was as bright as the sun itself.

Why hadn't I been born into a family that owned an apartment building down by the lake, or had a father who pushed me along, encouraging me to be a star athlete? Why had I been born so poor and so average looking, I often wondered.

"I'm gonna be a fuckin' fireman," Billy announced proudly, snapping me out of my depressing thoughts. "I'm gonna follow in my Daddy's footsteps."

I could easily picture big Billy being a fireman someday, pulling people out of burning buildings, playing the hero. Billy's dad had been tragically killed in the line of duty, serving as a fireman for the city of Chicago. I had heard rumors around the schoolyard that there was always "someone" looking out for Billy since his father had died on the job. So that path to becoming a fireman would probably be there when Billy decided to take it.

"What about you, Double G?" Billy asked as our eyes met.

"I want to be a sailor," I blurted out, in truth not really knowing what I wanted. I dreamed of someday going to Notre Dame and playing football but not much past that. The football dream seemed reasonable since I was a big-boned, husky kid who was already six feet tall and two-hundred pounds going into eighth grade.

"A sailor!?" Will questioned.

"Yeah, what better life than to live on the water like we are today."

"Where the fuck you gonna live in the winter?" Billy asked.

"Somewhere warm, baby!" I shot back with a grin from ear to ear.

Will announced it was time to get on our way so we fired up the engine again and headed for the Pratt Avenue pier, a mile further down the shoreline. After buzzing the fishermen at the tip of the pier, we made a sweeping U-turn, which positioned us several miles from shore. We then began our return journey to Belmont Harbor. None of us had a watch, but our best guesstimate placed the time at about four o'clock and our return to Belmont at around seven or eight.

As we made our way up the shoreline, I felt a queasiness in my stomach, not from sea sickness but from regret. Yes, we had a lot of fun out on the lake, but I knew that at this very moment my mother was at home worrying about me and wondering why I hadn't come home for dinner or at least called. If I got home at nine or ten she'd be furious. I knew I would get punished and had to admit to myself that I deserved it. Well, I guess that's the price I'd have to pay I thought, as I sighed deeply to myself.

The trip back to the harbor seemed to be taking longer than the trip out had taken. As the sun was beginning to set, we could see a dark, almost black cloud front approaching the lake from the west, the direction that usually brings storms to Chicago. I tried to reassure myself, the best I could, that we should be coming up to Belmont Harbor very shortly as I didn't even want to consider being out on the lake when it grew dark and stormy.

Then, just as we made out the harbor's opening, it happened. Our motor shut down. Will immediately tried to start it again, priming and pulling but nothing happened. Then he unscrewed the gas cap and trying as best he could in the increasing darkness, peered into the gas compartment.

"Well, guys, as best as I can tell, we're out of gas," Will announced.

"Oh, fuck!" was Billy's response.

"What are we gonna do now?" I asked.

"Since there's not a lot of boat traffic and it's getting dark, the chance of getting towed in is pretty slim," Will confessed. "Since we're not too far from the harbor, our best bet is to get into the water and try to swim the boat in."

When the last words left Will's mouth, I felt a lump in my throat. I wasn't a great swimmer and the thought of getting in the water, in the dark, scared the hell out of me. As if on cue, we heard a huge thunderclap in the distance and the wind, which hadn't been apparent all afternoon, suddenly reared its ugly head. Not only was it getting dark, but we were adrift in a small boat on a very dangerous body of water with a fast-moving storm approaching. Will's voice shook me out of my fearful thoughts.

"We're close to the harbor. If we start now, it should take us less than an hour," he stated matter-of-factly.

My mother's going to kill me, I thought.

"We'll take turns. Billy, you and I will get in the water and pull first. Then Greg will get in, and you can take a break. Then you can relieve me and so on until we make it to the harbor."

Billy and Will took off their shirts, shoes, and socks again and jumped into the water and swam to the front of the boat. I threw them the towline, and they began to swim toward the harbor. I looked toward shore and noticed, for the first time, the twinkle of lights in the buildings and skyscrapers as well as the headlights of the constant traffic on Lake Shore Drive.

Funny, I thought, probably less than a mile from civilization yet still in a world of trouble. I picked out a building on shore that we were parallel with so I could track the progress of my two friends. After a while of keeping my eyes on my point of reference, it seemed we hadn't moved toward the harbor very much, if at all. A little while longer the splashing stopped, and I heard Will make the announcement I didn't want to hear.

"Greg, your turn. Billy, take a break."

I helped Billy back onto the boat, asked him how the water was, half knowing what his answer would be.

"COLD, mother fucker!" Billy shouted.

I slowly took off my shirt, shoes, and socks as the first raindrops of the approaching storm began to fall. I jumped over the side of the boat and hit the cold, black water hard. I came back to the surface and immediately my breathing began to accelerate. A wave of panic gripped me as I couldn't see the boat and was completely disorientated.

When I heard Billy's voice asking me how the water was, I realized that I was facing in the opposite direction of the boat. I turned myself around, made out the silhouette of the boat, and swam toward it. I joined Will at the front of the boat and he handed me some of the rope and we began to swim together.

We kept rotating swimmers, over and over again. Each time I got back in the boat I was consumed by two things, exhaustion from swimming and guilt as my mind contemplated my poor mother and all of the worry that she must be enduring at home.

The rain began to come down in sheets and the wind began to howl, pushing us away from the safety of the harbor and further out toward the middle of the lake. The wave chop began to get so rough we decided the safest thing for us to do was to hunker down in the belly of the boat and ride the storm out. Back in the boat, we gathered together in the V of the hull as we bounced from wave to wave like a small cork bobbing on the ocean. Cold rain pelted our shivering bodies as lightning lit up the sky above us. Only hours ago, I was skipping down Belmont Avenue, wrapped in my youthful anticipation of spending an afternoon on the lake, on a boat. Now I was literally hanging on for my dear life.

Suddenly I felt a huge urge to vomit, probably from all of the up and down motion from the chop of the waves, I thought. As I felt my face go flush with heat, I decided better to heave my guts out over the side of the boat than on my two friends beside me. Just as I was lifting myself up to the top edge of the boat's sidewall, a huge wave crashed over the boat, catching me from behind.

The wave's power picked me up and catapulted me up and over the boat's side. I ended up out of the boat and below the water. I'm not sure if I had puked in mid-air or below the surface but the nauseous feeling was gone now, replaced by a feeling of sheer panic.

I broke the water's surface and couldn't see a thing. I heard Will and Billy yelling out my name but could not make out the boat.

"WE GOTTA SAVE EM!" Billy yelled to Will.

"YOU'RE A BETTER SWIMMER THAN ME. I'LL ANCHOR THE LINE. YOU GO AFTER HIM," Will shouted back.

Quickly tying a piece of extra rope around his waist, Billy found Will's hand in the darkness and handed him the other end.

"WHEN I YANK ON IT, PULL AS HARD AS YOU CAN. AND SIT LOW IN THE BOAT. WE CAN'T HAVE YOU FALL IN, TOO!" Billy shouted to Will above the storm's din.

Billy jumped into the water toward the general direction of where I had been swept overboard. I was trying to keep afloat as best I could, but between the huge waves and the incessant rain I thought for the very first time there was a distinct possibility I would never see my mother again. I had taken in a couple of mouthfuls of lake water and was beginning to choke. I was going to break my mother's heart just because I wanted to go for a ride on a boat. Then, out of nowhere, I felt something touch my chest.

"IT'S ME, GREG!" I heard Billy scream as he slid his arm around me. "JUST RELAX. WILL'S GONNA HELP DRAG US TO THE BOAT."

I couldn't answer as I was choking so badly. Specks of white light now starting to float about in my field of vision. I'm about to pass out, I thought. My mother!

Back on the boat, lying in the V of the hull, Will felt a sharp tug on the rope. This prompted him to sit up and position his two feet on the top edge of the boat's side in the direction from which the tug came. Will began to pull the rope with all his strength as Billy felt the line go taut.

"COME ON, WILL!" Billy shouted at the top of his lungs into the teeth of the dark, treacherous storm.

A burst of lightening allowed Billy to see an outline of the boat, only a few feet away now. Moments later, between his two feet, Will made out a hand grabbing the side of the boat. Will moved carefully toward the side of the boat, the wind, waves, and rain swirling all around him. Now peering over the side, Will could make out the outlines of two bobbing heads in the water.

"REACH OVER AND TRY TO PULL GREG UP," Billy shouted.

Billy then dove under the water and tried to push my butt up, out of the water. I had stopped choking by now but was barely treading water. As I felt Will's arm touch me, I instinctively grabbed it and tried to climb up, very weak from my adventure in the water. Now with me clinging to Will's arm, I felt Will's other hand grab my shorts at the waist. With one giant tug, Will yanked me back into the boat. I landed with a loud thud on the bottom of the boat and immediately passed out as Billy clamored back aboard the boat with Will's help. Once back on board, they both collapsed onto the hull of the boat as the thunder roared like a lion, the lightning lit up the pitch-black sky, and the wind and rain showed us no mercy.

* * * *

My mother had waited until seven o'clock that evening before she looked up Will's home number and gave his parents a call.

"Mr. Striker, this is Mary Garrity. I was wondering if my son Greg is there?"

"No, he isn't," Mr. Striker replied. "We're wondering where Will is as well. We haven't seen him since this morning."

"Oh, I see."

"Your son didn't have any crazy ideas about running away from home, did he?" Mr. Striker asked rudely.

"Oh no, Greg would never do that. He's a happy boy."

"Well, I just hope your 'happy' boy didn't lead my Willy astray. My boy's got quite a bright future, you know," Mr. Striker exclaimed.

"Well, if you see or hear from Greg, will you please call me?" my mother asked.

"Of course I will, but I imagine they'll show up any time now. Goodbye."

Not much comfort for a mother worried sick about her boy. After speaking with Mr. Striker, my mother waited until eleven o'clock, the official curfew for adolescents in Chicago, before she called the police. The police told my mother that someone was classified as a missing person only after they had not been seen or heard from in twenty-four hours, so there wasn't much they could do at that point. However, sensing the worry in my Irish mother's voice, the cop told her to come by the Twenty-Fourth District tomorrow morning so she could fill out a missing persons report. Extremely worried and frustrated, my mother hung up the phone, destined to spend a sleepless night listening to the intense storm roll through Chicago as she wondered where the hell her son was and prayed to God for his safe return.

At six a.m. the next morning, my mother walked the three blocks up to the Twenty-Fourth District police station in Rogers Park. Once there, she filed a missing persons report. A little later that morning, Will's dad also called the police. Since Mr. Striker was a big shot in the neighborhood, the police sent a squad over to the Strikers' apartment building so they could file a missing persons report as well.

One of the questions the police asked involved how many vehicles the family owned and if they were all accounted for. When Mr. Striker

14

mentioned he had a small fishing boat docked at Belmont Harbor, the officer asked him if Will knew where it was.

"Of course he does."

"Alright," the officer responded, "we'll have someone from that district go take a look to make sure it's still there."

The police sent a squad down to Belmont Harbor to verify if the boat was still there, and to Mr. Striker's dismay, found out that it was missing. This prompted the Coast Guard to launch a search and rescue mission along Chicago's lakefront. Meanwhile, one of the Chicago newspapers caught wind that there were three teenagers from the north side of Chicago possibly missing on the lake so the newspaper people asked their police contacts to keep them posted.

*　*　*　*

I think it was the seagulls I heard before the hum of the boat's engine. The shrill calls from the gulls had shaken me out of my dead man's slumber. I was the first one awake, and as I rose up out of the four or five inches of cold lake water that now rested on the bottom of our boat, I shivered uncontrollably as I squinted in the early-morning sun to see where we were. What I saw was a bright, white Coast Guard ship about a hundred yards away from us.

"AHOY THERE!" a loud voice boomed from the ship's bullhorn, waking my two sleeping companions. Within minutes, the ship was alongside us and the sailors were pulling us up and onto their ship. We were led to the ship's bridge and once there were introduced to the captain.

Dressed in a starched white uniform with various pins on his chest, the captain was probably about sixty years old with a finely cropped beard and an air of authority about him.

"How was that storm last night, boys?" the captain asked.

"Rough!" I blurted, still groggy from the night before.

"Understandable," the captain replied. "Let's get you three mates below deck, into some dry clothes, and find you something to eat and drink. How's that sound?"

"Fu...ah, awesome!" Billy blurted.

A sailor led us below deck and into a small utility room. He gave each of us a pair of overalls to change into. Once we changed, he led us to the ship's galley where we were given some water and bologna sandwiches.

"Hey, guys," I said between bites of my sandwich. "Thanks for saving my ass last night. I owe both of you guys big time."

"Hey, you would of done the same for us right?" Will asked.

"Of course, but I mean it," I replied.

Then, staring at both Will and Billy, I said the most serious thing I had ever said to them.

15

"I think I would have drowned last night if it wasn't for you guys. So I promise, one day, somehow, I will repay you both for saving my life, if it's the last thing I do."

"Well, fuck, it better not be the last thing ya gonna do," Billy said. "I don't wanna wait that fuckin' long."

We giggled at Billy's comment, extremely relieved to be out of harm's way and making our way to dry land. I realized now how foolish our little trip had been and how lucky we were to be alive. Will and I admitted our parents were going to kill us while Billy said he wasn't sure how his mom was going to react. What he meant was it all depended if his mom was drunk or sober when he faced her for the first time after our little adventure. Drunk, she most likely was going to beat the hell out of him, sober she was most likely going to just mumble something about being more careful next time.

The Coast Guard boat we were on eventually docked at Belmont Harbor, and we were escorted off the boat to an awaiting police car. Once in the squad car, we were driven to the local district house where we were placed in a room and told our parents were going to be called to come pick us up. A little bit later a rather portly sergeant with a kindly red face came in and told us he needed to get some info to close out the missing persons reports.

"So, boys, why were you guys in Mr. Striker's boat?" he started.

To my surprise, without hesitation, Will said, "Well, sir, we've been reading *The Adventures of Tom Sawyer* and decided that we wanted to be like Tom Sawyer and Huck Finn sir, you know, go exploring on the lake."

"So you guys were inspired by a book to take the boat out onto the lake?" the sergeant asked.

"Well, uh yeah, but not much past the mouth of the harbor sir," Will shot back.

Then, as he stared down the three of us the sergeant asked, "This is your story?"

"Yes, sir," we said as a team.

Why not, I thought to myself. Hell, if a kid can't be inspired by one of the greatest books of all time to go out and seek his own adventure, then what can a kid do. Besides, this story was better and might go down a lot easier with our parents than the truth, which was that we were three young, inconsiderate kids who did not even attempt to contemplate the consequences of our actions or the stress it would put our parents through. No thanks, the bullshit story about being inspired by Tom and Huck worked fine for me.

"You kids are lucky nothing bad happened out there on the lake. It can be very dangerous, ya know. OK, that's all I have. Sit tight. Your parents should be here shortly."

As the sergeant rose and left the room, we shot each other a sheepish grin as we waited in silence for our parents. A little while later, my mom and Mr. Striker arrived. Billy's mom was not with them as she had asked Mr. Striker to pick up Billy. My mom began crying when she first saw me and gave me a big, long hug. She then told me how worried she had been and how much she had prayed for my safe return. Looking up toward heaven, my mother exclaimed, "Thank you, Lord, for answering my prayers!"

Once we all had gotten into Mr. Striker's car, he began to give us all a lecture about how foolish we had been and how dangerous Lake Michigan can be for even experienced sailors.

"I don't know about Greg and Billy, but Will you should definitely have more sense than to do something like that."

"Yes, sir."

"And in the future if these guys are pressuring you to do something dumb, just walk away and come home."

"Yes, sir," Will replied again as he quickly glanced at Billy and me.

Mr. Striker drove to Billy's apartment to drop him off first, but when we arrived at Billy's apartment he discovered that Billy's mom wasn't at home. Mr. Striker then decided to drive over to my apartment, and drop my mother and me off and bring Billy back to the Strikers' apartment.

Once at home, I spent the rest of the day with my family, happy to be alive but also knowing in my heart that I had a huge debt to repay my two best friends.

The next morning came, and when I got to our breakfast table my mother pushed the front page of the *Chicago Tribune* newspaper towards me.

"LOOK AT THIS!" she said in a tone I couldn't immediately recognize. I looked down and saw Will sprawled out on his bed looking rather out of it while Billy sat on the edge of it with a copy of *The Adventures of Tom Sawyer* in one hand and a lit cigarette lighter in the other. The headline read "Chicago Boys, Modern Day Tom Sawyer and Huck Finn."

'It's not bad enough that you boys worried your parents half to death, but now the papers have to make you celebrities, too?!" my mother exclaimed.

According to the newspaper account, the boys had read the Mark Twain book recently and had been inspired to be like Tom and Huck and go for an adventure on the waters of Lake Michigan. However, the newspaper noted, their adventure had been cut short by the fact that they had run out of gas and had run into a major storm on the lake. What bullshit, I thought.

"You're right, mom," I said only half agreeing with her as I was very jealous that I wasn't in the picture as well.

Maybe Billy and Will weren't really celebrities, I thought, but they were definitely heroes in my book. Two heroes who had saved my life and who I was destined to repay one day in ways I couldn't even begin to imagine at this tender age.

3 THE CHICKEN GAME

Billy and Will became instant celebrities around the schoolyard. When the school year began in September, the Tom Sawyer, Huck Finn article was all everyone talked about. I cringed every time I heard a mention of it and reminded anyone who would listen that I had been part of the adventure as well.

Fall turned to winter and our eighth grade year hummed along. I had begun to notice the opposite sex more, and it seemed the shorter a classmate's skirt was, the more I noticed. Will, on the other hand, had been flirting with girls for years or, should I say, they had been flirting with him. After all, he was a good-looking kid with a great personality. Billy, on the other hand, would just as soon play basketball by himself as have an encounter with a member of the opposite sex.

I had an embarrassing moment along these lines one afternoon in Mr. Snyder's social studies class. It was my favorite class because we sat at tables and I happened to sit next to Shannon O'Reilly, the "fastest" girl in the whole eighth grade. Where most of us eighth graders were just daydreaming about touching a member of the opposite sex, Shannon, it was rumored, had already hurdled that fence and was moving right along the human highway of sexuality.

One afternoon as we sat at our tables waiting for Mr. Snyder to begin class, Shannon turned to me and asked, in a hushed tone, if I wanted to play a game.

"What game?" I asked naively.

"Well," she began, leaning in toward me, "it's a game called chicken."

"Chicken?"

"Yea, you see I put my hand on your knee under the table and you put your hand on my knee, see."

And with that I felt Shannon's small hand come to rest on my knee. My mind began to race as I began to feel strange sensations from the lower half of my body.

"Now put your hand on my knee."

"OK," I meekly replied as I reached under the table and placed my hand on her bare kneecap, which was just below her plaid, schoolgirl skirt.

"Now to play the game we take turns sloooowly sliding our hand up the other person's leg, a little bit at a time. The game ends when someone takes their hand off. That person is the chicken. Got it?" she asked.

"Yep," I replied as I wondered to myself what was more amazing, that Shannon, with her developing body and fire-engine-red hair wanted to play the "chicken game" with me or that it was all happening in Mr. Snyder's social studies class.

"Today we're going to begin with a geography game. Each table will be a team, and I will ask individuals from each team to come up one at a time and identify, on a map, the city I have given them," Mr. Snyder announced.

As Mr. Snyder droned on Shannon began our game by sliding her hand ever so slightly up my leg. Shannon glanced my way, smiled, and nodded her head in a yes motion, indicating it was now my turn. I moved my hand up her leg a little bit and could feel the edge of her skirt against my pinky.

Shannon moved her hand up further this time, and I felt a twitch in my groin as I began to become aroused. As I slid my hand up her leg I could feel that my hand was sliding up, under her skirt. Mr. Snyder rambled on, and for all I cared he could have been announcing that Jesus Christ was marching through our classroom door at that very moment and I wouldn't have noticed or cared at all as I was playing the chicken game! All I could think of were two questions: how far was she going to go and how far was she going to let me go?

Shannon slid her hand up my thigh a little further and was now just a couple of inches away from my crotch, which now featured a full-fledged boner. Shannon and I made eye contact, and I wondered if she knew I had a boner and if she was planning on touching it. Holy shit! As I took my turn sliding my hand, which was now fully under her skirt, up her smooth, naked thigh, I was shaken out of my "chicken game" stupor by the sound of Mr. Snyder calling my name.

"MR. GARRITY, ARE YOU DEAF?" he asked.

I felt Shannon's hand suddenly retreat from my thigh as I looked up at Mr. Snyder with a dumb gaze.

"No, no sir," was all I could muster as I pulled my hand off of Shannon's thigh.

"Then let's go, Caracas, Venezuela. Mr. Garrity, come up to the board and show everyone where it is on the map."

Caracas my ass, I thought to myself. In my aroused state I'd probably tip over the table if I tried to stand up. As I shot Shannon a glance I saw that she was beginning to giggle. She obviously knew I had a boner.

"Mr. Snyder, I'm, ah, not feeling so good. I'd like to pass," I said.

"Fine, Garrity, see me after class then," he shot back.

Hopefully by the end of class I'd be back to normal, and I didn't give much thought to what Mr. Snyder might do to me then. All I could think about for the remainder of class was the two or three minutes of our "chicken game" and the wonderful sensations Shannon's hand on my thigh had given me and how smooth her thigh had been. I also wondered how good it would have felt if she had slid her hand all the way up and what I would have felt if she had let me reach her crotch.

Class finally ended, and I stayed to talk with Mr. Snyder.

"You know, Mr. Garrity, the next time I catch you daydreaming in class I'm going to send you down to see Mother Superior."

Daydreaming I thought to myself, little did he know!

"I'm sorry, Mr. Snyder. I'll try to do better."

"Alright then. Get to your next class."

"Yes, sir."

That evening as I lay in bed, I replayed in my mind our game of chicken. I dreamed of Shannon's hand reaching my crotch, and as I did, I let my own hand do what I dreamed her hand would have done.

4 WINTER FUN

Fall ended and another harsh, Chicago winter arrived, which meant we could now engage in a couple of our favorite activities of the season, namely pelting and skitching.

Pelting involved climbing up to a rooftop of an apartment building, making snowballs, and throwing them off the roof at cars that drove by. When we began our pelting careers as seventh graders, we would get on the roof of the one-story-high Busy Beaver nursery school, which was directly across the street from the schoolyard.

Our pelting efforts were met with different reactions from various drivers. Some, even though their car had just been hit by numerous snowballs, would just keep on driving. Others would screech to a halt, jump out and look up at the roof, and scream obscenities at us. Usually we ducked and tried not to give away our position on the roof, but sometimes we just stood there on the roof and flipped the bird to the irate driver or even better, pelted him with more snowballs. On several occasions, the offended motorist came looking for us by driving around the block and coming down the alley that ran behind the Busy Beaver building. At these times, we would either just lie low on the roof or try to scramble down as fast as possible to escape.

One wintry Saturday afternoon, Billy, Will, and I were walking around the neighborhood when we decided to walk by the schoolyard. There were a couple of older guys hanging out on Loyola Avenue right in front of the schoolyard, and they called out to us asking if we felt like pelting some cars. We walked over to them and asked them if they meant climbing up on the Busy Beaver's roof.

"BUSY BEAVER!?" shouted Donny Daniels, a tall lanky high school junior who was a regular around the schoolyard. "That's kid stuff, my boys. It's time to move up to some serious pelting."

"You pussies up fer that or what?" chimed in Doug Eller, another schoolyard regular. Had we known then that Donny and Doug were referred to as the "nut brothers" around the schoolyard, we might have thought twice about going pelting with them, but since we considered ourselves pelting veterans we were ready to take on the challenge.

"Yeah, let's go," we chorused.

Donny and Doug led us off of Loyola Avenue and into the St. Ignatius schoolyard. On the west end of the schoolyard was the back of the grey, St. Ignatius Church building. The church's bell tower stood sentry over the schoolyard, silently observing all of the shenanigans that took place there.

On the east side of the schoolyard was the red, brick grade-school building, with entrances to the gym, auditorium, and school itself. Donny and Doug led us through the schoolyard and into the narrow gangway that ran between the church and school on the schoolyard's north end and that led to the alley located behind them. Once in the alley, they stopped us in our tracks and told us the plan.

"OK, we're going to walk down the alley and look at the back porches of the three-story apartment buildings and find one where we can easily access the roof," Donny explained.

Now a snowball thrown from a three-story roof has a lot more speed behind it at impact and can do a lot more damage than a snowball thrown from a one-story roof. I wasn't sure if Donny and Doug wanted to show us dumb eighth graders that fact or were just out to raise some hell with us.

We followed Donny and Doug in single-line formation until they found a building they liked and motioned for us to follow them into the backyard. We slowly climbed up the wooden, grey back staircase of the building and finally reached the third-floor landing. Carefully climbing the rickety, metal ladder attached to the red brick back wall of the building, Doug pushed the cover off of the hatch that led to the roof. One at a time, we made our way up to the roof via the rickety ladder. Once on the roof, we realized two things: We had plenty of snow for making snowballs, and we were pretty high up.

This particular building overlooked Glenwood Avenue, which was a very narrow, fairly busy, two-way street. The fact that St. Ignatius Church was only about three or four buildings to the south of where we stood did not make us think twice about what we were about to do.

We each bent down and grabbed handfuls of snow and formed them into snowballs, piling them near the edge of the building for easy retrieval. Once we had a significant arsenal of packed snow, we positioned ourselves near the edge of the front of the building. As a car drove down Glenwood Avenue, we all took aim, and as it passed the building we all threw our snowballs. The first volley missed the moving car but did hit a couple of parked cars. The sound the snowballs made when they hit the parked cars reminded me of the crack you hear when a baseball meets a bat.

"YOU GUY'S AIM IS TERRIBLE!" Donny shouted.

"HEY, YOU GUYS MISSED, TOO!" Will shouted back.

Another car came down Glenwood, and another volley was launched. We crouched down to hide our positions as two snowballs hit their target and the car came to a screeching halt. There was anxious laughter and giggling from the roof.

"Holy shit! Did you hear it when they hit the car!?" Donny asked as he stared at us eighth graders with his red face, wide eyes, and "crazy man" smile.

From my crouched position, I peered over the roof's two-foot outer ledge and saw the driver jump out of the car and scan the rooftops. I thought it a good idea to back away from the ledge so that our position would not be discovered and motioned to Billy and Will to do the same. However, Donny and Doug were a bit bolder and stood on the edge of the roof taunting the driver.

"FUCK YOU, MOTHER FUCKER!" Doug shouted to the driver peering up at our position.

The driver flipped Doug the bird and then got back in his car and sped off.

Another car came rolling slowly down Glenwood Avenue, and more high-powered snowballs were launched resulting in more direct hits. Once again, the driver got out and spotted us on the roof. This time instead of just yelling back at the driver, Donny and Doug started to throw snowballs at him. Realizing he was now the target of these young urban terrorists, the driver quickly got back into his car and took off.

The next car down Glenwood was a police car. We didn't pelt it, but I figured that sooner or later they were going to get the word there were kids on a roof pelting cars, and I decided at that point it was time to get down off of the roof.

"Hey, guys, it's just a matter of time before the cops find out we're up here. I'm heading down," I announced.

My suggestion was met with ridicule from Donny and Doug.

"You fucking pussy!"

"See if we invite you along anymore."

"I'm out of here, guys," I said as I turned towards the rear of the building and the hatch opening, which led to the rickety ladder.

"Me too," said Will.

Will and I made our way through the hatch opening and down the ladder while Billy chose to stay up on the roof with the nut brothers. As we made our way down the back porches, we heard someone below. When we turned the last corner on the stairway and reached the first-floor back porch, we came upon an ambush. A huge woman jumped out from her back porch door and literally tackled me. Another woman made an attempt to grab Will, but he was able to escape and booked out of the backyard and down the alley. The woman who had grabbed me had to have weighed at least three-hundred pounds and had a nice firm bear hold on me.

"YOU NEED TO SIT DOWN AND RELAX!" she ordered as she positioned me onto the top step of the stairway, which led to her first-floor landing. She released her bear hold, and I sat down as she had ordered. She positioned herself several steps below me and effectively blocked my path down to the last flight of stairs. Three-hundred pounds between me and freedom, I thought. What to do? What to do?

The other woman stood in the back doorway of her apartment listening for her front doorbell to ring. She told me she had called the police, and they were planning on having me arrested for throwing snowballs at cars.

"Don't you have anything better to do than to put the lives of other people in danger?" she asked.

I didn't respond as I was still thinking of how I was going to get out of this jam. The path in front of me was fraught with danger, being crushed to death by the over-sized woman a distinct possibility. Getting up and running back up to the roof was an option but only seemed to be a delay tactic at best, not a solution.

I heard the faint sound of the woman's apartment's doorbell ring, its echo filtering out her back door. The woman, who had been lecturing me on the evils of pelting, said it must be the police and left to go answer the door.

Just as a picture of me being led away in handcuffs flashed in my head, a loud noise was heard from up above.

CRASH, BOOM, BANG! It sounded as if a herd of elephants were suddenly stampeding down the back porch stairs of the apartment building.

Donny, Doug, and Billy had seen the police car pull up and realized it was time to get off the roof. But it wasn't going to be a quiet retreat but rather a very loud one. As they made their way off of the roof and down the stairs, they began yelling and knocking over garbage cans on each landing while the woman standing guard over me looked up and starting yelling to her friend.

"THERE'S MORE COMING OFF THE ROOF, HURRY!" the obese woman cried out as she gazed upward toward the commotion.

At that very moment I saw my chance. With all the strength I had and all the spring in my youthful legs, I jumped from my position on the porch landing and attempted to hop over the wooden banister of the stairs, which led to the ground below. Just as my feet landed on the banister I felt the woman's hands grab my ankles.

All the while the boys were descending down the stairs toward us, still making a racket as they came. They must have caught wind of my situation for just as I jumped from the clutches of the big woman, I saw Donny and Doug landing on the ground in front of me having made their leaps to the ground from the second-floor landing up above.

The woman's grabbing of my ankles had caused me to make an abbreviated jump/fall over the banister causing me to land hard on my hands, belly, and knees. For a split second, the wind was knocked out of me and I didn't feel like moving. However, realizing that the sumo-wrestler-sized woman was about to pounce on me and the police were walking through the apartment as well, I managed to drag myself up and run, run, run. I ran out of the backyard, down the alley, cut through the schoolyard, crossed Loyola Avenue, and ducked into the hallways of the apartment building that was across the street from our school. If anyone had timed me, I know I would have broken some type of world's running record.

As I tried to catch my breath, I gazed out though the glass door of the apartment building's hallway and spotted Sal Rigatoni's car coming down the street. Sal was another older guy who hung out at the schoolyard. I exited the hallway and waved him down and asked if I could jump in. He said yes, sensing that something was wrong. Once I was in, he asked me what had happened. I blurted out my story in spastic breaths as I was still trying to gain my composure. Sal started laughing as I came to the part involving the sumo wrestler and her strangle hold on me. We drove around for several minutes and then circled back and drove by the schoolyard again. This time we saw a police car parked by the curb. As we drove by, we spotted a single passenger in the back seat. It was Billy!

As Will and I would find out later from Billy, he had been the last one off the roof. When all hell had broken out as they were coming down the back staircase, Billy figured he didn't have a chance at escaping so he opted to go back up to the third-floor landing hoping the police would think all of the pelters had escaped.

But Billy's luck that day, as it often would be in the future, was all bad. The police took the time to walk up to the third-floor landing and found Billy hiding there.

"Where can we find your friends?" they asked him.

"I'm not sure," Billy told them.

"Alright then, we're gonna go looking for your buddies and you're gonna tell us where to look," the cops told Billy.

So Billy told the police we might be in the schoolyard hanging out. Of course Billy realized the schoolyard would probably be the last place we'd be, having just booked from the police. Just as Sal and I were spotting Billy in the squad car in front of the schoolyard, Billy was revealing to the officers another possible location where they might apprehend the other pelting suspects.

"We might try Little Kings," said Billy referring to a popular sub sandwich shop on Sheridan Road. Of course we weren't there either, so the search was eventually called off and Billy was brought home to suffer the wrath of his mom. Although it was the middle of the afternoon, Mrs. Smith was drunk when the police arrived with Billy so she decided to take out her pent-up anger on him.

"YOU MISERABLE LITTLE SON OF A BITCH. ALL I DO IS WORK MY ASS OFF FOR YOU AND YOUR BROTHER AND THIS IS WHAT I GET IN RETURN!" she shouted at him after the police had left.

Mrs. Smith beat Billy silly that afternoon, giving him a cut lip and black eye, which he sported for a week. Unfortunately for Billy, whenever Mrs. Smith drank she got angry for she was mad at the world for taking her husband away from her. When Billy's dad tragically lost his life fighting a fire the year we were in third grade, Billy's mom did not take it well and turned to the bottle to cope with his death and the responsibility, which she now had to face alone, of raising her two young sons. More often than not, she beat her boys at times like this and if that wasn't bad enough, Billy also got a regular beating from his older brother Sam for just being a dumb, younger brother.

We kinda cooled it with the pelting after this incident and decided to take up a different winter sport, skitching. Skitching involved a snowy street and a moving vehicle, which were the two essential ingredients. We had seen the older guys around the schoolyard doing it, so Billy, Will, and I decided to give it a try.

We would position ourselves in between two parked cars, usually near a corner where a vehicle coming down the street would have to stop. We would be in our position, crouched and ready to pounce like a big cat from the jungles of Africa. When a car or truck stopped, we would scurry out toward it trying not to be seen and grab onto the bumper or wheel well. Once the vehicle started moving, we would be dragged along as our combat boots slid over the snowy street surface. The snowier and icier the streets were, the better, and of course the faster the vehicle went, the more thrilling the skitch was.

The ideal skitch involved getting on the vehicle unnoticed, getting a good grip, and going for as long of a ride as you could. Several of us on occasion skitched on a variety of vehicles all around the entire neighborhood. Of course skitching also had its dangerous side. The wheel-well skitch was inherently more dangerous than the bumper skitch because of your close proximity to the turning car tire. Plus, if you fell off there was a chance that you might tumble into the side of a parked car.

One late winter afternoon, we were out and about after a real heavy snow. Ideal conditions for skitching. We were on Loyola Avenue and sneaking onto the bumpers of any vehicle that drove by. We'd skitch several blocks in one direction and then let go, cross the street, and get ready to pounce on the next car coming from the opposite direction.

Billy and I decided to go for a yellow Volkswagen bus, which had stopped at the corner. We grabbed onto the rear bumper, the driver hit the gas, and we were off. We skitched to the corner where we had been getting off, and I let go of the bumper and kneeled down in the street so the driver wouldn't see me.

"OH, FUCK!" I heard Billy yell.

27

Looking in his direction, I could see Billy was still holding on to the bumper.

"BILLY, WHAT ARE YOU DOING?" I shouted his way.

"MY GLOVES FUCKIN' STU….," he tried to say as the VW bus lurched forward and Billy fell on his backside with his right arm fully extended and his right hand still clutching the bumper.

Billy's skitch had ended, and he was now being dragged along by the bus. I quickly got to my feet and ran up to the slowly moving VW bus. I grabbed the bumper to skitch while Billy continued to be dragged along.

"BILLY, YOU GOTTA SLIP YOUR HAND OUT OF YOUR GLOVE WHEN HE STOPS. IF HE TURNS ON A STREET THAT'S BEEN PLOWED YOU'RE GONNA GET REALLY HURT," I shouted.

"I CAN'T, GREG," Billy shouted back to me as he was dragged down the street. "MY MOM WILL FUCKIN' KILL ME IF I LOSE A GLOVE!"

When the VW bus stopped at the next intersection I knew what I had to do. I let go of my hold on the bumper and dove toward Billy's feet. I grabbed them and gave them a big hard tug.

"NOOOOOO!" Billy screamed as his hand fell out of his glove and his body came to rest with a thump on the snow covered street. The VW bus lurched forward again and continued its journey down the street with Billy's army glove still caught on the bumper.

"WHY DID YOU FUCKIN' DO THAT?" Billy yelled at me as he got up to his feet. "My mom's gonna fuckin' kill me now," he continued with tears beginning to well up in his eyes.

Having taken a beating for the pelting incident earlier this winter, he knew exactly what would happen to him if he didn't come home with both gloves and his mom found out. So, since all of our winter outfits were basically made up of the same attire: combat boots, straight-legged blue jeans, black or blue tanker jackets, and army gloves, I decided to bail him out.

"Here, Billy," I said as I pulled off my army glove from my right hand and extended it to him. "Take it."

"But that's your glove, Double G."

"It's yours now, Billy" I said as I tossed it his way, forcing him to catch it.

"What's your mom gonna say?"

"I'll tell her I lost it."

"Won't she be mad?" Billy continued, a shocked look on his face.

"I suppose," I blurted as I thought that at least she wouldn't be beating the snot out of me because of it.

"You'd do that for me, Greg?" Billy asked, his eyes staring into mine now.

"Hey, you saved my life once, that's the least I can do, right?" I said as snowflakes began to fall from the sky, gently illuminated by the street lights, which had just gone on.

"Hey, this don't make us even," Billy said as the facade of seriousness left him.

"Hell no, I still owe you and Will big time," I said as I smiled at Billy and pushed him toward the sidewalk for our walk back to the schoolyard. Billy smiled back, with a grin from ear to ear.

5 THE TOURNEY

The long, Chicago winter finally broke and spring arrived. The big, annual spring event at St. Ignatius was the boys' intramural basketball tournament, which had been held annually in March for about the last sixty years. It was a real tradition, March madness in the flesh. Anybody who was anybody and had gone to St. Ignatius had participated in this annual event. My older brother had played in it as well as all of the older brothers of my friends. It was THE school year EVENT!

The way the tournament worked was every eighth grader on the varsity basketball team was made a captain. The head coach of the varsity team then placed kids from grades five through eight on the various teams, trying to make them as fair as possible.

When the teams for the tournament were announced, I was pleasantly surprised. Due to my lack of basketball talent, they had placed one of the best sixth graders, Bobby Bradley, on my team. So I knew I had at least one good player. I also had another eighth grader and a fifth grader, Ray Wilson, who would turn out to be the best player at that level.

The school supplied uniform tops for all the teams, and by the looks of them my brother, who as I mentioned was eleven years older than I, might also have actually worn some of them. Each team represented a real Catholic, college team. Due to the fact some of the teams seemed to win the tournament more often than others, certain team uniforms were believed to bring good luck. Therefore, the eighth grade captains all wanted to be the first one to pick their team uniform. The varsity coach addressed this by holding a lottery to see what order the captains would pick their uniforms in. I ended up with a bad lottery pick and as a result, picked Santa Clara, which really wasn't wanted by anyone else. As soon as I chose it, the ribbing began.

"Santa Claus for Greggie," or "Saint Claire, nice red uniforms," the other captains chided.

I was also informed by one of the seventh graders that the year before when his Santa Clara team had been knocked out of the tournament, his captain had ordered all the players to pile their uniforms into a shower stall so he could piss all over them. That's nice, I thought, I'll make sure I wash mine a couple of times before our first game.

The tournament finally arrived, and the games were to begin on a Friday night. My Santa Clara team, red, pissed-stained uniforms and all, were scheduled to open against Billy's Creighton team. The air in the gym that night smelled of popcorn and sweat, and was packed with school kids, players' parents, and alumni of St. Ignatius who had played in the tournament in previous years. There had to be two to three-hundred people packed into the tiny, elementary school gym. The old gym was quite impressive in its own right. Not only did it provide court-length bleacher seating on both sides of the court, there was also seating available in the balcony overlooking the court's hardwood floor which was the best in our Catholic school conference.

As we took the court for warm-ups in front of this large crowd, my stomach felt as if it was performing tumbling routines. As the captain I knew I couldn't just go through warm-ups and then take my place on the bench as I had done on the varsity team all season long. No, this time around I had to be a big contributor to the team.

Our basic game plan, drawn up by our coach George Kronos, an older schoolyard regular I had asked to coach my team, was to get our sixth grader the ball to shoot from the outside and for me to hang out around the basket for rebounding and inside scoring. We also wanted to play good defense and when needed, apply full-court pressure to turn the tide of the game.

Our game plan worked like a charm, and near the end of the game a very frustrated Billy Smith kicked the bleachers as he came off the bench during a late-game timeout. As Billy and I met after the game, I could see the tears welling up in his eyes. Losing one game had knocked him out of the chase for the tournament championship, but his team was still alive and would now compete in the consolation bracket.

"Good game, man," I said as we met at half court and shook hands. "Remember, you still get to play in the consolation tournament, good luck."

"Thanks, Double G," Billy said, "good luck playing Will. You'll fuckin' need it."

Having won our first game, we now advanced to the next round. This game was played on Saturday afternoon, and as I took the court I noticed how much emptier and darker the gym seemed compared to the night before. We won this game quite easily and were scheduled to play our next game that evening.

When I arrived back at the gym Saturday night, the electricity in the air, which I had experienced on Friday night, was back. Compared to that afternoon, the gym now seemed much better lit and the jam-packed crowd once again buzzed with excitement. The smell of popcorn and sweat was back as well!

Our opponent that night was Tommy Chen's team. Tommy was an Asian kid who was brilliant at math but couldn't play his way out of a paper bag when it came to basketball. Because the enrollment at St. Ignatius had been dwindling for years our eighth grade class was small, which forced our varsity coach to make Tommy a captain even though he had not played varsity basketball. This being the case, coach had put Derrick Washington on Tommy's team. Now St. Ignatius only had four black kids attending, and Derrick Washington was one of them. He was a very good seventh grade player with a big afro and a killer outside jumper. This was a huge game for both teams. Whichever team won advanced to the championship game.

In the locker room before the game, a bunch of older, schoolyard regulars stopped by and wished us well.

"Hey, Greg, can we have a word wit you?" one of them asked.

I got up from the locker room bench and walked into the adjoining washroom with the regulars, wondering what they wanted to talk about.

"Hey, we just want to wish you luck and tell ya we're rooting for ya."

"Yeah, man. You can't let Washington beat you tonight. You know that, right?"

"Hey, we're gonna try our hardest to win," I replied.

"We don't need no black kid from the south side playing in the championship game, do we, boys?"

"Hell no!"

"No fucking way!"

"And, Greg, YOU are the one that can make that happen, so don't let us down."

With that, the group of regulars turned and made their way out of the musty locker room.

I stood alone in the washroom, noticing for the first time the sound of water dripping from one of the faucets. Shit, I thought, I had enough pure competitive motivation in me to want to go out and beat Derrick Washington. I didn't need, nor would I have ever wanted, to use racism as my motivator. In this regard, I was definitely in the minority. Most of the people in the parish, including Billy and Will, held negative views toward blacks, but my view was different because of something that occurred in my fifth grade year.

That year, my father volunteered at work to put up a colleague for about a month, as the man was relocating to Chicago and would be initially looking for permanent housing for his family. The man's name was Stan Lyons, and he was black.

One Saturday afternoon while he was living with us, I got into a fight with some of the neighborhood kids. It was probably the most upset I had ever been in my young life, and I really wanted to hurt some of those kids. I went up to our apartment hysterical and complained to my dad who said he would go out and talk with the kids.

Stan Lyons, who was about to go out and do his laundry, suggested I go with him. After some resistance, I reluctantly agreed to go. As we walked, Stan talked to me in his deep, calm voice, asking me to explain what had happened. He seemed genuinely interested in my side of the story, and just knowing he was actively listening to me helped calm me down.

Having had this man live with us and having talked with him alone, I knew I had, at a very young age, learned not to generalize or pass judgments about a particular group of people, be it blacks, whites, men, women, Catholics, Jews, etc. Instead, I learned to judge the character of each individual within a group as I came to know that person. By having this black man live with us, I soon realized he wasn't any different from us. Unfortunately, a lot of the good Catholics of the parish hadn't learned this lesson yet and probably never would.

We took the floor for warmups, and as I looked around, I realized the crowd was really large, even bigger than Friday night's. Most of the older schoolyard guys were in the stands, all pulling for me. The game began, and we ended up playing pretty well that night. Luckily for us, Derrick Washington had an off night. My sixth grader, Bobby Bradley, was able to score from outside while I dominated the inside. We won easily and advanced to Sunday's tournament championship game. The racists in the crowd were pleased.

I was glad we had won, but I was quite disappointed with the reason some people in the gym that night cheered for us. As the final horn sounded, I made a point of running over to Derrick Washington and shaking his hand and congratulating him on a game well played. I felt it was my way of telling some of the people in the stands to go get screwed.

In the locker room afterwards, some of the schoolyard regulars stopped by and congratulated the team. I wanted to tell them we had played our hearts out and won the game for ourselves and not for them. We wanted to show everyone in the gym we were the better team, not because we were all white but because we had just played better, period! Unfortunately, I couldn't find the nerve.

Sunday morning arrived, and I went to church with my mom and sister. At the end of mass, the priest announced that the tournament championship games would be that night. As soon as I heard that, my stomach began to churn. I pictured the gym again packed as we took the court that night. Knowing I would face Will's team for the championship made my stomach churn even more. I knew this would be a tough, if not impossible, game to win since I would be going head to head with Will, who had been an all-conference player on the varsity team and had already spoken to some high schools about playing for them next year. I was a varsity bench warmer who would probably never play high school basketball. I would definitely have my hands full tonight, but at least I wouldn't have anyone pressuring me to beat him because he was black!

That Sunday afternoon seemed to drag on forever, like a long cross-country road trip. I couldn't think about anything else besides the game that evening. Finally the time arrived to head over to the gym. As I walked into the St. Ignatius gym, the excitement in the air was palpable. Again, the sweet smell of buttered popcorn and sweat drifted through the gym, while another capacity-room crowd filed in to see the three games and the tournament's award ceremonies afterwards. Our game was scheduled after the first two games, which consisted of the third/fourth place game and then the Consolation Tournament Championship game. Unfortunately, for Billy, he lost his first two games and had been eliminated from the tournament so now he was faced with the dilemma of which of his best friends to root for.

I sat in the stands during the first game and couldn't believe how enthused the crowd was. I got shivers down my spine thinking I would be out on this court in front of this huge crowd within the next couple hours. At half-time of the second game, we gathered our team in the locker room and got dressed. The second game ended, and we were ready to take the court for warmups. As we did, I felt the adrenaline surge through my body as I noticed that not only were the bleachers filled but the balcony was packed as well. In addition, many people who could not find a seat stood at the west end of the gym near the concession stand to watch the games.

As we took the court for the tip-off, Will and I shook hands at center court and I said, "Good luck, Will."

"You'll need the luck. I've got the skill!" Will shot back.

Will was different from me and Billy. He dripped self-confidence like a maple tree drips syrup in the spring. Maybe it was the fact he really wasn't working class like us but rather had been born into an upper-middle-class family.

Unlike Billy whose father was dead and me whose father was an alcoholic, Will's father was a big business executive whose income was significant enough to allow the family to own an apartment building near the lake and allow Will's mother the freedom to be a stay-at-home mom. Will's dad was also a big shot with the church, serving on many of its volunteer committees.

As an only child, Will was in many ways the center of his father's life. Sure, Will's father pushed him hard at times to be the best in everything he did, but he also wasn't above bragging about Will to anyone who would listen.

The game began with me losing the tip-off to Will. His team came down the court, and Will got a pass in the corner and put up a shot, swish. Two to nothing after five seconds of play. As it turned out, all of the momentum in the first half was in Will's Boston College's team's favor. The capacity crowd picked up on this, and halfway through the second period the fans began to chant and kick the wooden bleachers with their feet.

"BOSTON COLLEGE," stomp, stomp, stomp-stomp-stomp.
"BOSTON COLLEGE," stomp, stomp, stomp-stomp-stomp.

We really had a terrible first half, and I was the main culprit for our demise. I couldn't guard Will, and he knew it so he was absolutely controlling the whole game. The first half ended with us down fourteen points. We slowly made our way to the locker room. As I sat there, I imagined the crowd wishing that this damned Santa Clara team, which had been totally outplayed during the first half, would just concede so that the trophy presentations could take place and everyone could go home and go to bed to get a good night's sleep before Monday morning arrived.

The mood in the locker room was a very serious one, and the only bright spot was that Will had committed his third foul just before the final buzzer of the half. With our backs really up against the wall, we decided that the best strategy to start the second half would be to get Will to commit his fourth foul. Most likely, his coach would bench him for at least the remainder of the third quarter to avoid him committing his fifth foul and fouling out. This might just give us a chance to get back into the game. No team in the history of this tournament had ever come back from a deficit of more than ten points and won on championship night, so we knew things didn't look good.

My brother Jerry and Ray Wilson's brother, two guys who had played in the tournament when they attended Ignatius, came into the locker room and pulled me aside.

"Hey, you got to get tougher in the paint," my brother said.

"Yeah, man, don't let Striker push you around. You're bigger than him, man," Ray's brother added.

"OK, I will," was all I could say in response.

Just as we were going to leave the locker room, our coach gave us all one more instruction.

"I want you guys to run our full-court defensive press the rest of the game. Pressure the man with the ball no matter where he is on the court. We need some turnovers and some quick baskets to get back into this."

We all nodded our heads in agreement.

"You guys may get real gassed running it," Coach George continued, "but remember this is the last game of the tournament for you guys so there is no holding back. Give it all you got!"

As we took the court and began warmups, I thought about how I had something to prove after embarrassing myself with my play during the first half. The second half started, and we came down the court for the first time. I cut across the lane for a pass in the low post. Will was guarding me but didn't deny the bounce pass from my sixth grader, Bobby Bradley.

This is it, I thought as I faked to my left, then turned right and dribbled the ball once. Having stopped my dribble, I knew Will would expect me to shoot so I bent my knees and started to move upwards as if I was going to shoot. Will bit and jumped up, leaving the ground to block my shot. As he did I bent down again and then went back up. Will's body, which was coming down by now, collided heavily with mine, which was on its way up. The sweet sound of the ref's whistle filled the gym.

"FOUL ON NUMBER ONE," the ref shouted to the scorer's table.

"Yes!" I said out loud, knowing it was Will's fourth foul.

As I lined up to shoot my free throws, the scoring table's horn blew and Will's coach waved him to the bench. I made both of my free throws, which cut the lead to twelve points. We went into our full-court press and then boom, a steal and another quick basket. Now with only seconds gone in the second half, we were only down ten. Boston College broke the press and came down the court, but with Will on the bench they didn't have a scorer and ended up turning the ball over.

With a Bobby Bradley outside jumper, the Boston College lead was cut to eight and the crowd sensed they might be watching a major comeback in the making. After having screamed their lungs out and bruised their feet stomping for Boston College during the first half, the crowd decided to switch their allegiance and began rooting for the comeback kids.

"SANTA CLARA," stomp, stomp, stomp-stomp-stomp.

I heard the first chant and thought, we've got the crowd and momentum behind us. Here we go.

We continued to frustrate Will's team, and our press kept causing Boston College to turn the ball over. In addition, Bobby Bradley began hitting jumpers from everywhere. We crept and clawed our way back into the game, and with just over twenty seconds left in the third quarter, we tied the score. The crowd went wild. The quarter ended, and we all wondered in our huddle just when they would decide to put Will back in the game.

The fourth and final quarter began with Will on the bench. We took a two-point lead with just under a minute gone in the quarter and with that, I saw Will jump up from the bench and make his way to the scorer's table. On the next whistle, Will reentered the game as an audible buzz erupted from the crowd. Will walked out toward me for the restart of play, and as I looked him in the eyes, I saw he was so focused I felt as if he was looking right through me.

It was our ball with a two-point lead and just seven minutes left in the game. As we came down the court, our coach yelled to get the ball into me since Will was guarding me. The ball was passed into me, and I knew immediately what I had to do. I took a dribble toward the basket and felt Will on my backside, but the usual strong push from him was gone. Instead he stood flat footed with his arms raised in the air allowing me my path to the basket. I made the lay-up, and as I headed back down court I heard Will's coach yell at the rest of the team to help him out on defense.

Will got the ball and headed down the court swiftly. He dribbled through our press and pulled up and hit a twenty-foot jumper, showing no rust from sitting out the third quarter. Both teams traded baskets for the next six minutes as the crowd roared. With less than thirty seconds left, Boston College had the ball while we maintained a two-point lead. The crowd, now anticipating a Santa Clara victory, began to chant, "DEFENSE, DEFENSE," stomp, stomp, stomp-stomp-stomp.

Will came down the court and went to the basket hard. I went up with him and fouled him yet somehow his shot fell through the basket. Boston College had tied the game, and now Will was on the free throw line shooting one free throw that could give them the lead. Will made the free throw, and with eighteen seconds left, we called our final timeout.

"OK, guys, this is it," Coach George announced in our huddle. "Greg, I want you to set a hard screen on Bobby's man. Bobby, you streak down the court. Ray, you heave the ball into Bobby. Got it?"

"Yes."

"Yep."

"Got it."

"Hands in," Coach George shouted as we all reached out into the middle of the huddle and placed our right hands on top of one another's. "Score on three, Score on three. One, two, three!"

"SCORE!" we yelled as we broke the huddle and headed back onto the court.

When the ref handed Ray the ball to inbounds, I did as I had been told. I set a hard screen on Bobby's man and he was able to head down court unguarded. Ray lofted the ball to him and Bobby began dribbling with a clear path to our basket as Will closed quickly. At the last moment, Will caught Bobby, but I could see he wasn't going to try for a block but rather just try to intimidate the sixth grader with his presence. Bobby got the shot off clean, and as it went through the hoop the crowd's reaction was deafening. We now had a one-point lead as Will's coach signaled frantically for a time out with ten seconds left. The refs blew their whistles, and we jogged to our bench as the crowd continued cheering.

"OK, now we have to double team Striker," Coach George explained. "Greg and Bobby, I want you on him. Don't let him drive to the basket. If he's gonna beat us, let's force him to make a shot from way outside."

The shrill sound of the ref's whistle rang out, signaling to us the time out was over.

"Hands in. Defense on three, Defense on three," Coach George shouted. "One, two, three."

"DEFENSE!" we collectively shouted.

We retook the court, and the ref handed the ball to Will. He inbounded the ball to another player and then clapped his hands immediately, signaling to his teammate he wanted it right back. Bobby and I backed off a bit until he received it, and then we approached him as a team. The crowd was counting down the clock as Will began his dribble.

"SIX, FIVE, FOUR…"

Will tried to dribble around us, but we pushed him toward the sidelines. Realizing he was trapped, Will decided to step back away from our double team and put up a half-court shot.

"THREE, TWO, ONE…," I heard the crowd yell as the ball drifted over my head, toward the basket. I felt Will's shooting hand, finishing its sweet follow through, brush the side of my face as I turned to follow the ball's trajectory.

I swear the gym fell dead silent for just a moment that night, as every eye in the gym followed the ball's flight as it made its way through the air - a scene burned into my memory until the day I die. The next sound I heard broke my heart and caused the capacity crowd to erupt like a mighty volcano.

"Swish!" the net purred, as the ball passed through the basket and fell back onto the court, and Will began to celebrate his championship triumph.

The eighth graders, especially the girls, surrounded Will and joined in his celebration. With his good looks and athletic talents he was always one of their favorites, and he had just given them another reason to show it off. I slowly walked to our bench with my teammates as Coach George shouted to us to keep our heads up since we had played such a great game. He then suggested we go shake the hands of the players from the other team. I tried to make my way to Will, but his fan circle was too wide so I couldn't get very close. We never did shake.

6 GRADUATION

Will's popularity continued as he was given, once again, the lead role in the school's annual spring play. No one had ever had the lead role as a sixth grader, but Will auditioned and earned the lead two years ago and had done an excellent job. He repeated that feat as a seventh grader as well, and this year would be his tour de force, a premier of things to come. With his good looks and confidence, Will was a natural actor. Ever since he had starred in the school's play as a sixth grader, all he could talk about was moving to Hollywood and getting into acting. The funny thing was, the more he talked about it, the more we all believed he would do it someday.

This year's play was a huge success and again Will got all of the attention, and rightly so, as he was talented beyond his years. I believed his success would only be limited by his ambition, which in itself was huge. I wondered how it must feel to be Will, to be blessed with so many talents and to also have the admiration of so many. Both of these things I greatly craved, but I knew for me neither would ever come as easily as they had for Will.

I also wondered how I would ever be able to pay Will for saving my life. He already had everything he needed, and I was sure he was destined to live a charmed life. Coming to his rescue someday as he had done for me didn't seem like a real possibility. As I pondered these thoughts one afternoon as I sat in my bedroom, my body grew warm with anger. The root of the anger wasn't caused by the fact I realized that I may never be able to pay Will the debt I owed him but was formed from the realization, for the first time, that my life wasn't going to be as easy or as good as Will's. My eyes welled with tears as I sat there silently contemplating this fact.

* * * *

The greatest lesson my friends and I learned during our eighth grade year was one we taught ourselves. We discovered that if we put our heads together and worked as a team we could stick it to "the Man" who, in our little world were the good sisters of the Blessed Virgin Mary. This lesson once learned would serve us all well the rest of our lives.

In our English class, we had a series of lessons which were called the SRAs. I forget what SRA stood for, but I remember that when May 1 rolled around all, of the eighth grade boys panicked as we realized we only had one month of school left and about fifty SRA lessons still to complete. What we decided to do was to get organized.

"I have a plan," I announced to Billy, Will, and a couple of my other classmates in the schoolyard one day after school.

"We all have way too many SRA lessons to still complete by the end of the school year, right?"

"Right."

"Yep."

"Too fuckin' many!"

"OK, here's what we can do. We talk to Sister Anne, and we ask her if we can take some lessons home this weekend. Let's say each guy takes five a piece. My parents are gonna be gone this Saturday, so we all meet at my place and we form an assembly line."

"An assembly line!?" Billy blurted. "What the fuck ya talking about?"

"Picture this," I continued. "We sit around the table. Each guy does a lesson. When you are done, you pass the answers to that lesson to the guy on your left. He copies your answers and then passes them to the guy on his left. If five guys show up at my house with five lessons a piece, we all could knock out twenty-five lessons in one afternoon and all we are really going to do is five a piece."

"I LIKE IT!" Will shouted.

"So when you pass your answers to the guy on your left, then you get answers from the guy on your right?" Billy asked.

"Exactly!"

The next day at school we approached our English teacher Sister Anne individually and asked her if we each could take some SRA lessons home during the weekend so we could begin to get caught up. She wholeheartedly agreed, and since my plan had caught on like wildfire, ten of us each took five different lessons home.

On Saturday afternoon, the ten of us met at my apartment and once there we gathered around my dining room table and each of us completed our first lesson. When we were done, we passed it to the person sitting to our left so he could copy that lesson. This assembly line copying system was employed until everyone had completed all fifty lessons. Not only had we stuck it to "the Man," we had also erased any worries about graduating!

On the final day of eighth grade, we got out of school and a bunch of us decided to make our way down to Albion Beach. Billy, Will, and I decided to stop on Sheridan Road and bum a bottle of wine to celebrate our last day. We eventually got a young dude to go into Albion Liquors and buy us a bottle of Boone's Farm.

With our bottle of wine in tow, we made our way down to the beach. As we sat on a park bench gazing at the blue-green waters of Lake Michigan, we passed the bottle around like hobos and talked about what it felt like to be out of St. Ignatius and eighth grade.

"I'm going to be in every play my high school does and star on the b-ball team. And then once high school is done, I'm packing up and heading off to Hollywood, boys!" Will proudly announced.

"For me it's the fire department," Billy blurted out as he was lifting the brown bag to his lips. After a huge gulp of wine he added, "Just like my fuckin' dad."

I sat there in silence and listened, not really able to state any of my goals either short term or long. There was much bravado bandied about that afternoon, but I sensed uneasiness among us as well. We were all smart enough to realize that as high school freshmen, we were once again the low man on the totem pole and none of us really knew what to expect in high school.

Our graduation day arrived the following Saturday and was celebrated in the St. Ignatius church, which had been the school's tradition for years. I still remember the card my mom gave me that afternoon. It was very mushy and said something like "We know you're growing up and soon you'll be a man but no matter what we'll always be there for you."

I thought about what the card meant as I walked to the church alone that evening and realized, for the first time in my life, that I was growing up. A feeling of fear came over me, but I quickly squished it as I thought of my two best friends. I can always count on Billy and Will, I thought, and they can always count on me.

7 PINK BELLIES

The summer of 1974, between my eighth grade and freshman years, was long and hot as I spent most of my time hanging around the St. Ignatius schoolyard. That summer, some of the older guys hanging out at the schoolyard got bored and decided it was time to initiate the newly graduated eighth graders into the "Patch."

From what I had been told, the initiations of the past had been much more formal, but this summer's were more informal and consisted of just two events: the pink belly and poling. The pink belly involved being attacked and pinned to the ground by a group of guys. The guys would then pull up your shirt and slap your belly until they had achieved a nice pink color.

The pink belly wasn't so bad, but the polings always had potential for real damage. During a poling, four guys would each grab one of your limbs and carry you to one of the basketball poles in the schoolyard. While your legs were being spread apart, they would run you into the pole. Billy, Will, and I suffered these indignities together that summer and in doing so our friendships grew even deeper.

As us new recruits soon found out, drinking on the weekends was the major pastime of the schoolyard crowd. There were two favorite locations to drink at, the schoolyard or the beaches. The beaches we went to most often were Albion and North Shore, in that order. Billy, Will, and I didn't do a lot of drinking that summer as it was always a challenge to get someone of age to buy for us. The older guys would generally refuse to buy for us younger guys with the possible exception of George Kronos, my eighth grade tourney coach who usually exacted a fee of a couple of beers in return when he did.

The only other method of getting beer was "bumming" for it, which consisted of us standing on Sheridan Road and walking up to complete strangers who looked cool, and asking if they would be willing to buy us some beer. Every time you went to bum for beer, it had the potential to turn into an adventure.

One Saturday evening, Will, Billy, and I decided to buy and split a twelve pack of beer. The problem, as usual, was how to obtain it. So there we were, hanging out on Sheridan Road across the street from Loyola University trying to bum a twelve pack of beer, none of us older than fourteen. As the traffic hummed along Sheridan Road and the sun set in the west, we asked several people to do us this favor, but they immediately said no. I took it upon myself to approach another young guy who looked cool.

"Excuse me, would you mind doing me and my buddies a favor?" I asked.

"What's that?" the guy shot back.

Always a good sign, I thought.

"Well, we want to buy a twelve pack of beer," I announced.

With that, the guy answered, "Oh man, I just got out of jail and if I got caught buying for you guys, I'd be in big trouble."

"I understand," I said ready to let the guy go on his way.

But the guy, who himself must have experienced bumming for beer in the past said, "I'll tell you what. I'll give you my ID and let you try to buy it. How's that?"

"Sounds great!" I said, thinking here I am fourteen years old, wearing a tee shirt and a pair of shorts, going into a liquor store with an ID that describes someone else who doesn't look anything like me, and who has just been released from jail. What's wrong with this picture?

Undaunted but nervous as hell, I went into the liquor store with the ex con's ID and meekly made my way to the beer cooler. I grabbed a twelve pack of the cheapest beer they had and walked to the checkout clerk. Then I waited. The clerk looked at me for a second or two and then began to ring up the sale on the cash register. He looked up from the register and announced, "Four ninety-five."

Four ninety-five, I thought, what the fuck!? I've been screwing around for half an hour trying to find someone to buy this fucking beer and this guy ends up not even carding me!

I paid the clerk and left the liquor store astonished. Once outside, I thanked the guy for his ID and me and the boys made our way down to the beach. We laughed our asses off all the way there as I told them about my not being carded at all.

Unfortunately not all "bumming" stories had happy endings. Billy went out one Friday night and really having a thirst for a cold one decided to bum by himself, never a good idea. He headed up to Sheridan Road on his bicycle and began bumming for a six pack. He was not having any success when he encountered two older schoolyard guys, Sal Rigatoni and Mark Fields, walking down Sheridan Road heading for the Vic Star Lounge, a dive bar at the corner of Albion and Sheridan Road. Billy asked them if they would buy him a six pack, and they promptly refused and crossed the street and went into Vic's to start their evening of drinking.

Undeterred, Billy kept approaching strangers and knew that with every no, he was getting closer to a yes and therefore his six pack. Finally Billy approached a young black guy.

"Hey, man, can you buy me a six pack of beer?" Billy asked.

"What jus say man?" the young black guy replied.

"A six pack, man, can you buy me one?" Billy answered.

"Sure, man, I can buy ones fer ya. But I needs to use your bike man and cruise down the block where I can buy fer shures. Ya sees da man cards me over heres," the young black guy said pointing to the Albion liquor store, which was several store fronts down from where they stood.

In an instant Billy had thought about it, said OK, and proceeded to hand the guy his three bucks and his bicycle. The guy jumped on Billy's bike and headed out south down Sheridan Road.

"SEE YA'LL IN A WHILES, MAN!" the young black guy shouted over his shoulder as he rode off.

"OK," Billy said as he watched the black guy ride further and further away.

Where is there another liquor store on Sheridan Road, Billy thought to himself as the stranger, who had his three bucks and his bike, became a dot on the street's horizon? Several more minutes passed before the realization that he was getting ripped off swept over Billy like a huge Lake Michigan wave.

"SHIT!" Billy said out loud. "I'm getting ripped off! FUCK!"

Billy decided to seek help so he took off running and crossed the street and entered Vic Star's Lounge. As he inhaled the smell of stale beer, he let his eyes adjust to the dimness of the bar's lighting. Once adjusted, he saw Sal and Mark sitting at the bar and approached them.

"Dudes, you gotta help me, some nigger just stole my bike. Please come outside and help me," Billy pleaded.

Feeling sorry for Billy, Sal and Mark reluctantly left their stools and strolled out of the dimly lit bar and onto Sheridan Road, which was now awash with the ambiance of the setting sun.

"There he is," Billy said pointing a finger in the direction of south Sheridan Road.

"Where?" Sal and Mark chorused as they looked south down Sheridan Road.

"There," Billy said as he squinted and pointed south. "You see that little black dot about ten blocks away? That's the guy who stole my bike."

"Billy, how could you let the guy ride off with your bike when you were standing less than a hundred feet from a liquor store?" Sal asked sincerely.

"He said he couldn't buy there and he had to ride to another store," Billy answered with a sad look on his face.

"You dumb fuck!" Mark Fields said as he shook his head from side to side.

"Well, Billy, I hate to say it, but it looks like you're out a bike," Sal said. Then Sal and Mark, feeling somewhat sorry and maybe just a tad guilty for not buying Billy a six pack when he had asked, decided the least they could do was to buy him one now.

"Thanks, guys," Billy said as Sal handed it to him.

"Be careful, Billy," Sal said as he and Mark crossed the street to go back to Vic's and resume their drinking.

Later that night back in the schoolyard, Sal and Mark, who were pretty well oiled up by then, told of Billy's expensive bumming story to anyone who happened by the schoolyard. Many a hearty belly laughs echoed about the schoolyard that night, unfortunately all at Billy's expense.

*　*　*　*

None of us held a regular job that summer, but I did manage to work a bit. The apartment building that we lived in was directly across the alley from Brian and Mike Murphy's two flat. The Murphy brothers had both graduated from St. Ignatius the year before I did, and I originally met them both at the schoolyard. One night while we were talking, Brian mentioned that he had worked for this guy named Pete who was a maintenance man for several buildings and also had a carpet cleaning business on the side. Brian had gotten a job at a grocery food store, so he couldn't work for Pete anymore. Brian asked me if I would be interested in doing some work for Pete, and I said sure, after all, I really didn't get any money from my parents who were struggling themselves, and I was tired of always being broke.

Brian gave me Pete's number, and I gave him a call. Pete wanted me to start right away, and I told him that I could. The next day Pete picked me up in his white work van, and I became a working man. The work itself turned out to be pretty hard as I helped him carry in the carpet cleaning machine and move furniture around the apartment or house so that he could clean all of the carpet.

My other duty was to be the corner man. My role as corner man involved getting down on my hands and knees, with a bucket full of carpet cleaning solution and a large bristle brush, and clean by hand the four to five inches of carpeting that was right next to the walls. This allowed Pete and the machine to concentrate on the center of the room and also prevented the machine from getting too close to the walls and banging them up.

I worked for Pete about three or four days a week that summer. For my hard work, I was paid the minimum wage of two dollars an hour. The money I earned allowed me to buy a six pack on the weekends and play some poker and blackjack down at the beach or schoolyard.

The summer after eighth grade was also the first time I sat in a bar and drank a beer. There was a bar on Devon Avenue called Connolly's Tap, which was notorious for selling liquor to minors. Sure enough, the first time Billy, Will, and I dragged our fourteen year old butts into the joint and plucked a quarter down onto the bar, we were immediately served a cold mug of draft beer. No questions asked. Little did I know in that summer of '74 that an event would take place in the future at this broken-down, Irish watering hole, that would have a major impact on the rest of my life.

8 CAKE EATER

As the summer drew to a close, thoughts of going to high school began to emerge. My brother Jerry urged me to go to Loyola Academy, which was a very respected Catholic, Jesuit high school located in the northern suburb of Wilmette. The enrollment was comprised of boys from many well-to-do north shore families.

As Jerry put it, "You'll be going to school with the sons of really well-connected people, which can never hurt."

So the decision was made for me to attend Loyola in the fall. Will was going to Loyola with me while Billy would attend Gordon Tech, a gritty, Catholic high school located on the north side of Chicago. The tuition at Loyola in 1974 was a hefty thousand dollars, which was huge compared to other Chicagoland high schools whose tuition was about half that. Since Loyola was located in Wilmette, Will and I would have to take a school bus to and from school every day as well.

The school year started, and everything about it was very different than grade school. Instead of being hot-shot eighth graders, Will and I were now lowly freshman, and at Loyola the upper classmen liked to haze the freshman. One afternoon, I witnessed one freshman, who had been changing clothes after gym, get thrown outside into a snow bank in only his underwear. Luckily for me I was a pretty big freshman and nobody ever really messed with me. Although that's not quite true - I did have a run in with a sophomore on the bus one day.

As we were loading onto the school bus one afternoon, a sophomore tried to take the seat I was about to take. I shoved him out of the seat, and he shoved me back. That prompted me to give him a punch. The bus driver saw us scuffling and told us to knock it off. That was it for that day, but the very next afternoon the same thing happened again. Will, seeing I was about to go at it with the sophomore, gave me the "I got your back look," and I knew it was time to go at it as I had had enough!

I began to pummel the sophomore with rights and lefts. The kids on the bus, especially the freshman, loved it and started to yell and scream. The bus driver jumped up out of his seat and made his way toward us, screaming at the top of his lungs.

"I'M GONNA TOSS DA BOTH OF YOUS OFF DIS BUS, YA HEAR ME?!" he wailed.

Afraid he might be true to his word, I sat down in another seat. The driver returned to his seat, and as the bus started rolling, other freshman came up to me and patted me on the back.

"Way to take care of that sophomore"

"Nice job!"

Will turned to me and spouted, "You bad ass!"

That was the last time the sophomore tried to take a seat away from me or any other freshman.

While I was busy joining the freshman football team at Loyola, Will decided to join the theater group and the basketball team. Meanwhile Billy, at Gordon Tech, also became a football player.

We didn't have a very good freshmen football team, but we had fun. One of our opponents that season was Gordon Tech. I'll never forget the day that Billy and the Gordon Tech freshman team came out to Loyola to play us. Here we were, about a hundred guys on our sideline and their hundred guys on theirs.

The game began, and the Gordon Tech players began chanting, "BEAT THE CAKE, BEAT THE CAKE," as they considered kids who went to Loyola rich, spoiled, cake eaters. We began to chant, "BEAT THE GREASE, BEAT THE GREASE," as we considered the city kids who went to Gordon low life, greasers. We won the game in the end, and the way we celebrated you would have thought we had just won the Super Bowl.

I met Billy at the fifty-yard line for the post-game handshakes, and as we shook hands he said, "You fuckin traitor! What the fuck you doing out here with these cake eaters? You're a city boy!"

We laughed together, but deep down I knew he was right. I wasn't like my classmates at Loyola and as a matter of fact, I wasn't even like Will. They all came from families with money while I came from a lower, working-class family who lived in a dingy, roach-infested apartment in Rogers Park.

Fall gave way to winter and when it did there came weekend nights so cold we couldn't hang out at the schoolyard. Some of the older guys had cars, and they sometimes parked them in the schoolyard and partied in them. But as guys who were too young to drive, we would either have to hang out in the cold or hang out in the hallways.

The hallways were located in a four-story apartment building across the street from the schoolyard - the same ones I had ducked into to escape the police following the pelting incident. These hallways led to the back doors of the apartments, so there was never really much traffic there. Although they were not heated, they still beat hanging out and drinking beer in the sub-freezing temperatures. In total, we probably spent two or three winters hanging out in these hallways during our high school years, and it wasn't bad unless someone got drunk and started pissing underneath the stairway, which made the whole place stink like one big urinal.

On Christmas Eve of my freshman year, Billy, Will, and I found a Christmas tree in an alley so we decided to drag it into the hallway. We gently persuaded a locked laundry room door to open and then dragged the tree in and perched it in a sink. We decided we needed to decorate the tree so as we finished a beer we promptly hung the empty can on the tree. As we continued to drink, we became more sentimental about our tree specifically and Christmas in general.

Someone began to sing a Christmas carol, and soon we all joined in. So there we were, about ten of us now, drinking and singing as we celebrated the birth of Jesus Christ in a dingy, poorly lit laundry room of an old apartment building that none of us lived in, in the Patch of Green. We capped off the evening by walking a block west and attending midnight mass at St. Ignatius Church. Happy birthday, baby Jesus!

As the school year dragged on, we amused ourselves on the weekends by drinking beer and finding various ways to raise hell. One of the hell-raising activities introduced to us by some of the older schoolyard guys that winter was an activity we referred to as "blowing up" the L.

I made my way over to the schoolyard after dinner one Saturday night and found Billy and Will already there.

"What's up, guys?"

"Nuttin," Billy answered.

Several minutes later we were joined by the nut brothers, Donny Daniels and Doug Eller. Donny would grow up to be a very respected Chicago police detective who, while working undercover during a drug sting, got so badly beaten by gang members he came out the other side barely able to recognize his family and friends. For this, he was sent to Washington D.C. where the president himself bestowed upon him a special award. Doug, on the other hand, ended up in Montana working as a fish and game warden.

"What are you fuck nuts up to tonight?" Doug asked us.

"Nuttin much."

"Nothing so far."

"Maybe buying some beers."

"Yeah, well me and Donny are thinkin' bout blowin up the L. You guys ever do that?"

"My broder told me 'bout it," Billy replied.

"I never heard of it," Will said.

"Me either."

"OK, well the first thing we gotta do is go around the neighborhood and break off car antennas," Doug began to explain. "Once we got a bunch of antennas then we go hop the L at Loyola. Then we walk about a half block away from the station platform and crouch down next to the tracks."

"When the next fucking train rolls into the station," Donny interjected.

"BOOM!"

"BOOM!"

With their BOOMS fully expressed, Doug and Donnie starting laughing uncontrollably.

"You guys in?" Doug asked.

I glanced at Billy and Will.

"Fuck yeah!" Billy answered.

The idea of blowing up the elevated train sounded a little crazy, but at the same time it seemed like a cool thing to witness.

"OK then, you three head toward Devon and each of ya find at least three antennas. Me and Donny will head in the opposite direction. Plan on meeting back here in about twenty minutes. OK?"

"Yup."

"OK."

"Got it."

Will, Billy, and me headed down the deserted side streets toward Devon Avenue. We took turns breaking off the steel antennas on any car we found that had one. In just about fifteen minutes we had our quota and turned around, heading back to the schoolyard.

"What took you fuck nuts so long?" Doug asked us upon our return. "You're lucky you showed up cuz we were just about to leave without cha. Now it's time to head up to the station."

With that, we made our way up Loyola Avenue to the Loyola L stop as a group. Once we were just shy of the station entrance we threw our cache of antennas over the chain link fence and began to climb over it. Once on the other side, we gathered up our antennas in the darkness and with antennas in hand, we climbed the cement blocks that led to the opening at the track level where we could squeeze through and find ourselves on the train tracks.

Once we made it onto the L tracks, we followed Doug and Donny's lead as they walked down the tracks about a half block south of the station and then got off of the tracks and crouched down low in the darkness, between the south and northbound tracks.

"When we see the headlights of a southbound train approaching the station, get ready to throw your antennas on the third rail, OK?" Donny asked.

"Yup."

"OK."

"Got it."

We all sat in the darkness peering north just past the station, just waiting for the train to come rolling down the track. We didn't have to wait long. Several minutes later, before we could actually see the train, we could see the reflection of the train's headlight off of an apartment building that sat next to the tracks.

"Not yet," Doug commanded

Then suddenly the train appeared around the bend.

"NOW!" Doug shouted.

Rising to our feet we all threw our cache of antennas onto the third rail and stood back.

"BOOM! BOOM! BOOM!"

As every antenna found its mark, the pitch-black sky was shaken out of its slumber as electrical sparks, emanating from the third rail, streaked twenty feet high into the night sky. The reflection of the electrical fireworks show danced on the facades of the adjacent apartment buildings, which stood in stunned silence. What we had accomplished was in effect the shorting out of the third rail, which powered the train via a strong electrical current. The train suddenly screeched to a halt, while the lights in the station as well as the surrounding apartment buildings flickered on and off.

We didn't stick around long for as soon as the fireworks had subsided, Doug and Donny took off running toward the station, and we followed in quick pursuit as the police and the Chicago Transit Authority were probably going to arrive on the scene momentarily. We scrambled back onto the station's platform and headed straight down the exit staircase. We made our way out of the station and once we had safely made our way back to the schoolyard, we rehashed our little adventure, as the adrenaline it created was still coursing through our bodies.

* * * *

Winter finally passed and spring arrived, and to nobody's surprise Will was the star again. After being the star of the freshman basketball team all winter, he got the lead role in the spring play at Loyola. His performance was outstanding, and again I thought that his acting success would only be limited by his ambition. As we sat around the schoolyard the weekend after the play, I told him just that.

"I know what you're saying man," Will replied. "Hey, I got my plans. I'm going to Hollywood right after high school, fuck college."

"What about playing b-ball in college?" I asked knowing that he would probably be recruited somewhere for his talent.

"I like playing ball but the real thrill for me is acting and being on the stage and hearing people tell me how much they enjoyed my performance," Will answered.

"You gonna fuckin' send for us once you're rich and famous?" Billy asked with a grin.

"Fuck yeah, dude," Will answered as he wrapped his arm around Billy's neck and gave him a mild noogie to the noggin.

"Big mansion, means big parties," Will continued clearly feeling the effects of the beers he had consumed. "We're gonna party big time!"

Our freshman school year finally ended, and we came away unscathed except for Billy. He had been in and out of trouble all year long and then, when he got caught smoking on school grounds for the umpteenth time, the administrators at Gordon Tech had had enough. They expelled Billy from school right as the school year came to a close.

The Saturday after his expulsion, Billy came by the schoolyard. He had a nasty-looking black eye, which prompted some of the older guys to ask him who he had tangled with.

"I got in a fight at school with some Mexicans," Billy told them.

As I looked at Billy as he told the story of the fight, I knew it was all bullshit. Most likely his mother, in a drunken rage, had gone off on him after finding out about the expulsion. I felt bad for him as his story continued, realizing all I could do was pray his mother would never go crazy enough to kill him.

9 WHEN FUN GOES BAD

One mid-summer Friday night, after my freshmen year, we decided to make our way over to the Granada Theater, which was located on Sheridan Road near Loyola University. It was a big, old, grand movie theater, built in the days of vaudeville. A theater that had definitely seen its better days.

Billy told Will and me that we could sneak into the theater through a rear, fire exit door as he had done it with his older brother a couple of nights before. When we got to the theater, we walked down a gangway that ran alongside of it. Once in the back of the building, we climbed up three stories on an old, rusted, metal fire escape stairwell attached to the outside of the building that creaked and swayed as we made our ascent. At the top of the metal stairwell was a landing with a door to the theater. We jarred open the door, snuck inside, and in the complete darkness of the backstage area, we climbed back down the three stories on a rickety stage ladder. Now having descended the ladder, we found ourselves on the stage of the theater, behind the movie screen.

As I looked toward the movie screen, I froze. The movie had already begun playing and from my position the screen appeared transparent. I could see all of the people in the theater, and they appeared to be looking up directly at me. Billy shook me out of my frozen state by whispering, "They can't see you."

Now knowing this, I followed my buddies as we crawled on our hands and knees behind the screen. We had to crawl the entire length of the screen until we reached a stage exit. From there we simply stood up and walked down a couple of stairs that brought us to a small hallway that led us to the main floor of the theater. Nothing like a free movie!

On the Saturday night after we had snuck into the Granada, Billy arrived at the schoolyard in a really foul mood. That evening, just prior to leaving for the schoolyard, he had an argument with his mother. Billy told me she was drunk and had hit him over the head with a lamp before he had bolted out the door.

"I'm ready to do some drinking," he announced after telling us about the lamp story.

"OK," I answered. "Let's go get some beers."

We walked our way to a grocery store on Devon where we had discovered we could buy beers without being carded. We bought some beers and then headed back to the schoolyard and sat around and drank for several hours. After we ran out of beer, we went for another beer run. Back at the schoolyard we were all feeling good when Billy starting talking about going for a train ride.

"Leeet's fuckkinng go summwhere," he suggested, slurring and staggering around.

"Where to, big boy?" I asked.

"I don't fuckkinng care. As loonng as it's not my fuckkinng house," Billy answered.

"I get that," I replied.

"Come on, letz's go," Billy said as he started east down Loyola Avenue toward the L station.

"Will, you in?" I asked.

"I think I've had enough Tom Foolery for the evening, gents. I'm heading home."

"Pussy," I blurted out to Will with a smile on my face.

"WAIT UP!" I shouted out to Billy as I started out in his direction.

Billy and I made our way up Loyola Avenue and once we got near the train station, Billy announced he was hopping the L. Now hopping the L in daylight when you're sober is dangerous enough but doing it at night, drunk, is crazy.

"You're fucked!" I shot back. "Let's just pay and go for a ride."

"Fuuuck it!" Billy slurred as he started to climb the chain link fence.

"You're fucking serious!?" I shot back as I started to climb the fence as well.

Billy got over the fence first and in the darkness began to climb up the cement blocks that led to the level that ran beneath the L station platform.

"WAIT UP!" I shouted as I was just finishing my climb over the chain link fence.

Billy reached the top cement block and began to crawl underneath the wooden station platform. His next maneuver would be the hardest of all. Now he would have to crawl from out beneath the platform, onto the train tracks, pick himself up, and run to the end of the platform where he could climb a short ladder and make his way onto the L station platform.

Billy either hadn't taken the time to touch the train rail to feel for any vibration or just didn't hear it approaching, for as he began to pull himself from underneath the station's platform onto the train tracks, a northbound train was pulling into the station. As I saw Billy's torso disappear I heard, for the first time, the faint rumblings of the approaching train and instinctively shouted out, "BILLY!"

But it was too late.

The train, slowing as it entered the station, clipped Billy's right shoulder and knocked him back under the station's platform. Luckily for Billy, the train engineer had seen him coming up from underneath the platform and onto the tracks and immediately radioed for help when he realized his train had hit him.

I climbed the cement blocks toward Billy in a panic. As I reached him, I couldn't see much but felt his warm blood flowing from his shoulder.

"BILLY, CAN YOU HEAR ME?" I shouted.

No response.

"HELP! SOMEONE PLEASE HELP US!" I yelled out into the darkness of the night as I held him in my arms.

"You're going to be alright, Billy," I whispered as tears began to roll down my cheeks.

So there we were, all alone underneath the elevated station platform with the train that had just hit him sitting right next to our position, me crying like a baby and Billy lying in my arms dying.

As I sat there in the darkness, I thought about what the nuns had taught us in grade school. About how we are all born with original sin and only by having Jesus come back into the world could our wretched souls be saved. For the sisters had taught us our lives were destined to be a struggle between doing good and doing evil and they said the guilt a person felt when they did something evil was sometimes more than they could stand. Like how I felt now, knowing that I was the one who was guilty for letting Billy try to hop the L in his drunken condition. Damn those black-veiled monsters!

I'm not sure how long we sat there as time seemed to have stopped, like it does when your concentration is so acute that nothing else seems to matter. Suddenly the noise of sirens shook me out of my hellish thoughts, and I saw the glare of flashlights appear near the chain link fence below me.

"WE'RE UP HERE!" I shouted out into the darkness of the night.

"They're here to help you, Billy," I announced. "Hang on, buddy."

The police and firemen made their way over the chain link fence and arrived at our position. They decided to take Billy out the way he had come in, down the cement blocks. They got me out of the way and then a cop asked me what had happened. I tried to do my best to explain and after taking my statement the cop told me he would give me a ride home.

"What about my friend?" I asked.

"Here's hurt pretty bad, but he's in good hands now, don't worry," the cop replied.

Don't worry!? I thought as the cop drove me home. Guilt again welled up inside of me like hot lava inside an active volcano. I should have stopped Billy from trying to hop the L in the first place. This was all my fault. Billy was a guy I owed my life to, and what the hell did I do? I let him get killed!

When I got home, I woke up my mother and sitting at our dining room table I began, as best I could, to tell her what had happened. As I did, tears began to form in my eyes and finally made their way down my cheeks. My mom gave me a big hug and told me in the morning she would help me find out what hospital Billy had been brought to. She consoled me as best she could and then after a while suggested I try to get some rest. I went to bed but couldn't sleep, not knowing if Billy was alive or dead. I thought the worst but prayed for the best.

That morning I wearily got out of bed and went into the kitchen where my mother was washing some dishes. My mom had made some calls and found out that Billy was in a hospital on the southwest side of Chicago. Thank god he was still alive, I thought. I then decided to call Will.

"Dude, that's fucked up," was Will's response after I had explained to him what had happened to Billy.

"I know, it was my fault," I answered as I felt tears well up in my eyes once again.

"Don't say that, man," Will responded. "He was fucked up and you were feeling pretty good, too. He decided to try to hop the L and shouldn't have. It's gonna be alright."

"I hope so. The hospital told my mom he can have visitors. Do you want to go see him?" I asked.

"Hell yeah!" Will answered.

"Can you get your dad's car?" I asked

"I'm sure I can. I'll come by and pick you up in a little while."

"Alright, see you then."

I hung up the phone and made my way to the bathroom to take a shower, exhausted yet anxious to see Billy. Will came by a bit later and picked me up. We drove in mostly silence to the hospital and once there, made our way up to Billy's room.

As we walked into Billy's room, we could see he was awake and sitting up. His mom and brother Sam were also in the room. Billy's arm and shoulder were heavily wrapped and although very pale and heavily sedated, Billy was able to speak with us.

"Hey, guys."

"How you doing?" I asked not really knowing what to say.

"Been fuckin' better," was Billy's weak response.

As ironic as it seems, the alcohol that fogged Billy's judgment also saved his life. As his limp body went into shock, the alcohol acted as a sedative that slowed the flow of blood from his badly damaged shoulder saving him from bleeding to death in my arms right there beside the L tracks.

Will and I visited with Billy for only a couple of minutes and then we said good-bye. As we left his room, we were approached by a nurse who asked us if we would be willing to donate blood.

"Why would our friend need blood?" Will asked.

"Oh, just in case," she answered.

Will and I told the nurse we would and went down to the first floor and gave our pints.

Several days passed and the news grew dim. Infection had set in, and the doctors were concerned about gangrene. A day later, the most awful moment I would ever experience in the schoolyard occurred. I had been shooting hoops awhile when Billy's brother Sam walked into the schoolyard.

"How's Billy doing?" I asked Sam as he approached me.

"Not good. I just came back from the hospital."

"What's up?"

"They amputated his arm at the shoulder joint today."

I immediately dropped the basketball I had been holding, all of a sudden finding myself in a world of silence, with only Sam's words echoing in my brain. "They amputated his arm at the shoulder joint today."

I don't remember walking home but somehow I got there. I walked into my apartment crying, and immediately my mother asked me what was wrong.

"Billy," I blurted out trying not to cry anymore. "They cut off his arm today."

"Oh, my God!" my mom said as she came toward me and gave me a big hug.

"It's all my fault, mom. I should have never let him hop that train."

"It's not your fault, honey. If it didn't happen that night, it might have happened another night," she answered trying to console me as best she could.

But of course she didn't understand. Billy was a guy I literally owed my life to and instead of paying him back, I let him get hurt on my watch.

"I gotta call Will," I said as I left my mother's embrace and went into the dining room to use the phone.

During our conversation, we decided we wouldn't be real friends unless we visited Billy in the hospital now so we drove to the hospital the next evening not knowing what to expect. What we found upon arriving was Billy in relatively good spirits, but I suppose a psychologist would have said he was going through denial.

When we entered the room, Billy was sitting up in his bed with a blue, floppy, Cubs hat on his head.

"Hey, you guys, howd ja like my new hat rack?" Billy said as he placed the floppy hat on his shoulder stump.

Feeling extremely uncomfortable, all Will and I could do was respond with nervous laughter. We continued to visit with Billy for a little while, making some small talk and then a short while later we said our goodbyes. Will and I left the hospital and drove home in silence, shocked at what we had just witnessed.

"Shit, man, Billy's dream of becoming a Chicago fireman, it's over!" Will suddenly blurted out when we were about halfway home.

Will's words stung me like a hard slap to the face on a cold, Chicago's winter day.

"I didn't even think about that," I mumbled. "Now what's he going to do?" I asked out loud.

"Fuck if I know," Will answered.

Our eyes met, and I could see that Will was feeling as bad for Billy as I was.

Billy was released from the hospital several days later. For the remainder of the summer, Billy didn't come around the schoolyard but Will and I kept in touch by calling him and visiting him at his apartment. We didn't want to push Billy into going out and figured that once school started back in the fall he would get back to normal. What I didn't realize at the time was that normal was never really a part of Billy's world.

ACT II

10 CLOSER TO GOD

Riddled with the guilt about Billy's accident and seeing my working-class parents struggle with a high school tuition they really couldn't afford, I began to think about not going back to Loyola Academy for my sophomore year. The day Billy was kicked out of Gordon Tech, his mom decided to enroll him in a school called St. Vincent DePaul, which was located in Lemont, Illinois. Billy's cousin was a priest there, and I guess Billy's mom thought by sending him to this boarding school, they could keep him out of trouble. Ever since his accident, Mrs. Smith was more adamant than ever about getting him out of our neighborhood.

I thought since Loyola was a financial burden, I should at least check out what the deal was at St. Vincent since one of my best friends, who had saved my life and whose life I had helped to destroy, was going there. My parents and I drove out to Lemont during an open house day in mid-August. We soon found out St. Vincent was a seminary, basically exposing high school age boys to the Catholic priesthood. Maybe exposing is a poor choice of words, but you know what I mean.

The school and dorms were located on about fifty acres of wooded land, which really made you feel like you were out in the country. There were five main buildings on the campus. The school building was a large, old, red-brick, two-story building, which housed the priests' offices and living quarters and the classrooms, which we would attend. Directly opposite across the courtyard and running parallel to the school building was another large, old, red-brick, two-story building, which was the student dorm. Sandwiched between these two building were two smaller, more modern buildings. One was the mess hall and the other was the chapel. A very large, aluminum, hangar-like structure that was our gym was located on the opposite side of our dorm and across a parking lot. If you followed for about a mile the dirt road that ran past the far end of the gym building, you would find the major seminary in which men who were just about to become priests did their final studying.

I was told students at St. Vincent's had to attend church every day and were allowed to go home every other weekend. The class sizes were small, in fact the sophomore class, which I would be a member of, would consist of only twenty-four boys and the current senior class had only ten boys. The best part of the deal was the tuition, which including room and board, was less than Loyola's. I was sold. St. Vincent DePaul here I come!

When I arrived at St. Vincent DePaul late in August, I began to find out the "little" things they didn't tell me about at the open house. Things like being required to attend study hall every weekday night from seven to eight-thirty. Volunteer work, which consisted of waking up at five in the morning and driving to a local shopping mall and cleaning it up once a month. Now going in I knew that I would have to attend mass every day, but upon arrival I also learned that we had benediction service every Sunday night and met to pray the rosary once in a while as well. But, hey, I was saving my folks some money and more importantly I was going to school with Billy as he struggled with his new identity as the kid with one arm.

The freshman and sophomores at St. Vincent had a barracks-style, no walls dorm arrangement on the first floor while the juniors and seniors slept two or three guys to a private room upstairs. Since there were so few upper classmen this year, the administration decided to put some of the sophomores on the second floor, which the upper classmen resented since traditionally only upper classmen were allowed access to the second floor of the dorm building. They took out their frustration on us sophomores by hazing us, which involved raids into our rooms in the middle of the night during which we would be swatted by pillows and have glasses of cold water thrown on us.

One of the first nights at St. Vinnies my two roomies decided to have a cigarette. They got up in the dark and crouched down in the corner of the room. All I could make out was the glowing tips of their cigarettes in the darkness. A minute couldn't have passed when the door of our room was swung open and the light from the hall illuminated the room like a thunderbolt from heaven. In walked Fr. Fagan, who slept and maintained order on the second floor, to bust them. The next morning at breakfast I told Billy about what had happened and warned him to keep his smoking habit, which he had begun during his freshman year at Gordon Tech, on the QT. As punishment, my roomies were forced to stay at school and work during the first weekend we got to go home.

Billy and I soon became the leaders of our sophomore class even though we were newcomers. We introduced the other boys to card games and gambling. One of the greatest "cons" Billy and I pulled off involved playing the card game *Between the Sheets*. This is a fairly simple game in which everyone puts their share of ante money into one big pot, which all the players are trying to win. Each player takes a turn and makes his bet after seeing two of the three cards to be dealt. First, a card is dealt face up onto pile one and then another card onto pile three. The player whose turn it is then estimates the chances of a card being dealt to pile two that will fall somewhere between the cards in piles one and three. He makes his bet based on his estimate.

So, for example, if a two was dealt to pile one and a king was dealt to pile three, a player would feel pretty good about betting the entire amount in the pot. If a card that falls between the two and the king is dealt to the second pile of cards, then the player wins the entire amount in the pot. If a two, king, or ace was dealt then the player loses and has to put into the pot the amount already in there.

Billy and I always managed to get a couple of kids interested in a game. We would play *Between the Sheets*, and I would begin our little session by losing all of my money on purpose, leaving Billy and the other kids to play the game. I dealt and set Billy up by tipping him on how much of the pot he should bet and on occasion I also resorted to dealing off the bottom of the deck.

We would play these kids like a fiddle, eventually getting every cent of their money into the pot. Then I would deal Billy a five on pile one and a seven on pile three or something equally ridiculous, and then give him the signal, which meant go for the pot. Of course miracle of miracles would occur next (we were at a religious seminary after all).

"A SIX?!" one of the remaining kids would scream out, "BILLY SMITH, YOU'RE THE LUCKIEST FUCKER I'VE EVER SEEN!"

To some this might seem very unethical given the setting it was occurring in, but, hey, how else were Billy and I supposed to raise money for pop, candy, and pizza on the weekends we had to stay at school?

Besides boredom, St. Vincent's was also full of traditions. The building of a gigantic bonfire by the sophomore class was one of them. The entire class pitched in and gathered wood for about a month. One day Billy, Tom Hart, a.k.a., Boo Boo, and I went out into the surrounding woods to look for a dead tree. We eventually came upon one and decided to fell it with the two axes we had with us. I never realized how long it took and how hard it was to cut down a fair-sized tree using just hand axes. The tree was probably no wider than two feet in diameter, but it took the three of us all morning to chop it down, a total of three or four man-hours I would estimate. We left the tree where it fell as our plan was to return later that afternoon with Billy's cousin Father Grace. Father Grace was our sophomore class advisor, and he drove the pickup truck to drag the tree back to the bonfire pile.

Near the end of the month, the woodpile started to take shape. It was a towering monstrosity of wood approximately three to four stories tall. The day before the lighting, all of the members of the sophomore class climbed up onto it and had our picture taken. The following evening, a Friday, the ceremony began. The junior class presented a lit torch to the sophomore class, symbolizing the passing of school leadership from the upperclassmen to the sophomore class. The torch, having been passed, was then laid on the awaiting woodpile.

The red glow of the fire spread, illuminating the fall sky. The heat of the inferno grew fierce, and the crowd that gathered to witness its lighting was forced to back away from the growing flames. We sat and watched the fire burn for three or four hours that night and finally went back to the dorms with the fire still blazing. When we awoke Saturday morning, a group of us went back to see if the blaze was still going and sure enough there was still a strong nucleus of embers about two stories tall still burning. The fire wouldn't go out officially until Sunday morning when all that was left was a smoldering heap of charred wood about the size of a campfire.

When winter passed and spring arrived, our friend Boo Boo was asked to help give a retreat for some public school kids who lived in the town of Lemont. He asked if I would help him, and I agreed. The retreat was to occur over a weekend at the major seminary that was about a mile walk away from our seminary. Deacons, men who were two or three years away from being ordained priests, were in charge of the retreat.

About a week before the retreat, something came up at home and Boo Boo informed me he wouldn't be around to help me with the retreat, so I asked Billy if he'd like to join me. He said he would so the two of us met with Mr. Taylor, a deacon, who informed us we would be giving a presentation, by ourselves, in front of thirty high-school-age kids. Billy and I took a deep breath and prepared our presentation as well as two sixteen year olds could.

When the weekend of the retreat arrived, we were nervous as hell. There were other kids giving presentation too, and as luck would have it, the girl who gave her presentation just before ours was awesome.

"We're fuckin' screwed!" Billy whispered to me just before we were introduced.

"I know," I answered as Mr. Taylor introduced us to the group.

"There is no way that we can top her presentation," I said to Billy wishing I could just run away and hide back in the comfort of my dorm bed.

I don't recall much of our presentation other than rambling on about connecting with others on a spiritual level and then directing everyone to pair off and get spiritual. God, did we suck! In my opinion we bombed, and Billy agreed. Mr. Taylor, however, told us we had done a great job and a couple of the other deacons told us that at our ages they could have never even gotten up in front of a room of strangers and spoken. Yeah right, I thought, they're just trying to make us feel better.

Late afternoon arrived, and the retreaters were given a break before meeting for dinner. Mr. Taylor asked Billy and me if we wanted to go for a walk, and since we had nothing else planned, we said yes. Billy and I carried Bibles, which had been given to us during the retreat, as Mr. Taylor led us to the seminary's kitchen. Once there Mr. Taylor, to our great surprise, asked us if we would like a beer.

"Yeah, great," I said as I glanced at Billy who had the most stupefied look known to man on his face.

Mr. Taylor pulled out three long-neck bottles of Red, White and Blue beer from the refrigerator, opened them, and handed Billy and me one. The three of us proceeded to make our way outside.

It was a gorgeous spring day, and it felt great to get outside into the sunshine after having spent all day in the hot, stuffy gym. We stood outside a side exit of the large seminary building just kind of shooting the breeze, sipping our beers and looking out at the woods in the distance. As we talked, I felt the tension in me begin to evaporate. Just when I was beginning to feel relaxed, I noticed the pickup truck from our school heading in our direction. It looked like it had several of my classmates in it.

"Oh, shit," I said out loud. "I think some of our schoolmates are in the truck, Mr. Taylor." Just as I finished my sentence, the pickup made a left turn off the dirt road and headed right toward us.

"That's OK," Mr. Taylor said calmly. "Just use your Bible to conceal your bottle of beer."

Billy handed me his bottle and I gave him back his Bible that I had been carrying. I placed both of our beer bottles in my left hand and with my right hand positioned my Bible in front of them. I did this just as the pickup pulled alongside us. There were three St. Vincent students in the truck, and they explained to us they were on their way into Lemont to pick up some supplies for the school and since they saw us they decided to make a detour to say hi.

They didn't stay long to visit, and as the pickup disappeared from our view, Mr. Taylor, the future priest, turned to me and said, "Maybe at the next retreat I'll have you give a talk about how much the Bible has helped you in your life and you can begin by telling the story of how you once used it to hide a couple bottles of beer."

With that Billy and I completely lost it. Every ounce of tension left my body as I laughed uncontrollably for several minutes as tears welled up in my eyes.

That evening when all the retreaters were in the gym settling down to sleep, Mr. Taylor, Billy, and I went upstairs to the massive kitchen area and broke into the supply of Red, White and Blue beer. We sat in the kitchen for several hours and shot the shit as several other deacons walked in and sat for a while and shared our conversations. It was an eye-opening experience hearing some of these future priests talk.

One of the topics of conversation was about a couple of sisters who were attending the retreat. One of the deacons mentioned how completely opposite they were in personality. Another deacon mentioned how physically different they were and wondered aloud if they were really biological sisters.

"Ann is really big and fat while her sister Carol has a body that just won't quit," one of the deacons remarked.

"That's true," another deacon responded. "But Ann has a great soul."

"That's correct," the first deacon blurted, but then quickly added, "but you don't fuck their souls."

Upon hearing that comment, I almost sprayed the sip of beer I had just taken across the room. We sat drinking with the deacons a little longer, and then Billy and I went back to our room around midnight to go to bed.

"Do you think you'd ever want to be a priest, Billy?" I asked through the darkness of our room.

"Fuck no, Greg, I was born to be a fireman."

A one-arm fireman, I sadly thought to myself.

"How about you?" Billy asked.

"I don't know. I always thought priests were different, but after spending time here I think they are the same as you and me. So maybe."

With that, I drifted off to sleep.

* * * *

Several weeks later, our sophomore class was supposed to go over to the gym after dinner one night and put away a bunch of chairs that had been set up for a play. Father Grace was going to meet us there to supervise. For some reason, a bunch of us blew it off completely and instead decided to just hang outside along the road a short distance from the gym.

Father Grace, in the meantime, went to the gym and with the help of only a couple of the sophomores, put away all of the chairs. When Father Grace was finished, he got into the school's pickup truck and began to drive down the road we were standing alongside. As he approached, he recognized us and since he was rather pissed off at us for not showing up to help with the chairs, he flipped us the bird.

"Wow," I said out loud to no one in particular. "Now I've experienced it all. I've just been flipped off by a priest!"

I'm not saying I didn't like the priests at St. Vincent. In fact, once it proved to be very helpful having one on my side. Tom "Boo Boo" Hart and I had turned sixteen early in the school year. Now Boo Boo was very eager to get his driver's license, so eager he had been borrowing the priests' cars and driving them around the school grounds getting in plenty of driving practice. I, on the other hand, had very little practice.

Well after much badgering, Boo Boo finally got Father Grace to take us to a driver's license facility to take our tests. On the way there, Father Grace offered to let each of us take a turn at the wheel. Boo Boo readily accepted, but I declined knowing full well I wasn't ready to drive on the streets.

We finally arrived at the driving facility, and Boo Boo and I were assigned a tester who would accompany us on the road test. Unfortunately, I was assigned to a cranky, old guy. We went out onto the streets, and all this guy did was bitch about the way I drove. When we pulled back into the parking lot of the facility, he let me in on the bad news.

"Son, I'm not going to pass you on the road test. You failed to signal once when you made a right turn and your three-point turn was atrocious. You'll have to come back another day and try again."

"OK," I replied softly.

We walked back into the driving facility, and as we did I felt tears well up in my eyes as a result of my disappointment.

"HOW'D YOU DO, HOW'D YOU DO?" Boo Boo yelled as he ran up to me displaying his newly earned driver's license.

"I failed," I said as a tear rolled down my cheek.

Father Grace approached us and asked me what had happened. As I began to explain that I thought my tester was really a jerk, the tears really began to flow.

"Wait here a second," Father Grace declared as he walked toward the counter.

I could overhear bits and pieces of his conversation with the supervisor of the facility.

"He's a seminary student... won't be able to come back... nervous... another chance?"

Father Grace ended his conversation and walked back toward us.

"Greg, they're going to give you another chance," Father Grace announced.

Aha, I thought, the power of the collar!

"Great," I said as I tried to compose myself.

We waited a bit and then my name was called, and a young guy introduced himself as my tester. We walked out to the car and got in. To my surprise, instead of instructing me to pull the car out into traffic, my tester told me to pull around to the back of the shopping mall where there was no traffic.

"So what happened on your first test?" the young tester asked me.

"I don't know," I replied. "The guy said that I didn't do a three-point turn very good."

"OK, well let's see you do one."

I stopped the car and proceeded to make the most perfect three-point turn anyone could possibly make in a deserted parking lot.

"Great!" said the tester. "You've passed. Now let's go back into the facility."

I walked into the facility, and from the gigantic smile on my face Boo Boo and Father Grace knew I had passed. With my new license in hand, we left the facility and as we approached the car, I turned to Father Grace and thanked him for what he had done.

"It's OK, Greg," Father Grace said. "Sometimes in life we don't get things quite right the first time so we need a second chance to prove we can."

"Yeah," I said. "A second chance and an empty parking lot!"

Now armed with our licenses, Boo Boo and I borrowed the old station wagon the priests owned and took trips into town to run "errands." One afternoon late in the school year, Boo Boo, Billy, and I were given the wagon to go to town to pick up a birthday cake for a fellow student. Now Boo Boo was a little goofy to begin with, and I thought when we left the school that afternoon an adventure might be in the making. We made the trip to and back from town OK but then Boo Boo decided to go by the major seminary where there was a lot of open road and no real authority watching us.

We cruised around for a while as Boo Boo stopped and accelerated quickly, trying to scare the shit out of Billy and me. I finally suggested quite calmly to Boo Boo we should make our way back to our school. So Boo Boo positioned the beat-up old wagon on a very straight stretch of road, which ran directly in front of the major seminary, and then turned to Billy and me and announced he was going to try to do a super brake torque.

Wonderful, I thought.

The station wagon was so old that the speedometer actually went up to one-hundred-and-seventy miles per hour, and when the car was in neutral the needle moved when the driver pressed down on the accelerator. Boo Boo put the car in neutral and began to hit the gas. Fifty, eighty, one hundred ten, one hundred thirty, and finally as the engine began to give out a loud cry, as if it were in pain, the entire car began to shake. Boo Boo buried the needle past the one-hundred-and-seventy mark on the speedometer.

Right at that moment, Boo Boo shifted the car into drive. As I grabbed for the dashboard the whole car lurched forward and the tires began to squeal and smoke. The balding tires finally found a grip on the road and catapulted us quickly forward about one-hundred feet. Then the roar of the engine suddenly went silent, and we coasted for another five-hundred feet before the car came to a complete stop. Boo Boo's first reaction was to try to start the car back up, but the engine would not respond. We piled out of the wagon and looked back down the road. As if we were in a chorus performing at mass, we sang out a collective, "Oh, shit!"

With the smell of burnt rubber and motor oil heavy in the air, we saw lying willy-nilly all over this lonely stretch of road screws, pieces of metal, and ball bearings. Parts that just a moment ago had been part of the car's transmission. We had succeeded in killing the priest's beloved, old station wagon!

We grabbed the birthday cake out of the car and as we began the mile or so walk back to our school, we discussed how we were going to break the news to the good Fathers. Boo Boo, of course, wanted to tell them that all of a sudden the car just up and died. Billy didn't even want the priests to know he was in the car, which was fine with Boo Boo and me. I told Boo Boo whatever story the driver (Boo Boo) wanted to spin, I would go along with.

We finally reached the school and found our way to Father Grace's office. We entered his office and found him at his desk smoking as Boo Boo began his story.

"...And all of a sudden Father the car just quits and I can't get it started again," Boo Boo announced.

"Oh really," was Father Grace's reply. "Let's hope it's nothing serious. We've been trying to sell that wagon for a while, and just this morning somebody called and made us an offer I think we're going to accept."

Yeah, right, I thought as we left Father Grace's office. Accept that offer all you want, Father, but unless the buyer is looking for a car he can push around town, I don't think the deal's going to go down.

The following day I was in the rec room watching TV when Brother Ben came in.

"Garrity, were you with Boo Boo yesterday when the wagon broke down?" he asked.

Oh, shit! I thought.

"Yes, Brother Ben, I was," I answered as I began to feel my body tense.

"Good, then you can show me where it is. I want to tow it back and see what's wrong with it."

"OK," I said. Why me, I thought.

We walked out of the rec room to the pickup truck parked outside. As we were getting into the pickup, Brother Ben let out a low moan. I stared at him and noticed for the first time that he didn't quite look himself.

"Oh, my head," he murmured.

As we began to drive away from the school, Brother Ben confided in me he was taking me along just in case he got dizzy as he was trying to hook up the wagon to be towed. It seemed he had been at the basketball coach's house the night before, celebrating the end of the school year with him.

We finally reached the wagon. Brother Ben, being no dummy, surveyed the road and said, "What the hell were you guys doing? I see parts of this car scattered all over the place?"

My immediate thought was why weren't we smart enough to throw all the parts off the road thereby hiding all the evidence. But my reply was,

"What do you mean, Bro Ben?" (We always used Bro when we were trying to get on his good side.). "The car just died on us."

"Yeah, right," Brother Ben shot back as he bent down to hook up the towing cable. As he did, he let out a giant moan again, his head still spinning from the night before.

We got the wagon back to the school, and nothing else was ever mentioned of our one-hundred-and-seventy-mile-per-hour brake torque/transmission crunch. Of course the sale of the wagon never did go through and eventually it was sold for scrap.

*   *   *   *

The first time in my life that I sat down and weighed the pros and cons of an impending decision was at St. Vincent's. It happened the last week of school. The decision to be made was whether or not to return for the following school year. Boo Boo and I got to talking about this one day, and that evening we found ourselves in an empty classroom in the school building evaluating the situation. We didn't include Billy since we knew he didn't have a choice in the matter. Our discussion of the pros and cons was put up on the blackboard as follows:

Going to another High School vs. Coming back to St. Vinnies

<u>PROS</u>	<u>CONS</u>
1) Go to school with girls	Deserting Billy (Greg Only)
2) Being at home every weekend	Not as much individual attention
3) Go to school with girls	Probably just another athlete there and
4) No more Mass	not a star as we are here
5) Go to school with girls	
6) No tuition (Public School)	

The list wasn't a long one, but you get the point. By looking at the list, it was obvious that at some point during our sophomore year Boo Boo's and my libidos must have really kicked into high gear, as going to school with girls was our number one argument for leaving St. Vinnies. The only rub for me was leaving Billy here. We had really grown close living here together this past year, and we also had the chance to talk about his accident and the way he felt about it. For the most part, after Boo Boo's and my discussion, my decision had been made, but I knew I would have to tell Billy first.

On the second-to-last day of school, I asked Billy to take a walk over to the gym to shoot some hoops. Even with just one arm he could still shoot pretty good.

"Hey, I've been thinking," I said as we began to shoot around.

"'Bout what."

"Next school year."

"Oh yeah, what about it?"

"Been thinking about not coming back to St. Vinnie's."

With that Billy stopped his dribble and our eyes met.

"Where jah go?" he asked.

"Probably St. Greg's."

"St. Greg's eh."

"Yeah, what do ya think?"

"I think I'll miss ya, man."

"Well I'll miss you too, man. But, remember, I'll see ya every other weekend when you come home and we'll get together, just like we have been doing with Will this year."

"That's true. And we'll always be friends right, Double G?"

"Hell yeah, man, always!" I said as I walked over to Billy and gave him a great big bear hug.

11 ST. SULLIVAN BY THE LAKE

The school year ended and summer began. While Billy and I had been playing cards and attending mass at the seminary, Will was honing his acting craft. He was the star again in Loyola's annual spring play, and his parents had actually hired an acting coach to help him as well. In addition, he had been brought up to the varsity basketball team halfway through the season, so everything for Will, as usual, was golden.

I missed seeing Will during the school year, but we always made up for lost time when Billy and I came home for the weekend. This summer I'd be seeing him every day as he was able to get Billy and me jobs working for the company his dad worked for.

We worked most of that summer on the south side of Chicago's famous Loop or downtown area. The company shot pictures for store catalogs and magazines. Our jobs consisted of pulling merchandise from the warehouse and bringing it down to the studios to be shot. It wasn't hard work, and the three of us mixed some fun in with it.

There were some real characters at this place, which made the day even more interesting. One of the characters was Charlie, a huge black man who operated the freight elevator. He was about six foot two and three-hundred-and-fifty pounds and had what appeared to be a terrible scar from a burn on his head, which he usually tried to conceal with a fishing hat. We would get on the elevator and Charlie would mumble something unintelligible to us, and we would just shake our heads yes out of respect and fear, mostly fear. Often, Charlie would break out in song, singing "Ain't got no bread with my meatballs, not even little crumbs."

No problem, I thought to myself as I quietly rode the elevator. Whatever you say, old man.

Will had been seeing a girl from the neighborhood named Laura during the school year, and one summer night I was introduced to a friend of hers named Mary Anne. We started to see each other and sometimes got together with Will and Laura. When the summer ended, so did my relationship with Mary Anne.

Not everything that summer was rosy, as things at home weren't going so great. My dad had been sick, and my sister, according to my mom, was getting into drugs. My mom and I discussed where I would go to school the following year, and I told her I thought I wanted to go to St. Gregory's, a local co-ed Catholic high school. She said she would love to have me go there, but since St. Greg's tuition was more than St. Vinnie's we might not be able to afford it if my dad's health didn't improve.

Near the end of the summer my dad got so sick he had to take some extended time off of work, and our family's money situation got really tight. We had to change our plans, so I registered at Sullivan High School - a public school just a couple of blocks from our apartment building in the heart of good old Rogers Park. We Catholic school kids always referred to it as St. Sullivan by the Lake.

As the summer wound down, I got a job as a bagger with a grocery store in the neighborhood. I would get off my shift at around nine-thirty at night and ride my bike down to the schoolyard or beach to meet up with everybody. Although I wasn't making a hell of a lot of money, I gave some of it to my parents in an attempt to help them out.

The school year started, and the thing I noticed my first day at Sullivan was the girls. Girls, girls, girls! Boy, had I made the right decision! During my first week there, the school janitor followed me around with a mop so no one would slip and fall on all of the drool I was producing.

As I began my junior year in high school, things at home went from bad to worse. My dad wasn't working at all, so I had to work as much as I could at the grocery store to help my parents out. Some of my checks went to help them pay the rent. In addition, my sister had run away from home. My mother was sick about it and filed a missing persons report in hopes that the police could find her.

My junior year was the only year in high school I didn't play any high school sports, although not for the lack of being recruited. During my first gym class at Sullivan, I was approached by the head coach of the football team.

"You ever play any football?" he asked.

"Yes, sir," I answered. "My freshman year at Loyola Academy."

"Well then, how about joining Sullivan's team?" he asked.

"I would, coach" I began, "But I have to work to help my family out right now."

"I understand. If things change let me know, OK?"

"Will do, coach."

Classes at Sullivan were a breeze compared to Loyola Academy and St. Vincent. That was a good thing for me because I was working a lot of hours and always seemed to be tired. I also soon found I was losing my motivation to apply myself to schoolwork.

About two weeks into the new school year, something great happened. Billy was thrown out of St. Vinnie's for numerous smoking violations and as a result, joined me at St. Sullivan by the Lake! Billy's first impressions of Sullivan were quite similar to mine. We had found our high school nirvana!

Several weeks after Billy started going to Sullivan, I had a bunch of the guys over to my apartment for some drinking since my parents were visiting relatives for the weekend. Around one in the morning, we ran low on beer

so Billy and I volunteered to go to Jokers Pub to buy another six pack.
Jokers was a serious, open to four a.m., bust-out bar on Devon Avenue just
a block away from my parents' apartment.

We made the short walk over to Jokers, and once inside we saw some
guys from Sullivan so we decided to have a beer there. I started a
conversation with Tommy Pines, a senior at Sullivan and the football team's
starting center. Somehow we got around to talking about Billy who was up
at the bar talking to some other guys from Sullivan.

"Your fucking one-armed friend is a friggin fruitcake, isn't he?" Pines
asked.

"If ya know what's good fer you, I wouldn't talk about my friend that
way," I shot back.

"Oh, yeah," Pines replied. "Not only is he a fruitcake but so are you
buddy boy!"

And with that comment Tommy Pines decided to throw a punch at me.
I responded in kind. We ended up on the wet, sticky floor of the bar rolling
around, trading punches. Butch McCarthy, the owner of Jokers, who was
this huge, three-hundred-pound tattooed guy came over to break up the
fight. Butch picked me up in the air with his right arm and Pines up with his
left arm.

"YOU MOTHER FUCKERS WANT TO FIGHT IN MY BAR!?"
Butch yelled. "FUCK YA!"

And with that he threw Pines out the front door of the bar and then
dragged me to the bar's back door and threw me out as well. Because the
bar was jammed packed, Billy hadn't seen what had transpired so he
remained in the bar. As I started to walk down the alley that ran behind the
bar I thought to myself, man what just happened!?

I thought the fight between me and Pines was done, but little did I
know it was just about to begin. All of a sudden, Tommy Pines and his
older brother appeared in the alley. Pines came at me, and under the glow
of an alley light we began to trade punches and wrestle one another again.
We both fell down hard, Pines landing on top of me. I was able to flip him
onto his back, and just as I was about to raise my arm and start punching
his lights out, I felt a hard kick to my head delivered from behind me. It
was Tommy's older brother who began pummeling me with kicks and
punches for several moments. All I could do was to try to cover my head
and take it.

By this time a crowd had rushed out of Jokers and gathered to watch the
late-night alley-fighting festivities, and fortunately for me I had an ally in it.
Donny Daniels, my old pelting buddy from the schoolyard, was in the
crowd and having gone to Sullivan he knew the Pine brothers. He knew
that if nobody stopped Tommy and his older brother, they just might beat
me to death. So Donny jumped in and tried to calm the older brother

down, and a couple of other guys, including Billy who had just arrived on the scene, stepped in between Tommy and me. As I slowly picked myself up off the ground, I could tell I had gotten the worst of it. I was beaten and bloody and had a very swollen right eye that would soon turn quite black and blue.

Billy and Donny guided me back to my parents' apartment where the guys were wondering what the hell had happened to us. When the guys saw me walk into the apartment, one of them ran to my freezer and pulled out a frozen piece of liver sausage and handed it to me, instructing me to hold it against my bulging eye. Shortly afterwards, everyone left and I was alone in my misery.

I woke up early the following morning feeling and looking like hell. I had to go to work at the grocery store but decided to go in late. I needed time to get myself together and go ride my bike by Jokers. I hadn't come home from the brawl with my expensive letterman's jacket I had bought at Loyola Academy during my freshman year. I hoped I'd find it lying in the alley somewhere. Unfortunately, I drove down the now-deserted alley and found nothing.

I finally made it to work and went directly to my store manager to apologize for being late. He took one look at me and put up his hands and said I didn't have to explain. I worked my usual shift then went home and collapsed.

I'm not sure if this incident helped me gain any respect around my new school, but everybody knew me after that. Tommy Pines and I avoided one another, and I eventually become friends with his younger brother Willy when I played football my senior year.

Even though Billy and I were going to Sullivan and making friends there, we still hung out at the schoolyard with our Catholic school buddies, including Will. One weekend, a group of us bought a gallon of cheap vodka and went over to Jimmy Morgan's parents' apartment, which was across the alley from the schoolyard. Jimmy was three or four years older than us but loved to party and didn't care who he partied with. We mixed up a very lousy batch of vodka gimlets. They tasted like shit but did the trick. We were feeling no pain in just a short while. We started listening to tunes and before long we were belting out the best of the Beach Boys.

Having killed the vodka, we decided to make our way over to the schoolyard to see what was going on. Will, Billy, Jimmy Morgan, and I left the apartment singing at the top of our lungs. As we entered the schoolyard, Will dropped back saying he had to take a leak. We continued on around to the steps of the auditorium and continued our singing. Five or ten minutes passed when someone finally realized Will had never returned. We all got up and started to walk toward the rear of the schoolyard. As soon as we turned the corner, we saw Will hanging onto a pole outside the gym doors.

In a matter of minutes he had gone from a happy, singing drunk to a sloppy, barely able to walk and talk drunk. We rushed to his side to prevent him from cracking his head wide open should he fall off his pole. Several minutes later, Will passed out.

"What are we going to do now?" we asked one another.

Will's parents' apartment building was a good walk from the schoolyard, too long of a distance to drag a six-foot stiff. Even if we could drag him home, what would we tell his folks? As we sat discussing this issue, Donny Daniels pulled into the schoolyard in his parents' VW bus.

We quickly approached Donny and explained the situation.

"FUCKING, STRIKER," Donny shouted in the direction of Will, "LOOK AT YOU, YOU'RE A FUCKING MESS!"

After a little discussion, Donny agreed to drive Will home. Donny, Billy, and I loaded Will's limp body into the VW and we headed out. When we got to Will's apartment, it appeared no one was home.

Great I thought, we may pull this one off yet.

We half carried, half dragged Will to the vestibule front door. It was locked. We dug into his pockets and pulled out his keys and started trying each one in succession. Will, now becoming slightly aware of where he was and what was going on, managed to mumble, "Wrong key."

Finally we hit upon the one that opened the vestibule door, dragged him in, and walked up the short flight of stairs to his apartment door. Again we fumbled through his set of keys until we found the one that worked. Once in his apartment, we asked Will which bedroom was his.

"On the right," he meekly replied.

We dragged him down the darkened hallway and pushed open the door of the first bedroom we came upon, which was on the right side of the hallway. We walked in and laid him down on the bed.

"Wrong room," Will moaned softly.

"Don't worry, buddy, you're home," I answered.

"Wrong bed," Will sighed.

"Sweet dreams, Willy boy," Donny said as we made our way out of the room and down the stairs, laughing to ourselves as we thought about how funny it would be when the usual occupant of that bed came home and found a passed-out Will in it.

I didn't consider getting Will back to his parents' apartment safely that day as payback for him saving my life, but at least it counted a little bit toward it.

* * * *

It was about this time in our young delinquent lives that we came up with a brilliant idea for getting free beer. The scam involved Albion Liquors, one of the liquor stores on Sheridan Road. With Albion Liquors you could call them up and order some booze and an old guy, who we had nick-named Bob Albion, would ride up on his dilapidated, nineteen-forties-style bicycle and deliver the stuff to your house or apartment. He had an old-fashioned, wired basket on the front of his bike where he carried his liquor load. This delivery method made our scam possible.

One day while sitting around the schoolyard, we decided to put the new scam into action. We went over to Brian Murphy's parents' two flat and went down into the finished basement. Both of Brian's parents were at work, so everything was cool. We called Albion Liquors and ordered a gallon bottle of vodka to an address that was just north of Brian's two flat. Then a couple of minutes later, we called back and ordered a case of beer to an address that was four or five houses to the south of Brian's two flat.

We figured that good old Bob Albion would come with both orders and stop first at the apartment building that was north of Brian's two flat. When Bob walked into the building to deliver the bottle of vodka we would have a window of opportunity to run out from our hiding place, which was a gangway alongside the next building, and snatch the case of beer that was to be delivered next.

The plan worked perfectly. Bob Albion went in to make his first delivery and while he did, we jumped on the case of beer left sitting in his basket. We disappeared into the gangway between the two buildings and made our way into the alley, which ran behind Brian's two flat. A short distance later we turned into Brian's backyard and ran down the stairs leading to his basement. Once in the basement, we locked the door behind us. We made sure to drink a toast to Bob Albion, beer delivery man most extraordinary.

12 GOING MOBILE

Ever since I had gotten my driver's license at the seminary, I had wanted to buy a car and now, with some money I had been saving for a very long time, I eventually had enough to by an old beater. My dad and I went out to Skokie to look at a 1966 Chevy Caprice Classic. In its day, it had been quite the car with power windows, tilt steering wheel, and a very powerful 396, V8 turbojet engine.

I ended up paying the guy five-hundred dollars for it, and as I drove it back home I couldn't wait to show it off to my friends. The next day, I drove by the schoolyard and the usual gang was there. I let a bunch of guys in and we cruised around the neighborhood for a couple of hours. I'll never forget the sense of new-found freedom the car provided me. I felt as if I was no longer chained to the schoolyard, or the beaches or the neighborhood. With my car, the world was now truly my home and I could explore it as I saw fit.

After I had the car for about a month, I decided to give it a very thorough cleaning one day. As I was cleaning out the interior, I found a couple of marijuana pipes hidden in the ashtray compartment. I thought they must have belonged to the son of the old guy who had sold me the car. I knew a couple of the guys around the schoolyard who were into pot, so the next time I saw them I told them of my discovery and asked them if they might want to keep the bowls. They accepted and asked if I wanted to get high with them. I thought about it for a minute and decided that in some weird way maybe finding the bowls in my new car meant I should try pot at this point in my life. We got high in my car and then spent the rest of the afternoon driving around, listening to music. I didn't really like it because I was already nervous since I was an inexperienced driver to begin with. The pot seemed to just exaggerate my own anxiety. I wouldn't smoke it again until late in my senior year of high school.

Not long after discovering the pipes in my car, I was at home one Saturday night getting ready to go out when our apartment doorbell rang. I answered it and found Billy making his was up our staircase. I had called him earlier so we could drive to a party together and since he lived across the street just a couple of apartment buildings down, he had decided to walk over.

I finished getting ready, said good-bye to my parents, and then Billy and I headed out. We made our way out to the street and jumped into my beater. As I pulled away from the curb, I glanced down the side street, which dead ended at the street we lived on. Out of the corner of my eye, I saw my sister Maureen crossing the street. This was significant because my parents had reported Maureen as a missing person to the police, as she had not been seen or heard from for several months.

I slammed on my brakes and threw the car in reverse.

"WHAT THE FUCK, MAN!" Billy shouted.

I floored the accelerator and peeled backwards about thirty feet, smoke billowing up from my rear tires. I then threw the car in drive and pressed my foot hard on the accelerator, turning the wheel sharply to the left. Billy gripped the dashboard with all of his might as we peeled down the street.

"MY SISTER!" I yelled out as we raced down the street toward her.

When we arrived where I had seen her, I slammed on my brakes hard and threw the car into park just as my sister was reaching an entrance to an apartment building. I jumped out of the car and ran to her, grabbing her by an arm just before she made it through the doorway.

"LET GO OF ME!" she screamed as she tried to hit me.

"CALL THE POLICE!" I screamed to Billy who had followed me out of my car.

Billy took off running as my sister continued to struggle. As I fought to keep a grip on her, I told her how much our mom was worried about her and how much we thought she needed help.

Billy reappeared around the corner, and I asked him if he had made the call.

"Yep," Billy answered.

"Thanks, man," I said as I continued to struggle to keep a hold of my sister.

Several minutes later, a squad car pulled up and two cops got out.

"What's going on here?" one of the cops asked as he approached us.

"This is my sister," I began. "She's been reported as a missing person by my mother. You can check," I said.

"Let her go," the taller of the two cops ordered.

"I don't want to lose her," I said still holding my sister tight.

"She's not going anywhere. Now let her go," the tall cop repeated.

I let my sister go and as I did, I began to explain to the cops how my sister had starting using drugs and had fallen in with the wrong crowd. I told them all my mom wanted to do was to find her and get her some help.

The shorter cop went back to the squad and ran my sister's name through the system. She came up as a missing juvenile, so when he came back to us he announced that he was going to bring her to the station house and he wanted me to follow him there.

They loaded my sister into the squad car and Billy and I jumped into my car.

"Dude you just fuckin' had your sister arrested!" Billy said to me, looking incredulous.

"Dude, she needs help and my mother is worried sick about her. Now we might be able to get her the help she needs," I responded.

Billy said he understood and a short time later we arrived at the police station. Once there, the police asked me to verify my home phone number, and then they called my parents. My mother and father arrived a short time later, and my mom asked me what had happened. I told her I had stumbled upon my sister, and she gave me a big hug and thanked me. The cops told my mom she could see my sister and also told me I could go if I wanted to. So Billy and I left and headed out to the party we had originally intended to go to.

I couldn't stop thinking about my sister the rest of the night. Billy and I rehashed what had happened, and it all seemed so surreal. My parents eventually were able to place my sister in a drug rehab facility where she was able to get help and turn her young life around.

* * * *

On a Saturday night about three weeks later, Billy, Will, Brian Murphy, and I were cruising around the neighborhood in my Chevy Caprice just tossing back some beers and shooting the breeze. There was a Sullivan dance that night. We drove by but didn't go in as Billy and I had yet to really become friendly with the Sullivan crowd.

The end of our night found us all feeling pretty good, parked down at Albion beach, when we saw a taxi cab coming east down Albion toward us and the lake. The cab passed us and then proceeded about fifty feet further to the dead end of the street. On the other side of the guard rail, which marked the end of the street, was Albion beach. The cab began to make a three-point turn but the driver, having pulled parallel alongside the guardrail, turned the cab off and got out. As I watched through my side-view mirror, the driver began to walk toward us.

"What the hell does this cabbie want?" I said out loud.

"What cabby?" Will asked.

"The one that just drove by us!" Billy barked.

The cabbie walked up to my window, pulled out a handkerchief, and asked if we wanted to buy some pot. Seeing the opportunity to hassle the guy, we all hopped out of my car. Billy walked up to the guy and asked to look at the pot. The cabby carefully unfolded the handkerchief and when he was done unfolding it, held it up to Billy. Billy immediately knocked the hanky out of the guy's hand and the pot fell onto the street.

As Billy was capturing this guy's attention, two other events were taking place. I had slipped back into the car and pulled out a tire iron I kept under my seat and Will began to make his way to the guy's cab.

The moment Billy knocked the pot to the ground, the cabby realized he was fucking with the wrong group of guys. Disregarding the fallen pot, he began to make his way back to the cab. As he retreated, I yelled at him to get the fuck out of our neighborhood as fast as he could and held the tire iron up in the air to show him we meant business.

As soon as Will got out of my car, he made a beeline to the guy's cab, opened up the driver's door, and jumped in. Immediately we heard two screams from the cab. Will jumped out of the driver's side door as a black woman, the cab driver's companion, jumped out of the passenger's side. To this day I'm not sure who was more surprised or scared, Will at finding someone sitting in the cab or the woman at having a white guy jump into the driver's seat.

The driver began to sprint back to his cab as we all started walking slowly toward it, me still wielding the tire iron. The cabby jumped into the cab and motioned to the woman to hop back inside as well. Once she was in, he threw the cab into drive and accelerated. By this time, we were right on top of the cab, and I took a swing with the tire iron as the cab sped by me. I made contact with the left front headlight, and the sound of it shattering pierced the quiet of the lakefront night.

Unfortunately for me, we made one mistake. When we had first gotten out of my car to confront the driver, someone left my car's rear door open on the street side of the car. As the taxi driver screeched away, he made a direct hit on that door of my car and completely ripped it away from the body of the car. My car door tumbled, turned, and bounced a good thirty feet down the street in the wake of the fleeing cab. The four of us stood in stunned silence with our mouths wide open. Talk about your Instant Karma!

At that point I did the smartest thing all night. As the cab sped off into the night, I noted its identification number, 8287. After what seemed to be an eternity someone shouted out, "Let's get that nigger!"

My body shook in response. I turned and began to move toward my car. We were all in the car when I thought, yeah, right, I'm going to go chasing around some lunatic cab driver with one of my car doors missing. For the first time all evening, my sense of reasoning kicked in.

"No," I said out loud, "let's not chase him. Let's call the police and report him as a drug dealer. The first thing we need to do is to hide all of the remaining beers we have, guys, so everything out of the car."

The guys pulled out all of the remaining beers and carefully hid them in some bushes along the street. Everyone then piled back into the doorless car, and I pulled away from the curb. I decided that in order to preserve the crime scene, I should leave my car door lying in the street. I drove the three blocks to the Loyola L station, and we went inside to call the police. I dialed 911. When a dispatcher answered, she asked if it was an emergency. I told her it wasn't and was transferred to a non-emergency number.

"Hello," I began. "I was just approached by a drug dealer down at Albion Beach, and when I tried to make a citizen's arrest he resisted and sped away in his cab and tore one of the doors off of my car."

"Sir, are you trying to report a car accident?" the female voice on the other end of the line replied. "If you are, I suggest you drive to the nearest police station and fill out an accident report."

"No, I'm not trying to report a car accident. This cab driver was trying to sell me drugs, and when I tried to hold him until the police came he escaped and tore my car door off," I stated as the anger began to well up inside me.

"Sir, I'm not sure there is anything I can do for you," the dispatcher replied.

"Well," I said as the volume of my voice began to rise. "Maybe I'll just have to kill somebody to get a squad car down to Albion Beach!"

Will, seeing my exasperation, nodded to me and reached for the receiver. In a calm voice he asked the dispatcher if she could just direct a squad car to go down to Albion Beach to investigate the situation. Will then hung up the phone.

"The dispatcher said she would send a squad but it might be awhile before they got down there," he announced.

"Good," I replied.

We piled back into the doorless car and made our way back to the beach. As we turned on to Albion, we saw the reflection of the streetlight on my door, which was still lying in the street where it had ended up after its tumbling and bouncing routine. I parked my car exactly where it had been before and turned the car engine off. Turning to my buddies I said, "OK, time to get our stories straight."

"Right," my buds replied.

"We'll tell the cops that we came from the Sullivan dance and had just pulled up and parked when the guy in the cab approached us."

"Right," they chorused.

"He showed us some pot, which he wanted to sell us," I continued.

"Da pusha man!" Will said in his best smart-ass tone.

"We'll say we got out of the car and were going to hold him while one of us went to call the police."

"OK," they responded.

"But he made a break for his cab and in his haste tore the door off," I said.

"Right," they answered.

And then I added, "I think it would be wise not to mention Will's little foray into the cab or my little wielding of the tire iron. OK?"

"Oooh, but that adds a little humor and excitement to the story," Will said sarcastically.

Several minutes later the police arrived and we all hopped out of the car to begin our retelling of the night's events.

"Officers, we were trying to make a citizen's arrest," I began.

"Citizen's arrest?" one of them echoed with raised eyebrows.

"Yeah, you know," the other cop offered. "Like on the *Andy Griffith Show* when Gomer tries to arrest Deputy Fife for making an illegal U-turn. Citizen's arrest, Citizen's arrest," the cop then chirped sarcastically.

The other cop just shook his head as I went on recounting the events of the evening just as we had discussed, my buddies adding their own editorial comments along the way.

"OK," one of the cops said. "Now if this guy had some pot and you said you knocked it out of his hands then the evidence should be lying in the street, right?"

"Right," our chorus of voices rang out.

"OK," the cop continued. "Then let's search the street and try to find it so we'll have some evidence."

Now the street was only illuminated by a single streetlight and the chore of tracking down the couple of joints worth of pot that Billy had knocked out of the cabby's hanky into the street seemed impractical at best and in reality probably impossible. However, we spread out and gave it our best try anyway.

"I think I found it!" Billy declared at one point having picked something up from the street.

He then handed his find over to one of the officers. The cop walked over to the streetlight and with the help of its illumination declared, "God dammit, that's a little piece of hardened dog shit!"

With that, the search was effectively called off.

"Here's what I'll do," the officer started. "I'll file an accident report and include the number of the cab that you gave me. That way you should be able to get your car door fixed at least."

"OK, thanks," I said thinking that was better than nothing.

After completing and giving me a copy of the accident report, the police got back into their squad and drove away. Will and I walked down Albion and retrieved my battered door, brought it back to my car, and threw it into my trunk. By now it was pretty late, and we all had had enough excitement for one night. I drove the guys home and later found out that Brian Murphy's dad was awake and looking out onto the street when I had dropped Brian off.

Seeing Brian exit out of my doorless car his dad, a fireman who also happened to have numerous relatives who were cops, immediately thought we were cruising around in a stolen car. As Brian entered his parents' apartment, his father said, "Brian, tell me where you guys got that car or I'm going to kill you." Brian related to his father as quickly as he could the events of the evening so that his young life might be spared.

"Unbelievable!" was his dad's stunned reply.

Unbelievable indeed!

I made it back to my parents' apartment and spent a fitful night's sleep, dreaming about cabs, tire irons, and car doors tumbling down the street. The next morning I told my mother the pasteurized version of the story and assured her everything would be OK. I wasn't really sure what was going to happen, but I didn't want her to worry.

About a week after the incident, I was contacted by the cab company. An insurance adjuster called me and told me that he wanted to come out and take pictures of my car. I told him fine and several hours later he arrived. I had been driving around the neighborhood doorless in the interim, and it was quite the conversation starter.

A week after the visit from the insurance adjuster, I received a summons to appear in court. I was charged with attempted assault and battery by the cab driver who claimed I attacked him with a tire iron.

"How dare he!" I mumbled to myself as I read through the summons.

In the meantime, I got some estimates on repairing my door and finally got it fixed several months later. I settled with the cab company's insurance carrier for about four-hundred dollars. The actual cost to repair the door was about two-hundred-and-fifty dollars, so I used what was left over to tune the car up.

My court date was soon approaching, and I began to get nervous so I enlisted my older brother Jerry to appear with me in court. He was not a lawyer but was a good talker and I figured I didn't want to go down there by myself. My court appearance was at the Belmont Avenue police station, which also served as a court house. My brother suggested we get down there early and try to find the cab driver before we got in front of the judge. Jerry thought our best strategy would be if we could talk to the cabby and maybe offer him a little something to drop the charges.

We arrived a good hour before my scheduled appearance and stood out in the large hallway outside of the courtroom. With every new black male face that appeared in the hallway my brother asked, "Is that him?"

"I'm not sure," was always my response.

After several requests by my brother to identify the cab driver, I realized I didn't remember him well enough to be able to recognize him that day. My heart sank as I realized I would have to go in front of the judge without cutting a deal with the cabby.

Fortunately several people who had court dates that day did offer some comedic relief. My brother and I, who were both dressed in suits, were approached by no fewer than five individuals who asked us if they could hire us as their attorney.

"I should hang out here every day! I could make a fortune!" my brother exclaimed.

These interruptions, coupled with my brother's sense of humor, helped ease my tension.

Finally my time to appear in court came, and as I sat waiting for my case to be called, I could feel my mouth drying and my palms sweating. I heard my name announced by the clerk of the court and, as if in a dream, I walked up to the front of the courtroom and took my position in front of the judge. I glanced to my right to see if the plaintiff, the cabby, had taken his position. My eyes grew wide as I realized no one had walked to the plaintiff's position in front of the judge. The cab driver's name was called again. This time I glanced backwards toward the seated audience to see if I could detect any movement. Nothing!

"Your honor," the clerk of the court began, "it appears that the plaintiff in this matter is not in court today"

"I see," the judge replied. "Would the state like to make a motion?" the judge asked the state's attorney.

"Your honor, the state asks that the charges be dismissed against the defendant," the state's attorney replied.

"So ordered," the judge said as he slammed his gavel down and then added, "Next case."

With that, I looked at my brother who shot me the "let's get the hell out of here look." It felt great to get out of the courtroom and into the fresh air of the parking lot. All that worrying and the fucking guy didn't even show up for the court date.

13 "SHOW US YOUR TITS"

During Memorial Day weekend of my junior year, a bunch of us decided to go to the Indianapolis 500 for the very first time. It all started out with Jimmy Morgan as his sister, brother-in-law, and their kids had been going to the race on the Memorial Day weekend holiday for a number of years and when Jimmy told us about it, we decided to go, too.

Jimmy's brother-in-law, during a previous trip to attend the race, had hooked up with the Jones family who lived a couple of blocks from the Speedway. They allowed Jimmy's sister, brother-in-law, and the kids to camp out on their lawn and use their washroom. This year the Jones family had also agreed to allow us to do the same.

I was all of seventeen years old when I drove to Indianapolis with Billy, Will, Jimmy Morgan, and Brian and Mike Murphy for the first time. The ride from Chicago to Speedway, Indiana takes about three and a half hours. As we pulled off the expressway onto the main street that runs through Speedway, I could tell we were about to experience something we had never experienced before in our young lives.

There were people lining both sides of the road as far as the eye could see. RVs were spread out everywhere, and two things distinctly filled the air: the noise of people hawking tickets to the big race and the smell of barbecue.

We slowly drove toward the track then turned off of the main drag and onto a side street. Several blocks down the side street we turned right and made our way to the Jones' house. As we drove down the street, we saw that the friendly inhabitants of Speedway were renting out their lawns to racing fans as evidenced by the RVs, cars, and tents that filled the lawns everywhere.

We were greeted by Mr. and Mrs. Jones, an average-looking couple in their fifties or early sixties. I backed up my 1966 Chevy Caprice Classic onto their lawn and immediately we started to party because, after all, that's what Indy is all about. It's truly the world's largest party.

Our itinerary for the weekend was simple: arrive in Speedway early Saturday afternoon and spend Saturday night partying our asses off; wake up early Sunday morning and head to the track to watch the race and party some more; after the race, hang around for a couple of hours to sober up a bit before making our return trip to Chicago.

Around seven o'clock that Saturday evening, someone suggested breaking out the grill and cooking up some hot dogs and burgers we had brought along. I started the grill and after the coals got hot we threw on the meat. By this time, Billy was feeling no pain. I made the mistake, about twenty minutes later, of asking him if he thought the hot dogs were done.

"I'd don't fuckin knoooow," he slurred. "Led me cheeeeck."

Billy bent over the mini-grill and proceeded to snatch a hot dog off it with his mouth. He must have been really hammered because when he came up from the grill, he had the hot dog in his mouth and the outline of the grill grate burned into his chin.

"I TINK THEY'RE FUUUCKIIIING DUN!" he shouted to no one in particular, as pieces of charred hot dog flew out of his mouth, never once acknowledging the burn he had just experienced.

After dinner, in the heat and humidity of a late-May, Midwestern evening, we grabbed our coolers full of beer and made our way down to the strip. We soon found out one of the major events on the Saturday night before the race was TITS! We learned that the women who went to Indy and made their way to the strip on Saturday night found themselves the targets of much verbal abuse. The unofficial mantra at Indy that evening was "SHOW US YOUR TITS!"

One guy started up a collection among the onlookers to persuade an unusually endowed woman to show them. Other guys yelled at good-looking women on the street. "Show us some titty and win the kitty!" or "Big or small we love them all!" while dozens of other guys stopped in their tracks to see what the outcome of their request would be. Some of the ladies walking the strip that evening did, in fact, oblige these requests.

After several hours on the strip, people watching and drinking beer, we finally got tired and headed back to the Jones' house. As we arrived, it began to rain, which caused us to abandon the idea of sleeping on the Jones' lawn in our sleeping bags and instead forced us to fit six guys into my Chevy for the evening. During the night, as the humidity engulfed us like a sock on a foot, six drunk, hot, sweaty, and foul-smelling guys tried to catch some sleep as we also fought over whether the air conditioning should be on or off.

The following morning broke hot and humid but clear. One of Jimmy Morgan's nephews, a kid about six years old, walked up to our car and motioned for us to roll down our window. As I rolled down my driver's window, a toxic vapor of our own making, which we were unaware of having spent the night basking in it, escaped the car. The poor kid never knew what hit him. With one good whiff of the foul odor, the kid crumpled to the ground like a crushed paper cup. Several of the other kids who witnessed the first kid go down began to approach, but by the time they were within five feet of our car, they let out a scream, pinched closed their nostrils with their fingers, and fled the immediate vicinity of the car with their young lives. There was some talk among the adults who were also camped out on the lawn about calling in a toxic waste team to hose us and the car down, but it was just idle threats. As for the kid who was felled by the smell emanating from our car, no real harm was done other than the fact he had probably lost a good portion of his sense of smell for the rest of his life.

After escaping our tomb of stink, we washed up in the Jones' bathroom and went to a local VFW Post for some chow. There's absolutely nothing better for a hangover than a greasy meal. Once back at the Jones' lawn, we loaded up our coolers with more beer and made our way to the track to witness the "Greatest Spectacle in Racing."

Once in the grandstands Will realized that he should not have worn jeans as the temperature was about ninety-five degrees and he was dying from the heat.

"Anyone have a pair of scissors or a knife I could borrow?" Will blurted out to no one in particular.

"What for?" I asked.

"I want to cut off the legs of my jeans. I'm sweating my fucking balls off in these long pants."

"I don't have a knife but I do have a nail clipper," Mike Murphy said as he held it up.

"Let me see that," Will said as he took the clipper from Mike and began to try to cut off a pants leg while still wearing the jeans.

Will probably spent a good twenty minutes trying to convert his long-legged jeans into a pair of jean shorts. The results of his efforts varied greatly and were accompanied by some well-deserved comments from his friends.

"Dude, what da fuck happened with the left leg?" Mike Murphy asked.

Will did a fairly good job of cutting off the right leg of his jeans. Although not perfectly straight, the cut was straight enough and most importantly at a good position on his thigh.

The left leg's cut was a train wreck. It had started out at about the same position of the right leg's but when Will cut toward his inseam, the cut veered severely toward his crotch. The result was that when he stood up his left nut, which was covered by his white briefs, hung out of his new jean shorts.

"Dude, you better go into acting cuz you'll never make it as a tailor," I announced as I poked at Brian Murphy and Jimmy Morgan to make them aware of the results of Will's little adventure into the world of tailoring.

"Ya trying to get a little sun on your balls!?" Jimmy Morgan asked.

"Fuck you guys, I'm a lot cooler now," Will said as he grabbed another beer from a cooler.

"I bet you are!"

We spent the rest of the afternoon catching rays, drinking beer, and basking in the excitement of race cars passing by at over two-hundred miles an hour.

After the race, we headed back to the Jones' house, Will's left nut still swinging in the breeze. We stayed there a while sobering up and finally said our goodbyes. We piled into my car and began our trip back to Chicago.

On the way home, we continued to party. Billy, in particular, kept pounding beers, and it became quite evident he was cursed with a rather small bladder. It seemed like every thirty minutes Billy asked me to pull over so he could take a piss. I obliged him for the most part, but when we got close to Chicago I finally told him he had to hold it.

"I don't think I can fuckin hold it!" Billy answered.

"Then piss in an empty beer can," I replied. "I'm not stoppin' anymore on the highway."

I never imagined Billy would piss in a beer can, but sure enough the next thing I knew Billy was jostling around the back seat getting ready to take a whiz!

"GREG, THIS CRAZY FUCKER'S TAKING A PISS BACK HERE!" Will shouted.

"Are you fucking kidding me?!" I said as I glanced into my rearview mirror.

"Man, I got to fuckin' go," Billy replied.

As Billy began, we all shook our heads in wonder and amazement.

"I'm done!" Billy announced proudly a short while later. "Now I gotta get rid of it. How come my window doesn't roll down?"

"That's the fucking door that got torn off and replaced, ya fuck!" I replied. "The power window hasn't worked since."

"How am gonna dump this then?" Billy asked. "Here, Will, dump this out your window, will ya?" Billy asked as he lifted the beer can, full of warm piss, toward Will.

"Fuck you, I ain't touching that," Will said with his hands up in the air and a smile on his face.

Jimmy Morgan and the Murphy brothers started laughing out loud as they glanced at Will with his hands up.

"Billy, open your door a crack and just pour it out," I suggested. "Unfucking believable!" I added as I heard the car door open and realized that Billy was about to pour out the can of warm piss as we hurtled down the highway at seventy miles an hour.

"Mission fuckin' accomplished!" Billy announced a few seconds later, as he slammed the door shut.

* * * *

As my junior year wound down the grocery store I worked at closed, and I was out of a job. Fortunately I was able to find another job soon as an all-around goffer at Harry Kirschenbaum and Sons clothing store. Kirschenbaum's was a family-owned, men's clothing store that had been a fixture in Rogers Park for over thirty years.

I also decided to go out for spring football and made quite an impression on the football coaches. Upon returning from an away football scrimmage and as I was getting off our school bus, our defensive coach pulled me aside and told me that if I kept working hard, I could become the first senior in school history to come out for football for only his senior year and start both ways. His little message pumped me up, and I promised myself, come hell or high water, I was going to play football for St. Sullivan by the Lake the next fall.

14 FOOTBALL FEVER

The summer between my junior and senior year passed quickly, and when the end of August rolled around, I was itching to start school because school meant football and the start of my senior year. Our football coach had sent each member of the team a letter in the middle of the summer basically challenging each of us to make our goal a trip to Soldier Field to play in the city of Chicago, Public League Championship game. I took the letter to heart and became very excited about the upcoming year and the prospect of playing in the championship game.

We started practice the last week of August. These were referred to as captains' practices since it was against Illinois High School Association rules to conduct organized practices with coaches before school officially started. The coaches came to the practices but more as observers than coaches. We practiced on the shores of Lake Michigan at Loyola Park on a field that was more glass and dirt than grass. To this day I still have scars on my elbows from the nicks and cuts I got from the scrimmages on that field. During these captains' practices, we primarily did a lot of running and stretching. We ran along the lakefront and through the sandy beaches of Lake Michigan, which was a real killer. I always seemed to be one of the last guys to make it back to the field after a run.

"GARRITY, WHY AREN'T YOU HUSTLING?" Brad Meier, one of our captains, shouted to me as I finally arrived back to the practice field one afternoon.

"Dude…I'm trying my best…I'm just slow," I managed to get out as I gasped for air.

My six foot two, two-hundred-and-forty pound, big-boned frame wasn't designed for distance running but surprisingly, I possessed good quickness for ten or twenty yards. The best use of my body type on a football field was for hitting people, whether on the offensive or defensive side of the ball.

School started a week later, and our first game was scheduled for the second week of September. During one of our last practices before our first game, I received a challenge from a junior who was playing against me on defense. I later suspected the coaches might have been behind it, but at the time I didn't know what to make of it. We were only supposed to be going through the scrimmage at half speed, but the guy across from me went full tilt on every play. Not only did he make me look bad but I took some lumps.

"Kick his ass, Garrity!"

"Yeah man, go full speed on that dude," were a couple of comments I heard from guys when I came back to the huddle.

I let it pass for two or three more plays, but then I finally had enough. On the next play from scrimmage, I went full speed and just kicked this guy's ass. We were practicing on the school's blacktop, and I dropped the guy right onto the hard, hot, blacktop surface. I stood over him and as he got to his feet, I head slapped him. First a right, then a left.

"YOU WANT TO GO FULL SPEED, I'LL GO FULL SPEED BUT I'M GONNA KICK YOUR ASS EVERY TIME!" I shouted while pointing a finger into his chest as we stood face guard to face guard.

"Relax, dude," the junior blurted out as I turned to go back to the huddle.

"Way to go, Garrity!" I heard from the rest of the guys as I returned to the huddle. I believe this might have been my final test before the season to see if I really belonged. I think I proved I did.

Our first game of the season was the first Chicago Public League game played at night in over twenty-five years. As our coach Mike Block put it, it was going to be an event and he didn't like losing events.

Our opponent was Dunbar High School, a predominantly black school located on the south side of Chicago. The game was at Hanson Stadium on Chicago's near northwest side and scheduled for seven o'clock. Since it was such a big deal, the local Chicago news stations sent reporters to cover the event. Because of this, we went onto the field at five o'clock and ran through some pre-game warm-ups so we could be seen live on the five o'clock news.

The game began, and it was a hard-fought contest. I started at right defensive tackle but did not play on the offensive line. The reason I didn't play any offense that night was because about a week before the game, I injured my right knee and the doctor told me I was suffering from some strained ligaments. The doctor recommended I not play at all for four weeks. I tossed out his advice but mentioned to my coaches that the knee was bothering me. They decided to rest me by moving me from my right defensive end position to right tackle and not playing me at all on offense.

The score was six nothing in favor of Dunbar about midway through the game when I recovered a fumble on Dunbar's twenty-five yard line. Several plays later, we scored and made the extra point. Seven to six, St. Sullivan by the Lake in the lead!

Dunbar scored again in the third quarter and the score was twelve to seven Dunbar. Time was running out in the fourth quarter, and Dunbar had the ball fourth and twenty from their own three-yard line. Our coaches thought for sure they would take a safety, give us the two points, and then take the free kick from the twenty. We'd end up with the ball at around mid-field with just seconds remaining.

Instead, their quarterback dropped back into their end zone and looked for a receiver. I beat my man badly on the play and forced my way up the middle and into the end zone. The quarterback, feeling my pressure, rolled to his left and found no resistance from our right defensive end. Fifty yards later, their quarterback was brought down from behind by one of our defensive backs. Game, set, match. We lost the event!

As we walked off the field, our defensive coach, Mr. Johnson, came up and grabbed me by the facemask.

"From now on, YOU'RE my defensive end! OK?" Coach Johnson shouted.

"YES, SIR!" I shot back.

I was thankful I had survived my first varsity game, a little sad we had disappointed Coach Block, and somewhat giddy that my fumble recovery had set-up our lone touchdown.

After the game, I went to Albion beach and drank some beers with the Saint Ignatius schoolyard crowd and talked about the game, as many of them had attended. The following morning, I woke up early to see if my name was mentioned in the newspaper. I deposited my fifteen cents into the newspaper dispensing machine and pulled out a *Chicago Tribune*. I quickly found the sports section and sure enough found a story about the game. My name was mentioned in a blurb about the fumble recovery. I deposited another fifteen cents into the machine and grabbed about ten more editions. I was a high school, football jock, celebrity!

I started the next game at right offensive tackle and right defensive end. My knee wasn't giving me any pain, so all systems were go. We had more luck this time around and won by a large margin, savoring the sweet taste of victory for the first time. As the season went on, one thing became quite clear, our squad was much improved over the team from last year, which had won just a couple of games. The coaches were excited to be out there with us, and I think their enthusiasm rubbed off on us as we started to pile up the victories.

I had my best game of the year when we played Prosser High School at Hanson Stadium. Playing at Hanson was both good and bad. The playing surface was astro turf, which I liked because I felt quicker on it. But it was bad because it was less forgiving than grass, and if you were ever caught on the bottom of a pile of human flesh your wind was surely to be squeezed out of you, a lousy feeling I had experienced on several occasions.

Prosser's best player was a big kid who was their center and because of this I was moved at game time from defensive end to nose guard so I would play right over him. I had never even practiced at nose guard let alone played the position in a game. The battles between me and this kid were pretty fierce, and I eventually knocked him out of the game for a while. He was replaced by a second stringer, and on the first play against this kid I knocked him back into their quarterback who was back pedaling to set-up for a pass play. Just as the quarterback was about to pass, I jumped as high as I could and extended my left arm and felt my fingertips on the ball as it sailed past me.

Because of my deflection the pass missed its mark and instead found its way into the arms of one of our defensive backs. A local newspaper photographer captured the moment of my deflection and it appeared about a week later in the local Rogers Park paper. Again, I couldn't help but procure about ten copies for myself.

With about two minutes left in the same game, Prosser had the ball on our fifteen-yard line, fourth and five to go for a first down. We were leading by one so they decided to kick a field goal to take the lead. They had a good field goal kicker who had won the game for them a week ago by kicking a thirty-five yarder, so things were looking pretty grim.

The ball was snapped, and I made my forward push. Much to my surprise, I didn't feel much resistance. I was able to get my left arm extended and felt the ball ricochet off of it. It bounced about twenty feet straight up in the air, and when it came back down one of my teammates pounced on it.

Now all we had to do was make a first down and the victory was ours. Unfortunately, Prosser's defense played us tough on the next three downs and we were forced to punt with only seconds remaining. Prosser tried a long pass play on first down that was unsuccessful and then brought their field goal kicker back into the game. This attempt was going to be from about forty yards, and our head coach decided to call our final time-out in order to ice their kicker.

As we lined up for this final play, I felt confident their kicker wasn't going to make the kick. It was an awful long one, and I'm sure in the back of his mind he knew I would be hauling my big ass up the middle toward him to try to block another. The ball was snapped, and once again I made good penetration. I just missed getting a piece of this one but immediately realized it had an awful low trajectory and appeared to be shanked to the left. As it went past me, I turned around to see where it was headed. As I came around, I saw time expire on the end zone scoreboard just as the kick died a premature death at our fifteen-yard line.

We had won a tough, big game, and I was the hero! I was congratulated by coaches, teammates, and fans as I left the field. It had been an awesome game, and with a season that had many high points this was probably my personal pinnacle.

We went on to have a very good season, ending up seven and two overall and six and one in our conference coming in second to Lane Tech. We won our homecoming game against Westinghouse, something a

Sullivan team hadn't done in several years, and it seemed to be a morale booster for the whole school.

When the regular season ended, we were scheduled to play CVS, otherwise known as Chicago Vocational High School, for our first opponent in the opening round of the Public League playoffs. CVS was a very large, all-black high school on Chicago's south side and it also happened to be the alma mater of famed Chicago Bears middle linebacker Dick Butkus. On the day we were scheduled to play CVS, we had a huge pep rally at school the morning of the game and then made our way over to Hanson Stadium.

It was a bitterly cold, November afternoon with some snow and sleet falling at game time. I hurt my left wrist early in the game but decided to gut it out. It hurt so much that at times I played with tears in my eyes.

CVS had a terrific running back and on one play during the second quarter he came right at me and as I attempted to wrap him up he just bounced off of me, broke several other tackles, and ended up scampering about forty yards for a touchdown. The score was thirteen to six very late in the fourth quarter when we failed to make a first down, which would have kept our final offensive drive alive.

"KEEP YOUR HEADS HELD HIGH, GUYS. WE'VE HAD A GREAT SEASON AND WE PLAYED AS HARD AS WE COULD TODAY," I shouted out to my defensive teammates as CVS ran out the game clock.

As time expired, I quickly congratulated the CVS players and then, with tears streaming down my eighteen-year-old cheeks, ran off Hanson field for the last time. I was the first player in the locker room, and as I entered it I threw my mouth piece across the room and began to really cry. The rest of the team soon filed in. All of the coaches went around the room shaking hands and congratulating everyone on a fine season. I showed my swollen wrist to the coaches, and they recommended I go get it x-rayed. I did but everything was negative, just a painful sprained wrist.

Prosser, the team we beat when I had my heroic afternoon, played our archrival Lane Tech for the city championship two weeks later. Lane beat Prosser soundly, and I wished we had had a second chance to play Lane. Unfortunately for me, our second chance against Lane Tech came a year later after I graduated, when Sullivan met Lane at Soldier Field for the city championship and beat them.

* * * *

In addition to the on-field action during my senior year, there was plenty of extracurricular action. From playing football, I got to know a whole different group of public school kids. I found out about different parties and hung out sometimes with a different bunch of guys. The most important question at St. Sullivan by the Lake every Friday afternoon was "Where's the party at this weekend?"

One Friday afternoon, the scoop was that a girl who attended one of the local, all-girl, Catholic high schools was having a bash and supposedly people from Sullivan were invited. The girl lived in Rogers Park so of course a bunch of us planned to attend. Billy, Will, and I drove to the address that had been circulating and found a group of our Sullivan buddies already there. Many of them were already pretty well lit up. What hadn't been mentioned at school that day was that a bunch of guys from Gordon Tech also knew about the party and planned to attend.

We were all in the basement of this girl's house drinking and listening to music when Will started to punk out, slam dancing, bouncing up and down and all around, and running into everything that got into his way. Soon a couple of other guys were doing it, and before long guys were shoving each other around and into things like chairs, tables, and lamps. Finally a table got smashed, and the girl whose party it was had had enough.

"SULLIVAN PEOPLE, YOU GOT TO BE COOL OR ELSE YOU HAVE TO LEAVE!" she yelled as she stood in the middle of the basement.

The room fell silent.

"I'm cool, I'm cool," Will, instigator par excellent announced as he proceeded to break into his most vicious punk out of the evening.

Several other guys joined in, and the general mayhem was back at full throttle.

"I'M CALLING THE POLICE!" the girl whose party it was announced.

Now that statement got our attention. We figured at that point we had truly worn out our welcome so we made our way up to the first floor and out onto the front porch of the house where we encountered a bunch of Gordon Tech football players who were just arriving.

To this day I'm not sure who started what, but in a flash, punches were thrown between the two factions. Someone fell and the mass of humanity that was now a tangled pile of human flesh, lurched toward Billy's and my position at the far end of the porch. Billy caught the full force of the lurch and unable to steady himself with only one arm, was knocked backwards off of the porch. Lucky for him, the fall was only three or four feet to the ground.

Before anyone could get seriously hurt in the scuffle, the police pulled up and everything broke up pretty quickly. What no one knew at the time was that the father of the girl whose house we were partying in happened to be a Chicago policeman, so it was a seriously bad place to decide to get rowdy.

The police ordered us all to disperse and disappear. Billy, Will, and I started walking away from the house when Will decided to shout something at a squad car that had just pulled up. The police jumped out of their car and immediately grabbed Will and put him under arrest. Just then another squad car pulled up and a sergeant got out.

"HEY, WHAT'S WITH ALL OF THE POLICE BRUTALITY?" I yelled at the sergeant, in all of my youthful wisdom.

My comment didn't go over very well with the sergeant.

"I'll give you police brutality!" the sergeant responded as he approached me and then swung and hit the left side of my face with a glancing blow.

Luckily I saw the punch coming and had a chance to duck somewhat and did not receive the full impact of the punch. My initial reaction was one of self-defense, and as I came out of my ducking position I began to raise my fist up in the air.

"GO AHEAD, TAKE YOUR BEST SWING, PUNK!" the sergeant yelled at me.

I quickly realized this was exactly what he wanted me to do so he would have an excuse to kick my young ass right there and then. I kindly declined his offer and instead surrendered peacefully and was promptly handcuffed, arrested, and shoved into a squad car.

When we arrived at the Foster Avenue police station, Will was put into one cell and I was put into another. Will's cell was empty, but mine was already occupied by an older, black man who was larger than me. He was sleeping on a metal bench in the cell with one cigarette and a book of matches resting near his head. He had numerous tattoos and scars on his arms, and his clothes appeared very worn and tattered. The type of character I wouldn't want to mess with.

After a while, Will, who was in the cell directly next to mine, asked if I had a light for his cigarette. I told him to hold on and reached down and very gingerly snatched the book of matches from my sleeping cellmate and passed them through the bars to Will's awaiting hands.

Several minutes passed when all of a sudden my cellmate awoke and bolted straight up into a sitting position, startling the hell out of me. Without saying a word, but with his dark eyes focused on me, he reached down slowly and grabbed his lone cigarette, and put it in his mouth. He glanced back down to where his book of matches had been resting and when he discovered they had vanished, looked up and stared coldly at me. Without saying anything my cellmate made a very effective communication, which I interpreted as something along the lines of "Where the fuck are my matches, white boy?"

With his eyes locked on me I held up my right index finger up and said in my kindest voice, "Just a second, buddy. I'll get those back for you."

As I walked to the corner of my cell, which was closest to Will's, a newspaper headline flashed in my brain. "Party-Going Teenager Strangled By Cellmate Over Matches Dispute."

In the calmest voice I could muster, given the circumstances and thinking that my fate might actually hinge on getting those damn matches back, I said, "Hey, Will, can you please hand back the book of matches I let you borrow?"

"Fuck you, Greggy," Will replied in a cocky voice.

"No, man, you don't understand," I began, a slight trace of panic now in my voice. "My nice cellmate here just woke up, and he'd really like to enjoy a cigarette."

All the while my cellmate just sat there, staring at me with his cold, dark eyes.

"What will you give me if I give them back?" Will asked.

"Oh, I don't know," I replied. "How 'bout I don't kick you're fucking ass when we get out of here," I said, panic now clearly conveyed in my voice. "Now just give me those fucking matches back, Will!"

Will must have finally caught on to the desperation in my voice because his hand poked out of his cell and he handed me the matches back.

"Allow me, good sir," I said as I turned to my silent cellmate, with matches now in hand.

I struck a match and held it up and lit his lone smoke. No "thank you" was forth coming, but as he took a long, deep drag of his smoke I knew my life no longer hung in the balance.

Will and I were bailed out several hours later by Billy, and eventually the charges of disorderly conduct were dropped.

"You saved my ass again, Billy! My cellmate was one bad looking dude!" I said as we left the police station together that night.

"Nothing you wouldn't have done for me, Double G," Billy replied.

15 SOYBEAN CAPITAL OF THE WORLD

My coaches at Sullivan sent my name to some colleges, and a few of them had contacted me. Mostly letters but also a few phone calls from coaches who wanted to know what my football plans were for the next year. I received a handwritten note from the head football coach at Millikin University in Decatur, Illinois. He seemed interested in me, and since the round trip bus fare from Chicago to Decatur was only about thirty dollars I decided to go for a visit.

After about a three-and-a-half-hour bus ride through the corn and soybean fields of central Illinois, I finally arrived in Decatur. I was met at the bus stop by the offensive line coach who was a slightly built, friendly guy with a blond mustache and short blond hair.

"Hi, Greg, I'm Coach Williams," he said as we shook hands.

"Nice to meet you, sir," I replied.

We got into his car and began driving to the campus. As I looked out the window, Decatur appeared to be just another sleepy, central Illinois, small town to me.

"How was your bus ride down?" Coach Williams asked.

Wonderful, nothing but corn fields and soybeans, I thought in the split second before I answered.

"It wasn't bad. Time passed pretty quickly," I replied.

"Good to hear. I'm going to take you over to our athletic complex so you can meet Coach Perkens, our head coach."

"Sounds good!"

Once we had arrived at the athletic complex, Coach Williams escorted me in and led me to the waiting area outside of the head coach's office.

"Sara, Coach is expecting this young man," Coach Williams announced to the woman sitting at the desk.

"OK, I'll let him know he's here," she answered as she shot me a quick smile and picked up the phone to relay the message.

"Greg, you enjoy your stay here and I will see you at nine Sunday morning at your dorm room to give you a lift back to the bus station. OK?"

"Thanks, Coach," I said as I shook hands with him.

As Coach Williams left, Sara got up from her desk and said, "Right this way."

Opening the coach's door she led me into his office. Coach Perkins was a large, older, grandfatherly type of guy who spoke in a slow, slightly Southern drawl.

"I'm very glad to meet ya, Greg, and was hopen' you might allow me to give ya a tour of our athletic facilities."

"Of course," I answered. "I'd love to see the facilities."

Coach Perkins led me on a tour of the fairly large and new athletic complex, and then we headed back to his office where we each sat down at his desk.

"Greg, I hope ya give Millikin University seerus consideration," he said.

At that point I knew it was time to mention money.

"Coach, I know the school doesn't offer athletic scholarships, but I understand some grant money may be available," I mentioned gingerly.

"That's right, young man," the coach replied. "Grants are usually based on financial need. Many of our football players are receiving em. Some get as much as half their tuition paid fer."

Not bad, I thought, considering at the time the only school in the state of Illinois with a higher tuition was prestigious Northwestern University.

"Well, Greg, it was nice to meet ya," the coach said as he stood up and extended his right hand toward me.

I reached out and shook it.

"Now I'd like to introduce ya to one of our players," Coach Perkins announced after the handshake.

Once outside his office, the coach introduced me to James Gordon, a junior wide receiver who was a starter on the varsity. James was a tall, muscular kid, with an all-American face. As James and I left the athletic complex to begin a tour of the campus, it began to rain. James' mood seemed to match the dark, gray weather perfectly. Overall, James admitted not being real happy at Millikin, and I soon discovered why.

Millikin had a student population of about fifteen hundred students, of which a good seventy-five percent belonged to a fraternity or sorority. James did not, and I sensed this was at the root of his unhappiness, as he seemed to be an outsider. Sure, he shared a nice rented house with a couple of other guys, but he wasn't part of the large, frat house social circle that existed on campus.

We ended our campus tour at James' house, and as we arrived there he told me he was going to turn me over to a couple of other football players who were going to show me around that evening. He made a call and shortly afterwards the two players came over to the house to pick me up.

Once they arrived, I was introduced to Tubes and Joe. Tubes was a starting middle linebacker on varsity, not very tall but solid as a rock. Joe played offensive tackle and was built like me, tall and husky. I also soon discovered they were both frat boys, Delta Sigs to be exact. Then the best news I had heard all day hit my ears.

"Say, Greg," Tubes began, "our frat is having a party tonight and we would definitely like you to come to it."

"Sounds great!" was my senior-in-high-school response.

But first we had to eat, they told me, so we made our way to a local supermarket, which was about a four-block walk from the campus. Tubes and Joe bought some stuff for dinner, and as we were walking out of the store, Joe pulled out several sticks of butter from his jacket sleeve.

"JOE!" Tubes declared in fake astonishment. "Now you don't want old Greg here thinking that we're nothing but a couple of common criminals, do ya?"

"Nothing common about us," Joe shot back without missing a beat. "Besides," Joe continued, "I didn't think we had enough money for the butter, and how could we dare try to fry up those mushrooms we bought without any butter?"

We continued our walk until we arrived at an apartment building located directly across the street from the main entrance of the campus. We made our way into the building and went upstairs to a second-story apartment. I was told the apartment belonged to a friend of theirs who happened to be out of town that weekend. We ate dinner there, and then it was time to go over to the frat house for the party. The party was held downstairs in the basement of this immense, old house that served as the home base for the Delta Sigma Phi Fraternity.

At the party was beer, loud music, and girls. I was in heaven! Although I felt somewhat uncomfortable not really knowing anyone, I knew this was the type of environment I could warm up to in a hurry. Many of the Delta Sigs were football players, and upon hearing I was a recruit many of them came up to me during the party and shot the shit with me. At one-thirty in the morning I found myself to be a little geezed and decided to walk back to campus to find my room in the dorm. Sober I probably would have had a hard time finding the dorm and my room, but given my current condition, the task seemed to be next to impossible.

As it turned out, I started my journey back to the dorm in the wrong direction and after about a mile, I turned around, having realized my mistake. After retracing my steps, I stumbled upon a late-night, fast food place and went in and bought a bag of grease. While there I asked a couple of people in the restaurant directions to Mills Hall, the dorm I was staying in. They were able to point me in the right direction, but my troubles didn't end there.

Once I made it back to the dorm, I couldn't find my room. I went into the TV lounge and asked a couple of the brothers who were in there if they could help me out. They did and I finally made it to my room about an hour or so after leaving the frat house. My journey should have taken all of about ten minutes!

Even though this was late April, the temperature outside was close to freezing. My room, however, seemed unbearably hot to me so I turned on the air conditioner and then sat down and enjoyed my bag of grease. That was the last thing I remembered.

I woke up the next morning, and my room was like an icebox. The temperature outside had dropped overnight, and several of inches of snow had fallen. I hadn't taken but two bites out of my greasy burger before passing out. What I woke up to was a room cold enough to be a meat storage locker, which also reeked of greasy burgers and stale beer farts. To add to this pleasant scenario, I was scheduled to be picked up by Coach Williams promptly at nine for a lift back to the bus station but had woke up at ten to nine.

Great, I thought, I'll be the only football recruit rejected by a college while still on his recruiting visit.

I hurriedly got my stuff together while trying to ignore the intense sensation that felt as if I had an ax deeply imbedded in my forehead. When the coach came knocking I met him at the door and quickly stepped out, leaving the stench of the room behind me.

"So, how'd you like your visit, Greg?" Coach Williams asked.

"I liked it," I answered as my beer breath enveloped both of us.

I liked everything, I thought, except this fucking headache! We walked out of the dorm together, got into the coach's car, and drove in relative silence for the five or so minutes it took to reach the bus station. At the bus station, we got out of the car and Coach Williams helped me get my suitcase out of his trunk.

"Well I hope you give Millikin serious consideration when you're deciding on what college you want to attend and play football for," he said as he handed me my suitcase.

"I will, sir," I responded as I shook his hand, already knowing in the back of my mind I could definitely handle four years of partying here. As I rode back to Chicago on the bus, nursing my hangover, I promised myself I would become a member of the Millikin Big Blue football team next year.

16 GOODBYE, ST. SULLIVAN BY THE LAKE

The very final month of my senior year passed by fast, like an express L train did when it wasn't making a stop at your station. There was a lot of partying, so many of my memories of those days are a blur. It wasn't uncommon for Billy and me to go out at lunch time and buy a six pack and then drive back to Sullivan and park my car in the student lot. We would "borrow" a couple of paper cups from the lunchroom and pour ourselves a couple of cold ones during lunch. After lunch, it was time to go back to classes.

When my senior year ended, my high school graduation came with no big emotional high for me. My mom made a big deal out of my graduation and said I would probably be her only child that she would see graduate from high school since my brother had skipped his ceremony and the verdict on my sister was still out. The graduation ceremony went off without a hitch. Afterwards there were some parties I stopped in at for a while but no major blowouts. I had to work the next day at Harry Kirschenbaum and Sons and arrived the next morning a little hung over.

The summer began and plodded along slowly, like thick syrup oozing its way down the trunk of a maple tree. Activities that used to occupy my time didn't seem as exciting anymore as partying at the schoolyard, and the beach had grown old. I wasn't sure if this was because I was maturing or just looking to get out of the old neighborhood and experience something new and different.

Billy's dream of becoming a fireman ended the day his arm was amputated and because of this he had been depressed on and off for several years now. Billy's mood swings, which had always been a part of his persona, had gotten more severe since the accident. Now depressed because he faced an uncertain future, you could never tell which Billy Smith was going to show up. I really felt bad for him, but I knew some of his dad's friends had some influence with the city of Chicago so I held out hope something good would come Billy's way very soon.

Will, on the other hand, was experiencing the dilemma of the smorgasbord. During his senior year, Will was offered basketball scholarships from some very good schools and was approached by some Chicago theater companies that wanted him to audition for roles in some upcoming productions. I knew wherever he wound up he would experience success.

With each passing summer day, I looked more and more forward to going away to school. At the end of my senior year, I had visited Elmhurst and North Park Colleges both located in the Chicagoland area. Since they were so close to home, I decided I should go to Millikin to force me to get away from the old neighborhood. Although I had been dating a girl for most of my senior year, I broke up with her when I knew I was going away to college.

That summer I continued to work at the clothing store and helped it close its doors for good after some thirty-five years in business. Rogers Park was a neighborhood in change. Predominately Jewish during the last forty years, it was now transforming into a very ethnically and racially mixed neighborhood. The Jews were moving out to Skokie and Highland Park while the East Indians, blacks, and Hispanics were moving in. Mr. Kirschenbaum, the owner of the clothing store, claimed he just couldn't make it with the new neighborhood composition. The newest members of the hood just weren't into going to a local clothing store and spending three to five-hundred dollars on a Hart, Schaffner, and Marx suit.

The neighborhood I grew up in, my "Patch of Green," was changing and so was my life. Not knowing what lie ahead made me excited and anxious, all at the same time.

17 COLLEGE BOUND

Once the clothing store closed, I found myself thinking even more about the upcoming school year. Because of university rules, I couldn't take my Chevy Caprice with me to school so I sold it to a mechanic who wanted the engine. I was actually able to recoup my initial investment of five-hundred dollars.

I was scheduled to report to double session football practices in mid-August, about a week and a half before the rest of the students arrived. The Millikin football coaches sent me a summer workout program, which included some personal, timed goals that I hadn't taken very seriously. I started working out about August 1 and just prior to leaving, ran some of the drills. I came up pretty short of the coaches' goals and wondered, probably for the first time, whether or not I could hack it playing college football in Decatur.

On the August morning I was to leave for college, the sun shone bright. I said good-bye to my mother, hugged and kissed her, and told her I loved her. She had tears in her eyes as I turned away from her and headed out the front door of our apartment.

My dad drove my two beat-up suitcases and me to the Loyola L station. Not much baggage for eighteen years of living and a nine-month school year ahead of me, I thought as we drove in silence. At the L, I would catch the train that would take me downtown to the Greyhound bus station. Once downtown I would catch the bus that would take me to my future.

We made our way, in my dad's Ford Galaxy 500, through the deserted streets of the neighborhood I had grown up in. As we passed the empty schoolyard, I thought about how much time I had spent there in the last ten years. All the good times shared with Billy, Will, and my other buddies from the Patch.

Part of me was happy I was about to start a new life adventure that would take me away from here, but there was also a part of me that was sad because the schoolyard had been my home away from home. It had been a refuge where I could share my thoughts with my peers, a place I was welcomed, and a place I felt that I belonged.

Upon arriving at the L station my dad, who was not a man who showed much emotion, helped me get my bags out of the car's trunk. He turned to me and reached out his hand to shake mine. I instinctively grabbed him and gave him a big hug, and as I did I heard him, in a voice that I perceived to be choking back tears say, "You be a good boy now."

Fighting back tears, I responded with a meek, "I will."

I proceeded into the Loyola L station, and as I paid my fare and walked up the long flight of stairs, I felt like the loneliest guy on earth.

Here I am, I thought, leaving my parents and friends for what? FOR WHAT!? I didn't know. COLLEGE!? I really didn't have a clue what collage life would be like. FOOTBALL!? I'm not in the greatest shape, and I will be playing against guys three years older than me.

As I reached the L platform and staked out my position to wait for the train, I looked out over the old neighborhood. Directly west of my vantage point, I could see St. Ignatius's Church steeple, which loomed so boldly over the schoolyard. I again thought of all the good times I had had there with my friends, and how much I was going to miss those good times.

I thought back to that fateful night, where just yards away from where I now stood, Billy had his brush with death. But then a moment later a more cheerful thought entered my head. Hey, I thought, if things don't work out at school, this old neighborhood and my friends will be waiting here for me.

Suddenly I was shaken out of my deep thoughts by the sound of the approaching train. I boarded the train and glanced out the window for one last look at the hood, and I then knew I was ready to begin my adventure. I was ready for college after all, I decided. Ready or not Millikin University, Decatur, Illinois, you fucking soybean capital of the world, here I come!

*   *   *   *

I arrived in Decatur four hours later. One of the coaches met me at the bus station and gave me and another freshman football player a ride to the dorms. I found my way to my room and walked in. The room was about the size of a large bedroom. There were beds on each side and small desks at the end of each bed. There was one window, which was in the middle of the wall that faced the door.

"So this is where I'm going to live with another person for the next nine months," I said out loud.

I unpacked my meager possessions and lay down on my bed. I was tired from the bus ride and wanted to take a nap. But the room, without air-conditioning, was very hot and I was too uncomfortable to sleep.

At six that evening, there was a football team meeting so at the appointed time I walked the short distance from my dorm to the athletic complex. The coaches welcomed everyone and passed out a practice schedule. The next day was equipment day and the following day double-session practices began in earnest. Meals were available to us at the school's cafeteria even though school had not officially started. The coaches dismissed us, and I went back to the dorm and watched some TV in the lounge area for a while and then went to bed.

The next day, equipment was issued. Equipment was issued in class order priority, seniors, juniors, sophomores, and then us lowly freshmen. The whole deal took about four hours. The best part was when it was over we got to go to lunch. I thought about tomorrow and the start of double sessions as I walked alone to the cafeteria. I decided then and there I would go to bed early again so I'd be fresh in the morning.

The next morning arrived, and I got up and made my way over to the locker room, got dressed in my practice gear, and made my way out onto the practice field. It was about nine in the morning and just beginning to get hot. Practice began, and once we started drills I really got heated up.

In mid-August, the humidity in Decatur was a killer. At least at Sullivan we practiced on the lakefront so we got a little breeze off the lake. No such luck here. In Decatur the air you breathed felt thick, like a warm milkshake, as you waded through it during your drills, sucking and gasping for more of it. And the sun, hanging in a cloudless sky like a vulture flying over road kill, beat down on us mercilessly, as if mocking us at our strenuous foolishness.

We practiced for about two hours, and just before we were dismissed the coaches told the freshmen we would be tested later that afternoon on the fitness goals we had been sent during the summer.

Great, I thought upon hearing the announcement. I couldn't do any of the drills back in Chicago when I was fresh let alone try them after a two-hour workout in super-humid conditions.

We broke for lunch, but I knew I wasn't going to eat anything. I figured the fitness tests, which consisted of running a four-forty for time and then completing a calisthenics obstacle course that involved running around the four corners of the football field, would probably kill me and if it didn't it would at least make me heave. I went to lunch and watched some of my fellow freshmen wolf down huge portions of food as I sat quietly sipping my water and fruit juices.

We were back on the practice field by one, and the hot, late-summer sun, now hanging in the sky directly over us, showed us no pity. A small group of freshmen were pulled off of the practice field every fifteen minutes or so and brought over to the playing field. Once there, they were first timed in the four-forty on the running track, which circled the football field. When they were finished, they were given thirty seconds of recovery time before they began their run of the obstacle course.

As I stood waiting to get into a drill, I watched a group of freshmen come back from the tests. Most of them looked dead with a few fresh faces plainly sticking out. I thought to myself the guys who had gone through the tests with no problem were probably the down-state guys who grew up in the middle of a cornfield and didn't have anything better to do all summer but to get in shape for these tests.

When it was my group's turn, we jogged over to the testing area. As we got closer, I saw a couple of freshmen players near the end of the obstacle course puking up their lunches all over the field. That's nice, I thought, just what I want to see before it's my turn to wade through hell.

I lined up on the running track with four other guys, and the coach announced, "Ready, set, go!"

I was the trailer in my group, but I wasn't too far off the pace. In my mind once around the quarter mile track didn't seem far but about three quarters of the way around, having sprinted all out so far, I suddenly felt like someone had just placed a piano on my back. I pushed on as hard as I could and as I crossed the finish line I heard the coach yell, "Sixty-eight."

Although I had finished last in my group, I had hit my four-forty running goal time exactly. The bad news was I had only thirty seconds to recover before I had to run the obstacle course and I felt absolutely exhausted. We all slowly jogged over to the beginning of the course, still sucking and gasping for air. Once we arrived at the beginning of the obstacle course, a coach started barking some instructions to us. Still hurting from the four-forty run, I wasn't really able to pay him any attention.

"Ready, set, go!" the coach yelled, and we were off.

Through a series of calisthenics, small sprints, agility drills, push-ups, etc. I finished the course on legs of rubber and lungs, which burned intensely. I failed the test, but on the bright side I wasn't the only one and most importantly, in my mind, I hadn't gotten sick.

"OK, you guys," a coach said as we stood doubled over sucking air like crazy. "The guys who didn't pass the obstacle course get to do it again before practice tomorrow."

Oh great, I thought, now I've really got something to live for, another torture session.

We were the last group to be tested that day, and as we were jogging back to the practice field the head coach blew his whistle and called the entire team in for a small talk before dismissing us. He briefly talked about how each of us had to give a hundred percent in everything we did whether it be a practice, a game. or our studies. After his little pep talk. I walked slowly back to the locker room feeling really thirsty and exhausted. I think that night I must of drank about ten gallons of water as I sat around my hot dorm room and recuperated from my day.

The following day just before practice, a bunch of us out-of-shape freshmen, obstacle-course flunkies, met out on the playing field to have another shot at it. We ran the course again and didn't do much better than the day before. To our surprise the coaches didn't tell us we had to do it again. They just said we needed to work extra hard to get into better shape and then told us to get back to the practice field. As I jogged back to the practice field, I thought about how tired I was and the fact I now had to go through a two-hour practice and then another two-hour practice later in the day. Fuck! So you wanted to be a college football player, I thought, as the beads of salty sweat began to roll down my forehead and into my eyes.

Practice that day, both morning and afternoon, proved to be a bitch, but I managed to survive and in doing so I gained some confidence and thought, hey, if I could survive today I could probably survive anything. This newfound confidence helped carry me through the rest of the season.

The other students arrived about a week later. I met my roommate and discovered he had lived in Berlin, Germany with his parents over the summer. His dad was some big wig, corporate type on business there. His grandparents lived in Illinois and had driven him to Decatur to start school. He was a real egghead type, pleasant enough, but we really didn't hit it off and I knew we wouldn't end up hanging out together.

I met some other freshmen on my dorm floor during the early part of September as well. One guy, Pete Walters, had gone to St. Pats High School in Chicago and knew some of my buddies from Rogers Park who had also gone to St. Pats. One night we were sitting around having a few beers and got to talking about people we knew who were really big drinkers. I told Pete about one of the older guys from Rogers Park who could drink anybody under the table.

"A 'natural' alcoholic if I ever saw one," I said to Pete. Pete, not to be out done, boasted of a fellow he knew who was a friend of his brother.

"This guy could drink all night and through the next day," Pete exclaimed. "In fact," he continued, "his parents tried to get him to stop drinking by having a doctor prescribe Antabuse medication! But this fucker took the medicine and still went out drinking anyway. He got sick as a dog but at least he didn't miss a Friday night's worth of drinking!"

"That's wild," I exclaimed. "The same thing happened to the guy I know. Schmidty's parents fed him this shit, which made him as sick as a dog."

"Hold on," Pete interrupted, "Did you say Schmidt?"

"Yeah, Benjamin Schmidt," I replied.

"I DON'T FUCKING BELIEVE IT," Pete yelled while grinning from ear to ear. "We're talking about the same fucking guy! Benjamin Schmidt is a good friend of my older brother!"

"No shit!" I said in amazement. "Well then," I continued, "Are we agreeing then that the biggest drinker that we have ever known is Benjamin Schmidt?"

"Here, here, Benjamin Schmidt, it is!" Pete said as we raised our beer cans and clanged them together still reveling in the fact that we were both describing the same guy.

"Here's to you, Schmidty, wherever you are, you drunk fuck," I said as Pete and I drained our beers.

I also became friendly with some other freshmen on my floor. Ted Day and Terry Holstrom were roommates who lived in the dorm room directly across the hall from mine. They both lived in the suburbs of Chicago and both liked to smoke dope. In fact, Ted Day had practically turned smoking dope into a near-religious ceremony. We spent many a nights in their room passing around the bong and listening to albums and cassettes.

One night a bunch of us were in their room partying, and we were all pretty buzzed. Somehow we got onto the subject of bathrooms and the fact that since our rooms were situated at the far end of the dorm building and the johns were in the middle of the building we had to travel farther to the johns than anyone else on the whole fucking floor except for the poor suckers whose rooms were located where ours were except on the opposite side of the dorm building.

"Sometimes I'm so stoned and lazy I feel like taking a piss right out my dorm room window," said Ted who was sprawled out on his bed.

"Fuck that," I replied. "If you're gonna take a piss you may as well take a shit out the window as well."

"Fuck you, Garrity!" was Ted Day's reply. "I'll fill a party bowl with my best weed and let you smoke it all by yourself if you take a dump out my second floor dorm window right now."

With Ted's dare hanging in the air, the room erupted in laughter as everyone drew a mental picture of me hanging my ass out the window and taking a dump. I hesitated for a moment and then replied, "OK, but I don't feel the urge right now." The OK part was all they needed to hear.

"Come on, Garrity, a whole party bowl," Ted shot back.

"Do it, Greg!" "This I got to see!" others added.

"All right, you assholes," I said as I got up out of my seat. I walked slowly to the window as my partying companions began to whoop it up. I got to the window and opened it slowly. I then turned to the boys and said, "If I try to shit I'll probably end up pissing all over the floor so I better take care of that first."

With that said I turned around to face the open window, pulled down my zipper, pulled out my pecker, and proceeded to piss out of Ted Day's dorm window. My stream of piss, illuminated by the lights of the parking light and cascading gently down two stories to the earth below actually made quite a beautiful sight. Too bad the boys are missing this, I thought.

With that done, it was now time to get serious. I deposited my unit back into my shorts and turned to face the boys.

"OK," I said, "one party bowl is what's on the line here, right?"

"You got it, you sick bastard," Ted Day replied.

"All right, boys," I said. "I think Mother Nature is calling."

With that I proceeded to unbuckle my pants and pull them and my underwear down enough to expose my ass. I then backed up into the opened window and began to push. As I mentioned earlier, I didn't really have the urge to take a dump, but I couldn't let the boys down. As I sat with my bare ass hanging out the window I thought how funny it would be if someone walked by at that moment and saw me shooting them a moon out a second-story dorm window.

After about five minutes and some serious pushing I finally accomplished my mission. I took a dump out of a second-story dorm window! The actual event wasn't really noticeable by the guys inside of the room, and as I got up from the window I was met with disbelief and derision.

"See I told you that you wouldn't do it, you fuck," Ted Day barked.

"Oh, but I did do it," I replied.

"You took a shit out the window?" Ted Day's roommate Terry asked incredulously.

"Oh, yes," I responded. "Now how about that party bowl, buddy?" I asked looking directly at Ted Day.

"I need proof," Ted demanded.

"Oh, there's proof. Take a look for yourself," I said as I motioned toward the still-open window.

Ted Day got up off his bed and gingerly walked over to the open window.

"How the hell am I going to see it down there on the ground where it's so dark?" he said as he peered out the window.

"Oh, you don't have to look all the way down there," I replied slyly, knowing that the turd that I had expelled hadn't quite made its way to the earth below. "Take a look on your window ledge."

Ted Day stuck his head out the window again and stared at the ledge.

"UGH!" he yelled upon making his discovery. "YOU DID IT, YOU SICK BASTARD! GARRITY SHIT OUT MY DORM WINDOW!"

A chorus of "ughs" rose up in the room as all of the fellows rushed over to the window to check out my turd. As the conversation turned into a debate as to where I ranked in the world of truly sick bastards, I made my way down to the john to wipe my ass. Meanwhile Ted Day sat back down on his bed and began packing the party bowl. As I reentered the room after my soiree to the john, I was greeted by Ted who said, "Here, sicko, enjoy," as he handed me the fully packed party bowl.

While I was enjoying my reward, several other inhabitants of our floor, who happened to be walking by, were invited in to see the newest attraction of dorm life. After a while the uniqueness of the whole deal wore off, and Terry, the neat priss that he was, declared he probably wouldn't be able to sleep that night knowing a turd lurked just outside his dorm window. So he decided to fill a pitcher of water and pour it over my turd in hopes of dislodging it from its window-ledge home. His first attempt was unsuccessful.

"Stubborn turd!" I declared as I giggled out loud, beginning to feel the full effects of my just-completed party bowl. Terry tried again, and this time managed to dislodge it and watch it tumble to the grass below thus bringing an end to the pooping-out-the-window incident in Ted Day's room.

*   *   *   *

I didn't pledge a fraternity during the first semester of school, and I don't really recall why. I think I didn't really quite get the whole concept of rush and pledging until the fall season was over and someone explained it to me. As far as academics, I got off to a poor start and it was all downhill from there. During registration, I wanted to sign up for a pre-med schedule because I thought I wanted to become a physical therapist. When I got to the registration area, the pre-med line was really long, so I looked around for the shortest line and ta da, there was pre-law. I went over and signed up - so much for my desire on wanting to become a physical therapist.

As for my classes themselves, things weren't too great. Unfortunately my last two years in high school at Sullivan were very easy, and I wasn't academically challenged at all. Now here I was attending an academically demanding quality institution of higher learning, and I couldn't handle it.

I ended up totally blowing off my freshmen Spanish class as it was an early-morning class, and I couldn't get my ass out of bed to attend it. In my other classes, I did the least I could to get by. Partly out of laziness and lack of discipline, and partly out of not having the skills to handle the workload.

Meanwhile football became an after-school job. We were forming a junior varsity team that would be scheduled to play about four or five games. Great, I thought, when I first heard about it, thinking that I would really get some quality playing time on it. But as it turned out, I got very little playing time and became discouraged. The couple of games I played in saw me getting very little action, a couple of plays at the very end of a game or maybe playing on the kickoff return team, other than that, not much.

My football week consisted mainly of playing right offensive tackle on the scout team, which ran that week's opponent's offense against our first string defense. So I practiced all week and let our first string defensive tackle kick my ass, and then came Saturday. If it was an away game, I got to sit in my dorm room and listen to the game on the university's radio station. If we played at home, my fate was a little bit better. I got to suit up for the game, and if we were winning big near the end, which fortunately was usually the case, I got in for at least a whole series of downs.

Every Monday at practice the coaches passed out little decals in the shape of footballs to the players who had done well in practice and the game the previous week. The decals went on your helmet as a kind of badge of honor. On the last Monday of the season, before our last game, I was surely expecting to receive my first decal. I was the only member of the scout team who had yet to receive one and figured I couldn't be overlooked this, the final week. The coaches gathered us together at the beginning of practice, like they always did, and began talking about each player who would receive a decal that day. After they mentioned all of the players who received a decal because of their play in last week's game, they started to pass out decals to guys for their efforts in practice.

Finally Coach Perkins, our head coach said, "And now our final football goes to a freshmen member of the scout team who gave a great effort all week and who has really been giving a hundred percent all season long in practice."

Here it is, I thought in that split second before the coach announced the recipient's name. Receiving this decal just might make this whole damn thing worthwhile.

And then just as I was about to make my way forward through the crowd of players, I heard the coach say, "Marty Maker, where are you?"

As Marty Maker made his way through the crowd to receive his decal, I just stood there with my mouth wide open, frozen in disappointment and disbelief. The rest of the practice was just a blur as all I could concentrate on was the fact I had gone to every practice and meeting during the season, busted my ass all season long, and wasn't, in the eyes of the coaches, worthy of one lousy, stinking, football decal.

After practice I went back to my room and thought about the whole situation. I knew I had to make a statement, but I wasn't sure how. After a while I came up with a game plan, deciding that I would go to practice Tuesday, Wednesday, and Thursday, but I would skip Friday, which was when our game jerseys were issued. I also decided I would skip our last game, which, if we won, would give us a share of the league championship.

I did this for two reasons. The first reason was I wanted to make the statement to the coaches that, hey, if you don't need me I sure as hell don't need you, and second, I wanted to find out where I really stood. Would I be missed? Would I receive a phone call from a coach asking me where I was for the last game?

I did exactly what I planned, not even attending the final game as a fan. Instead, I sat in my room alone, brooding. After the game, I ran into a couple of freshmen football players, and they told me we had won big and they actually saw some playing time early in the fourth quarter. They told me I should have suited up because they thought I would have definitely seen some extended playing time.

So now with the football season over, I waited to hear from a coach. And waited, and waited, and waited. I never did hear from a coach, and as things turned out, I never spoke to a member of the football coaching staff again. So this was my fall semester at Millikin and my first taste of college life. Taking dumps out windows, getting stiffed in football, and slowly but surely flunking out of my classes.

18 DIFFERENT PATHS

While I was being tortured and in general fucking off in Decatur, Billy and Will were making their own paths out into the world. Billy graduated from high school with no real plans for his future. However, several months after graduation one of his father's friends had contacted him and asked if he would be interested in working in some capacity for the city of Chicago. Billy said yes and filled out a job application with the city. About a month later, he was called for an interview. He was hired to work in the accounting department for the city, making a very decent wage and working in the Daley Center building in the heart of the Loop.

The day he got the job he called me at school and told me the great news. From the sound of his voice, I could tell it was the happiest he had been since his accident. He told me his first goal was to save enough money so he could move out of his mother's apartment. This came as no surprise to me. I told him I was jealous because at least he knew what his future held where as I felt I was kind of adrift on an ocean of opportunity but not knowing which direction to sail in.

Will also had a clear-cut idea where he was heading. He had confided in me, one drunken night near the end of high school, that his passion in life was acting and his long-term goal was to be a famous actor on the silver screen. I told him at the time I was sure he could reach his goal, and in order to do that, he had to follow his dream, wherever it led him. I'm not sure if what I had said that night influenced him, but when decision time finally came, Will opted to not accept any scholarships for basketball but rather to get involved in the Chicago theater scene while taking acting lessons with his ultimate goal to one day end up in Hollywood and make it big.

Will's dad wasn't thrilled that he turned down some serious scholarship opportunities to pursue acting, but he eventually worked through that and gave Will his full support, including working his West Coast connections to help Will find a Hollywood agent who would represent him once he made his way out there.

19 HELL WEEK

During my second semester at Millikin, the campus fraternities held a second rush to recruit another pledge class into their respective houses. Representatives of various fraternities made the rounds to see who might be interested in pledging their frat. Pledging simply means you show a desire to become a member; however, you can't become a member until you have gone through the frat's Hell Week.

I was actively recruited by several frats during this rush. One was the TKE's (pronounced Teek's) who were the largest Greek organization in the country at the time and on campus were a well-respected house. The other frat that recruited me was the Delta Sigs, the frat house whose party I attended on my recruiting trip and a frat house that didn't enjoy as respected a reputation as the TKEs. The Delta Sig's membership was primarily made up of football players, which was probably part of the problem.

I thought long and hard about which frat house to choose but finally decided on the Delta Sigs. The Delta Sigs were a wild bunch of guys, and at this time of my life that was what I was into, wildness! The TKEs were more laid back and also seemed to carry an attitude that everyone else was inferior to them, which definitely turned me off.

About a week after pledging the Delta Sig house, my pledge brothers, four in all, and I were told our house was hosting an ice cream social for the pledges of our sister sorority house. Since I worked in the school's cafeteria, I was asked by one of the house members to see if I could "borrow" some spoons to use at the ice cream social. I knew that wouldn't be a problem, and I told the house member so.

The day of the ice cream social finally arrived, and as I left the cafeteria after dinner, a hundred metal spoons accompanied me. I met up with my pledge brothers, and we made our way over to the Delta Sig house for the social. When we arrived at the house, we were quickly whisked down into the basement where I turned the spoons over to one of the house members. After a couple of minutes, more of the frat members filed down into the basement.

All of a sudden, one of the frat guys came rumbling down the basement stairs and once he reached the bottom he announced, "Oh, oh, pledges, bad news. The sorority has just canceled the ice cream social."

His announcement was greeted by a loud chorus of "AAAGHS!" that resonated from the other members of the house.

"DAMN!" one of the members shouted. "WHAT THE HELL ARE

WE GOING TO DO NOW?"

"HOW ABOUT WE HAVE THE PLEDGES DO SOME EXERCISES?" another member shouted out.

As the last syllable of the word exercises fell from the member's mouth, a barrage of spoons were hurled toward us pledges from every member who had made his way down into the basement.

We pledges began to do exercises on command and spent the next two hours doing so. I was pretty much out of shape, the football season having been over for a couple of months, so there were points during the two hours in which I felt I was going to collapse, but I willed myself to be strong. At the very end of the two-hour session, we were told this was nothing compared to what we would go through during Hell Week. Oh great, I thought, what the hell was I getting myself into this time?

The end of our little workout finally came, and as I began to walk toward the stairs that led to freedom, I became nauseous. Luckily, the john was right there by the stairs, and I quickly ran inside and heaved my guts out. So you wanted to join a fraternity eh, I thought, as I filled the bowl.

The week before Hell Week arrived the house gave us pledges a short list of things we needed for it. The Hell Week list comprised of a burlap bag, women's panties, and a toothbrush. Interesting list, I thought upon reading it. We procured our burlap bags from a local hardware store and then made our way to a department store to buy the panties. We all assumed at some point we probably would end up wearing them, so we tried hard to get a pair that would fit.

Just prior to Hell Week, the pledges were supposed to do something called a walkout, which traditionally meant attacking the frat house late at night, trashing it, kidnapping a member of the house, and then driving to the nearest college campus that also had a Delta Sig house. Once there, we would call our frat house and make a ransom demand, which was a party in our honor.

The way we figured, the more we trashed the frat house, the more we would have to pay for it during Hell Week. With this in mind, we had a very low key walkout. We attacked the house one night and emptied a fire extinguisher in the main hallway and dumped a couple of bags of garbage there, too. As far as kidnapping a member, we considered kidnapping a gorgeous little sister who belonged to our sister sorority but decided that might not be too cool. We eventually didn't do any kidnapping and were later told by the frat members that our walkout was rather weak. I guess it was a kind of damned if you do, damned if you don't type of situation.

For the actual beginning of Hell Week, we were told all of us pledges should gather in one of our dorm rooms and await the arrival of the pledge master who would escort us over to the frat house. The actual Hell Week was only scheduled to run from Wednesday afternoon through Saturday evening, so with our shopping bags full of our Hell Week supplies, we all sat silently in one of our dorm rooms awaiting the pledge master. He finally arrived and asked us if we were ready for Hell Week. The five of us said we were.

"Good, let's go then," he announced.

We left the dorm building and made our way across the deserted campus. As the frat house came into sight, we saw a bunch of the frat brothers standing out on the lawn that ran along the side of the house. Some of them had beers in their hands, a definite bad sign I thought.

Once we got to the lawn, we were verbally assaulted with every bad word I had ever heard and a few I hadn't. We were ordered, by various members of our reception committee, to get on all fours and crawl around the lawn. As we did this, we were purposely ordered to crawl through mounds of dog shit that had obviously been strategically placed on the lawn. It was at this point we heard for the first time the Hell Week mantra, which we were destined to hear a million times over the next three days.

"You gotta do it cause every member of this frat house has done it and now it's your turn. We're not asking you to do anything we haven't done ourselves," we were told repeatedly.

With this morale booster in mind, we followed their commands. Through the shit we crawled. After a while they told us to get up and run to the side of the house. As we did we were hit by a barrage of eggs, which were thrown down onto us from a second story window of the house. After the egg shower, we were all thoroughly hosed down with cold water, which was emanating from a garden hose held by one of the members. Now soaking wet, we were ordered to go down into the basement of the house.

Once in the house, we were separated and each of us were assigned our own little team of tormentors. We were then given a mouthful of chewing tobacco and ordered to begin exercising. As I started doing jumping jacks I was shown a piece of cardboard, which had scribbled on it my own personal Hell Week saying.

As I exercised, I had to repeat the saying over and over until I had it committed to memory. During the next three days if any frat brother asked us for our saying, we had better know it and recite it for them. Each pledge's saying ridiculed them in some form or fashion. My saying had to do with the scarring on my face from my acne, something about my face being like a dartboard because of the pockmarks I had incurred. We all eventually memorized our sayings, and after about an hour or so of exercising, we were asked if we were hungry. Of course we told the brothers what they wanted to here.

"YES, SIR!" we all yelled.

We were then presented with the "Apple of Brotherhood." The apple turned out to be the largest yellow onion I had ever seen in my entire life.

"You guys pass that apple around and take a bite out of it until it's all gone," the pledge master instructed.

We did as we were told, each of us taking a nice chunk out of it, chewing it, and then swallowing our onion bite. As soon as I had swallowed my last bite, I began to feel nauseous, and I told the pledge master I felt sick to my stomach. He led me to the bathroom, and I immediately heaved up my portion of the Apple of Brotherhood plus all of the tobacco juice I had also swallowed during my exercise session.

I wearily came out of the bathroom and joined my fellow pledge brothers as we were led upstairs to the first floor of the house. A bedroom door was open, and inside our shopping bags full of our Hell Week supplies were waiting there for us. We were told to take out the burlap bags we had brought and to cut out neck and armholes. The burlap bags were going to be our official Hell Week uniform top, and we were sternly told that whenever we were in the house the bags had to be on. So we made our Hell Week tops, and once we managed to get them on, found they were quite itchy, warm, and very uncomfortable.

Once dressed in our Hell Week finest, we were led downstairs again for some more calisthenics. After about an hour or so, we were brought back up to our bedroom and somebody brought in some sandwiches, which consisted of two pieces of bread and one piece of bologna. After our feast we were led to the kitchen of the house where we cleaned dishes and scrubbed the floor. After that it was downstairs again for another marathon session of exercises.

Finally, hot, smelly, wet, and exhausted, we were led to our room to get some rest. The problem with that concept was that every hour or so throughout the night, we were awoken by different frat brothers in varying degrees of sobriety. Some frat members would walk in and ask us to stand up and recite our Hell Week saying or ask us for a quick twenty-five jumping jacks. While others said they had stopped by just to see how we were doing.

I was never so happy to see morning come at Millikin as I was that following day. Morning meant shedding my burlap bag, putting on clean clothes, and heading over to the cafe for some real food. We were under strict orders by the house not to skip any classes during Hell Week, but I was so tired after I had eaten my breakfast that I made a beeline to my dorm room. Once in my room, I set my alarm to wake me in two hours and I then quickly fell asleep.

It seemed as if I had just put my head down on my pillow when the alarm buzzed, waking me from my coma. I got up slowly and made my way back to the frat house where once inside I slipped back into my burlap bag. Since some of my pledge brothers were still in class as well as many frat brothers, there wasn't a lot of terrorizing going on so I was ordered to clean up around the house for a while, which I did trying to be as inconspicuous as possible.

Finally after all of my pledge brothers had gotten back from their classes, we were led downstairs where another exercise session broke out. While we were exercising, one of the frat brothers suggested that we dictate what exercise we should do and sing a little song as we did them.

When it was my turn I ordered us to do twenty-five jumping jacks. At that point the brother who had been ordering us to do all kinds of really hard drills began eating a fillet of fish sandwich. I began my exercise ditty innocently enough but ended it with a very dramatic line. Something to the effect of, "Oh if I could, I surely would, stick that fish sandwich right up your ass."

My comment made all of the frat brothers roar with laughter, and the brother eating the sandwich pulled down his draws and, while shooting us a moon, feigned sticking the aforementioned fish sandwich up his aforementioned ass.

"SHIT, GODDAMN IT!" the sandwich-wielding brother exclaimed. "I GOT GODDAMN TARTAR SAUCE ON MY UNDIES."

"Yeah right, sure that's tartar sauce," some of the other brothers chided him.

We continued on with our exercises for a while and then were led upstairs to our room. We were served some more delicious bologna and bread sandwiches and then told that tonight was the fashion show.

Around eight o'clock that evening we were ordered to put on our women's underwear. Once we were all dressed in our underwear and burlap bags, we were marched down into the basement. We were pranced around the basement in front of the whole house in our frilly best. Rude and lewd comments erupted from every corner of the room, and we were told at least none of us had made the mistake of buying a pair of crotchless panties as one unsuspecting pledge had done several years ago. Once the crude comments had subsided, we began yet another exercise session, ladies undies and all.

One of my pledge brothers started to talk back to some of the brothers during this session, and I could sense the whole Hell Week ordeal was starting to get to him. When the exercise session was over, we were ordered to clean up the house. At this point one of the brothers pulled me aside and brought me up to his second-floor room.

"You've really set a good example for your pledge brothers," he began.

"Thanks," I replied humbly, ever on the Hell Week defensive.

"But," he continued, "I want you to know if any of your pledge brothers quit in the middle of Hell Week, it's a direct reflection on all of you who are left. Understood?"

"Yes," I replied.

"Here," he said as he handed me a big sandwich full of assorted cold cuts and cheeses. "Eat this before you go downstairs."

"Thanks," I said as I began to devour the offering.

Once I got back downstairs I found my pledge brothers had been sent to our room so I joined them and found they were already talking with the one brother who was wavering in his conviction to go through with Hell Week. I could tell he wasn't being very receptive to their arguments so I added one I thought was worth mentioning.

"Hey, man, just think about it, we're halfway home. We get through tonight, tomorrow, and then the next night it ends!"

"I don't care if it's half over," my pledge brother shot back. "I can't bring myself to be humiliated by some of these guys just to get into this frat. Especially by some of these guys who I know are real pussies."

"Hey, don't think of it that way," I countered. "Remember, all of the brothers who are putting us through Hell Week have had it done to them and one day it will be our turn to put some pledges through hell."

"I don't want any part of that," he responded.

"Fine," I quickly answered, "you know you don't have too but if you really want to be a Delta Sig you gotta put up with some bullshit for a little while longer. Don't quit now man, we can get through this together."

"Just think about it," another pledge brother added.

Just then a brother popped his head in and announced, "Lights out." He turned off the lights and closed the door. Lying in the darkness, I wondered how long my pledge brother would last. I didn't have to wait too long to find out.

The nightly disturbances began about two hours after we had gone to bed. The same shit as the night before, indiscriminate interruptions of our sleep. Brothers waking us to see how we were doing, waking us to see if we needed anything, waking us to see what time in the morning we wanted to be awoken, and waking us just to wake us.

Finally my wavering pledge brother reached his breaking point. After he almost came to blows with one of our sleep interrupters, he demanded to use the phone. Being a local kid from Decatur, we all figured he was calling his folks to come get him out of this nightmare. Unfortunately, we were right. We wouldn't see or speak with him again until after Hell Week.

After our pledge brother left, some of the frat brothers came into our room and told us how disappointed they were in us and how angry the other brothers would be since we let one of our pledge brothers quit. Great, I thought, he quits and we get fucked. That was the thought on my mind as I fell back into an uneasy sleep.

I awoke the next morning feeling like shit. Two days and two nights of humiliation, sleep deprivation, and little nourishment left me feeling like a zombie. As I was slowly waking up and shaking the cobwebs from my mind, I questioned for the first time if it was all really worth it.

Fuck it, I thought, even if it turns out that being a Delta Sig isn't worth all of the crap I've endured, it's really too late to turn back now. If I quit now, then I've put up with all of this bullshit for nothing. No way! I'm going through with this thing until the bitter end. Bring on the bullshit, frat brothers. This badass from Chicago can take anything you boys can dish out.

I left the frat house that morning with renewed determination and actually went to all of my classes. When I returned from my classes, I got into my burlap bag and started cleaning up the house. A couple of the brothers I saw mentioned the Hell Week Olympics, which were scheduled for that evening. As I heard them talk, I wondered what they had planned for us.

As the afternoon passed, things were strangely quiet around the house. There was no marathon exercise session as there had been the two previous afternoons.

"Something's up," I whispered to my fellow pledge brothers. "I got a feeling that tonight's gonna be a bitch."

Around seven that evening, we were herded into our room and told we were going to go through the Hell Week Olympics.

"Here we go," I said to my pledge brothers.

We were all led downstairs to the basement where most of the frat brothers were gathered. It appeared they had been boozing it up for a while. They all gave a loud cheer when we entered the basement. They lined us up shoulder to shoulder in front of them and told us they had "special" Olympic uniforms for us to wear, so we all should strip down. We all stripped down and stood in front of the frat brothers buck naked as comments were shouted out about our various anatomies and our manhoods or lack thereof.

Then suddenly one of the brothers burst forward and asked, "You guys want your Olympic uniforms?"

"YES, SIR!" we all shouted back

"THEN HERE, ASSHOLES!" he shouted as he threw a bunch of six pack ring holders toward us.

"LET THE GAMES BEGIN!" another brother shouted at the top of his lungs.

A loud cheer went up throughout the basement as a hose was brought out and we were all sprayed down and a good half inch of water gathered on the basement's concrete floor. The one "Olympic Event" that I can distinctly recall was the lemon drop roll, which involved a brother placing a lemon drop piece of candy in front of each pledge and instructing us to push it with our noses across the basement floor. The concrete floor was rough and following their directions earnestly caused me to scrape off a good layer of skin on my nose as I participated in the competition.

As I rolled my lemon drop across the floor, I was cheered on by an almost fanatical fervor that erupted from a large group of the brothers. Suddenly Joe Kilborne, who was my designated Big Brother and in theory supposed to help me get through Hell Week, appeared in front of me. Before I knew it, Joe pulled out his unit and began to take a long, leisurely piss right into the puddle of standing water I was about to roll my lemon drop through.

"Come on, pussy," Joe said as he finished his piss.

Looking him straight in the eye I said, "No problem, big brother." I went ahead and pushed that lemon drop through the awaiting puddle clear across to the other side of the room. As I did, a wild yell erupted from the brothers.

A bit later the Olympics ended and we were brought upstairs to the first floor of the house, still in our birthday suits. Standing in the hallway that ran along the entrance of the basement, we heard one of the brothers shout out to us, "WHAT IS HELL WEEK?"

We all shook our heads from side to side not really understanding his question and afraid of his answer.

"WHAT IS HELL WEEK? HELL WEEK IS A BUNCH OF YUKS! SO YOU PLEDGES, IT'S TIME FOR YOU TO START YUKKING IT UP!" he responded.

With that announcement we were all shoved into a small, unlit bathroom on the first floor. As the door was being shut, leaving us in total darkness, we were ordered to start chanting the word or maybe better yet the sound "yuk."

"Yuk, yuk, yuk, yuk, yuk, yuk, yuk, yuk, yuk, yuk, yuk, yuk, yuk, yuk , yuk," we began.

Every so often, a brother would open the door and shout at us that we were chanting all wrong or weren't loud enough. Several times the door opened and we were dowsed with a rather putrid-smelling substance whose composition I really didn't care to think about. After a while in our small, dark bathroom cell I began to lose all sense of time and space and began to see various images appear in the darkness of the room. The images bounced and danced in the dark, and as I became mesmerized by them I also started to distinguish each of my pledge brother's distinct voices from the chorus of yuks emanating around me.

Finally, the door opened a crack, and we were told we could stop yukking.

As we exited the dark bathroom and made our way into the well-lit hallway, I felt I now knew what it must be like being a coal miner coming out of a mine and seeing the sunshine again after a hard day on the job. As we walked to our sleeping room, one of the brothers asked us how long we thought we had been yukking it up for. None of us could offer a very concrete answer but our best guess was that we had been in the bathroom for at least a couple of hours.

The brother whom had asked us the question then extended his arm to show us what time it was. One o'clock in the morning we read with astonishment. We had been put into the bathroom and started yukking at about seven-thirty that evening. So we had been chanting for over five hours! My sense of losing touch with time and space hadn't been imagined I and my fellow yuk mates really had lost our sense of time.

Once we were in our sleeping room, a brother came in and told us that during the Vietnam War, the North Vietnamese would put captured G. I.s into dark, little huts and make them yuk until they broke down. Fortunately, we were told, we weren't pushed to our breaking points! Being too tired and disorientated to ask a question or offer a comment, we all just kind of shrugged our shoulders and then lay down to go to sleep.

Probably because of the yukking we were allowed to sleep through the rest of the night until six the following morning. We were awakened and told we had to clean up the house and then go out with a brother and clean up a party site that had been sponsored by the university the night before. We obliged, and as we did I think we all thought about the yukking session from the night before.

One of my pledge brothers confided in me that if we were made to do another yukking session that evening, he was going to call it quits. I told him I didn't think they would make us yuk anymore since tonight was the end of Hell Week. I tried to encourage him by adding that I thought the worst of it was probably behind us, hoping I was right but in reality half doubting my own words.

After we were done cleaning up the party site, we were brought back to the house. We were assigned various chores and after they were done sent back to our room for several hours. We tried to catch up on our sleep the best we could; however the excitement of knowing we were going to face our last Hell Week hurdle in a matter of hours kept us from sleeping very soundly.

Suddenly the door to our room burst open, and several of the frat brothers, including the house's president and vice-president, walked into our room.

"We've got something we feel you guys have got to know about before you go any further with Hell Week," they announced.

At this point, being so sleep deprived and exhausted it was difficult for any of us to separate fact from fiction. We could have been told anything and would have probably believed it, but what the president told us sounded pretty believable.

"Guys, a couple of nights ago, three of our brothers got pretty tight and decided to make a visit to the sorority house across the street," the president began.

"MISTAKE NUMBER ONE!" the vice president announced with emphasis.

"Now upon arriving at the front door of the house, they decided that instead of simply knocking on the door they were going to gain entry to the house by a rather unique method," the president continued.

"MISTAKE NUMBER TWO!" added the VP loudly.

"They decided they were going to make like medieval knights and use a battering ram against the front door of the sorority. The battering ram consisted of the smallest of the three brothers, who was fitted with a football helmet, being held up in a horizontal position by the other two. With a running start, they banged his helmeted head repeatedly against the door. All of this took place after all of the coeds had gone to bed," the president explained.

"MISTAKE NUMBER THREE!" the VP shouted as he held three fingers in the air.

"I guess the noise that the human battering ram made against the front door of the house woke up all of the sorority sisters who responded by calling campus security. The whole event, unfortunately, was reported to the dean of students who is already at odds with the Delta Sig house. So the 'news' that I want to share with you before you decide to go on with Hell Week is that the dean has put the entire house on social probation. This means we can't participate in the upcoming Greek Games, which are a kind of Greek organization's end-of-year Olympics party. But even more importantly, guys, the dean has put the house on notice that if one more wild escapade occurs he would try his hardest to have the house's charter revoked and the house closed down for good," the president explained.

With the announcement made, the two brothers left us alone to make our final decisions. My decision was made rather quickly.

"My mind's made up," I announced. "I've come too far and been through too much to give up now."

The rest of my pledge brothers agreed with me. We were determined to become Delta Sigs! We called the president of the frat back into our room and told him of our intention to go through with the rest of Hell Week.

"Great," he said. "Then you guys just relax, and I'll see you in a little while."

About an hour later, a couple of brothers came into our room and I thought, here we go, this is it. We were marched out into the hallway and brought to the doorway of the bathroom where we had spent last night yukking it up. Then one of the brothers asked us what Hell Week was all about. In unison we meekly replied, "It's a bunch of yuks."

"THEN START YUKKING IT UP!" he shouted back to us.

Oh, shit, this is too much, I thought. Not for me, but I knew some of my pledge brothers were on the verge of cracking and another yukking session would surely do the trick.

Just as I began to try to say something in protest, another brother opened the bathroom door and began to push us in. This time, however, something was different. The bathroom light was on so we wouldn't be yukking in the dark.

We all marched into the bathroom as we yukked it up and just as the door was about to be closed, a brother popped his head in and whispered to me, "You guys hang tight. You won't be in here very long. We're just getting the basement ready."

Thank god, I thought.

We didn't yuk very long before our pledge master opened up the bathroom door.

"SHUT THE HELL UP YOU YUKKING BASTARDS!" the pledge master shouted. "Follow me downstairs where the rest of the house is waiting for you. This is the last part of Hell Week, the Hell Week Celebration Dinner!"

When we got to the top of the basement stairs, we heard a strange humming noise emanating from the basement below. As I walked down the stairs and entered the basement, I could see that the lights were dimmed and through the smoke that swirled about I could see all of the house members dressed in costumes and smoking cigars. As all of the brothers hummed in a low monotone I thought to myself, what a truly eerie sight to see. We were lined up at one end of the room and told to strip so we were bare-ass naked, shoulder to shoulder in front of the whole house.

"Since we have put you guys through so much crap, we will now allow you to get a little even by ordering us to do some exercises," the pledge master announced.

He then told us we had one minute to decide what exercise it would be. We huddled together and each of us had the same thought. No matter what exercise we choose, we're gonna get fucked! So with that in mind, we told the brothers we had decided they should do one hundred up downs, a truly tortuous exercise that we borrowed from our football practices.

"All right, brothers," our pledge master announced. "The pledges demand we do one hundred up downs. Ready, begin."

To our surprise all of the brothers begin counting off up downs. But, this being Hell Week, we knew in our hearts it couldn't last and we were right. After about four up downs, the entire house of brothers began to pull marshmallows from underneath their costumes. They then began to whip them at our exposed genitalia. The "Celebration Dinner" had begun!

After being pelted by the marshmallows, we were ordered to put our hands on the shoulders of the pledge brother in front of us and march around the basement to the chant of "Fuck your brother, fuck your brother," all the while receiving verbal abuse from the house members.

After several minutes, we were ordered to begin a mini exercise session, which probably lasted about fifteen minutes. Finally we stopped and each of us were escorted to a table, which was actually a large piece of plywood supported by four cement blocks. We were ordered to kneel down at our respective places and each of us was assigned a brother who was there to make sure we ate our festive meal.

The meal began with a soup that I swear was one hundred percent hot sauce. We were ordered to slurp it as fast as we could. Then a brother, dressed in a complete formal waiter's outfit, brought in the main dish. To this day I can't even imagine what the main dish consisted of, and at the time I was too afraid to ask. As we each began to dig into our meal, the brothers who were assigned to us at the table began to smear some type of concoction on us that made our skin burn. The more I ate the more nauseous I felt.

As a chant of "EAT! EAT! EAT!" started among the brothers, my personal dinner companion whispered in my ear that the end was near. Thank god, I thought.

Finally some liquid concoction was brought in and the brothers made a toast welcoming us all into the Delta Sig Fraternity. We downed our glasses and then were told to get up and run out the side door, the same door that we had entered when Hell Week had begun.

I made my way out the door and up the stairs and at the top was shoved, bare-ass naked, out into the night. Each of us had a turn being hosed down with a cold stream of water from a garden hose. Once hosed down we were told to run around to the front of the house.

As we got to the front door, each of us was met by several brothers who congratulated us on making it through Hell Week. They quickly escorted each of us through the house and to a brother's room where they encouraged each of us to take a shower.

I jumped into the shower and began to soap up my skin, which was still stinging from whatever it was that had been rubbed on me. Every few minutes, my shower was interrupted by brothers ducking their heads in and congratulating me for making it through Hell Week and becoming one of them. The whole scene was very exhilarating, and I can only compare it to a locker room scene of a professional sports team that had just won the

Super Bowl, the World Series, an NBA Championship, or the Stanley Cup. It was truly a triumphant moment, which all of the pledges and brothers celebrated in.

After our showers, we were gathered for what would be best described as a debriefing session. We were told we still had to go through nationals, which was a hazing actually sanctioned by the national office of the Delta Sig Fraternity. It only lasted a day we were told, and it wasn't anything to really worry about. We were also told we had just endured one of the, if not the most demanding Hell Week of any Greek organization in the country.

Specifically, the brothers mentioned the TKE fraternity and said they didn't have anything to compare to our Hell Week. As a sign of how tough our week was, it was suggested that we leave a little something at the TKE house next door. That something was our beloved burlap bags, which by now had become encrusted with sweat and all kinds of garbage.

"I'm up for that," I piped up. "And let's not just lay them there," I continued. "Let's torch em and leave them burning right at the front door."

"Yeah!" my other pledge brothers chimed in.

"Now hold on," one of the house members replied. "Remember we just got put on social probation and we can't afford getting in any more trouble this semester."

We nodded our heads in agreement. Then one of the brothers added, "But if maybe you went to the backdoor of the TKE house and torched the burlap sacks there, then I don't see any problem."

"Yeah, that's it. Leave them at the back door," I said.

And that's exactly what we did. We sneaked over to the TKE house and we found their back door. We threw our burlap bags into a big pile and lit them on fire. We banged loudly on the back door and then turned and ran like hell. As I ran, I glanced back and saw the door open and several of the TKE brothers emerge.

"TKE's are pussies!" I shouted at the top of my lungs as I made my way back to the safety of our frat house.

A week or so later, the entire house went out to a Sunday brunch to celebrate our triumph. It was kind of strange dining with the very guys who a week ago put us through hell, but there were truly no hard feelings between the pledges and the brothers as we were all Delta Sigma Phi brothers now.

20 A BROTHER SAVES THE DAY

Late in the school year of my freshman year, I had a very focused discussion with Pete Walters, the guy on my floor from St. Pats High School in Chicago. The topic was our future and whether or not to continue our education. Pete was planning to quit school and become an apprentice in one of the trades. His goal was to become a carpenter, plumber, or electrician.

I thought long and hard about my options. If I came back to Millikin, I didn't want to play football, and since I didn't want to play I wasn't sure I wanted to come back to Decatur to go to school. I didn't feel I was getting very much out of school, so I thought maybe I should quit school, try to find a decent-paying job, and save up enough money to buy an apartment building or maybe start my own business.

With those thoughts in mind the last month of school rolled around and every night and sometimes even the days were a party. One afternoon, a bunch of us were sitting around drinking when we ran out of booze. My dorm neighbors, Terry and Ted joined me as we left my room for our short trek up to the liquor store for some reinforcements. But we didn't get out of the dorm before we ran into or should I say caused some trouble.

We all ducked into the washroom on our floor to take a leak, and as we entered we saw Rudy Jones, a fellow freshman, rip a sink from the wall. We would find out later Rudy had just gotten into an argument with his girl back home and had decided to vent his anger in the washroom. The three of us saw what he had done and decided it looked like fun so we grabbed a sink and gave it a great, big tug.

Unfortunately, the force of three of us was a little too much for the sink's plumbing and instead of just unseating the sink from its pedestal, as Rudy had done, we actually ripped it away from the wall, plumbing and all. Water began to spray from the wall at an incredible rate. We all ran like hell from the washroom, made our way down to the ground floor of the dorm, exited, and walked up to the liquor store. By the time we returned to our dorm, the school police, Decatur police, and the dean of students were on our floor.

We carefully made our way back to my room pretending to be oblivious to all the commotion going on around us, but eventually the dean knocked on my door.

"Hello," I said to the dean as I opened the door and let him in.

"Do any of you know anything about the damage that occurred in the bathroom on this floor?" the dean asked.

GREG KAUP

"No, I don't know anything. We actually just got back to the dorm a couple of minutes ago," I answered.

"Yeah, we were surprised to see all of the cars parked outside," Terry added.

"OK, well, if you hear of anything, please let me know," and with that said the dean left our room.

Several days later, the dean issued a memo to all of the residents of the floor. In it he itemized all of the damage that had occurred during the school year. The biggest item, of course, was the recently dismantled sinks. The memo stated that since no culprits could be found for the damaged sinks, the cost to repair them both would be spread among the entire floor. Each person would be billed something like sixty bucks. I, of course, didn't have a problem with that as I knew I was getting off easy.

That night a bunch of us went out drinking at a local saloon, and somehow the conversation turned to the sink incident. Thinking I could speak in confidence with the guys I was with, I mentioned I knew who had done the damage to the sinks. Well the next thing I know, Andy Baker, a fellow freshman football player, announces at the table that he is going to go visit the dean the following day and tell him I know who damaged the sinks.

"You're joking," I said to Andy.

"No," Andy responded, "I don't want to have to pay for those sinks. If you know who did it, you should go tell the dean."

"Hey," I said, "how about I pay you for your share and you forget about the whole deal."

"What about everybody else on the floor?" Andy continued.

"Don't worry about them," I answered sharply.

"No," Andy said, "I'm going tomorrow."

You're making a big mistake, I thought, as I pictured myself kicking Andy's ass after his visit to the dean.

The next day passed and nothing. Andy was just bullshitting me, I thought. I'm in the clear. Just one more week of school and then I'm outta here.

The next day my dorm phone rang, and who's on the other end but the dean of students' secretary. I got a shiver down my spine as she told me the dean would like to have a word with me. As I left my dorm room and slowly made my way over to the dean's office I resolved to deny, deny, deny.

The dean began our conversation by telling me a fellow student had implicated me in the sink incident.

"Who?" I asked, "I feel I have a right to know who my accuser is."

"All right," the dean said, reluctantly agreeing with me. But before he told me, he warned me that if anyone took retribution upon this individual I would be automatically thrown out of school.

"It's Andy Baker," the dean announced to me.

The prick really did it, I thought.

The dean continued to tell me everything I already knew, that while we were all out drinking I had mentioned I knew who had damaged the sinks.

"That was just beer talk," I said trying to reassure him I really didn't know anything.

"I don't believe that," the dean answered. "I believe you really do know who did the damage to the sinks so I'm going to give you twenty-four hours to think about whether or not you're going to tell me. Be back in my office tomorrow, at the same time," the dean announced.

"OK," I replied meekly.

Deny, deny, and deny some more, I thought, on the way back to the dorm. The next twenty-four hours passed by agonizingly slowly and seemed to last an eternity as I spent a fitful night trying to sleep, but a guilty conscious knows no rest.

The next day I met again with the dean, and he had me go over my entire day on the day of the sink incident. He first tried the soft approach and then tried the tough approach.

"All right, if you're not going to cooperate then I'm going to officially accuse you of doing all of the damage yourself. The next step is to take the incident before the University Disciplinary Review Board and let them decide your fate," the dean finally announced.

I left his office and immediately made my way back to my dorm room and found my copy of the student handbook. In reading it I learned I had the right to appeal any decision the board made, and since there were only three days of school left I figured if I appealed their decision there wouldn't be enough time to hold an appeal hearing and everything would be carried over to next year.

The next day I was called back into the dean's office and he informed me the Disciplinary Review Board had recommended I be expelled from the university. In my most compelling legalese, I demanded an appeal hearing in which I could testify before the Disciplinary Review Board directly. The dean responded that the board had taken that into consideration and, given the timing of the whole affair, had decided to deny any appeal requests I might make.

So much for that brilliant idea, Perry Mason, I thought to myself.

As I left the dean's office, a feeling of numbness came over me as I tried to decide what to do next. If I'm expelled, I become the scapegoat in the whole deal, but on the other hand, I felt a loyalty to my buddies and since it was my big mouth that got me into this situation I should be the one to shoulder the blame.

Being very distraught and not knowing what to do I decided to make my way over to the Delta Sig house to see if any of my frat brothers had an idea. As I walked into the house, I ran into John Foster, a senior who was about to graduate. John was wearing sandals, cut-off blue jean shorts, a sleeveless T-shirt, and a Chicago Cubs, blue plastic batting helmet. From the looks of his bloodshot eyes and the smell of his beer breath, he was also seriously hungover.

"Hey, buddy, what's up?" John asked.

Without hesitating, and much to John's surprise, I blurted out my whole story.

"Jesus Christ, buddy, you're sure knee deep in shit! Well, do you want to be expelled?" John asked me point blank.

"No," I answered.

"Then you gotta roll, buddy. But before you do, you gotta make it clear to your buddies what you're up against. That way they can't be pissed off at you."

"Yeah, you're right," I said as I began to see for the first time a light at the end of the tunnel and this time it wasn't an oncoming train.

"OK," John said. "Here's what I want you to do. Go find your accomplices and tell 'em you're getting the boot unless you come clean. Ask them what they think you should do. I guarantee they will tell you to fess up. In the meantime, I'm gonna call the dean and arrange a meeting with him in two hours. How's that sound?"

"Great!" I answered, already feeling better than I had all week.

I quickly made my way across campus and back to the dorm. I found my buddies, and as I explained the events of the last couple of days to them they quickly grasped the seriousness of the situation.

"OK, Garrity, what happens to us if you come clean? Do we all get expelled then?" Ted Day asked.

"No," I quickly answered. "I'm gonna tell the dean, before I give any information, he's got to agree none of us will be expelled. I mean, guys, we're gonna get punished in some way, but I think the dean will spare us from expulsion if he can just get to the bottom of this whole thing."

To their credit, the guys all agreed I shouldn't have to take the fall all by myself. As I left the dorm for my meeting with John Foster and the dean, I got a feeling that everything just might turn out all right.

I walked across campus and met up with John at the Delta Sig house. John, still dressed in his hangover best, and I made our way over to the dean's office. Once there, we were ushered into the dean's office by his secretary. John, the dean, and I sat down at a conference table and John began the meeting by saying, "Dean, I know you and I have butted heads during my five years here at the university."

Butted heads?! Five years?! I thought to myself. Who the hell did I pick to represent me!?

"But I just want to thank you for keeping me in line and helping me to graduate," John continued.

"Well, John, I must admit there were times I wondered if you would graduate but you made it and that's what counts. Good luck to you in the future," the Dean replied.

Great I thought, I've got a guy who's been on the dean's shit list for the past five years representing me.

"Now Greg here is a pretty good guy and has pledged to the Delta Sig house. He came over to me for guidance and has explained the whole situation. I guess the reason I asked to meet with you is to see if we couldn't come to some type of agreement that both parties could live with. Dean, Greg really doesn't want to be expelled," John explained.

"Are you aware of what Greg is accused of doing, John?" the dean asked.

"Yes, I am," John answered.

"Well then," the dean continued, "what type of 'agreement' did you have in mind?"

"Well, dean, let's just say hypothetically Greg could provide you a very accurate picture of the events involving the damage to the sinks, including the names of any students who were involved. Could you and the Disciplinary Review Board see it in your hearts to not expel those involved and perhaps just make them pay restitution?" John asked.

"Let me make a call, I'll be right back," the dean replied quickly.

The dean then got up out of his brown, leather chair and walked into an adjoining room. Several minutes passed by as my stomach knotted up and the possibility of heaving right there in the dean's office loomed large. The dean finally returned with his secretary in tow.

"I've spoken with the chairperson of the Disciplinary Review Board," the dean began. "And he wants complete restitution from all parties involved. In addition, each individual will be put on social probation for the entire first semester of next year and a formal notice will be sent home to all of their parents."

With that said, John turned to me and asked, "Well, Greg?"

"I'd like it all put in writing," I quickly shot back.

The dean took a step back, obviously physically taken aback by my brashness.

"Ooooh, I don't think that's necessary," John quickly blurted out as he flashed a big toothy grin the dean's way, hoping to smooth things over. "What's next, dean?" John asked.

"I've brought my secretary in here in order to transcribe what Greg is about to tell us. OK, Greg, anytime you're ready," the dean said as he stared into my eyes.

I began to relay the details of that fateful day. With each word I spoke, I felt a little more weight lifted from my shoulders. The dean interrupted every so often asking me a question in order to clarify something. When I was finally finished, I began to cry. I'm not sure why, maybe it was because I felt bad about telling on everyone but more likely because I had just seen a very emotional week come to a conclusion and my crying was a manifestation of all that pent-up emotion.

"You've done the right thing," the dean said as we stood up to leave. "John, I want to thank you for helping Greg make the right decision."

"My pleasure, sir," John said as he shook the dean's hand.

"Good luck to you, John," the dean said smiling.

John and I left the administration building and stood for a moment out in front of it.

"All right, buddy, that's it," John said. "Pay the bill, stay out of trouble during first semester of next year, and this whole thing will be behind you."

"Thanks, John," I said as I looked him in the eyes. "I really appreciate you coming to see the dean with me."

"No problem, that's what brothers are for," John replied with a smile. And with that John turned and began to walk in the direction of the Delta Sig house. I didn't know it at the time, but that would be the last time I would ever see or speak to him.

I slowly walked across campus and back to my dorm. I met with the guys and debriefed them on my meeting with the dean. The basic feeling was hey, we fucked up, got caught, and now had to pay our dues. Fuck it, I thought, as I got back to my room. Another couple of days and I'll be back home. I can't wait!

21 THE STEEL FACTORY

Good-bye Decatur, Illinois you soy bean capital of the world and hello, Chicago, you toddling town. School was over, and it felt good to be home. Just before Christmas my parents had moved out of Rogers Park to an apartment just west of Western Avenue off of Lawrence Avenue. It was a two-bedroom apartment so I had my own room, albeit a small one.

I wasn't sure if I was going to be going back to Millikin in the fall, but at this point that wasn't one of my major concerns. My major concern was finding a summer job so I could make some money. My dad told me there was a possible position open at the screw machine company he worked for, so I filled out an application and a week later was hired. My job there was to be an all-around factory helper. Primarily this meant I caught finished parts, which came off of an automatic screw machine, for ten hours a day.

The work was monotonous, and since the factory wasn't air conditioned it was hot as hell during the summer months. In addition, hot oil ran through, over, and sometimes out of the machine so it was really a hot, smelly mess. Some days I left work caked in oil and couldn't get rid of the smell until I had gone home and taken a good shower and blown my nose thoroughly.

I had been thinking about quitting school but decided the only way I would do that would be if I could find a really decent-paying job. The father of my friend Brian Murphy was a big shot with the steel company located just behind the company I was working for. I asked Brian to ask his dad if there were any openings. He did and his dad told him I should go see the personnel director to fill out an application and see what was happening.

So one day of the following week, during my lunch break, I went over to see him. The personnel director had me fill out an application and then told me he was anticipating an opening on the graveyard shift in the big punch press room. He told me the position paid twelve bucks an hour and he would contact me when it became available. Twelve bucks an hour! Screw college I thought, this is some serious cash! I left the personnel office elated and with the prospect of a good-paying job on my horizon I felt I could finally decide on my future. College was out, I decided. Working full time was in!

I enjoyed the fact that working allowed me to always have money in my pockets, but I didn't like the fact I had to take a bus or a train to get back to the old neighborhood to drink with my buddies. With a new-found feeling of confidence, I decided it was time to look into buying some transportation so I thought of various scenarios and consulted with my friends.

Billy told me he had some money saved up and he would be willing to make me a loan if I promised to repay him a hundred bucks a paycheck. I thought about buying a motorcycle, and since I couldn't get either my parents or my older brother to cosign a loan for it, I took Billy up on his offer.

Here I was trying to repay Billy for saving my life, but instead I relied on him for a loan to help me buy some transportation.

"Billy, I now owe you even more than I already do," I said one night as he handed me over the fifteen-hundred dollars in cash, which I needed to purchase the motorcycle.

"I know where you live, Double G," Billy shot back.

I'm not sure why Billy gave me the loan other than he was trying to help a buddy out. He was really taking a big risk when you consider I had never driven a bike before. Had I killed myself on it, Billy would have been out the cash and only had the wrecked remains of my bike to show for it.

I went to a Honda dealer in Rogers Park to look at some bikes. The one I liked was called a Nighthawk. It had about a four-hundred-and-seventy-five c.c. engine, which is not really that powerful when you consider the big bikes are one-thousand to fifteen-hundred c.c. But I felt it was good for a beginner, which certainly described me.

I made arrangements with one of my old Sullivan football buddies to pick up the bike. My football buddy told me he knew how to drive one and was willing to teach me. We picked up the bike and cruised over to his dad's apartment.

My buddy showed me the basics of accelerating, shifting, and braking, and then I practiced. First going up and down the alley and then around the block. I wouldn't say I was an accomplished rider by the end of that first night, but I did manage to drive myself back to my parents' apartment, about five miles away. The bike brought me the freedom I wanted, and I was now able to zoom to work, zoom home, take a shower, and then zoom to Rogers Park to hang out by the schoolyard or the beaches.

In late summer, the steel company I interviewed with contacted me. The punch press operator position on the eleven-to-seven graveyard shift had become available. Seeing the opportunity to make some real money, I gave the company I was working for my two weeks' notice. During my lunch break, I went over to my new employer next door for a routine physical and to buy a steel-toed pair of work boots, which were required. I spent my last two weeks at my dad's employer anticipating my future and lucrative position and wondering what working the night shift would be like. I was scheduled to start at eleven the following Monday night.

Monday night came, and since it was raining I opted to take the L and a bus to the factory instead of riding my bike. How eerie it was, I thought, as

I walked the last couple of deserted blocks to the plant in a light, misty rain. The streets were so quiet yet I could hear the pounding of the giant punch presses, like a great, thumping heartbeat emanating not from a human chest but from inside the building I soon learned I would be working in. It seemed so odd to be going to work at this hour, in the darkness of night.

I checked in at the guard station, and the guard telephoned building 37, the building that housed the three-story punch presses. The assistant foreman came to pick me up and showed me the way to the building. He introduced himself and asked my name. I told him, and he responded with, "Well, at least you speak English."

We walked in silence through the darkness and rain to building 37. As we approached the building, I felt the ground beneath my feet shaking and heard the loud thud of the three-story presses and the high-pitched tink, tink, tink of the smaller presses as they punched out steel laminations from the sheets of steel that were being fed into them.

The assistant foremen opened the door and led me inside. It's hard to describe the level of noise inside building 37 when all of the presses were running. I had been told this building, where I was to work eight hours a day, had been rated as the second highest producer of noise pollution in the state of Illinois only to be out done by O'Hare International Airport.

Once inside, I could believe it. To speak to someone, you had to cup your hands around your mouth, lean toward the person's ears, and shout your message. A forklift truck, normally a fairly loud vehicle, could drive right up along next to you and if you didn't see it, you would not realize it was there. Given this noise level, I soon learned both interesting and dangerous things were bound to happen here.

I immediately became aware the workers had developed a very functional sign language of their own. For example, placing your fists in front of you, thumb touching thumb and then moving your hands in a motion that resembled breaking a stick in your hands meant you were going to go on break. If you first pointed to your press and then did this motion, it meant there was a problem with your press. A wipe of your forehead with the back of your hand meant you were working your ass off and putting an open hand over an ear and then rotating it back and forth meant someone or something was crazy.

Since a lot of the workers didn't speak very good English, the fact we were not able to communicate by spoken word wasn't really a major problem as we primarily relied on our homegrown sign language to communicate.

The first couple of nights on the job I was shown the ropes by one of the veteran machine operators. The press I was trained on was one of the biggest in the building. It was approximately three stories tall, which meant much of it was below the removable floorboards we stood on.

There wasn't a lot to the press itself. A heavy, metal, cast die sat in the opening of the press and was secured there with a series of large bolts. The die determined what kind of punches would be made into the steel strip, which unwound slowly from a two-thousand pound roll of steel.

As the press ran, steel laminations were created via a series of punching operations applied to the steel strip from within the die. The finished laminations were punched down into a chute, which was connected to the die. The chute ran in a slowly curving angle underneath the machine and then ran up and out from underneath the floor, about fifteen feet from the machine. At that point, the chute angled upwards and emerged through the floor and extended about four feet above it.

The punch press eventually pushed, or should I say punched, out a steady stream of laminations through the chute to where I waited. As I held the handle of a short steel rod, I inserted the rod into one of the holes in the laminations and then took a metal ruler, which had a sharp metal "tooth" at each end, and pressed it into the stream of laminations. This enabled me to measure off about eight inches of laminations, which I would lift out of the chute and place on a table in front of me. I inserted a wire through each side until it extended through the fifty or so laminations, which made up my eight inches. Using common household pliers, I twisted the wires together tightly insuring the laminations stayed together for the next process, which involved exposing them to intense heat. Once wired, I lifted the bundled laminations, which weighed about fifteen pounds, onto a cart. Once the cart was full, it was hauled away by a forklift. My new job was hot, hard, and mind numbing, but the paychecks went a long way to ease my pain. This was my new career.

It was strange getting off of work at seven in the morning and heading home as everyone else was busy going to work. I usually went home to my parents' apartment and would take a long, hot bath while I listened to the radio. My parents had already left for work, so I had the run of the apartment. What this meant was I could break out my bong and get high while I listened to some tunes.

As I eventually got into a routine, this is how my days and nights were spent. I came home from work at seven thirty. Bathe, party, eat, and go to sleep around noon or one. I woke up around eight, watched some TV, and left for work at ten thirty. On the weekends when I didn't work, I partied my ass off with Billy, Will, and all of the other usual suspects.

*   *   *   *

One Saturday night around this time I had just bought an ounce of weed and met up with some of the guys at the schoolyard. Will drove by in his car, so a bunch of us piled in and cruised to the liquor store and bought a couple of six packs. We cruised around the neighborhood, shooting the shit, listening to tunes, and drinking. Will decided to cruise to North Shore beach to see if anything was going on down there. Since it was late fall, we really didn't expect to see anybody, but it was a way to kill time.

The police had been turning up the heat on people drinking at the beaches, so we didn't plan to park and drink there. As we pulled up to the beach, we saw an unmarked detective car parked there.

"Just turn around, Will, and get us the fuck outta here," I whispered to Will as if the cops could hear me.

"That's all I need, to get pulled over with a bunch of open beers in the car," Will replied as he began to turn the car around. Will completed his legal U-turn at the beach's dead end and headed back toward Sheridan Road. About a half a block away Will yelled, "FUCK, THEY'RE COMING AFTER US!"

As I slowly turned my head, my eyes quickly confirmed his observation.

"Will, maybe they just got a call," I said trying to rationalize why they would be directly behind us. Just then I heard the announcement from the detectives' loud speaker.

"You need to pull your vehicle over," came the command.

The sound of clanking, empty beer bottles emanated from the back seat as Billy tried to hide them under the car's seats and floor mats. At this point, I remembered I had a fresh ounce of weed in my pocket. Fuck! What do I!? Quickly I realized I had two options. I could leave the weed on my person or I could try to hide it in Will's car somewhere. As I considered my options a picture of us being busted for open beers formed in my mind. Then another picture popped up as well, one of me being searched at the police station after our arrest and being found in possession of weed, which would result in additional charges.

Without hesitation, I pulled the ounce out of my jacket and shoved it underneath my front passenger seat as far back as I could reach. Will pulled over to the side of the road and within seconds the detectives were upon us. With their flashlights pointed in our faces, they demanded we all get out of the vehicle.

"What are you guys up to?" a detective asked.

"Oh, just cruising around officer," Will replied.

"I got some beer bottles in the back seat area," one of the detectives announced as he began searching Will's car.

Oh boy, I thought, here we go.

"OK, let's see some ID from everybody," the bigger of the two detectives ordered.

As I pulled my wallet from my jacket I saw the other detective, with flashlight in hand, begin to look around the front seat area where I had been sitting. My heart began to race as the beam of light illuminated the seat and foot area where, just beyond the light, underneath the seat, lay my ounce of weed. Then, just as I thought the detective was going to end his search, he bent over and pointed his flashlight directly under my seat.

I'm fucked, I thought, as my heart practically burst through my chest. Then suddenly, inexplicably, the detective stood back up and began to lecture us about drinking and driving.

After the lecture the detectives confiscated all of our beers but decided to let us go on our merry way. We piled back into the car, and Will pulled away slowly. As soon as the detectives were out of sight, I reached below the seat and found my ounce. With trembling hands, I twisted up a doobie, lit it and hit it hard.

The guys started talking about how they all thought for sure we were going to be busted for the open beers. I interrupted their conversation to make a confession.

"Guys," I began, "I thought for sure we were going to get busted for the brews and thinking that, I thought it would be better to stash the reef under my seat than in my crotch."

"You fucking asshole, I don't believe you did that in my car," Will responded immediately.

"But they looked under your seat," Billy said with astonishment in his voice.

"I know, man," I responded. "Either the dick saw it and didn't want to deal with it or my guardian angel made it disappear as the guy was looking under there. Either way, I'm one lucky dude."

"Yeah, but it's in my car so I get busted," Will muttered.

"Will," I began, starting to feel the intoxicating effects of the reefer, "I would never have let you take the rap for me. If they find it I confess that's its mine, OK?" I said, meaning every word.

"OK, if you say so," Will replied not completely convinced. "Double G, just do me one favor."

"Anything, dude."

"CROTCH THAT SHIT!" Will yelled.

I responded by bursting out in laughter, which seemed to be contagious as everyone else in the car joined in. And then as the laughter subsided, I dutifully stashed the weed down my shorts and passed the joint.

* * * *

Some work mornings I deviated from my normal routine of going straight home to party and instead hit a bar close to the factory. For breakfast I would have the "Breakfast of Champions," which consisted of a Greyhound (vodka and grapefruit juice) and a small frozen pizza. A couple of times I sat drinking with some of the guys so long that my dad would show up for his lunch and find me sitting there half in the bag.

"Don't you think you should go home?" he'd ask.

"Hey, I got off of work at seven and its only noon now. It's like getting off work at five and now it's ten at night," I would respond.

He didn't argue with my logic but sat down instead to enjoy his liquid lunch.

As the days went by, I learned more and more about the guys I was working with. Most of them were first-generation immigrants who did not speak or write English very well but weren't afraid to work hard. There were Koreans, Peruvians, Puerto Ricans, Mexicans, Cubans, and Eastern Europeans.

I became friendly with one Puerto Rican guy who had worked in the factory for years. He was missing about half of his index finger on his right hand. I've failed to mention this aspect of the job. There were a number of guys who were missing various parts of fingers and hands. These were the results of the steel getting jammed up inside the die within the press. We did have steel magnetic hooks to help us pull out the big pieces but sometimes a really small scrap would get stuck to the underside of a punch and a guy, already exasperated by a recurring jam up, would stick his hand in to get the last, small piece of scrap metal. These presses, which were controlled by hydraulics, would sometimes slam closed by themselves. If this occurred while you were pulling that last piece of scrap out with your hand it was good-bye finger or worse. And all around me were the maimed workers to prove it.

One morning after work, my Puerto Rican friend invited me to go to another guy's apartment to party. He told me to pick up some beers and meet them there. When I walked into the apartment, I saw my Puerto Rican buddy along with two other guys who worked on our shift, a young guy from Peru and an old guy from Cuba. We sat down around a dining room table in the apartment, drinking beer and bullshitting as best we could.

Much of the conversation was in Spanish, but they tried as best they could to update me on what was said. After a while one of them went into another room and came back in with a silver tray full of cocaine. They passed it around, and each guy did as much as he wanted. I really hadn't done coke before, so I took it easy. As the tray made the rounds, the level of noise from our conversations seemed to rise in direct proportion to the amount of coke we had done.

The little old guy who I learned had fled from Cuba during Castro's takeover, became especially agitated when he re-told his old war stories. As he spoke in rapid, loud Spanish I became very interested in what he was saying. My Puerto Rican buddy translated as best he could. The old Cuban told us about how he had left Cuba and how a guy caught him as he was trying to escape and told him he was going to turn him over to the authorities. Fearing he would be thrown in jail for a very long time or worse, he did the only thing that he could. He pulled a gun on the guy and put a bullet in his brain, killing him instantly.

As the old Cuban told the story, I could not understand a word of it, but

I saw the fire and desperation in his old, tired eyes, the same fire and desperation that must have been present the day he fired that fatal shot so many years ago.

After a while, I felt it was time to go so I said my good-byes and headed home. On my way, all I could think about was the old Cuban and his story. His taking of another human life, his flight from Cuba, and how it all led him to this hard, hot, factory job in Chicago.

"The modern American dream," I said out loud to myself.

* * * *

As the winter drew near, I realized I wasn't going to have any transportation once the rough weather started. Coupled with this was the fact that one recent afternoon while cruising on my motorcycle down Touhy Avenue, a car had pulled out of its parking space right in front of me. At the speed I was going I had three options. The first was to ram into the car, the second was to lay the bike and myself down, which was also not a very pleasant thought. The third choice was to swerve around the car into the oncoming traffic lane. Luckily, (guardian angel again?) there wasn't a vehicle traveling in the opposite lane as I made this maneuver so I escaped unharmed. However, the experience left me shaking in my boots, and a lot less fond of my bike. So with that experience in my mind, I called Billy and Will one Saturday afternoon and asked if they would like to join me in visiting some car dealerships to price some vehicles. They agreed, and we soon found ourselves on the showroom floor of a local Chevy dealer.

I looked at vans, which were really detailed but the steep prices drove me away. Then the salesmen showed me a gray-on-gray Chevy Nomad, which came equipped with AC, four captain's chairs, and interior carpeting in the rear. The van had been used a bit by dealer personnel and therefore was slightly discounted. When I considered the price of the totally detailed vans with that of the Nomad, I thought the Nomad was a pretty good deal.

In what was the biggest rash decision of my life, I exclaimed to the salesmen, "I'll take it!" Since I was so new on the job, my parents had to co-sign the loan for me, and since I didn't have much in the bank for a down payment I had to trade in my bike. As Will drove me back to my parents' apartment I dreamed of how cool it would be to actually own a nice van like the Chevy Nomad.

Back at the apartment I presented to my parents the best argument I could in favor of buying the van.

"Just think I won't be riding that motorcycle anymore," I said.

That statement above all won them over. We drove back to the dealership, my parents in their car, Will and Billy in Will's car, and me on my bike. The papers were signed, and I left the dealership with a brand new Chevy Nomad van.

Having my Chevy van meant having a home away from home, a living room/bedroom on wheels if you will. If the fucking thing had a john with a shower my parents, would probably have never seen me again!

* * * *

The winter rolled around finally, and I continued to work my night shift and partied as usual. One night, a bunch of us were at Will's parents' apartment just sitting around partying when they unexpectedly came home. They told Will, in no uncertain terms, that we all had to leave. The most likely place to retreat to was my van, which was parked out back in the alley. We all exited the apartment and climbed into my van and continued to party, drinking and smoking as if we had never been interrupted.

About a half hour after we had arrived in the van, a squad car turned into the alley and approached us very slowly. I reached for the volume-control knob on the booming stereo and told everybody to keep quiet. The squad pulled up alongside and the officer rolled down his window.

"We got a complaint about noise coming from the alley," he said.

"Oh really?" I answered back.

"How many people you got in that thing?" he then asked.

"Oh I don't know officer, ten, maybe fifteen guys I suppose," I answered.

"Holy shit!" was his startled response. "If I wanted to bring you in, I'd have to call in a paddy wagon just to get everyone to the station. Listen, just do me a favor and take off and go somewhere else. OK?"

"You got it, officer," I quickly replied.

The cop pulled down the alley and I relayed our conversation to everyone in the van. Being the good Catholic boys that we were, we schlepped our booze and other party materials to a new location to continue our festivities without further interruption.

22 A LONG GOODBYE

Will had grown tired of the Rogers Park scene and although he had been very successful in the Chicago theatre productions he had participated in while going to school part time, he felt he needed a change.

"I'm moving to Hollywood next month," Will announced nonchalantly during one of our Risk games in Billy's bedroom.

"Really!?" I shot back, truly surprised by the news.

"What's your fuckin' old man say about this?" Billy asked.

"Yeah, how's he feel?" I chimed in.

"He wants me to succeed in what makes me happy and he understands that acting is my passion so he's OK with it. In fact, he has some connections out there that I'm gonna meet with so I might be able to get some work right away."

"That's awesome!" I said only half meaning it. I knew I would really miss Will once he moved away and that trying to repay him for saving my life was now going to be virtually impossible. Deep down, I also felt that once he left us we wouldn't be seeing much of him ever again since he was destined to make it really big out there.

"We gotta have a fuckin' party," Billy announced. "Just guys, to send you out in style!"

"Sounds good, gents, just let me know where I need to be," Will said with a smile on his face.

In the next couple of days, Billy and I passed around the idea of a going away party to our other buddies and Brian Murphy responded by volunteering his parents' two flat for the event. On the day of the party, we rented a quarter barrel of beer and on a whim, I bought a fifth of Jack Daniel's whiskey so we could do some shots as we toasted Will's departure.

We gathered in Brian's backyard on a bright sunny day - me, Will, Billy, Brian and Mike Murphy. Later on, some other guys from the hood dropped by as well. We started drinking around mid-afternoon, and by five o'clock we had polished off the fifth of Jack. Billy decided to make a quick run to a liquor store on Devon Avenue, and when he came back he proudly showed us his purchase. Not a fifth of Jack Daniel's this time but a quart. Already feeling no pain, we all cheered his return and gladly took another shot of this magic elixir.

Not long afterwards, Jimmy Morgan arrived and low and behold yet another fifth of Jack was tucked under one of his arms. Another mad cheer went up and the words "Just in time," muttered as we drained the quart and opened the new fifth.

Right about then Mrs. Murphy, Brian's mom, appeared at the back porch window of their apartment, just above where we were, and asked Brian if we could quiet it down a bit. Not out of disrespect but rather out of intense drunkenness we all shouted, "YEAH WE'LL BE QUIET!" and then proceeded to hoist the family picnic table up over our collective heads and march around the small yard while each of us hummed our own marching tune.

The situation deteriorated from there, if that was possible. We polished off the fifth Jimmy Morgan had brought and made a run to purchase another. It was shortly after the arrival of the fourth bottle of Jack that Brian Murphy's system decided to shut down. We got Brian to one of the couches in the Murphys' basement, and he slept there like a baby until the following morning. The party didn't stop just because one of us had hit the wall. Not at all, we finished off the fourth bottle, and that's when the real fun began.

Will, the guest of honor, went out to the alley to take a leak against a telephone pole. When he hadn't returned in several minutes, I stumbled out of the yard to check on him. I spotted Will standing alongside a telephone pole with his legs spread apart, about shoulder width, his hands on his hips and a cigarette dangling from his mouth.

"Will, whatcha doing?" I asked as I approached,

"Pissssing, Double G, what da fuck does it looook like I'mmm doing?" he drunkenly responded.

As I got a little closer I did in fact see that Will was pissing. However, there was one problem. In his drunken stupor, Will had forgotten to lower his pants zipper. In other words, he had just pissed in his pants. After his "piss" I suggested to Will he join Brian down in the basement for a little siesta. As he was led down the basement stairs, Will mumbled rather indignantly, "What the fuuuck got spilled on mmmmy crotch?"

With our welcome long worn out at the Murphys' place, the guys who could still stand went to Billy's mother's apartment's backyard, which was just one block away, to continue the party. The details of any of the scholarly conversations that ensued once we arrived in Billy's backyard were fuzzy to me at best, but I remembered the next day a couple of the shenanigans that occurred.

For some reason, upon arriving in Billy's backyard, Jimmy Morgan took his shoes off and laid them down on Billy's back porch. A little bit later Billy felt the urge to vomit. Unfortunately for Jimmy, Billy's urge occurred just above Jimmy's shoes resulting in a full afternoon and evening of drinking beer and lord knows how many shots of Jack Daniels being deposited into Jimmy's gym shoes.

When Jimmy Morgan got up to leave, despite our shouting out protest to the contrary, he put his vomit-filled shoes on and walked the five or six blocks home, sloshing all the way! Jimmy didn't realize what had transpired until he woke up the following morning.

The next day we also found out about Sean O'Reilly's long walk back home to his parents' apartment. Sean another guy who had graduated from St. Ignatius and the brother of Shannon, who was my chicken-game-playing companion in eighth grade, stopped by just as the second bottle of Jack was opened.

As Sean later recalled, "I don't remember much after leaving Brian's backyard but all of a sudden, I'm standing on Sheridan Road and a bank alarm is going off. There's broken glass on the ground and my arm is bleeding. The next thing I know a cop pulls up and asks me what I'm doing. From what I was told I guess I mumbled something about a late night deposit."

After being taken to the emergency room for some stitches in his arm, Sean was promptly put under arrest for disorderly conduct.

And so ended the goodbye party for Will and to a certain degree, a chapter of my life. The next day as I lay in bed nursing my massive hangover, I thought about all of the good times Will and I had shared. Our early grade school days, our freshmen year together at Loyola Academy, and all of the crazy shit we did together as teenagers around the neighborhood.

I also thought how if it wasn't for Will and Billy I wouldn't be here now, experiencing the bass drum pounding in my head. I laughed out loud at that one but gathered myself as I realized again that there was now very little, if any chance, of repaying him for saving my life on that stormy, summer evening years ago. I vowed to myself then and there that if I ever made it out to California or if Will ever moved back here, I would try my hardest to pay him back.

23 A SHORT LIVED CAREER

After Will's departure to the bright lights of L.A., I continued working at the steel factory at night and partying heavy on the weekends. On one very hot, early-June night, the temperature in Building 37, the one I worked in, was somewhere between ninety-five and a hundred degrees. Several months before I had been unofficially promoted to die setter as one of the Hispanic die setters on our shift had quit quite unexpectedly. I was taken off the machines, given his toolbox, and put in charge of four of the biggest punch presses.

My job as a die setter was to help pull out the dies that fit into the punch press machines when jobs were changing over and then put the new die in place for the next job. This was necessary because each die was made differently in order to punch out the steel in a unique pattern and shape to fit the customers' specifications. In addition, when a punch press jammed up badly, it was my responsibility to clear the jam and get the machine going again.

My assistant foreman, who had lost the tips of his fingers to the presses, helped me a great deal in learning how to change over jobs, set dies, and clear out jams. On this particular night, a rather unique type of jam occurred. A conveyor belt, which ran beneath the three-story machines and carried the punched out scrap pieces of steel to an awaiting freight car, became jammed. The jam occurred underneath the third machine away from the freight car and one of the machines that I was responsible for.

The machine operator somehow saw the jam up through the floorboards and quickly made me aware of it. As we really couldn't hear each other speak, I signaled for him to 'kill' his machine by pointing at the machine and then making a slashing motion across my throat. I then walked over to the operator of the machine that was furthest from the freight car and signaled to him to 'kill' his press as well because the steel scraps from his machine were being dragged by the conveyor belt into the already huge jam up.

The machine operators and I lifted the heavy, timber floor boards that made up the portable floor. All this action in an environment in which a yell was almost inaudible because of the loud din of the still operating punch press machines. The heat and humidity that night caused me to sweat profusely, and by the time we had lifted the floor to get to the conveyer belt I was drenched in sweat.

Once the floor was lifted, I got a pitchfork we used to remove the piles of tangled, sharp edged, steel pieces that got jammed on the conveyor belt from time to time. I handed the pitch fork to one of the machine operators and motioned to him that I was going down beneath the floor onto the still-moving conveyor belt. I then hopped down through the hole in the floor.

Once I was on the conveyor belt, he handed me the pitchfork and disappeared from my view. Probably to get a cold drink, I thought, as I began to wage battle with the steel pile by dislodging the sharp-edged pieces of scrap steel with my trusty pitchfork. Because the conveyor was still moving, I had a very difficult time getting enough leverage to enable me to dislodge any sizable portion of the eight foot high by five foot wide heap of steel scraps. After about five minutes of trying, I began to grow tired in the intense heat.

Then, while trying to dislodge a large chunk of the pile, I lost my balance and instead of falling off of the conveyor belt and down to the ground about ten feet below, I fell forward onto the pile of steel scraps and felt a sharp piece of steel pierce my chest. Luckily I was wearing work gloves and was somewhat able to break my fall and quickly able to regain my balance on the moving belt. Looking down at my chest I saw a small rivulet of red ooze through my tee shirt right where the steel piece had pierced me. I must be crazy trying to dislodge this heap while the conveyor belt was still moving, I thought to myself.

I scrambled up, out of the hole in the floor and went to the next two machines in line that were closest to the freight car but past the jam up. I made eye contact with the machine operators and showed them the slashing motion across my neck as well, our understood sign for them to "kill" their machines.

Once their machines were off, I went to the main switch of the conveyor belt and turned it off. I then went back down into the hole by the machine that had the original jam up. By this time, my clothes were so drenched in sweat I felt as if I had jumped into a swimming pool and had spent the last thirty minutes swimming in it. The ninety-five-plus temperature coupled with the unrelenting humidity felt more like one hundred and ninety-five by now.

Once on the now-still conveyor belt, I went back at the huge mound of steel debris with my pitchfork. I felt much better with a solid, stationary position in my battle with the jam up and was now able to get enough leverage so I could begin to pull small amounts of steel scraps off the pile and drop them down to the concrete floor below.

As I worked on removing the scrap pile, I heard a faint noise above me and looked up. It was the Chinese steel cutter who probably had the lowest position in the whole building. His job was to go around and pick up the five-to-ten-foot-sized pieces of slightly bent steel that came off the beginning and ends of each roll of steel. He dragged these pieces over to an electric steel chopper and then fed them by hand into it, cutting them up into one or two-foot sections that fell onto the conveyor belt and then were deposited into the awaiting freight car.

From the gestures he was making, I gathered he thought the conveyor belt should be turned back on. I gestured back by shaking my head no and pointing to myself. I wobbled and then pointed to the concrete floor ten feet below me. He disappeared from my sight so I went back at the pile with my pitchfork, confident he had understood my message.

I was beginning to make real progress when all of a sudden the conveyor belt jerked forward. I lost my balance and fell back onto the conveyor, landing on my butt. I had to quickly scramble to get to my feet lest I be dragged into the steel scrap pile.

I was furious the Chinese steel cutter had turned on the conveyor belt while he knew I was standing on it and had seen me gesture for him not to. Caught up in the heat of the moment, both literally and figuratively, I boosted myself up and out of the hole to find him. As I came around the machine I saw him walking away from the conveyor's main switch toward his cutting machine. I ran toward him and when I reached him I gave him a shove in the back, which sent him flying about five feet forward, landing on his hands and knees.

He quickly got up, turned, and now facing me struck what I considered to be some type of martial arts pose.

"OH, YOU WANT TO FUCK WITH ME SOME MORE?" I shouted loudly, although with the noise of the still-running presses no one could hear me. I then moved toward him.

I moved so fast he didn't have time to block my right-hand roundhouse, which caught him squarely on the jaw. Upon impact, teeth flew from his mouth as he fell to my left. He hit the ground but to his credit gamely got back up and faced me again.

"MORE!?" I shouted, as again my words were lost in the roar of the presses.

I lifted my fist again and began to move toward him, intending for this one to knock him into tomorrow. Just as I was about to deliver the blow, I felt two hands grab my arm. I wheeled around to see the foreman, who was in charge of the smaller presses, holding my arm. He pulled my arm down and pulled me away as several of the other workers grabbed the steel cutter.

He brought me to my foreman who brought me outside and asked me what had happened. With the din of the punch presses in the background of this hot, summer night, I explained the whole situation to my foreman who told me to wait outside as he had to go back inside and make a call from his office. My assistant foreman, who had been my mentor, came outside and asked me what had happened. I retold my story and asked him what he thought would happen.

"Well," he began, "when I first started here a couple of guys got into a little fight and they fired them on the spot saying there was no room for fighting on the job. But maybe because of your situation they will be a little more lenient. Maybe you will just be suspended for a while and make you pay for the Chinaman's dental work," he said with a slight smile. "How many times did you hit him?" he asked.

"Just once," I quickly and honestly replied.

At that moment my foremen came back out and told me I had to go see the shift supervisor in another building. I walked slowly over to the other building in my sweat-drenched clothes and recounted my story to him as he wrote it all down. The shift supervisor told me to go home and report to the personnel director in the morning.

As I left the shift supervisor's office and walked to my van in the darkness of the night, I wondered how this whole thing would shake out. I had just bought my expensive, new, Chevy van so I just couldn't lose my job. Maybe I'll just get suspended for a month, I thought, as I lifted my hot, sweaty, bloodied body into the van. As I turned the ignition on, I suddenly realized I couldn't go home since it was only about four thirty in the morning and my parents would ask me why I was home so early from work. So instead of going home I cruised down to North Shore beach to plunge into the cool, refreshing waters of Lake Michigan.

After about fifteen minutes of driving down the deserted, early-morning streets of Chicago, I turned off Sheridan Road onto North Shore. Half way down the block I spotted Katy O'Brien, a cousin of my friend Brian Murphy. She was sitting on the front stoop of the three flat she lived in. I pulled up in front of her and asked her if she could get me a bar of soap and a towel. She went inside and quickly reappeared with both. I motioned for her to get into the van, and she did.

I drove a bit further down the block and parked at the dead end, flush up against one of the cement blocks with the rear end of my van facing the lake. I stripped down and then waded into the water as Katy looked on. The cool water of the lake against my overheated body truly felt like a gift from the gods.

I took my bath as the first light of the morning's dawn broke over the eastern horizon of Lake Michigan. My body temperature cooled as I submerged myself into the chilly, early-morning waters. Finally washed up and feeling human again, I waded back to shore and got dressed. I packed a baby bong I carried in the van with some weed and smoked a bowl as I told Katy of my night.

"So now I have to go see the personnel director. If he cans me, I don't know what the hell I'm gonna do," I said as I finished my story.

Katy just shook her head upon hearing my predicament. A little later I said goodbye to Katy, thanked her for the soap and towel, and drove off, heading back to the factory. I went inside the building that housed the personnel department and told the director's secretary who I was and that I was told to report to him this morning. I waited about five minutes and was led into the director's office. As I entered it, flashbacks of the dean's office at Millikin appeared in my mind.

The director began our conversation by asking me about my duties on third shift. I told him I had been working as a die setter the past two or three months, ever since the Hispanic die setter had quit. When I told him I even had his toolbox, he seemed a bit surprised.

He asked me to tell him what happened on my shift last night. I explained the whole deal just as I had to my foreman and the shift supervisor. Then he asked me a question whose answer may have decided my fate.

"If you had to do it all over again, would you do the same thing?" the director asked.

"Yes!" I answered without hesitation. I went on and explained to him that at the time, I felt the steel cutter had put my life in danger by doing just the opposite of what I asked him to do.

"I see," was the director's unemotional response. He then asked me to step outside of his office for several minutes.

The several minutes stretched into ten and then fifteen. I began to sweat profusely as my stomach knotted up and my mind raced. Why was this taking so long? After several more agonizing minutes, my torturous wait finally ended when the director popped his head out of his office and asked me to come back inside. This is it, I thought, the moment of truth. I sat down, and the director began to speak.

"I've taken into consideration everything you have told me, what your foremen has told me, and what the steel cutter has told me. Based on this information, I will have to terminate your employment effective immediately."

I reached for the edge of his desk, something to hold on to, as I was physically shaken by the news.

"No suspension?" I managed to ask rather meekly.

"No, the company's owner himself reviewed this incident this morning, and it is his firm belief that violence in the workplace is not tolerable," the director explained.

"What about the steel cutter?" I asked.

"He will be terminated also," the director replied.

"OK," was all I could say in response.

"Now there are two other things I must say," the director continued. "The first is I must make you aware that the steel cutter has several teenage sons who were in here this morning with their dad and they were very upset. I'm quite sure they would love to get a piece of you and they might be waiting for you when you leave here."

Let them, I thought, as adrenaline began to pump through my body while my soul filled with anger. I'll rip their fucking heads off and shit down their throats.

"The other thing is," the director continued, "I'd like you to return the die setter tool box. Is it in your car?"

"Yes, I'll go get it," I answered numbly.

As I left the personnel director's office I managed to quickly snap out of my state of shock as I realized there was a distinct possibility I could be jumped by a couple of pissed-off punks and therefore had to ready myself for anything. I made my way to my van without incident and got the toolbox from the back of it. As I did, I also grabbed my tire iron and brought it up to the front of the van, carefully positioning it under my driver's seat.

I went back inside and returned the tools to the personnel director. Just as I was about to leave his office the director said, "Good luck to you in the future."

"Thanks," I said, thanks ASSHOLE! I thought.

I made my way safely to my van and headed home. I didn't know how I was going to break the news of my firing to my parents, so I just decided to wait. As it turned out, I didn't have to break the news to them at all.

That day at lunch my dad went to the saloon near work, which was also a hangout for the guys who worked at the steel factory where I had been employed. One of the guys who knew who my dad was approached him and said something like, "Gee, I was sorry to see your son was let go."

My dad, of course, didn't know what to think. He came home that night and asked me for an explanation. I told my parents the whole story and other than the fact I had a brand-new van to pay for and now was without a job, they didn't seem too upset.

"You'll have to find another job right away if you want to keep that van," my mother said.

"I know," I replied as I nodded my head in agreement, having already realized I needed to go job hunting immediately.

24 WHAT A WORLD

That Sunday I scoured the want ads in the newspaper looking for a new job. One ad caught my eye. It read:

"Van or truck owner wanted. Unlimited earnings while you have fun.

We're looking for 10 rock & rollers who enjoy making money while they have fun.

Call Mr. Jones at blah, blah, blah."

I decided to call first thing Monday morning. When I did, I was asked what type of vehicle I had. I told the woman that I had a Chevy Nomad and without hesitation she asked if I could come by the following morning. I said sure and began to get very excited by having the prospect of getting a new job so soon.

I arrived at the address I had been given early the next morning. The address was a small strip of offices a business could rent fairly cheaply. The name of the business was ABC Distributors, very generic I thought. Once inside, the receptionist had me fill out a rather short and quite simple application. As I was filling out the application, I heard shouts and cheering-like noises from behind the door, which led to another room. The very last cheer I heard before the door was opened was "JUICE, JUICE, JUICE!" When the door opened, ten or so people walked out. Their ages ranged from twenty to fifty years old and they all looked raring to go.

One of the guys who emerged from the room walked directly up to me.

"Hi, I'm John, are you the eight o'clock appointment?"

"Yes, sir, I am. My name is Greg Garrity."

"Good. Could I see your application?" he said as he extended his hand toward me.

He looked briefly at my application and then gave me a very sketchy outline of what the business was all about. The "distributorship" dealt in factory overruns, he explained, and it was my job to go out and sell them. The more I sold, the more I would make he added.

"That's simple," I said after having heard his pitch.

"Good," said John. "Let me go find Harry. He's the person I want you to tag along with today."

Several minutes later I was introduced to Harry. Harry was probably in his early thirties with a beard and slightly long hair. He said we had to go into the warehouse in back of the office and load up his van with the products. Harry and I went around back to the small warehouse where most of the people who had emerged from the cheering room could now be found loading up their vans, trucks, or cars with different products ranging from perfumes and jewelry to pots and pans.

Harry and I loaded up his van with boxes of ceramic plates and bowls. Once the van was loaded, we got in and drove away.

"It's too early to hit the streets, so let's stop for breakfast first," Harry said as he kept his eyes on the road.

"OK," I replied.

We stopped at a breakfast joint a little farther down the road, and once we were seated I asked Harry questions so I could find out more about the job.

"So how do you sell the merchandise to people?"

"Well, I drive around and basically approach random people that I see on the street," Harry began. "I like to tells 'em that I deliver merchandise for one of the big department stores in the area. You know, like Sears or J.C Penney."

"OK."

"So I tells 'em that I just made a delivery for the store and I have some extra items left that weren't listed on my delivery sheets."

"OK."

"So I tells 'em I'm just trying to make a couple of extra bucks to go fishing by giving them a great deal on some expensive ceramic dishes."

As Harry unveiled the scheme, I began to have my concerns, but what the hell, I thought, I've come this far let's see how this thing plays out.

After our breakfast, we left the restaurant and began driving around in no particular direction. As we drove Harry showed me some catalog pages that advertised some really nice ceramic cookware.

"Not what we're carrying, but close enough," Harry said as he added a brief laugh and a shit-eating grin on his face for emphasis.

A while later, as we drove down a residential side street, some workmen came into view.

"The first fish!" Harry announced as he pointed at them.

The men were working around a sewer and therefore had helmets and masks on. But that didn't stop Harry from approaching them. He pulled over and motioned to them to come over to his truck. One of the guys did, and Harry went full throttle into his little speech.

"Surprise the wife, fully microwaveable, we deliver for Sears and these items aren't on our delivery lists so they won't be missing. Me and my buddy here just want to make a little fishing money," Harry announced to the sewer worker.

By the time Harry was done with his little presentation, two other workers had stopped what they were doing and had walked over to see what was going on. Harry, being the professional con man that he was, repeated his little speech for the late-arriving fish. When it was all over, two of the three guys had bought about twenty-five dollars' worth of the third-rate, ceramic dishes, which weren't even microwaveable.

As we got back into the van after the sale Harry turned toward me, smiled, and said, "Pretty easy to reel the fish in, eh?"

"Yeah," I answered flashing a plastic smile as I began to see what this "job" involved.

We drove for another half hour when all of a sudden Harry made a quick left turn.

"I think it's lunch time," Harry announced. "Time to see if some people are on their lunch break. I saw some picnic benches yesterday outside this office building, so let's see if we can go fishing there."

As we approached the office building, I saw the tables full of workers enjoying the summer day as they took their mid-day break. Little did they know they were about to be approached by a con man.

Harry pulled up, got out of the van, and presented the catalog pictures to a table full of women. One of the women mentioned she had a wedding to go to and hadn't yet bought a gift. She and several others got up and walked over to the van with Harry and me.

After a couple of minutes of price haggling, the ladies agreed to purchase several sets of plates and dishware. I handed one of the ladies a box and she gave it a good shake. Everyone present could hear the rattle of broken china as she shook the box.

"I think there are broken pieces in this box!" she exclaimed to Harry.

"No problem," said Harry without skipping a beat. Harry then reached into the van for another box and as he brought it out he shook it gingerly and then announced, "This one's O.K."

The woman grabbed the box from Harry and went on her way. Harry and I got back into his van, and as we drove away I asked him if the higher priced dishware he had sold to the women were microwaveable.

"Hell no, but by the time they find out we'll be a faint memory," Harry remarked as he let out a belly laugh.

My questioning continued.

"What about that box with the broken dishes? Will you bring that back to the warehouse and exchange it for a good box?"

"Noooo," Harry blurted. "I'll sell everything! Broken, chipped it don't matter."

We drove around for a little while longer down the nameless side streets of suburbia when suddenly Harry spotted an elderly woman in her front yard doing some gardening.

"Hello, ma'am," Harry said as he eased his van up to the curb. "Me and my buddy deliver for Sears, and the boys at the warehouse overstocked our truck. I was wondering if you might be interested in some fine Sears' ceramic bowls or dishware, all fully microwaveable. I'll give you a great deal. We're just trying to make a little extra money so we can go fishing this weekend."

"For Sears?" the elderly woman asked.

"Yes, ma'am," Harry said as he held out a page from a Sears catalog.

"Well, my granddaughter just bought a new home and I suppose she could use something. Let me see what you have," the elderly woman said.

Instantly Harry sprang from the van and escorted the old woman to the rear of it. He repeatedly pointed out to her the biggest dishware set on the catalog page and told the woman that it retailed for three hundred dollars but he could give it to her for a hundred and fifty dollars.

"Now ain't that a deal, ma'am?" Harry inquired cheerfully.

"Boy, it sure is!" the old woman exclaimed. "Let me get my pocketbook. You've got a deal, sonny."

As the old woman walked slowly back into the house, Harry turned to me and asked, "Where'd you put that box that bitch shook at our last stop?"

"The one with the broken dishware?" I asked.

"Yeah, that one," Harry replied.

In silence I pointed to the box with the broken dishware that was sitting in the furthest corner of the van. Harry reached into the van and grabbed it just as the old woman emerged from the house.

"My granddaughter can really use this," the old woman said as she handed Harry the cash.

"I'm sure you will make her day," Harry replied as he stuffed the cash into his pants pocket and then handed the old woman the box of broken dishware.

We drove around for several more hours and approached some other people but found no buyers. Eventually Harry decided to call it a day and drove us back to the warehouse. I helped unload what was left in the van, said good bye to Harry and then went around the front of the building and inside to talk to John.

John invited me into his office and asked me to sit down.

"So how'd your day go?" John asked.

I wanted to tell him I thought he and his merry group were a bunch of con artists and thieves, but unfortunately I didn't have the guts to do so. Instead I just said, "It went all right."

"Great!" John replied, "Then if you want to start tomorrow just show up at the same time and we'll get you started."

"All right!" I replied knowing as I stood up to leave I would never see John, Harry, or this fucking place again as long as I lived.

I made my way outside into the heat of the summer day and slowly got back into my van and started my ride back home. As I drove, I replayed the events of the day in my mind and couldn't get the picture of the old women paying a hundred and fifty bucks for a box of junk.

As I drove I also wondered if I would ever get a real job again or if I was destined to lose the van. I arrived home a little bit later and dejectedly climbed the three stories up to my parents' apartment. As I walked in, my mom cheerily asked me how my day was so I told her of my experience with Harry.

With every sentence I grew angrier and more emotional. When I got to the part where we knowingly sold the broken dishware to the old woman, I actually began to weep.

"She reminded me so much of grandma," I said through my tears. "I just didn't feel right. I may as well rob banks if this is the kind of work that is out there!"

My mom reassured me by telling me I would eventually find something else and not to worry about what had happened today. I felt a little bit better after talking with her and letting go, but I also knew my ride with Harry that day had knocked off a huge chunk of what innocence I had left and increased my cynicism of the world.

* * * *

A couple of days later I heard through the grapevine that George Kronos, my former eighth grade tourney coach and a schoolyard regular, who now worked in the roofing business was looking for some help on his roofing crew. Jimmy Morgan called me and said George had suggested he and I go down to the roofing company's office and fill out an application. We did, and a day later we were called and told we could start working the following Monday. Thus began my life as a roofer.

I would roof that summer and fall. The work at times was backbreaking, dangerous, and often very hot, as we were required to wear long-sleeve shirts and pants even on the hottest days to prevent getting burned by the hot tar we poured into buckets and mopped onto the roof.

I ended up on a crew working with a bunch of guys from the St. Ignatius schoolyard scene who were all several years older than me but whom I knew fairly well. Since I was the youngest guy on the crew, I think that certain guys looked out for me but I always carried my weight and earned my paycheck.

The camaraderie we enjoyed having known each other from the Patch of Green made it bearable and fun at times. We always got the jobs done on time and the quality of our work was high, but since we all knew each other there always was a certain amount of screwing around.

My duties were that of a general laborer. I helped haul roofing rolls up to roofs using ropes and pulleys, and once the work on the roof began, I poured into buckets the hot, liquid tar, which was usually fed through an iron pipe up to the roof. I then carried the buckets over to the guys who were rolling out the roofing paper and mopping out the hot tar. Overall not very intellectually stimulating work, but at the time it helped make my van payments.

We did roofing jobs all over the city of Chicago and surrounding suburbs that summer and fall, anything from a two-story apartment building to a ten-story office building and everything in between. We roofed in good neighborhoods and bad. When we were doing a job, Cy, our only black crew member and our kettle man, stayed on the ground and fed the solid, tar "pigs" into the kettle so they could be melted by the kettle's intense heat and the resulting liquid tar could then be sent up to the roof. When we were working in a bad neighborhood, Cy always kept a half-filled bucket of "hot" (liquid tar) by him just in case somebody came by and tried to fuck with him while the rest of us were on the roof.

I usually gave Jimmy Morgan a ride to the job site and then a ride home. Jimmy was a wild man, and we often split a six-pack of beer on the ride home. That was usually the extent of my drinking for the night unless it was a Friday. Jimmy, however, usually went out every night of the week, and the next day he would be on the job sweating out all of the beer he had drunk the night before.

On the roof we always kept several gallon jugs of water, which we all drank from. It wasn't the most sanitary practice but when you're working your butt off on a roof in the middle of the summer, who gives a rat's ass where the cold water comes from and who has been drinking out of it. On many a day, Jimmy began guzzling from a water jug and between sips tell us in a loud voice about his previous night's escapades.

"Yeah, I fucked dis broad pretty good last night, but I think what she liked best was when I stuck my tongue way up her ass," he would beam as he stuck out his tongue just prior to drinking out of the communal water jug.

Jimmy's remarks were usually met with a resounding chorus of, "Shut the fuck up!" from the other members of the roofing crew. I guess we were lucky that we were all buddies and could more or less put up with each other's bullshit otherwise I'm sure someone would have been tossed off of a roof at some point.

25 THE TRAIN RIDE FROM HELL

During this time in my life, my older brother Jerry moved out to Round Lake, Illinois, about a forty-five minute train ride from Chicago. One summer weekend he invited my sister Maureen, her boyfriend John Jameson, and me there.

Since my parents were using my van that weekend, we took the train early Saturday morning and my brother met us at the train station in Round Lake. He showed us around Round Lake, and then we picked up some beers and headed to his house. We partied and barbequed at his house the rest of the day and had a really good time.

We all got up late the next morning and decided if we hurried, we could catch the eleven-thirty train back to Chicago. Unfortunately, as we arrived at the station the train was pulling away. The next train was in two hours so we picked up some beers and went back to the house to kill some time. So we sat around and drank for a while at my brother's place, and after an hour or so got ready to go back to the station. On the way, we stopped at a liquor store and bought a six-pack for the ride into Chicago.

We said our good-byes to my brother as the train pulled in. Maureen, John, and I got on board and made our way to the upper level of the car since usually on a weekend it was deserted. However, that wasn't the case. What we soon realized was that the reason the train was so crowded was because everyone had chosen this Sunday to head to Taste of Chicago, Chicago's annual food festival along the lake. The people in our train car were primarily our ages and out to party and have a good time just like us.

There were others beside ourselves who were enjoying a couple of beverages on board the train. After several miles, an old dude dressed in shorts, a Hawaiian shirt, and a straw cowboy hat lit up a big joint and passed it around. As we were blowing the joint, a conductor walked by, and although he didn't say anything, I think he was wise to what was going on. After the joint was smoked the noise level in the train car began to rise. A bit later the same conductor came by and looking at the upper level, but speaking to no one in particular, said, "You'll have to keep the noise down. People are complaining."

His comment didn't cause much reduction in the noise level. A little while later, the same conductor returned and this time looking directly at me said, "Since you wouldn't listen to me, you'll have to get off of this train at the next stop."

Taken aback, I didn't know how to react. I think I said something like "You're joking right?" But by the look on his face I could tell he wasn't.

155

I turned to my sister Maureen and told her I wasn't planning on getting off at the next stop. Unfortunately for me, when we pulled into the next station, my plans got changed. The conductor, escorted by several Glenview policemen (a northern suburb of Chicago), looked and pointed right at the three of us and said, "These are the ones causing the commotion, officers."

"All right, you three, come with me," one of the policeman ordered.

I stood up in disbelief, not able to comprehend what was happening to us. We were being thrown off this train a good three stops before our stop because we were singled out in a group of at least thirty people who were all partying on the train.

We exited the train with the policemen and once outside we saw there were actually three squad cars parked at the station. A slow Sunday afternoon in Glenview, I thought. Once off the train Maureen, John, and I stood shoulder-to-shoulder facing the two officers who had told us to follow them off the train.

"I need to see some identification from you," one of the cops said as he moved and positioned himself directly in front of me.

"Why don't you show me your ID first?" I responded quite belligerently to this cop who was dressed in full uniform.

By his reaction I don't think he took my remark too kindly. He threw a nice, right roundhouse, which caught me square on the jaw and knocked me to the ground. The next several minutes were a blur as people began screaming and more punches were thrown. My part in the fiasco was to remain lying on the ground, unwilling to react to this type of police brutality.

Maureen's boyfriend, John, however, a former Marine, jumped to my rescue and took a swing at the cop who had hit me. This action resulted in him being pummeled by the rest of the policemen. With the policemen's attention directed toward John and me, my sister did the smart thing. She took off running and didn't stop until she was far away from the station and sure she wasn't being chased.

John was dragged, kicking and screaming to the nearest squad car. All this time I remained on the ground motionless. When the cops had successfully gotten John into a squad car it was my turn. A couple of cops told me to get up but I told them I thought I had hurt my back when I was knocked down.

"BULLSHIT!" one of the cops shouted.

"Fuck you," I answered. "If you dicks are going to arrest me I want to be brought to a hospital first for a full evaluation."

"Listen prick, if you don't get up right now and walk to my squad car, I'm gonna snap your arm in two," one of the cops said as he bent down and grabbed my arm.

"Go ahead, asshole, I'll own your fucking badge," I responded having had enough of their Gestapo tactics.

"OK, let's go. We got a dead one here," the officer announced to the others as he let go of my arm and stood up.

With that said, two officers approached me and grabbed my legs while two others grabbed my handcuffed arms. They picked me up, and carried me to a squad, and threw me inside.

After a short drive, during which I asked to be brought to a hospital again, we finally arrived at the station house. A paramedic came by the car and took a rather quick look at me and pronounced me fit for incarceration. I refused to get out of the squad on my own and once again had to be lifted out by four officers. I figured, since I weighed in the neighborhood of two-hundred-and-fifty pounds, if they were going to arrest me I was going to have them work their asses off for it. The cops dragged me through the stationhouse and threw me on the floor of a cell.

Meanwhile my sister, the escapee, was slowly but surely making her way back to Rogers Park by alternately walking and hitch hiking the five-mile journey. Maureen knew she had to find some money to bail John and me out of jail. She eventually made her way to Rogers Park. Once there, she found a pay phone on Sheridan Road and called John's mother and made arrangements to get some cash and bail him out.

She hung up the phone and began walking down Sheridan Road when suddenly she spotted Billy and Brian Murphy crossing Sheridan Road heading toward the beach. Maureen ran after them and once she caught up, quickly blurted out the whole story of our arrest. Billy said he would put up my bail money, and Brian volunteered to drive to Glenview.

Some time had passed since my arrest. I fell asleep in my cell and awoke hours later not really knowing how long I had been sleeping or what time it was. Several minutes after I woke up, a guard came in to check on me and I asked him the time.

"Seven-thirty," he replied.

"Has anyone come to post my bail?" I asked.

"Not that I know of," was his gruff response.

"What if no one does?" I added.

"If no one posts your bond, then you go before the bail judge at eight tomorrow morning and he determines whether or not you should be released on your own recognizance or be sent to the Cook County Jail to await a hearing," he explained matter-of-factly.

"Cook County Jail," I said quietly, the words burning in my ears.

Just my luck, I get busted for partying on a damn train and end up going to Cook County Jail where I'll probably be ganged raped by a bunch of hard-core criminals. Beautiful, fucking beautiful, I thought.

I had been locked up once or twice before in Chicago on disorderly conduct charges but had never spent more than a couple of hours in a cell, and on both occasions I was accompanied by a friend. But this time was different. I was alone and I had already been in the cell for about five hours.

As I looked around my cell, I got a terrible feeling I would never get out. I thought about calling my parents, but I didn't want them to know about the arrest. I also thought about calling my brother, but it didn't feel right bothering him. I hoped that Maureen and John would be able to get someone to bail them out and then they would get me out.

But so much time had passed I was starting to wonder about that. I sat back down on the steel bed and lay my head against the concrete wall. Two years ago I was thinking about going away to college, now I was thinking about going away to Cook County Jail.

"What the hell has happened?" I asked myself out loud.

Several more hours passed when suddenly a guard appeared outside my cell.

"Let's go," he announced as he unlocked the cell door.

"Did someone post my bail?" I asked, half afraid of his response. He nodded his head in the affirmative, and I let out a deep sigh of relief. The guard led me to a desk where I signed a release form. Then he escorted me to the main lobby of the police station. My battered jaw dropped wide open when I saw it was Billy and Brian who had bailed me out.

"Dudes, how did you know I was in here?" I asked them as I walked toward them.

"Your sister, she ran into us on Sheridan Road and told us what happened. She asked if we could get together some cash to make your bail," Billy said.

"Thanks, man," I said as I grabbed both of their hands and shook them enthusiastically. "I was looking at a possible trip to Cook County come this morning."

We walked out of the station house into the warm, summer night air. The smell of freedom had never been so strong or sweet for me. Thank God I'm out, I thought.

John Jamison and I hired an attorney to represent us for our day in court, which came about two months later. We asked our attorney to see if she could work out something with the Glenview police to see if they would drop the charges. Since John owned a roofing company, we thought if we offered to do some free roofing work for them they might let us slide. Our attorney spoke with the officers the morning of our case, and they flat out refused to make any kind of deal. Instead they told our attorney that they planned to have us prosecuted to the fullest extent of the law. Oh great, I thought, as I heard the words fall from our attorney's mouth. What the hell does that mean?

Our attorney assured us since this was our first offense and a relatively minor one, we wouldn't see any jail time. Fortunately for us, she was correct. John received a fine and six months' probation during which he had to report to a probation officer every month. I didn't have the cash to pay a fine, so I had to settle for a year's probation.

After our hearing we left the courthouse and I couldn't help but feeling we got screwed. A little partying on a train gets you kicked off, beaten up by the police, and then as the grand prize I get twelve months of probation. The only real change in me because of all this was that I became even less trustful of authority figures, if that was even possible. I knew if my family had come from one of the wealthier suburbs of Chicago and if I had some political connections, I would have gotten off scot free. I guess I was just being taught yet another lesson about the innate unfairness of life.

I served out my year of probation, which didn't turn out to be all that bad. Probation meant leaving work early once a month and going to the Belmont Avenue police station where my probation officer was stationed. I finished out my probation and appeared before a judge a year later to get my release. I later paid an attorney to have the charges expunged from my permanent record so in the end, it was much ado about nothing. Although, it proved I could always rely on my family and friends, especially Maureen, Billy, and Brian Murphy to get me out of a jam.

26 THE BEER, THE DOT, AND THE HOOKER

One Saturday afternoon during the summer I roofed, I was cruising the beaches and ran into Billy. He asked if I knew where he could score some weed. I told him I thought all of our usual connections were dry, but if he just wanted a little bit, the lakefront, just off Lake Shore Drive near Irving Park, was a good place to go.

Billy thought it was a great idea so he hopped into my van and we cruised south, out of Rogers Park, and got onto Lake Shore Drive. Several minutes later I got off of LSD and pulled onto a road that led to the lakefront. Once we reached the lakefront, I pulled into a parking space about fifteen feet from the water. We both got out and checked out the situation.

There wasn't much happening so we walked toward a group of people about fifty yards away. I made eye contact with one of the black guys in the group and made the motion as if I was hitting on a joint. I then held out my hands as if to say, "You got any man?" The guy I motioned to slowly began to walk toward us.

"Yeah, man, I got some weed. How much ya looking fer, joint, nickel bag, ounce, pounds you name it," he said having reached us.

"I don't know," I said being honest, since I really wasn't the one buying.

"How much for an OZ?" Billy asked.

"Da mores you buy da cheaper it is, my man," was the guy's reply. "I can buy a pound for two hunded twenty and roll it all up and sell each joint for a buck you know and make almost four hunded dollars."

"No shit!?" Billy and I responded.

"I've been looking for a way to make some extra cash, maybe I've found it," Billy joked as he smiled at me.

The guy then lit up a joint and passed it to both of us.

"This ain't bad stuff," he said as he expelled bluish, white smoke from his lungs. "But I can getcha betta."

Once the joint was gone the guy asked us how much we needed.

"How much for a pound?" Billy asked.

"Well," the guy began, "if we gonna stablish a bidness relationship then I guess I should be good to you da first time so how bout two-fiddee. But we're gonna have to go somewhere to get it."

"No problem," Billy replied. "I don't have the cash right now anyway."

"I'll tell you what," the guy continued, "drive me to my crib, and then go do your thing and meet up wit me back at da crib."

"All right," Billy said.

All three of us then hopped into my van, and I drove away from the lake.

"Yeah, man, my connect is a dude I went to school wit up at da Univercity of Minnasotow, you know what I'm saying, man?" the dealer blurted.

"Sure, you go way back ha," I replied.

"Man, I know dis dude's sista too and she's kinda of a wild child, you know what I'm saying, man?

"Sure," Billy replied from the back seat.

We drove about five minutes away from the lake, all the while receiving directions from the dealer on how to get to his crib. We ended up in a near north side neighborhood known for being a little on the dangerous side.

"This is my stop," our newfound friend announced. "Can you guys meet up which me back up here bout six o'clock?"

"Yeah," Billy answered. "That'll give us enough time to drive back to my house, get my bank book, cruise to the bank, and get some cash."

With that the dealer got out of the van and disappeared into an apartment building. We drove back to Rogers Park and got Billy's cash. We then drove back to the guy's apartment building and waited. About ten minutes after six, he emerged from the building and got into the van.

"You guys ready?" he asked.

"Yes," we replied.

"Now here's da deal," he began. "We gots to drive over to Broadway and park da van. Now my connection never meets clients during the first buy no matta how nice yous is. And dammit if I haven't told em how nice yous is but still he said noooo dice. So it's got to be mees by myselfs dis time. Now I wouldn't expect you guys to give me all da dough and just leave da van. Hell, we just met! So I brought a little sumpin for you to hold on toos while I's gone."

With that our dealer friend pulled out a small, brown envelope and handed it to me.

"Take one if you want," he said as I opened the envelope up. Inside were hundreds of purple colored pills or dots, not the kind you get at a pharmacy but ones which looked as if they had been made by hand. Some were cut unevenly and others had odd shapes.

"Go aheads," he said, "take one but not two, cuz then you'll be completely out of yer's head."

Billy and I both shook our heads no.

"Dis is premium quality purple micro dot acid," the dealer explained. "Probly worth a tousand dollars on the street. I'm gonna leave it witchyas so you know I'm coming back."

It all made perfect sense to us.

We cruised over to Broadway and pulled into a parking spot on the street, which was across from a McDonald's. We sat there awhile and then the dealer suggested we buy a six-pack so we could party while we waited for him. As he was getting out of the van to get the six pack he called out to a black woman, who judging by the way she was dressed, was probably a hooker. She walked over to the van and the dealer introduced us to her.

"Hey, fellas, dis is my friend Candy"

"Hello," Billy said

"Pleasure to meet you," I replied.

"I'm fittin to get a six pack, you want to hop in da van and party with da boys?" the dealer asked Candy.

"Sure, but only fer a little whiles," she said as she climbed in the front passenger seat.

Several minutes passed before the dealer reappeared with the six-pack. We all were passed a beer and then he told us in a few minutes he was going to take a walk around the corner and meet his connection. He also added he was sure next time we would have the privilege of meeting his guy. Billy then gave the dealer the two-hundred-and-fifty dollars, which he had just withdrawn from his savings account.

The dealer left the van several minutes later leaving Billy and me alone, with the beer, the dot, and the hooker. The hooker soon finished her beer and told us it was nice to have met us but she had to be on her way. With that she exited the van.

Billy and I sat and waited, and after about ten minutes I began to get a little nervous. Another five minutes passed, and I told Billy I had to walk around the corner to see if I could see anyone sitting in any of the cars parked on the side street. I got out of the van and slowly walked to the corner and just before peeking around it crossed my fingers for luck. I peeked around the corner and carefully looked up and down the row of parked cars on either side of the street. I saw nothing!

"Fuck! We're screwed!" I said out loud to myself.

I then walked back to the van bracing myself for the bad news I was about to tell Billy. I climbed into the van and told him I hadn't seen anyone.

"NO WAY!" Billy exclaimed.

"Dude, go look," I said half hoping I had made a mistake. Billy left the van to go take a look for himself. Several minutes passed and then he came back and got into the van.

"I don't fuckin' believe it!" Billy said. "This is just like the time I was trying to bum a six pack and got my bike ripped off."

"I know," I replied softly realizing Billy was out two-hundred-and-fifty bucks and I was at least partially to blame.

"But what about the micro dot?" I blurted

I pulled it out and looked at it closely.

"I wonder if this is just bogus shit? If I wasn't driving, I'd take one just to find out."

Just then a terrible thought made me panic.

"Hey, man, if this guy just ripped us off who knows what else he'll do," I said as I looked at Billy.

"What do you mean?"

"Well, what if he calls the cops and tells them that a couple of white boys, parked in a van on Broadway just tried to sell him some acid."

"Oh shit!" Billy said. "We're sitting ducks. Let's get outta here!"

I started up the van and quickly pulled out of the parking space.

"Let's go back to where we picked him up. Maybe we'll see him on the street," I said.

"Let's hope," Billy offered.

"I'll tell you man," I continued. "If we find this guy I'm gonna beat the fuck out of him. So please stop me if it looks like I'm gonna kill him."

We drove by his apartment building but had no luck. We even drove back down to the beach where we had first met the guy but it was deserted. As we turned to go back to Rogers Park, I apologized to Billy about the whole fucking mess.

Billy told me not to worry about it, as the decision to put up the money for the weed had been his. As we drove I told him I would try the micro dot later and if it was any good maybe we could try to sell some to cover his losses. I dropped him off at his mom's apartment and drove home.

I had dinner and then took off for the schoolyard. The usual gang was there, and after a while I told a couple of guys the story of Billy and me being ripped off that afternoon. They suggested I try the micro dot to see if it was worth anything.

"Yeah, good idea," I told them, not really wanting to try it.

After a while Jimmy Morgan came by the schoolyard and I told him the whole story, too. Jimmy told me he had been ripped off several weeks ago, too, so he knew exactly how I felt.

"What about the acid?" he asked.

"I don't know, want to try some?" I asked.

"I will if you will," he said as he smiled at me.

I pulled out the little envelope, pulled out two of the little, purple, oddly shaped pills, and handed one to Jimmy.

"Here goes nothing," I said just prior to eating the dot.

As we waited for the acid's effect to kick in, we drank a beer and bullshitted with everybody in the schoolyard. After about forty-five minutes, I walked over to Jimmy and asked him if he was feeling anything.

"No, Double G, 'fraid not," Jimmy said.

"Me neither," I mumbled back, knowing for sure now that the microdot was worthless.

27 LOOK OUT ELVIS

One Friday night not long after the drug dealer rip off, I met up with some guys down at the beach. Instead of beer, I was drinking vodka, and that's probably where the trouble began. Billy and I started talking about taking a road trip in the van, and pretty soon we contemplated a trip to Memphis, Tennessee to see Graceland, the home of Elvis Presley.

A couple of more drinks, and we drove to Billy's to get some supplies for our journey. We grabbed some soap, towels, and snacks and decided we were pretty much ready for our nine-plus-hour ride to Memphis. I let Billy drive as I climbed into the back of the van and passed out. An hour or two later I was rudely awakened by an empty pint bottle of vodka, which clonked me on the head as it rolled around the back of the van.

I dragged myself to the front passengers seat. Looking out at the dawning morning, I realized we were several hours south of Chicago.

"Are we really going to Memphis?" I asked groggily to Billy. The previous night's vodka-induced euphoria had worn off.

"Sure, why not," Billy replied. "It'll be an adventure."

The day broke hot, and the temps eventually reached the mid-nineties. We didn't have a lot of cash so we decided to save some gas by driving with the windows down and the air conditioning off. As the day grew hotter, I suggested we stop and get some ice-cold beer. A bit later, as I was dozing in my captain's chair, Billy pulled the van off of the interstate and into a rest area that sold gas and had a large tin shed where they sold ice and beer.

"JUST BACK IT UP A LITTLE," I heard a voice shout out through my half-comatose state.

For Billy, with his one arm, driving forward was a challenge so I could imagine backing up was really an interesting endeavor. We began to roll backwards, and the next sound I heard was a loud thud as Billy managed to back the van right up against the tin shack. Loud "WOES," could be heard from several voices.

"PULL IT UP A LITTLE," someone shouted.

Billy pulled the van up several feet, and I managed to extricate myself from my seat, get out of the van, and make my way reluctantly to the rear to inspect for damage. Fortunately it was only the van's bumper that made contact with the shed, and neither the shed nor the van seemed to have suffered from the minor collision. We gassed up and bought two six-packs and a very large bag of ice.

"Next stop is Graceland and no more backing up, please," I announced to Billy once we were back in the van.

We kept on driving, and the further south we traveled, the hotter it got. The air hung heavy with humidity, which caused us to immediately sweat out the ice-cold beer we were drinking. As we drove, we talked about Billy's future and his past.

"You know, Double G, there's times I wished you had just let me bleed to death the night I got hit by that train," Billy said, with emotion in his voice.

"Don't say that, man," I replied as I took a big hit of my ice-cold beer.

"I mean, man, all of my fuckin' dreams went up in smoke that night, yah know. I mean, my dream was to become a fireman and I can't be a damn one-arm fireman, yah know."

"I know, man," I replied meaning it. "But it's not what happens to you in life that is important. It's how you react to what's happened to you that's important. Think about that for a minute, man."

"Dude, is this some of your psychobabble bullshit or what?" Billy asked as he glanced at me with a smile.

"Hey, bad shit happens to everyone, man," I continued. "You can either say I'm done or make the best of it. Now you got that job with the city, which is giving you a good income and security for the rest of your life if you want it. And what about that girl you met at work, Holly. Man that chick digs you, so you may have someone who you can spend the rest of your life with. And then you got your dear old drinking buddy Double G, and don't forget that Hollywood jackass Will. That fucker's gonna get rich and bail all of us out, man. Hey, let's drink to that fuck nut!," I said as I raised my beer can and Billy, momentarily letting go of the steering wheel, grabbed his beer and clacked it against mine.

As Billy continued to talk I sat in the passenger's seat, listening intently, sweating profusely and sipping my ice-cold beer. Billy continued talking, telling me how he had these feelings sometimes that everyone was out to get him and he felt that he couldn't trust anyone.

"You trust me don't ya, man?" I asked earnestly.

"Of course I do, I just don't know how to explain these feelings, Double G. It's weird, man."

"Dude, relax and let your life come to you," I said trying to reassure him.

"Double G, promise me one thing, will yah?"

"Sure, Billy, what's that?"

"No matter what happens to us or where we end up in life, let's promise to always be there for each other, no matter what! OK, man?" Billy asked.

"You got it, buddy," I said as I raised my beer can and clanked it against Billy's head this time.

"You know, Billy, I still owe you big time for saving my life from that time on Will's dad's boat. Dude, I haven't forgotten about that."

"I know you haven't," Billy replied.

The miles passed by quickly, and soon we found ourselves on the outskirts of Memphis, Tennessee, home of Elvis. We started to get excited as we talked about actually getting a chance to see Graceland. Once we arrived in Memphis, we stopped at a gas station and asked for directions. We got back in the van and drove to our destination with much anticipation.

When we arrived, we pulled up to the wrought-iron gates and discovered they were locked. For some reason Graceland was not open to the public that day. I guess because our entire journey had been born on a whim and a lark, we weren't greatly disappointed. We took comfort in the fact we had at least seen the wrought-iron, musical-note-draped, front gates that Elvis had passed through so many times during his life.

Strictly out of curiosity, as we were too broke to buy anything, we decided to visit the Elvis Presley shopping center across the street. After exploring several shops, we climbed back into the van and decided it was time we found somewhere we could wash up at. The nine-hour van ride through sweltering heat had left us a little rank.

As I drove, I saw a liquor store and pulled into the parking lot so we could buy another six-pack. As we got back into the van, a Hells Angel-type dude pulled up on his Harley. As he got off it, I approached him and asked if he knew anywhere we could wash up.

"Well, what I've done before is gone to a hotel and crashed their pool scene, man," the biker told us.

Oh great, I thought. Now knowing that filthy bikers were crashing hotel pools to freshen up made me feel like I would probably never use a hotel pool again. I thanked him for his advice and climbed back into the van.

We pulled out of the parking lot determined to find somewhere to take a bath or shower. We drove around a while and then came upon an apartment complex that had a large pond positioned in front of it. Billy and I gave each other the "what the hell" look, and I quickly turned into the complex's parking lot.

We clamored out of the van and stripped down to our underwear. We each had a bar of soap and a towel so we felt right at home. We waded into the water up to our chests and began our "baths." About midway through, a jogger came by and shouted out something about us coming out dirtier than when we went in. I don't know what that pond was for or how clean the water was, but believe me after traveling in ninety-degree heat for nine hours just to immerse myself in water to get the various layers of sweat off felt like heaven. Once we were washed up, we waded back to shore and opened up a fresh, ice-cold beer as we got dressed.

We got back into the van and decided to drive to Beale Street, which is the real nightlife area of Memphis. We bought some more beer and hung out in the van for a while. We decided to call Jimmy Morgan back home to tell him where we were. While I was speaking to him, I asked him to call my parents just to let them know I'd be home the next day. We sat around for a while drinking and checking out the people, but since we were flat broke by now we decided we may as well start driving back to Chicago.

I began driving out of Memphis and as the sun began to set, I saw Billy was about to do the same. I drove and drove and drove. About nine o'clock I felt myself falling asleep at the wheel. I nodded off several times, and when I opened my eyes caught myself drifting across the lane divider strips. I acknowledged the fact I was falling asleep at the wheel, and if I continued to drive I would probably end up killing both of us. So I decided to pull over at the next rest area and try to get some sleep. I soon came upon one and pulled off of the interstate and into a secluded parking lot.

Instead of getting some peaceful rest, Billy and I were intermittently awakened and pestered by swarming mosquitoes. Somehow they found their way into the van and ravaged our bodies. Our baths in the pond water probably had something to do with their excessive attraction to us. After several hours of providing the mosquitoes with a feast, I couldn't take it any longer. I got up, slid open the side door of the van so all of the damn mosquitoes would get blown out when I zoomed back out onto the highway. Better to fall asleep at the wheel and die instantly in a fiery crash than to be eaten alive by a swarm of mosquitoes, I thought. I would later painfully discover I had no less than one hundred individual bites on each of my feet and ankle areas as did Billy. We vowed next time to bring bug spray!

We finally made it back to Chicago just as the sun was rising on Sunday morning. I dropped Billy off and headed back to my parents' apartment. My mom and dad greeted me with surprised and relieved looks on their faces. My mom immediately asked me where I had been, having not seen or heard from me since around seven o'clock Friday evening.

"Oh," I stammered. "Didn't Murphy call you?" I asked meekly.

"No, he didn't," my mom responded.

"Well, Billy and I decided to take a road trip to Memphis, Tennessee to visit Graceland," I said.

"Graceland?" my mom replied. "We were worried sick. You should have at least called. How thoughtless of you!"

I nodded my head in agreement and wandered toward the back of the apartment and my bedroom.

"Thoughtless," I said to myself. That word kind of summed up our whole adventure, I thought, as I lay down on my bed for some much-needed rest. Come to think of it, thoughtless was a word that summed up many of the days of my ill-spent youth.

28 WHEN I SAW HER STANDING THERE

If ever there was a time in my life when I was completely without direction, this was it. Billy had his city job, which would keep him secure for the rest of his life if he chose to stick with it, and a girlfriend named Holly who I felt was really in love with him.

Will was out in Hollywood doing his acting thing. As it turned out, an old friend of Will's dad was a big Hollywood agent and had taken Will under his wing. Not that Will needed much help as we all knew he had the talent and looks to make it big out there. Hell, he was already getting bit parts in some TV shows.

I, on the other hand, was like a boat adrift on the ocean, not really sailing in any one direction. I knew the roofing work would end in the late fall and even though I lived with my parents, I still had a huge van payment each month. As the fall approached, I wondered what would happen next as I didn't really have any plans for the future. However, little did I know that the not-too-distant future would bring an event that would change my life forever.

I don't really remember what I did that Indian summer afternoon during the fall of nineteen eighty, but I probably hung out at the beach with some guys, drank a few beers, and watched the girls go by. So what else is new!

Late in the afternoon, I drove to my parents' apartment and decided to have a lone barbeque since they were not home. I started the small grill they had out on their third-floor veranda, and once the coals were hot I put on half a chicken and a couple of burgers. A moment later the apartment's buzzer rang. It was my sister Maureen and her boyfriend, John Jameson.

My sister had really turned her life around since she was younger and ran away from home. That didn't mean, however, that she and John wouldn't strategically stop by the parents' apartment every so often around dinner time hoping to get a free meal off dear old mom. This time instead they got even luckier when they had found dear old brother Greg about to prepare a feast on the grill and wash it all down with some beers.

I gave an obligatory invitation to stay for dinner, and of course, they accepted. After dinner, they asked me what my plans were. I told them not much was on my agenda other than cruising down to Rogers Park and checking out Connolly's Tap. Maureen and John said they thought that Connolly's was a good idea since draught beers only cost fifty cents and they only had five bucks on them. I told them not to worry about the dough situation as I had just been paid, and so our plans were made. I took a shower, got dressed, and we took off for the twenty-minute ride to Rogers

Park and Connolly's Tap.

We arrived around nine o'clock, and the place was already fairly crowded with most of the usual characters, that is, my friends. I started knocking back some Old Style longneck bottles as I bullshitted with Maureen, John, and some other people.

Several hours later I caught a glimpse of this short, blond standing near the bar. All I could see was her back, but I was attracted to her long, flowing, blond hair. I decided I would start a conversation with her by buying her a beer so I ordered a couple of longnecks and walked over to her.

"Hey, blondie, how about letting me buy you a beer?" I said from behind her.

She turned around, and as she did I saw her pretty blue eyes reflected in the bar's lights. I introduced myself and she then told me that her name was Elizabeth Hamilton.

"Hamilton," I said out loud. "I know a Terri Hamilton."

"That's my older sister," Elizabeth explained.

Just then my sister Maureen approached us and said, "Elizabeth, Elizabeth Hamilton?!"

"Maureen?" Elizabeth asked.

They both laughed, and I said, "Now wait a minute, how do you two know each other?"

"Spanish class at Sullivan!" they answered in chorus.

They went on to tell me they had been buddies in Spanish class, and Elizabeth often helped my sister with her homework. They had partied together on more than one occasion, they also confided. Elizabeth and Maureen reminisced for a while as I kept the rounds of cold beer flowing.

When I finally managed to get a word in, I discovered that Elizabeth was a student at the Devry Institute of Technology pursuing a degree in computer science while working part time for a company her mom worked at. We seemed to hit it off well as the night went on, and at closing time, approximately two in the morning, I asked her if she needed a lift home. She said both she and her girlfriend Patty, who Jimmy Morgan had been talking with while I was hitting on Elizabeth, could use a ride back to her parents' apartment.

As we left Connolly's, I bought a six-pack of beer to go and suggested we go to the beach to talk more. Everybody thought it was a good idea so we drove down to Albion Beach and parked. Elizabeth and I sat in the front captains' chairs of the van while Jimmy and Patty retreated to the far back of the van.

Elizabeth and I talked for a couple of minutes and then got down to what we both knew we were really there to do. Elizabeth moved from her seat and sat on my lap. We started to kiss and then started to let out hands roam over each other's bodies. I tried to unsnap her jeans, but she whispered we couldn't do anything else as she already felt uncomfortable with Patty and Jimmy present.

"No problem," I said quietly and a little while later I rousted Jimmy and Patty from the back of the van and then drove the two girls to Elizabeth's parents' apartment. Before she got out, I asked Elizabeth for her phone number, which I wrote down on a small piece of scrap paper. I drove Jimmy home and then drove back to my parents' apartment. As I drove, I reflected on the events and conversations of the evening. I pulled up to my parents' place just as the sun's rays of a new day began to appear on the eastern horizon.

While getting out of the van I became aware of the chirping of birds as they greeted the new day. I picked up off of my dashboard the sheet of paper with Elizabeth's phone number and gave it a glance before I safely tucked it up between my sun shade visor and the van's interior roof. I'll have to give this one a call back, I thought to myself as a grin came across my face.

I called Elizabeth sometime during the week, and we made plans to get together the following weekend. We went out to eat at a local diner and ended our Saturday evening by parking down at the beach and rolling around the back of my van. The passion and lust between us was unbelievable. I could tell she wanted to make love to me as bad as I wanted to make love to her. During our moment of passion Elizabeth, whispered that she would be getting her prescription for the pill the following week. I interpreted this to mean that next time, baby, I could expect the real thing!

The weekend passed and the following week seemed to drag on. It was October by now, and Halloween night was the coming Saturday. I had been invited to a costume party and asked Elizabeth if she wanted to join me. She asked me if she could bring her friend Patty along, and I told her it was no problem, although I really wanted to just be alone with Elizabeth.

I picked both of them up at Elizabeth's parents' place, and we made our way over to the party. I was dressed as a gangster while Elizabeth was dressed in her brother's army fatigues. Although the fatigues were kind of big on her, since she had long blond hair her imitation of Goldie Hahn in the movie _Private Benjamin_ was quite believable.

Given our conversations of the previous weekend, I had thought about this evening the entire week and daydreamed about making love to her that night. The party was nothing special, and around midnight I suggested to Elizabeth we leave and head down to the beach in my van. She first made sure her friend Patty had a ride home and then told me we should be on our way. With that said, a great feeling of anticipation came over me.

Once we made it down to the beach, I parked and we quickly found ourselves in the back of the van. We started making out and as I began to rub her between her legs I could feel how hot she was.

"If you want me, you'll have to undress me," she whispered.

In the darkness of the van I fumbled around, as I first had to take off her "costume" and then had to mess with her jeans and blouse. Once that had been accomplished, she laid down beside me in her bra and panties.

"Tonight you can give me the real thing," she whispered.

I positioned myself on top of her and made my penetration. I was so excited that I was actually "doing it," I really didn't concentrate on my technique or how long it was going to last or how much she was enjoying it. I exploded deep inside her in just a matter of minutes and rolled off of her exhausted but in ecstasy.

As the weather grew colder, our lust for one another grew hotter and our affections for one another grew deeper. We saw each other every weekend and talked on the phone almost every day. Elizabeth was becoming the center of my universe, a phenomenon that occurs when you are falling in love with someone.

*   *   *   *

One very cold, winter-like morning I realized that the roofing season would come to a close soon. A mild snowstorm during the second week of November caught our roofing crew by surprise and inspired us to break into a rousing, spontaneous rendition of _Merry Christmas_ while still up on the roof. After our performance, I quickly scrambled off of the roof with the crew, knowing that the roofing season would soon be coming to its end. As I made my way down, I wondered to myself what type of work I would be able to find in the very near future.

29 FACTORY LIFE WITH THE CAMBODIAN

My dad, who still worked at the screw machine shop next to the steel factory I had been fired from, told me he would see what he could do to get me rehired there. One Friday evening he came home and told me there was an opening in the parts cleaning/degreasing department, and I could have the job if I could start on Monday. I felt kind of bad that I wouldn't be giving the roofing company any notice and I wouldn't be able to say goodbye to the crew, but I figured I needed a full-time job during the winter so I decided to go for it.

I arrived at the screw machine shop with my dad the following Monday. He dropped me off at the front office so I could fill out the necessary paperwork before beginning my first day. Once the paperwork was filled out, Henry, the manager of the screw machine shop, led me to my work area.

He brought me to the parts cleaning area, which was located just outside the main entrance to the screw machine shop. I was vaguely aware of this area, having worked in the screw machine shop the summer after I had quit college. Henry introduced me to Bunchi Min who worked in the parts cleaning department by himself.

Bunchi was about five foot eight a hundred and forty pounds and all muscle. He had a dark-brown complexion with thick, black hair that sat on his head like a Brillo pad. His face had several scars that looked like someone had extinguished a lit cigarette on it and his knuckles and forearms had several tattoos. I once asked him about the tattoos, and all he could say was they gave him power. I don't think I ever really found out his true age, but I suspect he was much older than I thought. Bunchi was a living, breathing refugee of the killing fields of Cambodia. A freedom fighter loyal to Prince Sihonuak who took it on the chin when the Communist Khmer Rouge gained control of Kampuchea in the nineteen seventies and began their mad rule and systematic genocide of millions of rural Cambodian peasants.

Bunchi had humped the boonies fighting the Khmer Rouge, sometimes living on insects, river water, and uncooked rice. Through his very heavy accent, he told me how he had packed an AK47 rifle, which he said had probably come from Vietnam. He told me the AK47 was the best weapon he had ever fired and better for a guerrilla fighter like himself than an American-made M1 with its close tolerances. Bunchi told me an AK47 could be dragged through a riverbed and still fire if needed.

Bunchi had eventually grown tired of fighting the civil war in which he had killed many. He told me in halting English that the war had also claimed the lives of most of his relatives. He finally decided to join his wife and child in a refugee camp in Thailand. He and his family lived there for three years before he received sponsorship to the United States. Once in the U.S., he moved into a slum apartment in the near north side neighborhood of Uptown in Chicago. Here the enemies - poverty, robbery, murder, rape, and drugs - were less obvious but just as lethal as the Khmer Rouge. Sometimes, when I visited his rat and roach-infested apartment, I wondered if Bunchi ever wished he were back in Southeast Asia fighting Communists.

I found out soon enough that Bunchi and I were the only employees in the parts cleaning/degreasing department. We were responsible for collecting all of the parts that came off the screw machines the day before, cleaning them, counting them, and finally bringing them over to the final inspection department. This I would soon find out was the dirtiest, hottest, hardest job in the entire plant.

Each morning I led Bunchi, who drove a forklift, into the screw machine shop. We slowly proceeded down each aisle and stopped at each of the fifty screw machines, picking up the pans that held the previous day's production of parts. The pans were eighteen inches long, five inches wide, and four inches deep. I stacked them on a metal pallet that the forklift carried. The parts, whether they were miniscule screws or large, heavy rods, all shared one characteristic. They were all covered in machine oil and metal chips.

After our morning pick-up routine, we carried the load out of the screw machine shop and to our cleaning area. Once there, we divided them into two groups, large and small parts. The small parts were fed through an automatic degreasing machine by Bunchi. The large parts were stacked next to a large vat of mineral spirits.

It was my job to place a manageable amount of the larger parts onto a large, circular, wire basket and then dip and shake them in a vat of mineral spirits. Once the machine oil had been rinsed off, I utilized an air hose to blow off the metal chips that remained in the basket. I then placed the now-clean parts into a container that allowed us to count the parts later by weighing them on a large scale.

This was a dirty, backbreaking job, especially during the heat of the following summer when the foul smell of machine oil hung in the air. I often went home with an aching back, the smell of oil in my head, and my clothes covered in machine oil.

It was at this point, since my parents had been helping me out during the past several months, I realized with my reduced salary there was no way I could afford the van's monthly payments. I dreaded the day I would have to part with my beloved van. Perhaps my biggest fear was that once the van was gone, I imagined Elizabeth would also give me the heave ho. I reluctantly resigned myself to accepting this fact and decided that whatever happened, happened.

The day finally came and my Chevy van was sold. So there I was, living at home with my parents, twenty minutes from Rogers Park, and worrying about losing my girlfriend who I was quickly falling in love with. Fortunately for me, Elizabeth proved to want me for me and not for my van. So for the time being I got a lift to work from my dad and on days when he was too hungover to work or just feeling too lousy in general, I took the L and bus to work.

As fate would have it Elizabeth's part-time job was located at a company that happened to be just a couple of blocks from where I worked. Elizabeth and I often met outside my workplace and ate lunch on the steps of the factory. Every so often, I asked my dad if I could borrow his car to take her out to lunch. He would give me the keys to his car, but little did he know we had another agenda planned.

There was a large cemetery several blocks away and a very quiet side street that ran along side of it. This street was mostly deserted except when people drove to work in the morning or left in the evening. At lunch, Elizabeth and I would drive to this street. I would find an inconspicuous place to park, and then the fireworks would begin.

We would begin by making out, which almost always led to Elizabeth dropping her jeans and panties while I scooted my pants and underwear down as well. Then she'd climb on top of me and go for the ride of her young life.

The most daring lunchtime rendezvous we ever enjoyed occurred one wintry afternoon. My dad and I arrived to work late that morning, so he had to park the car on the street right in front of the factory. In the morning it began to snow really hard, so by lunchtime his car was covered with three or four inches of snow. I borrowed the keys for lunch and suggested to Elizabeth we not bother driving anywhere since the blanket of snow on the car would keep us concealed from any outside eyes. She agreed, and we got into the car and began talking.

My lunchtime was nearing its end, and we had yet to fool around. I really wanted to make love since I felt it was really adventurous given the circumstances. I pulled her close to me and began to kiss and touch her.

Now the sidewalk we parked alongside was the walk the employees of the factory used when they returned from lunch. That included my father who, despite the snow, had made his daily two-block walk to the local tavern to drink his lunch. Just as Elizabeth and I began to get into some serious lovemaking, I heard some voices near the rear of the car.

"HEY, WHAT'S GOING ON IN THERE?" I distinctly heard one of my co-workers shout.

"HEY, WHATEVER YOU'RE DOING IN THERE, YOU BETTER CUT IT OUT," another voice called out.

The usual lunchtime crew was returning, I thought as I reached climax.

"Just in time," Elizabeth said as she rolled off of me with a huge smile on her face.

30 MY FIRST PAD

As the weather turned colder I realized I wasn't going to enjoy taking public transportation to Rogers Park to see Elizabeth, so I figured what the hell, I may as well find a cheap, studio apartment there. The apartment I found was located on Pratt Avenue and Clark Street in Rogers Park. Realizing that I was in love with Elizabeth, I moved out of the comfort of my parents' place and into a cockroach-infested building, which the locals referred to as Beirut North, just to be close to her.

The apartment consisted of a main living area with a small fridge, sink, and stove just off of it, as well as a small bedroom and bathroom. The building's parking lot was just outside my first-floor door. Judging from the entire layout I guessed the building originally had been a cheap motel.

I furnished my apartment with hand-me-downs from all over the neighborhood. Will's dad gave me a chair, TV, and a nice beer lamp to brighten up the place. I don't recall where my couch came from, but the coffee table and my bed came from my parents' place. Just for good measure and to give the place the true ambiance of a bachelor pad, I bought a set of shower curtains that had a naked woman pattern on them.

These were some of the stormiest days of our budding relationship as well. I was living in this apartment when Elizabeth's best friend Patty suggested I meet her for drinks some night after I had walked Elizabeth home so I could get to know her better. After I informed Elizabeth of Patty's suggestion, their friendship pretty much ended.

I also lived in this apartment when Elizabeth called early one morning only to hear a groggy, female voice answer the phone. Fortunately for the female voice her exit was swift as Elizabeth ventured into the apartment about fifteen minutes later and awoke me with screams and punches.

I spent a little over a year and a half in this dump and decided to throw a party on the last night I was there, which happened to be a very cold February night. I figured it would probably be quite a while before I could host another party, as I was moving in with my sister and her husband John Jamison.

I was forced to make this move because I had just been fired from the parts cleaning job at the factory. Bunchi Mi, the Cambodian, and I had both been let go. Supposedly the company was moving to the suburbs, and our jobs were to become obsolete in the new plant. Anyway, I had to move because I couldn't afford the dump anymore, which brings me back to the party.

I rented a keg for the party and told everyone I knew about it. A really good crowd of twenty or thirty people showed up, cramming themselves into my tiny apartment. The party was in high gear when one of my friends came in around midnight and announced the police were on Clark Street issuing parking tickets and towing cars. There was a no parking after midnight law during the winter, which the cops were enforcing and of course many of my friends were parked out there. We made a mad dash the short distance to Clark Street and were able to rescue everyone's vehicle before they were towed.

After we had re-parked the cars elsewhere I began my way back to the apartment with several of my friends. Suddenly Bobby Bradley, who had played on my eighth grade tournament team at St. Ignatius and who was at my party, came running up the alley toward us.

"Guys," Bobby blurted out between breaths. "A bunch of guys just hassled me as I was making my way back to the apartment."

As Bobby was telling us this, several guys appeared a ways down the alley and began walking toward us.

"Bobby, are those the guys that hassled you?" I asked

"Yep, that's them," Bobby replied without hesitation.

"OK," I said, "let's give these guys a dose of their own medicine."

We walked toward them, and when we got about five feet away I said, "My friend here says you guys roughed him up."

"So what?" the larger of the two guys replied.

"So what?" I replied. "This is so what, mother fucker!"

While the "ucker" in "fucker" fell from my lips, I let go with a side-kick to the guy's groin, which felled him instantly. The other guy got knocked down as he was pummeled by two of my other buddies. The two guys quickly scrambled back to their feet and began running in the opposite direction.

"AND DON'T COME BACK," I shouted out as they ran away.

My buddies and I then walked back to my apartment laughing our asses off. Once we got back inside the apartment, we related the story of our little alley encounter to everyone inside. I sat down on my couch, which was next to the apartment's front door, with some chick and Will who was in town visiting his parents. As we passed around a bottle of amaretto, we laughed and carried on about our alley encounter.

About ten minutes had passed when suddenly my apartment's front door swung wide open and a guy without any shoes, socks, or a shirt, wearing only a pair of jeans let go with a karate kick as he stepped inside the apartment. Once inside, he made a slashing motion with his right arm, and as he did we saw a large knife clenched in his hand.

Without bothering with pleasantries, such as formal introductions or inquiring as to whether or not he had the right apartment, Will, holding a couch pillow in his hands, leaped up off of the couch and charged the guy. I followed Will off the couch and moved toward the door as others also began to move toward the intruder.

Will, who was the first to reach the guy, blocked his knife-wielding hand with the pillow while grabbing the guy by his hair with his other hand. With a massive display of strength, Will slammed the intruder's head into the concrete block wall of my apartment. The sound of the thud, as the guy's head smashed against the wall, resounded throughout the apartment.

As the guy collapsed to the ground, Will was joined by no fewer than eight of us partiers who were willing to take up the cause in the defense of the apartment. Fists and feet pummeled the guy from all directions as the human instinct of self-preservation, which had been threatened by the knife-wielding intruder, took control of us and blocked momentarily our reasoning powers. Bedlam reigned supreme for several minutes as the guy struggled to get to his feet while punches and kicks greeted his rise only to knock him to the ground again.

Above the din of the scene, a shout of reason could be heard.

"STOP, YOU'RE GOING TO KILL HIM, STOP I DON'T WANT MY BROTHER GOING TO JAIL!"

The voice was my older brother Jerry's, and as he continued to shout, the frenzy began to subside. When a semblance of order had been restored, Will and I held the guy, who now had blood flowing from his mouth, nose, and forehead and who had both minor and major gashes on other parts of his face and body. He wobbled like a drunken sailor as we brought him to his feet.

"GREAT!" I shouted. "NOW WHAT DO WE DO WITH THIS MOTHER FUCKER?" I asked out loud.

"Let him go!"

"Call the police!"

"Kill him!"

"Elizabeth," I called out. "Call 911 and tell them that we've captured a home invader."

Elizabeth went to the phone and did just that.

"The cops will be here shortly everyone, so let's hide the pot and bong and anything else you think we should and let's get this fucker outside," I announced.

As we began to walk him through the doorway, the guy began to struggle. I could feel the adrenaline and anger swell inside of me again.

"YOU WANT TO FUCK AROUND SOME MORE, MOTHER FUCKER?!" I yelled at the guy. "YOU HAVEN'T HAD A GOOD ENOUGH BEATING. THEN FUCK YOU," I shouted and swung as hard as I could. My fist flattened his nose and knocked him out through the doorway of my apartment. Several people grabbed me as Will and some others picked the guy up off of the ground.

"Call the police," the guy moaned as he was being picked up off of the ground.

"WE DID, PRICK!" I shouted back,

Several minutes later the cops were on the scene. When they got out of their cars and saw the intruder, the police entered my apartment and began to look around.

"You have no fuckin' right to search this apartment," Billy announced to the police in a loud voice bolstered by numerous draws of the keg.

"Be quiet," a female officer responded.

"I'm not going to be fuckin' quiet if you're doing something that you shouldn't be doing," Billy answered.

"DAT'S IT," a male cop shouted. "YOU'RE GOING TO JAIL," and with that two cops grabbed Billy and led him outside into the parking lot.

By now everyone was outside telling the story of the intruder to the cops. The cop I talked with said they needed to bring the guy to the hospital emergency room before they brought him to jail. Then he grilled me on whether or not I wanted to press charges and if I did, would I go to court. At this point my brother-in-law John Jameson, who was standing out in the parking lot, said something that pissed off the cops. A sergeant who heard his comment pointed to John and said "Put him under arrest, too!"

Hearing this John, who had run track in college, bolted down the alley with the police in chase. This temporary distraction allowed Billy, who was just about to be put into a squad car, to break free of the hold the two cops had on him and take off in the opposite direction. The cops ran and drove off in both directions as I gazed on the surrealistic scene.

The cop who had been taking down my information suggested everyone go back into the apartment and directed Elizabeth and me to get into his squad car. We got in, and several moments later so did the cop. He pulled out of my apartment's parking lot and headed down Clark Street for the short ride to the Twenty-Fourth District police station.

On the way, the squad car's police radio crackled and we heard a distant voice say, "DOA at 2100 West Pratt," my apartment building's address. Elizabeth and I looked at each other with "Oh shit!" expressions on our faces. I then turned to the cop and asked, "Did he say DOA?"

"Yeah, but it's not your bloody pulp," the cop answered referring to our bloodied intruder. "Somebody else died in your building tonight."

I had never been so relieved at someone else's death as I was at that moment when I realized the voice on the police radio wasn't referring to our invader, the bloody pulp.

We got to the station, and I filed a complaint against the guy. When I was done the cops gave Elizabeth and me a ride back to the apartment. The whole trip took about forty-five minutes. I opened the door to my apartment only to find a handful of people left. We were all quite jacked up about the events of the evening and couldn't stop talking about them. Then, out of nowhere, we heard a knock on the door.

"Don't open it," I said as I got up and walked to the window. Glancing out I could see Billy, shirtless but with what appeared to be a towel wrapped around him. I opened the door and he walked in.

"Dude what happened?" I asked.

"Those fuckin' cops! They never had a chance finding me!" Billy answered merrily. "I cut through a couple of gangways and then yards and then came out when I thought the coast was clear. But those jags tore my fuckin' shirt off when I made my escape and oh, shit!" he stammered reaching for his throat. "My gold chain, it's gone, fuck!"

With that, Billy opened the apartment door and walked outside. Several minutes passed before he came back in with the biggest shit-eating grin you could ever imagine.

"I found it," he proudly announced holding a gold chain up with his left hand. "This just proves they were wrong in hassling me." Then, looking up at the ceiling of my apartment Billy announced, "Somebody is looking out for me."

Shortly afterwards, everyone left for the night, leaving Elizabeth and me alone in the apartment. We were still wide-awake from all of the excitement so instead of lying there trying to fall asleep we decided to expend some energy by making love.

We did it on the couch, which was up against the wall, just below the front window, which looked out onto the parking lot. When we were done, we smoked a joint and since we still weren't tired one thing led to another and we ended up doing it again, this time with me sitting in a leather chair while Elizabeth bounced up and down on top of me. Finally, we collapsed into each other's sweaty arms on the couch for a short, fitful night of sleep.

The following morning arrived cold and bright. John Jameson, who had also successfully escaped from the cops, and my brother Jerry came over to help load my stuff into Johnny's truck for the short ride over to Maureen and Johnny's apartment. We were all quite hung over and moved at a snail's pace.

"God damn, if moving just your small pile of crap is turning out to be so painful given our hangovers, imagine what it would have been like if we had to move your crap AND dispose of a stiff corpse today. What a pain in the ass that would have been!" my brother Jerry remarked.

A smile came over my face as I thought that had to be the best line of the weekend.

And so my tenure at 2100 West Pratt, my first apartment, came to an end. I never went to court to follow up on my complaint, thinking that the less the guy knew about me the better. Several days after the party, I ran into Will at Hamilton's, a neighborhood bar. As I approached him, Will held up his right arm and showed me a cast on his wrist.

"Yeah, my wrist was killing me the next day so I went and got it x-rayed and sure enough the fucking thing's fractured - must a happened when I was slamming the guy's head into the wall," Will explained.

I downed the rest of my beer as I smiled and shook my head in agreement. A week later Will headed back to Hollywood.

I lived with my sister Maureen, her husband, and their infant son for a little over two months. She put me up in the bedroom in the rear of their apartment. We all got along for a while until one night I heard Maureen and her husband arguing about my staying there. I guess John didn't think I was giving them enough money for staying there or something like that. As a short-term solution, I went out that night and bought about a hundred dollars' worth of groceries, but I realized I couldn't live with them forever. I didn't want them fighting because I was there, so I started to look for an apartment the next day.

31 THE STAR AND THE SUIT

So there I was, twenty-three years old, unemployed, basically homeless if it wasn't for the generosity of my sister, and without much optimism for the future. My two best friends, on the other hand, were experiencing successes that I could only dream of.

Will was now under contract in L.A. with a studio and was slated to be cast in some minor roles in some of their upcoming projects. I knew it wouldn't be long before he got his big break and become a Hollywood name known throughout the world. We talked numerous times on the phone, and he told me that he was slowly but surely making his way into the, as he called it, "Hollywood in-crowd club," which meant he sometimes attended parties and social events with some of the biggest stars in Hollywood. Deep down, I knew that's where he belonged. Extremely handsome, charming, and a God-given talent for acting - Will was the total package, and it was just a matter of time before he was recognized for it.

Billy's work success wasn't quite as dramatic and didn't have as great a potential as Will's, yet I was jealous of his situation as well. He made good money at his job with the city and confided in me that the work was easy and that as long as he kept showing up, his job was secure. And as if that wasn't enough, it also came with a great pension package, which would allow him to retire in his fifties.

In addition, Billy's primary goal of moving out of his mother's apartment was also about to be realized as his relationship with Holly had really taken off. Billy asked Holly to marry him, and she accepted, so now happily engaged they were currently looking for an apartment to rent so they could move in together.

I, on the other hand, besides realizing I couldn't live with my sister anymore, concluded that I needed to begin looking for a job. What kind of job, who knew? Without more than a high school diploma, my pickings would be slim, but I was determined to find one and see where it would lead.

32 THE MOVE

It took me several weeks but I finally found another dump I could afford on my limited income, which at the time consisted of unemployment checks and a small reserve of cash. This apartment was located at 1666 W. Pratt, about a half block west of Lake Michigan. The apartment was in a ten-story, old hotel building, and the roaches were included in the rent.

I once again asked my sister's husband to help me move. I figured since he wanted me out of his apartment he couldn't say no, and I was right. I moved on a Saturday afternoon with the help of John, Elizabeth, my sister Maureen, and two of her friends, Sherry and Val. We drank as we moved, and by the time we were done, we all felt pretty good. John had to go somewhere, so the girls and I sat around my new apartment for a bit and continued to party.

Maureen's friends eventually said they had to be going and asked if they could use the phone to call a cab. I told them it was fine and once the call had been made, they said good-bye and went downstairs to wait for the cab. A little while later, someone pounded on my apartment door. I opened the door, and Maureen's friend Sherry stormed in.

"You're not gonna believe this but when the cab showed up and the driver got out Val jumped in and drove it down to the lake," Sherry blurted out.

"What?!" I responded. "Are you kidding me?!"

"I wish I was," Sherry answered

I knew I had to do something, so I ran out of the apartment and got into the building's old, creaky elevator. I finally reach the ground floor and made my way out into the street. The cabbie was standing out in front of the building and cursing up and down as he looked in the direction of the lake.

"Where did the girl go?" I asked the cabbie.

"I called polisa, dat girl she a kazy, I called polisa for her!" the cabbie answered in broken English, through a heavy, middle eastern accent.

"OK," I said trying to calm him down. "I'll get your cab back, OK, then no problem?"

"OK," he said as he shrugged his shoulders. "Dat girl she go da beach," he continued pointing in the direction of Pratt Beach.

"OK you stay here, I'll be right back."

I began a sprint toward the lake and the dead end of Pratt Avenue not really knowing what I was going to be able to do once I got down there.

As I reached the dead end, I saw the cab parked haphazardly at the curb in a semi-turned-around position. As I approached the cab, I saw Val in the driver's seat doing something.

"VAL," I called out so I wouldn't surprise her.

She turned her head in my direction.

"Greeeeg, looook, moneeee!" she slurred as she smiled and lifted up a cigar box full of bills, which I assumed was the cabbie's cash register.

I reached for the door handle and opened the driver's door quickly.

"Come oooon Greeeeg, giiiit iiiin!" Val slurred.

"The police are coming, Val. You better get the hell outta here!" I said as I simultaneously pulled her out of the driver's seat and took the cigar box away from her. I jumped into the driver's seat and threw the still-idling cab into drive. I floored the accelerator and headed back up the half block to my apartment building. I glanced in the rearview mirror as I drove and saw Val staggering down the street in my wake.

I quickly reached the front of my building and threw the cab into park. I got out of the cab, leaving the cigar box on the front seat. The cabbie walked toward me and cursed something to me about "Dat kazy girl."

I ran back into my apartment building and hopped on the elevator. The ride up the three floors seemed to take forever as I thought about the police who would be arriving shortly. I got off the elevator and sprinted down the hall to my apartment. Elizabeth opened the door, and I began to rant and rave about the whole situation.

"I think I've got to get out of here for a while just in case the cops come looking for me," I finally announced.

Elizabeth said she understood and in a blink of an eye, I was out the door. I made my way down the stairwell, which ran down the rear of the building and made my way out to the alley, which ran behind the building. I decided to walk the seven or eight blocks to Connolly's over on Devon Avenue.

Once at Connolly's, I ordered a beer and tried to calm down. My greatest fear was the building's manager, who lived on the first floor of the building, might have seen the whole incident and would be able to identify me to the police. Although I knew I had done nothing wrong, I still didn't want anything to do with the police.

While I was taking my stroll over to Connolly's, the police had finally arrived and had quite easily apprehended Val as she stumbled up Pratt Avenue toward my building. Upon interrogation, she told them she had a friend in the building and led them straight to my apartment. The police knocked on the door, and Elizabeth answered it.

"Hello," the shorter of the two cops began. "This woman says that you're a friend of hers and she's been hanging out here all afternoon. Is that true?"

"No, officer," Elizabeth responded while Maureen and Sherry shook their heads no as well, fearing they might be implicated in the cab jacking.

"THEY'RE LYING!" Val shouted through her drunken stupor as she also started to wrestle away from the taller cop's hold.

"That's it, sorry to have bothered you ladies," the cop holding Val said.

He then cuffed her and began to lead her toward the elevator. Once downstairs, they placed Val into their squad car parked out in front of the building and drove away.

I called the apartment later and was informed of the whole affair by Elizabeth. I asked Elizabeth to let me speak to my sister Maureen. Once she got on the line, I blasted her for bringing her deadbeat friend to my apartment and jeopardizing my new living arrangement. Our conversation ended with Maureen sobbing and me fuming. As I hung up the pay phone, I ordered another beer.

After a while, I walked back to my apartment. I slipped into the building as quietly and inconspicuously as possible. I opened my apartment door and found Elizabeth sitting there by herself. Once inside, I began to yell and exact my still-simmering rage on her.

"It's over, let it go. You've already made Maureen feel like shit," Elizabeth blurted out, which stopped me dead in my tracks and made me realize my bitching wasn't going to change anything.

"I wonder if the building manager knows what happened with the cab?" I said out loud.

As it turned out, I didn't have to wait long for the answer to that question. As I was coming into the building the next day, the manager of the building intercepted me. She asked me what had gone on yesterday and how I was involved. I told her the truth as best I could, hoping she would give me the benefit of the doubt. Once I was done with my story, she told me she wouldn't tolerate any riff raff and informed me she would be watching me closely from now on. I promised her there would be no more trouble. As I walked away from her I thought, oh great, now I'll be able to experience life living in a fishbowl where my every move will be monitored by this old hag!

I settled into the apartment after a while and came to find the place was infested with roaches and psycho tenants. I tried to keep to myself and for the most part did. Once the warm temperatures of summer arrived, I thought life would be great since I lived near the beach and had enough money to live on for awhile. I pictured myself taking the summer off and enjoying it at the beach with all of the other beautiful people.

However, that summer Chicago experienced one of the wettest and coolest summers of all time. My walks and runs down by the lakefront were more often witnessed by seagulls than by any humans. So my days were rather lonely since Elizabeth was going to school and working, but every night she came over to visit for a while. Some nights I walked her home, a distance of about two miles round trip. Other nights I put her in a cab and had her call me when she got home.

It would have been a quite forgettable summer if it wasn't for the big event that occurred in Vegas at the end of it.

33 SNOWSTORM IN VEGAS

Two things happened the previous winter and neither really surprised me. Will landed his first role, although a small one, in a major motion picture and Billy had announced his engagement to Holly, the girl he worked with downtown.

Holly's elderly parents lived in Las Vegas, so she and Billy decided the wedding would take place there in August. They invited a small group of friends to be part of the affair. Elizabeth and I, along with some other friends from the neighborhood, planned to attend. Will was going to drive in from L.A. and meet us there.

We all flew out together, and once everyone from Chicago was settled in, we met in the casino at our hotel, the Flamingo. We had gambled there for a while when we got a message from Billy to meet him at the Riviera Hotel where he and a handful of Holly's distant relatives were staying. So Elizabeth and I gathered up the other couples, piled into a cab, and headed to the Riviera.

We met Billy and Holly and spent several hours socializing, gambling, and having fun. The wedding ceremony was the following day in the early evening in the backyard of Holly's mother's condominium.

At about one in the morning, Will made his grand appearance on the floor of the casino. He strutted up to us looking like the movie star he was developing into. As I greeted him, Will hugged me and whispered to me, "Hey, man, when we can, let's go up to Billy's room for a minute."

"Ah, OK," I answered not knowing what was up.

After about an hour, Billy nudged me and said it was time to take a walk up to his room. I told Elizabeth that Billy wanted to talk to me and Will alone about something so we left the casino floor together and headed to Billy's room. We made our way to Billy's room, and once we got there Will pulled out a huge baggy of cocaine. Now it was the nineteen eighties so seeing someone pull out some coke at a party wasn't that unusual, but I had never seen that much coke in one place before!

"Time to party, boys!" Will announced.

"Holy shit!" I answered. "That's a lot of blow, man."

"Dude, in L.A. it's easier to get blow than it is to get weed. Everybody has a coke connection," Will explained.

"But, man, the money," Billy blurted out.

"Well I have an announcement, boys," Will began. "But before the announcement let's find something to chop this shit up on."

Billy went into the bathroom and came back with a small, rectangular mirror and handed it over to Will who proceeded to spread some coke onto the mirror and then pulled a razor blade out of a folded-up piece of magazine.

"You, gentlemen, are looking at the next film star who will be coming out of Universal Studios!" Will announced as he began to chop up the mound of white stuff.

"What the fuck do you mean?" Billy blurted out.

"I have just signed a contract with the studio," Will began. "I have a two-movie deal with an option for a third. They are going to see how I do in the supporting role in the first one, and if I do well I may end up with the lead in the second."

"Dude, that's fucking awesome!" I said high fiving Will.

"That's really fuckin' cool, man," Billy added.

Will rolled up a hundred-dollar bill and passed it and the mirror to me. I took the bill and bent down and snorted up one of the chokers Will had laid out. I then passed the mirror and bill to Billy.

"Dude, this blow had to cost you a small fortune," I said feeling the intense taste of the coke as it dripped down my nasal passage.

"Man, I'm under contract. When you sign a studio contract, you get a big, fat bonus! This blow is complements of that bonus!" Will explained as he then took the mirror from Billy and did a line.

"Now, Billy, I'm very happy you're settling down. I think Holly is a great girl. Double G, you on the other hand, although dating someone, have not made a commitment yet. So, if you ever want to come out to L.A. and see how the other half lives, you just let me know."

"So how does the other fuckin' half live?" Billy quickly asked.

"Lots of parties, lots of girls, lots of blow," Will answered. "As long as you don't overdo it, show up to the set on time and be ready to work things are wonderful."

"I'll think about it," I answered as the euphoric effect of the cocaine began to kick in.

Leaving Chicago and Elizabeth for L.A. wasn't something I had ever thought about before, but now I might want to consider it knowing I had a movie star friend who would love to have me out there. After all, I wasn't going to be able to repay him for saving my life if I stayed in Chicago forever.

We passed the mirror around one more time and then headed back down to the floor of the casino. We partied until the sun came up and then made our way back to our hotel rooms to get some rest.

The next day, Elizabeth and I woke up around noon. We ordered room service for breakfast and made our way to the hotel pool to hang out and let our hangovers wear off. We had arranged for a limo to pick us all up at five o'clock at the hotel. When it was time, we all met in the lobby, jumped into the limo, and headed out together.

Just before I left my hotel room, Billy called me and asked if I would be part of the ceremony. His older brother was going to be his best man but something came up at the last minute and he couldn't make it to Vegas. I felt really bad for Billy when he told me this because I knew his mother wasn't coming either. Billy asked me if I would stand in for his brother and be his best man, and of course I told him I'd be honored to do so. The actual ceremony was short and sweet and afterwards we ate, drank, and danced for three or four hours at Billy's mother-in-law's condo.

Several of us started to get the itch to head back to the casinos, so we said our good-byes and headed back to the strip in a limo. We ended up back at the casino in our hotel, and the rest of the night was spent drinking, gambling, and making excursions up to my room to do blow with Will. The cat had gotten out of the bag the night before, so now Will was turning everybody on. We took turns heading up to my room, determined to make a dent in Will's stash.

When the sun again was on the rise, Elizabeth and I decided to head up to our room for the night. Once there we couldn't fall asleep because we were so high, so we did the next best thing. We turned on some porn and began to make love like two rabbits in heat.

We eventually managed to catch a couple of hours of sleep that morning, but then we had to get up and get ready to catch our mid-day flight back to Chicago. On the way out of our hotel, we ran into Will who had a really attractive blond on his arm. It was pretty obvious he had not yet gone to bed from the night before.

"Double Gggg, dis is Teresa who I met dis moorng. Isn't she lovely?" Will asked through his liquor breath.

"Nice to meet you," I replied as I shook Teresa's hand.

"Hey, man, we got a flight to catch," I said as I wrapped my arms around Will and gave him a big, long hug.

"Cum seeeee me in L.AAAAA, mudddder fuuuckker!" Will blurted out as I let go of him.

"I will, man, take care of yourself."

Will smiled and waved goodbye and then walked away with Teresa.

*   *   *   *

On the fight home to Chicago, I thought about how much I missed Will. That thought was tempered, however, when I remembered how we always managed to keep in contact, especially during every baseball season. Billy had organized, not very long after we had graduated from high school, a Rotisserie Baseball league in which he reigned supreme as the commissioner of the league. Other members of the league included neighborhood guys like Brian and Mike Murphy, Jimmy Morgan, Bob Garcia, Sean O'Reilly, a couple of guys Brian worked with, and me and Will.

When Will moved to L.A., we consolidated our teams and he became my remote partner. As partners, I spoke to him every week about baseball strategy, women, work, politics, and world affairs, and the conversations we had during this period of my life I will never forget.

One of the strangest things that ever happened in Rotisserie was a meeting that occurred at Bob Garcia's house one Saturday afternoon. This was the first meeting after our annual draft and Billy, the Murphys, Jimmy Morgan, Sean O'Reilly, and I were all there. Will was participating as well, having called Bob's house from L.A.. Just as the meeting began, Bob's front doorbell began to ring frantically. Bob answered it and in walked this young boy. The kid was crying hysterically so me and Bob tried to calm him down.

"Hey, little man, what's wrong?" I asked the kid.

"The, the man," he began.

"What man?" Bob asked.

"The man outside, he hit me."

"A man outside hit you?!" Billy asked, as he got out of his chair and joined us in the interrogation of the kid.

Having heard that I went to Bob's front door, walked out onto his front porch, and looked up and down both sides of his street. I then walked back into Bob's house.

"See anybody, Double G?" Billy asked.

"No," I replied. "What did this man look like?"

"He has kinda long hair. A beard. And he was," the boy stopped momentarily to wipe away some tears, which had just rolled down his cheek. "He was carrying a yellow bag."

"Well, that's a pretty good description," I said to the boy. "Billy, you want to take a walk with me and see if we can't find this guy?"

"I'm with ya, man," Billy replied.

All the while Will, who was still on the phone with Brian Murphy, was getting updates on our conversation with the little boy.

"Billy and Double G are gonna take a walk down the street to see if they can find the shit head who hit the kid," Brian Murphy announced into the phone.

Billy and I headed down the street, and once we reached the corner of Bob's block I suggested we turn and walk one block to Montrose Avenue, which was a busy, main street. Once we reached Montrose, we turned and began walking down it. As we were approaching the next corner I saw a guy with long hair sitting on a bench in front of a drugstore, appearing to be waiting for a city bus to arrive.

"Billy, check out the dude on the bench."

"You think that's the guy?"

"Let's get closer."

We approached the bench and could now see the guy had a beard.

When we got right next to the bench we could also see a yellow bag sitting next to him. I motioned for Billy to move about ten feet away from the bench with me.

Whispering to Billy I said, "That's the guy man. Go into the drug store and call the cops. If a bus comes, I'm not going to let the guy get on it."

"Cool."

With that, Billy took off for the drug store entrance and I walked back to the bench. I looked at the guy again, and to me it looked like he was either drunk or on something else that was pretty strong. Several minutes passed when I looked up the street and sure enough, saw a city bus approaching. I realized then I was going to have to prevent this asshole from getting on the bus so I decided to not waste any time.

"Hey, buddy," I said as I walked from behind the bench and now stood right in front of him.

"I hear you like to punch little kids in the face, is that true?"

"Fuuuck yuooo!"

Just then the bus arrived at the corner, and the guy with the yellow bag started to rise up off of the bench.

"Sorry, pal," I announced, "you're gonna have to wait for another bus."

I shoved the guy back down on the bench, sat down alongside him, and grabbed both of his wrists.

"Me and you are gonna wait for the police to arrive. They want to speak with you about a little incident that happened around the block."

"I AIN'T WAITING!" the guy shouted as he tried to break my hold. I pushed him back down onto the bench again just as Billy walked up to us.

"The cops are on their way," Billy announced

A minute or two later, a cop car arrived and we briefly explained why we had detained the guy with the yellow bag. The cops loaded him into their car and told us they were going to drive around the block to get the kid to positively ID the guy. As they took off, Billy and I walked back around the block, hi fiving each other along the way.

By the time we reached the front of Bob's house there were several squad cars parked there and the kid was standing on the sidewalk with several cops and a woman who appeared to be his mother. Just then one of the cops walked to one of the squad cars, opened up the rear passenger door, and pulled the guy with the yellow bag out.

"THAT'S HIM!" the kid shouted. "DON'T LET HIM HURT ME!"

And with that the kid grabbed his mother by the waist and began to bawl his eyes out.

"Oh, honey, it's OK. That man is a bad man, and we won't let him hurt you again. But, honey, look," the mother said pointing to Billy and me. "There are good men, too. These men helped the police find the bad man."

Through his tears, the young boy glanced up at Billy and me. The mother thanked us, and then Billy and I made our way back into Bob's house where we spent the next twenty minutes recounting our man hunt and apprehension of the man with the yellow bag to everyone in the room as well as to Will who was still on the phone from L.A..

In the years that followed, Billy and I often reminisced about the time we captured the bad man with the yellow bag during one of our Rotisserie baseball meetings. Little did I know at the time that it would be at a future Rotisserie meeting that my friendship with Billy would change forever.

34 MY BIG DECISION

So Billy was now married to a great gal and had a very secure future with his job with the city, and Will was under contract in L.A., ready to make his fortune in movies. I, on the other hand, was jobless and needed to find one fast!

Once back in Chicago, I scanned the Sunday want ads and answered an ad for an administrative assistant for a North Michigan Avenue law firm. The law firm was located on the thirty-sixth floor of a high-rise building on Michigan Avenue just north of the Chicago River. The reception area I sat in was gorgeous, and as I sat there for my interview I wondered what the hell I was doing there.

An older gentlemen walked into the reception area and introduced himself to me as James Williams. James, with a large mane of silver hair, was dressed in a very sharp, baby-blue, three-piece suit and was probably in his late sixties or early seventies. I could tell he liked me from the start, and James told me during the interview that I would have to meet with the chief partner of the firm before he could hire me. The chief partner's name was Elias Richardson. James mentioned that Richardson had graduated from Sullivan High School just as I had.

"You should be a lock, being a fellow alumnus," James said as he let out a loud belly laugh.

I met with Mr. Richardson in his swanky office that overlooked not only Michigan Avenue but the Chicago lakefront as well. He was younger than James Williams but not much, with thinning hair and a kind face. He asked me a little bit about Sullivan and my previous job experience and then said he would let me know about the job. About a week later, James Williams called and offered me the job. I accepted.

It was while I was working at the law firm that I decided to ask Elizabeth to marry me. The more time we spent together, the more I fell in love with her and felt I wanted to make a life with her even though Will's invitation to live with him in L.A. was enticing.

Summer turned to fall in Chicago, and I decided I would pop the question around Christmas time. So I saved up as much money as I could from my paltry salary, and one day during lunch, I went to Cartier Jeweler's at the corner of Madison and State Street in the heart of Chicago's Loop. I picked out a small diamond engagement ring and put some money down on it. As I walked back to the office on Michigan Avenue, I began to formulate a plan on how to present it to her.

I decided I would take Elizabeth downtown for dinner on Christmas

Eve. Once we got there, I would suggest that before dinner we go for a ride in one of the horse-drawn carriages, which meander along the north shore of Chicago's downtown area. At some point, I would present her with the ring and ask her to marry me.

The days on the calendar and my installment payments for the ring passed in a blur. Finally, December arrived, and one afternoon I went to the jewelers and paid off the final balance on the ring. I walked back to work that afternoon and showed it off to all of the women at the firm. They told me I had done well. When I explained my carriage ride plans, everyone remarked on what a romantic I was. This, of course, helped bolster my confidence about the entire undertaking.

When Christmas Eve arrived, Elizabeth and I drove downtown in her parents' car. We parked and then found a carriage on the street to hire. We got into the carriage and began our journey into an unseasonably warm and rainy December night. As we made our way through the side streets of Chicago, I had a hard time deciding at what point to present the ring to Elizabeth. Finally, as we turned on the street that runs between the Drake Hotel and Lake Shore Drive, I got up enough courage to pull the small, wrapped box from my pocket and give it to Elizabeth.

"Merry Christmas," I said as I handed it to her.

"What's this?"

"Open it!"

She carefully removed the wrapping paper. As she opened the box, her mouth dropped open and she looked up at me. At that moment our eyes met.

"Will you marry me?"

"Of course I will!"

Elizabeth's tears began to flow from her eyes and make their way down her rosy cheeks. As they did, I reached over and gave her a big hug and kiss.

Several minutes later, our carriage arrived at the entrance of the Drake Hotel. We got out and entered the hotel for our dinner reservations at the Cape Cod Room. Once inside the Drake, Elizabeth wanted to find a phone so she could call her mother. When she returned from the phone call, I asked what her mother had said.

"Oh," Elizabeth began, "she asked me what my answer was."

"That's nice," I said. "You told her that you said yes, didn't you?"

"Of course I did," was Elizabeth's response.

Slightly perturbed but undaunted, I escorted Elizabeth into the restaurant where we enjoyed a delicious meal.

*　*　*　*

Christmas day broke sunny and bright. In fact, the temperatures rose to the mid-sixties that day, very unusual for Chicago. I woke up early and took a jog along the shores of Lake Michigan from Pratt Beach to Touhy Beach and back. It was a glorious morning. I felt great as I reflected on the events of the previous evening. Once back in my apartment, I showered and made my way to my sister's apartment where my family was gathering for Christmas. Elizabeth was also going to meet me there as well.

Once Elizabeth arrived, everyone wanted to look at the ring. My sister broke out a bottle of champagne and everyone drank a toast to our future together. After several hours of eating, drinking, and opening presents, it was time to go visit with my future in-laws.

I was given a hero's welcome at Elizabeth's parents' apartment and made to feel right at home. After we visited awhile, we sat down for Christmas dinner and afterwards Elizabeth's father broke out a bottle of brandy and poured everyone a small amount. He made a toast to our future, and we all downed the brandy. Round after round of brandy went by and at some point I lost all of the color in my face.

"Are you feeling all right?" Elizabeth asked.

"I think so," I answered. "But I need to go to the bathroom."

I excused myself from the table and lurched toward the bathroom. The day's festivities, especially the liquid kind, had finally caught up to me and it was time to pay the piper. My recollections of what happened next are foggy, but I did make it to the bathroom only to puke in the bathtub. A bit later Elizabeth opened up the bathroom door and came in to help me clean up. Elizabeth's sister, who was visiting from Florida and pregnant, was the next person at the bathroom door.

"Hey, you two," she said, "you're not married yet. I really need to go."

"Just another couple of minutes," Elizabeth said through the locked door while she fought off my drunken advances as she cleaned me up.

Once the cleanup was complete, we exited the bathroom together. I mumbled something about needing air and quickly made my way to the back door of their apartment. I let myself out and stumbled home and went straight to bed.

I woke up the next day with the phone and my head ringing. Elizabeth was on the line. She said she had been really worried about me since she tried contacting me at home after my swift departure and I hadn't answered my phone. She then reminded me of my bathroom performance.

"Oh no, what are your parents thinking of me today?" I moaned into the phone.

"Don't worry," Elizabeth said. "They knew it had been a long day for you, and I told my dad he shouldn't have been giving you all those shots of brandy."

"That's it!" I announced as a sharp pain raced through my brain. "Blame it on the brandy!"

One of the reasons I had asked Elizabeth to marry me, besides the fact I loved her, was that we wanted to move in together and she thought if we were engaged her mother wouldn't have such a hard time accepting it. So after Christmas, we began to make plans to move in together in May of the upcoming year.

At this point I was still working full time at the law firm as an administrative assistant and entertaining the idea of going to school to become a paralegal. Elizabeth had graduated from Devry the previous June and had been offered a full-time position at the company she had been working at part time since she was sixteen years old.

We took our time looking around Rogers Park for an apartment that spring before we found one we liked. The apartment we chose was actually in West Rogers Park located at the southeast corner of Warren Park. The apartment was an old, large, one-bedroom affair with wallpaper and shag carpeting right out of the pages of color blind, interior decorators monthly. But we were young, in love, and excited to be moving in together. Elizabeth's mom, however, didn't share our enthusiasm as evidenced by her response when Elizabeth told her about our apartment.

"Biggest mistake you'll ever make," Elizabeth's mom commented when told of our plans.

We moved in May 1, though the term moving in might be a stretch. We really didn't have any furniture to speak of although our beach and folding lounge chairs worked well as living room furniture initially. Elizabeth and I bought a queen-size bed so at least we had something nice to sleep on. The apartment had a good-size dining room. We eventually bought a table and four chairs that we used for years to come. We eventually bought a couch and a love seat, but I don't think we bought them for about a year.

Not long after we moved in, I applied to Roosevelt University in hopes of enrolling in their paralegal program. I made the partners of the law firm aware of this and was told they would be willing to pay for some of my tuition. As soon as they were aware of my intention to become a paralegal, my job duties expanded. Mr. Richardson, the senior partner, began to have me work on client cases in the role of a paralegal. Once he even had me go to court and appear before a judge to ask for a continuance for one of the firm's clients - a fact that shocked the associate attorneys when I told them about it.

I didn't mind acting as a paralegal until two facts became apparent to me. The first fact was that any work I did in my newfound paralegal role was billed to the clients at thirty-five dollars per hour while I was still paid about seven dollars an hour. The second fact, which really pissed me off, occurred when I was informed that the firm was going to contribute a measly two-hundred dollars towards my paralegal tuition bill, which came to about four thousand dollars total.

Aware of both of these facts, I had a change of heart concerning A) going to Roosevelt University for paralegal training and B) working for

Elias Richardson. I decided fairly abruptly to make a change so I hit the want ads hard, and the following week responded to an ad for house painters.

Since one of my roles at the law firm had been to come in on weekends and paint the offices, I thought that this experience might give me a good chance of being hired as a house painter. What I didn't know at the time but would find out later, was that an absentee owner who couldn't care less how his employees were paid or treated ran the painting company. I interviewed for the painting position a week after applying for it and was hired on the spot. A red flag for sure!

35 TRYING ON SOME JOBS

I gave my two weeks' notice the following day, and Elias Richardson seemed genuinely stunned that I had such a dramatic change of plans. I worked my last two weeks then said my good-byes. I started my new job as a house painter the following week. I was called on a Sunday night by the foreman of the painting crew and given an address of a house in Evanston that we were contracted to paint.

I arrived there early Monday morning and met the guys I would be working with. There was my foreman Kyle, a slightly built Asian who was about my age, and another painter named Manny. From the looks of Manny, he had worked outdoors his entire life as the wrinkles on his face were as deep as the tan he had on his leathery skin. The house we were going to paint was an old, three-story Victorian, owned by a Northwestern University professor. We began the project, and as we worked I found out how the company made its money and how my wages were determined.

My hourly wage was determined by what percentage of the customer's total payment had been allocated to payroll. The payroll allocation amount was then divided by the total man hours worked by each man on the crew. We spent about two weeks painting the house because there were several days of rain, which of course delayed our work schedule. For my efforts during that two-week period I was paid three-hundred dollars, and according to my calculations had earned somewhere between four and five dollars an hour. I called the head office of the company to see if I could negotiate a more equitable rate of pay but was always told the owner was out of town.

Since I felt I was being screwed and hadn't exactly fallen in love with house painting, I decided to seek employment elsewhere. I searched through the want ads again and applied at several different places, eventually landing an interview at a screw machine shop for a position working in their shipping department. I would be working for the shipping department manager who also happened to be the owner's son. I was offered the position, and although I wasn't all that enthused I accepted it as Elizabeth and I really needed the money.

I went to my first day of work on a Monday and met with my new boss. His name was Sonny and he was a gruff character who swore like a sailor. Sonny who had long, greasy hair and a Fu Manchu mustache was just a year or two older than me. He seemed to be perpetually annoyed at something or someone. He treated me like I should already know everything about the job and seemed put off when I asked him a question. He told me we could never take our lunches together as one of us should always be there to man the shipping and receiving dock. I thought that was fine since I probably wouldn't want to chitchat with an asshole like him anyway.

When lunchtime rolled around that first day, Sonny told me he would take lunch first and that I was to man the receiving dock. Manning the dock included loading and unloading trucks with a forklift, which I had never driven before. So there I was, having worked for this company for all of three or four hours, and I was running the loading dock. And sure enough, once Sonny left for lunch, a truck pulled into the dock with a small load to deliver and a load to pick up.

After initially panicking, I calmed myself down by thinking that I'd been placed in a very unfair position by Sonny and should I make any mistakes in my job such as drop a load, drive the forklift off the dock, or kill someone, I'd make sure to place the blame squarely on his shoulders.

I reluctantly hopped onto the forklift and fortunately quickly figured out how to drive it. Luckily the truck driver came to my aid by directing me into and then out of his truck. I picked up the skid of parts to be loaded onto the truck. As I entered it, I almost drove the skid right through the sidewall of the truck because I accidentally pressed my foot on the accelerator instead of the brake. I finally got it positioned correctly into the truck then maneuvered the forklift back onto the dock. As I was wiping the sweat off of my brow, Sonny reappeared and began to yell at me because I hadn't put the skid I had unloaded from the truck onto the correct side of the dock.

I asked Sonny if I could go to lunch. He grumbled back to me that I could but also reminded me that I only had thirty minutes and I better not be late. As I walked out of the building to my car, I had the fleeting thought that I should get in, drive home, and forget about this place forever. I fought the urge my entire thirty-minute lunch. I reasoned that maybe things would get better that afternoon and if not I could at least say I had stuck it out the entire day with Sonny the asshole.

After lunch, Sonny was even more gruff and abusive than he had been in the morning. I guess he's really warming up to me, I thought sarcastically. At three-thirty I punched out and told Sonny I'd see him the next day but knew in my heart I had worked my one and only day there. As I made my way to my car, I wondered how Elizabeth was going to react to my short-lived shipping career and also wondered what I was going to do with the rest of my life.

As I drove home, I thought about my future both short term and long. I thought about Will and Billy's situations and wished I could find a direction for myself. The movie Will had mentioned while we were in Vegas had recently come out, and his supporting actor role had been critically acclaimed. I had always been a little jealous of Will, his good looks, athletic talent, and popularity with the girls, but now I found myself even envious of Billy, my one-armed friend. After all, Billy had a good job, a wife, and was saving money to buy a home.

I finally reached home and told Elizabeth about my day. She wasn't very happy with my decision and stated rather emphatically that I had to start bringing some income in or we wouldn't be able to pay our rent. I could tell by the tone of her voice she was serious.

I decided that evening to work as a temp while I continued to look for a full-time position. The next day, I went to a local temp agency and got registered to work with them. Since they didn't have anything currently available, I decided to go down to Wilson Avenue and Broadway the next day and sign-up with Manpower, a day labor organization that employs on a day-to-day basis.

The next day I made my way down to the dicey Wilson and Broadway neighborhood and walked into the Manpower offices at six in the morning. There were approximately twenty or thirty men already in line. Most of the men in line were black or Hispanic. Another guy and I were the only white guys in it. When it was my turn to register, I was told that since I had a car, a beat-up Dodge Dart Elizabeth and I had bought used, I'd be paid a little more each day if I drove other workers to the job site. Sounds good, I thought, and told the interviewer I wouldn't mind doing that at all.

That morning I was assigned, along with three other guys, to a job sight at Motorola in Schaumburg. We were to report there and help breakdown a huge, temporary tent that had been put up for some special corporate function. As we drove out there, I found out a little bit more about my fellow workers. One guy collected welfare and did some day labor to get a little extra money. Another guy hadn't been able to find a job for months so he decided to try day labor. The third guy was on permanent disability pay and did day labor every so often to make ends meet.

We made it out to the work site and began to help dismantle the tent. The work was physical, and I worked a lot harder than any of the other day laborers. When our workday was done, I had to drive all the way back to Wilson and Broadway and drop off my fellow workers.

I reported again the next day, and we were assigned to another tent job. Things went about the same as the day before. Friday rolled around and I was to get paid for all of the days I worked that week as soon as I got back to the Manpower office that evening. Our job that day ran long, and I got back to the Manpower office a little late. The place was deserted except for the guy who registers everyone and another guy who was dressed in a business suit and, from the smell of it, was drinking a glass of scotch.

I walked into the dimly lit office and told them I'd come to pick up my check. They asked me my name.

"Greg Garrity."

"Oh," they chorused.

"A woman called for you wondering where you were," the registration guy said.

"That was probably my fiancée."

"She probably wants you to come straight home with that check," the guy in the business suit said as he smiled and raised his glass to take another sip of scotch.

They went on to tell me it was their practice to bring all of the checks down the street to a corner saloon so they could be picked up by workers after their office closed and throughout the weekend. As I left the Manpower office and began my walk toward the saloon, I laughed to myself at the irony of sending the checks down to a saloon. Kind of a vicious circle for most of the Manpower workers, I thought. Work, pick-up check at saloon, drink up check at saloon, go back to work again.

I arrived at the front of the saloon and thought that it was the kind of place I would never set foot in unless I had a paycheck waiting for me behind the bar. As I entered I saw a dark, dirty, dingy bar that fit in with the rest of the neighborhood quite nicely. As my eyes adjusted to the lack of light in the bar, I spotted a couple of the guys I had worked with during the week and walked over to them.

"Hi, I was told my paycheck would be here."

"Yeah," they both replied.

"Just ask the bartender for it," one of them continued.

I did just that and once the barkeep had produced the check he asked me if I wanted him to cash it.

"No, thanks," I said as I remembered what the Manpower guy had said about Elizabeth's call. The bartender handed over my check, and I began my walk to the door.

"Hey, man, you want a drink?" one of the guys I had worked with asked.

"No, thanks," I answered. "I've got someone waiting for me."

With that said, I opened the door to the street, stepped out, and breathed in deeply the cool, clear evening air. As I walked to my car I thought how I'd finally reached the bottom as far as a job was concerned and I realized any job I took after this would have to be an improvement.

I continued to work day labor for several more weeks while I sent out resumes and applied for full-time positions. I spent one day by myself unloading a semi-trailer truck full of manure and afterwards prayed to God my days as a day laborer would soon come to an end. God seemed to have been listening as the next week I received a call from my mom. She told me a friend of hers, who worked for a large company in the area, had told her about some long-term temporary jobs at the company. I decided at that point anything was better than day labor, so I drove out to the company and filled out an application. I was interviewed, and the next day I was called and told I could start working the following week.

I arrived the following Monday along with some other temps who had also been hired for this long-term assignment. We quickly found out our jobs involved verifying information for one of the company's publications. The work was done in an office environment, which sure beat the hell out of unloading trucks full of manure.

The other temps were an eclectic bunch ranging from full-time students to bored housewives and everything in between. The duration of our "temporary assignment" was always the subject of rumor, but at the time of our hire most of us were told it would last at least four months. Now that I knew where my paycheck was going to come from for at least four months, I decided to do some soul searching and think about my future. I reflected on my varied past experiences and decided that the one thing I had really enjoyed the most was when I volunteered to be a youth football coach the year after I quit college. Inspired by this realization and having thought about it for quite a while, I decided that I wanted to go back to college and pursue a teaching degree.

I applied to Northeastern Illinois University but was rejected because my grade point average at Millikin University was so low. I then applied to Wright Junior College and began by re-taking a couple of classes I had flunked during my freshman year at Millikin. Working days and going to school a couple of nights a week was hard, but I felt that finally I was moving in the right direction with my life.

About four and a half months into the temporary assignment, the company decided to lay us all off. That evening, Elizabeth and I talked about things and we both agreed - I needed to find a job ASAP. That Sunday, I saw an ad in the paper announcing the opening of a new sporting goods store in Skokie, a suburb just north of Chicago. The following morning I drove out to Skokie to apply. I was interviewed on the spot, as were many other applicants. At the end of the interview, I was told I would receive a phone call later in the week if they intended to hire me. I got the call two days later and was asked if I could start work immediately as they had trucks arriving the next day so that the store could be set-up. I told them I would be there the next morning and hung up, happy as hell to be employed once again.

I arrived at the store at eight in the morning. The doors weren't open yet but some of the other new employees had also arrived. As this was going to be a brand new sporting goods store, the first month of our jobs was going to be dedicated to setting up the entire store. This meant everything from putting up shelving and racks to pricing merchandise, stocking shelves, and creating eye-catching displays.

Shortly after I had arrived, the store manager arrived and greeted us all. He explained that a semi-trailer would be arriving shortly and asked that we clean up the parking lot and alley while we waited for it. He also told us that depending on how people worked during this initial month, some of us would be offered department manager positions when the store finally opened.

That first month proved to be full of hard work and long days. We spent numerous hours just setting up the store's fixtures. Once that was done, it was time to begin stocking the shelves and finally filling up the store's stockroom with reserve merchandise. I worked hard, coming in early, and staying late when asked. My hard work was rewarded when I was asked to become the manager of the store's sporting goods department, which carried all of the workout machines, treadmills, rowers, weight sets, and all team sports equipment.

I was usually scheduled to work four days during the week and then either Saturday or Sunday. I had spoken with my store manager after accepting the manager position and made him aware I was going to continue going to school in the evenings. He told me he would schedule me around my school hours.

My life had finally reached a point where all aspects appeared to be heading in the right direction!

All that was left was to find a way to pay back my debt to Billy and Will.

36 OH WHAT WEBS WE WEAVE

During my life, I've often wondered if the events in a person's life are predetermined or just a series of chaotic situations that are not part of any master plan. There have been times when I could connect the dots between events in my life and see that one led directly to another and that everything seemed to happen for a reason. At other times, shit would happen and I couldn't for the life of me explain why or how it fit into the flow of my life. Shannon O'Reilly reappearing in my life at this point was one of those times.

Shannon was the girl from Mr. Snyder's eighth grade social studies class who I had the privilege of playing the hand on the thigh "chicken" game with. After about a year of working for the sporting goods store, they decided to go on a hiring spree and one of the part timers hired was Shannon. Even though I sometimes hung out with her younger brother Sean, I had lost contact with Shannon after eighth grade and believe I had only seen her once or twice during our high school years. After high school, I heard through the proverbial neighborhood grapevine that she had gotten a bartending job on Rush Street, and that she went through men about as fast as she could pour drinks.

Shannon's first night at the sporting goods store was memorable. I was not aware she had been hired and ended up literally walking into her when I came back into the store from my dinner break. I opened the door in the back of the store that led to our time clocks, and as I opened it I clobbered the person behind it who was carrying two large boxes. The boxes went flying, and as my eyes moved from the boxes to the person carrying them they met Shannon's.

"Shannon O'Reilly?"

"Greg Garrity?"

Shannon reached out both arms to give me a big hug, and I instinctively reached out to hug her back. The sweet smell of her perfume overwhelmed me. The small scrawny girl from eighth grade had grown into a well-endowed, curvy woman. Her red hair radiated while her blue eyes sparkled with life. We both expressed shock on meeting each other this way and laughed out loud on how I had just, "Run her over."

That evening, when we could, we spent time chit chatting and catching up. I found out Shannon was doing well tending bar downtown but wanted to work a part time job so she could save enough money to buy an apartment building in Chicago.

After we closed the store and had cleaned it up, one of my duties was to let the employees out. Shannon was the last one to leave that night, and as I unlocked the door for her she told me how great it was to see me.

"You know, Greg, we should go out one night after work for a drink and really catch up," Shannon suggested.

Really catch up, I thought, what the hell does that mean?

"That's a good idea. Let's do that some time," I answered as I let her out of the store.

As I drove home that evening, I thought about how weird it was seeing Shannon after all this time. How strange it was that one of the first girls to ever get my sexual juices flowing would reappear some thirteen years later and be able to pick up right where she had left off.

A week or two passed, and as it turned out Shannon and I were not scheduled to work together very often. On the one night we did work together, she asked me if I had given any thought to going out for a cocktail. I knew our store's inventory night was approaching and people from the store would be going out drinking afterwards so I suggested we get together then. Safety in numbers, I thought to myself.

Inventory night came around two weeks later, and it was our job to inventory all of the merchandise under the store's roof. There was a great deal of preparation involved with this event as the entire store had to be first organized and labeled. Once this was done, all employees were expected to spend the better part of a Saturday evening and Sunday morning counting all of the store's merchandise. The deal was no one could go home until everything had been counted.

Once the store was closed, we all got down to counting merchandise throughout the various departments. As a team we did a great job and actually finished early. We had expected to work into Sunday morning, but when we finished it was only about eleven-thirty on Saturday night. Most of us had been in the store since eight o'clock that morning so a group of us decided it was time to go out for a well-deserved drink.

I asked Shannon if she was going, and she answered that she wouldn't miss it for the world. We drove over to a local sports bar separately and once there met up with several other department managers and some full and part-time employees.

I don't remember how one thing led to another, but the end of the evening found Shannon and me sitting in her car talking. It wasn't long before our talking was replaced with passionate kissing and petting. I eventually pulled her blouse up and unsnapped her bra exposing her supple breasts. I began to kiss them passionately while I reached down and began to unbuckle her jeans. She helped me pull her jeans down and then it was my turn. I sat up and unbuckled my belt and pulled my jeans down. Shannon crawled on top of me and as she did, began to kiss me passionately. As I slipped into her she bit my lower lip and then began to bob up and down on me. Her sweet perfume danced about my head as I thought how hard it was to believe that the girl I had played the "chicken" game with in eighth grade was now moaning in my ear and riding me like a cowgirl trying to break a wild horse. Little did I know at the time, but this would be the first of many similar wild encounters with her.

Although Elizabeth and I were living together at this time, things weren't going so well. Our initial period of infatuation had evaporated into a period of adjustment and acceptance and things were getting rocky. I loved Elizabeth, but we were having some relationship issues and I wasn't sure if asking her to marry me had been a good move. I don't think that was a valid excuse for being with Shannon, but I'm sure it helped me down that path.

It's very hard to describe the relationship I had with Shannon. We started working together a lot and on some nights that we closed the store together, we would either hang out in the store's parking lot or go out for a drink and talk. Shannon had a boyfriend, but she confided in me their relationship was not going well either. Sometimes we would just talk, and at other times it was all about the sex. We would sometimes rent a hotel room for the sole purpose of having sex for hours at a time. Other times we would steal away an hour, sometimes during the day, meet in a parking lot somewhere, and end up having a quick interlude in one of our vehicles.

I had never felt more alive than during this period of my life and never more disgusted with myself. It was an interesting dichotomy I managed to live with for quite a while.

37 IN COLD BLOOD

The madman had been in and out of psych wards and jails all of his life. Diagnosed as a paranoid schizophrenic with psychotic tendencies, he was unable to hold a steady job so instead lived a rough-and-tumble existence out on the streets. Lately he had been living in a small, raggedy tent, tucked away in a canyon.

Having had a successful morning of begging on the streets, the madman decided to spend his precious funds on MDA and malt liquor. Once back at his campsite, the madman consumed three quarts of beer that afternoon and decided to take the MDA as the sun set in the west. When darkness fell, the voices started talking in the madman's head.

"The anti-Christ is among us, you know."

"It's really up to you to save the world, you know."

"But what can I do?" the madman asked out loud to the voices in his head.

"Find him and kill him of course!"

"He's in the area, not far from here."

"How will I know him?" the madman asked.

"Don't worry. You are destined to do this. The whole purpose of your life is to kill the anti-Christ."

"YOUR TIME IS NOW!"

"DON'T HESITATE!" the voices screamed.

"OK, OK. I know what I need to do," the madman replied.

Entering his tent, he searched in the pitch-black darkness for his most prized possession, a ten-inch hunting knife he had owned since he was a child. The same knife he had used to kill his pet dog, Luke, when he had barked too much. As he crawled out of his tent, the voices spoke once again.

"The lights, see the lights?"

"Yes," the madman responded as he peered off in the distance toward a subdivision located on a hill above the canyon.

"That's where he is!"

"Follow the lights. It's as easy as that."

"OK."

And with that the madman, carrying his ten-inch hunting knife, began to walk toward the subdivision on the hill. Twenty minutes later and having climbed up a steep hill, the madmen fell to the ground, exhausted from the climb.

"That's right, get up your strength," one of the voices whispered. "You're going to need all of your strength to kill the anti-Christ."

"But how do I know which house he's in?" the madman blurted out into the dark, night air.

"Look for the house with the open door or window."

207

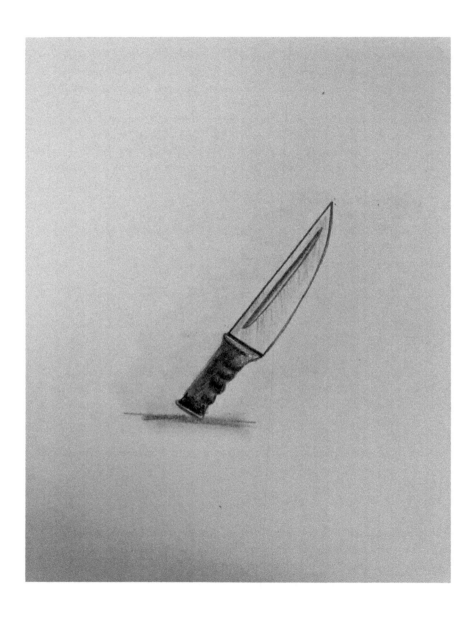

"You'll find him there."

The madman rose to his feet and approached the first house. Through the windows of the house he could see some people sitting at a table so he decided to continue on with his search. The next house was dark, but as far as he could tell there were no open doors or windows. As he turned the corner of this house, he saw that the next house had a window that was about a third of the way open.

"THAT'S THE ONE!" a voice shouted.

"NICELY DONE, SIR!" another chimed in.

The madman made his way to the window and carefully slid it wide open. He then grabbed a chair from the home's patio and positioned it under the window. Climbing up on the chair, the madman was able to lift himself onto the window sill and slide into the home.

"He's in the bedroom," a voice announced.

"Be quiet, you'll need to surprise him," another added.

The madman walked from the dining room to the living room where he thought he could make out a stairway that led to a second floor landing. He could also make out three doorways on the second floor.

"HE'S UP THERE!" a voice shouted.

"YES HE IS, HAH, HAH, HAH!" another laughed.

The heart rate of the madman accelerated as he slowly, quietly made his way up the staircase, one step at a time, hunting knife in his right hand, careful not to wake the anti-Christ. Once he reached the landing, he heard a noise.

"Zzzzzpuff, Zzzzzpuff, Zzzzzpuff, Zzzzzpuff."

"He's sleeping," a voice whispered.

"Kill him now!" another added.

The madmen slowly, carefully opened the door of the room from which the snoring sounds had emanated. The room was slightly illuminated by the full moon that hung in the sky, allowing the madman to see a silhouette of a man sleeping in a bed.

"Don't wait," a voice whispered.

"KILL HIM BEFORE HE WAKES!" another shouted.

The madman raised the hunting knife above his head with both hands and took two steps toward the bed. He brought his arms down hard, plunging the knife into the belly of the sleeping man. So hard that the tip of the knife came out the man's back.

"MORE, MORE!"

"HE'LL KILL YOU!"

To the sleeping man's credit, he awoke and instinctively reached out and grabbed for the madman. The madman pulled the knife out of the man's belly and then drove it down again, plunging it into the man's thigh, severing the femoral artery. The man on the bed now had his hands around the madman's neck and was trying desperately to push himself up and off of the bed.

"HE'S GONNA KILL YOU!" a voice shouted.

"DON'T STOP NOW!" another added.

Yanking the knife out of the man's thigh, the madman swung wildly and was able to *plunge it into the man's side. The man, who now had a good choke hold on the madman, swung his legs off of the bed and pushed the madman backwards.*

"HE'S STRONG!"

"BE CAREFUL!"

The madman was pushed by the man completely across the room and into the wall. The madman couldn't breathe and realized at that moment, he was going to die.

"DO SOMETHING!" a voice shouted.

"STAB HIM AGAIN!" another commanded.

The madman pulled the knife from the man's side and as specks of white light began to dance in his field of vision, due to a lack of oxygen caused from the man's choke hold, the madman managed, with one final attempt, to plunge the knife into the man's neck penetrating his carotid artery. A warm wetness splashed onto the madmen's face as the man began to bleed out. Immediately the madman could feel the pressure of the man's choke hold loosening.

"WELL DONE, SIR!"

"BRAVO!"

The man dropped to his knees and then fell backwards.

"He could be tricking you," a voice warned.

"Good point, stab him some more, you must make sure the anti-Christ is dead!" another voice advised.

The madman knelt down beside the still body of the man he had found sleeping and stabbed him another fifty times, until he was too exhausted to continue.

* * * *

The sleeping man's roommate had been working late that day and was just now arriving home to the rented house they shared. Upon entering the house, the roommate turned on the lights of the living room and couldn't help but notice on the second floor landing above a stranger standing there.

"WHO ARE YOU?" the roommate called out as he stared up at the stranger.

The madman responded by holding his bloody hunting knife in front of his face and then proceeded to lick the sleeping man's blood off of it.

"SHIT!" the roommate exclaimed as a huge chill ran down his spine.

Without hesitation he turned, opened the front door of the house, and ran to his car. With knife in hand the madman began to rumble down the staircase to follow the roommate outside. However, by the time the madman reached the driveway, all he could see were the tail lights of the roommate's car in the distance.

"That's OK, your work is done here," a voice announced to the madman.

"Time to go home and enjoy that last quart of beer you have. You deserve it!"

"Huh, I do!" answered the madman as a smile came over his blood spattered face. And with that, the madman disappeared into the darkness of the night.

* * * *

"Los Angeles Police Department," the voice on the phone announced.

"Hello I need help."

"What's the matter, sir?" the dispatcher asked.

"I just came home from work and there was this man in my house who had a knife with blood on it and, and, he was licking it."

"A knife with blood that he was licking sir?" the dispatcher asked.

"Yes! I'm not sure if this was real because I ran out of the house right away and called you."

"Where are you now sir?" the dispatcher asked.

"I'm at the Texaco gas station on Hillside Drive, about a mile from my house."

"OK and what is the address of your house sir?"

"3333 Canyon Way Drive."

"And, sir, can you give me a description of the man with the knife?"

"Aaagh, he had a beard and long hair and, oh no, he was also covered in blood too, now that I really think about it."

"Is anyone else at home right now?" the dispatcher asked.

"I'm not sure. I share the house with my roommate, but I'm not sure if he was home or not."

"OK sir, I'm going to send a squad over to the house. Stay where you are. After we investigate we'll have a squad drive over to your location and update you. OK, sir?"

"OK, thank you," the roommate replied.

ACT III

38 COMING BACK HOME

I woke up that morning like I always do. Made some coffee and turned on the radio to catch some news. That's how I found out.

"Breaking news out of Los Angeles, California this morning. Will Striker, the up-and-coming actor, recently recognized for his work in the movie *All About Cathy*, was found dead in his rented home, which he shared with a roommate. The cause of death has not yet been confirmed by officials, but anonymous sources have indicated that Mr. Striker died as a result of a home invasion. Mr. Striker was twenty-seven years old."

"What?" I said out loud to myself, "Did I just hear that?"

"ELIZABETH!"

"What?" she called out from the bedroom.

"It's Will. He's dead," I barely got out as tears began to pour from my eyes.

"What, honey?" Elizabeth asked as she walked into the living room.

"I just heard on the radio. They found him dead, don't know the cause. Maybe a home invasion"

"Oh, my god, no!"

"I need to let Billy know," I said through my tears.

Picking up the phone, I dialed Billy's number. The phone rang twice before it was answered.

"Good morning, Greg!" Billy said.

"Billy, I got some bad news," I started. "It's Will, Billy. They found him dead in L.A."

"WHAT THE FUCK!?" Billy blurted out. "ARE YOU SURE?"

"It was on the news, man. They don't have any details yet, but it's him, man. He's gone, and I can't fucking believe it!"

Billy and I talked a bit longer, always coming back to how utterly shocked we both were. What a waste, we said to each other. Our golden boy who had the world by its tail, who was going to put Rogers Park on the map was now gone. All that talent and charisma, just gone. And me, with a double pain of sadness and emptiness knowing that not only was Will gone forever, but he had left this world without me ever being able to repay that huge debt I owed him for saving my life when we were kids. I vowed then and there, that no matter what, I would find a way to repay Will and also promised Billy that somehow, some way, I was going to find a way to repay him as well.

*　　*　　*　　*

They shipped Will's body back to Chicago for a funeral service at St. Ignatius, in the heart of the Patch of Green. The golden boy would return not as a hero but rather as a reminder to all of us just how fragile life really is. Will's wake was attended by hundreds and depressing as hell. His friends tried to console one another as best they could. Billy had taken the news especially hard, so hard that he couldn't bring himself to even attend Will's funeral.

The day of Will's funeral broke grey and dark, like the feelings in my soul. St. Ignatius Church that day was packed for the funeral mass. There were a few celebrity types there, but for the most part it was people from St. Ignatius, Rogers Park, and Loyola Academy. The people Will had grown up with.

Will's father asked me to be a pall bearer, and I had told him I would. As we stood outside the main entrance of the church, waiting for the signal to lift his casket from the hearse, a light rain began to fall. I thought about all the times I had spent with Will. I thought of our grade school days, all the time we spent hanging out at the schoolyard and the beaches, and the night we chased a cabby who ended up taking my car door off. All these memories seemed like they had occurred just yesterday when in fact they had happened at least a decade ago.

A nudge from a fellow pall bearer brought me out of my day dream. We gingerly lifted the casket out of the hearse and made our way up the stairs that led to the church's main entrance. Even with six grown men supporting the weight of the casket, I couldn't believe how heavy it was. We made our way in as the church's organist began to play a hymn.

As I walked beside the casket I glanced into the crowd and could see men and women weeping. Better to look straight ahead, I thought, or else I might start crying like a baby as well. The funeral mass began, and to me it was all a blur, all too surreal to absorb.

Then it was time again to fulfill our duties as pall bearers and carry Will's casket out to the waiting hearse. This time when we lifted the casket, I could not believe how light it felt. As the church organist played _Amazing Grace_ and we proceeded slowly down the long aisle to the rear of the church, I wondered if Will's soul had abandoned all of its worldly weight and departed for heaven during the mass. To this very day, I believe it had.

God speed, my dear friend I thought, as we placed Will's coffin into the hearse in the now-driving rain. I'll pay you that debt I owe you one way or another, and we'll enjoy another beer together when we meet again. I promise!

39 WHY!?

On the Saturday after Will's funeral, I received a phone call from Billy.

"Hey, man, what's up?"

"Nothing, Billy, just kinda hanging out."

"Listen I'mma…, feeling kinda bad about not going to the funeral," Billy confessed.

"Oh…well, it was really depressing, man, so don't feel bad," I replied, remembering how Billy had explained to me how he was too upset by Will's death to attend.

"I can imagine, but what I need is to say goodbye, man… you know, some closure," Billy blurted out. "I was wondering if you would like to head out to the cemetery with me today so I could pay my respects."

"Ah yeah, what time were you thinking about going?" I asked.

"I got some stuff to do, so how about we head over around four this afternoon?" Billy suggested.

"That's cool," I replied. "You want me to pick you up since you're on the way?"

"That will work, Double G, I'll see you around four then."

"Sounds good, take it easy."

"Bye."

I went about my day as usual, but around three thirty I began to get ready to head out and pick Billy up. The sunshine, which had been abundant all morning and early afternoon, disappeared behind the grey, ominous clouds that now hung in the sky. I better wear a windbreaker and bring my golf umbrella, I thought, as I looked out my living room window.

When I arrived at Billy's house, I saw him sitting on the stoop by the front door of his home. Billy waved and got up and started to walk toward me. He carried a brown paper bag in his arm.

"Hey, man, what's up?" I asked as Billy got into my car.

"Hey, it's gonna be the fuckin' cocktail hour when we get to Will so I thought I'd bring a couple of six packs."

"Not a bad idea, dude," I replied as I shot Billy a quick smile.

We drove mostly in silence as the sky darkened and the wind began to pick up. Will was buried in a cemetery in Evanston, Illinois, which was Rogers Park's neighbor to the north. A section of the cemetery was on a hill overlooking Lake Michigan, and that's where Will's grave was. We made our way into the cemetery, and I drove up and parked my car on the hill. We got out of my car, and I helped Billy carry the beer toward Will's grave.

"Here it is," I announced as I led Billy to Will's gravestone.

"Will Striker 4/20/1960 to 9/11/1987," Billy read out loud. "A loving, caring son who brightened the world."

"That's nice, ha?" I remarked.

"I need a beer," Billy replied.

I reached into the bag Billy had brought and pulled out three cans. I handed one over to Billy as the first drops of rain began to fall from the sky.

"You remember Bunchi Min, Billy, that Cambodian dude I used to work with?"

"Yeah, I remember meeting him once at your apartment on Pratt."

"Well he told me once it was a Cambodian tradition to always pour a drink during a party for all of your deceased friends so that they could enjoy the party, too. So I'm gonna crack open this beer and set it next to Will's gravestone."

"Cool," Billy replied.

I opened the beer, bent down, and placed it next to the gravestone. When I stood up, I looked toward the east.

"It's a great view from this hilltop, isn't it?" I asked. "It's cool how you can see the lake from here. Check it out. There're white caps on the lake right now."

"Yeah, man," Billy replied still looking at Will's gravestone.

As I looked at Billy, I could see tears welling up in his eyes.

"You OK, man?"

"Why did this have to happen?" Billy asked. "Will never hurt anyone," Billy added and then proceeded to guzzle down his first beer.

The rain began to pick up a bit. I thought of running back to my car and grabbing the umbrella but instead I stayed, frozen in time like a statue.

"Wrong place at the wrong time, Billy."

Billy bent down and pulled another beer out of the brown paper bag and proceeded to open it.

"Why would God let this happen?" Billy continued. "Will had so much going for him."

As the rain began to strengthen, I could see tears now rolling down Billy's cheeks.

"Do you want to head out?" I asked Billy.

"No, I'm not done paying my respects. Is that all right?"

"Sure, but I'm gonna run back to the car and grab my umbrella. The rain's really starting to come down."

With that said, I took off, with beer in hand, toward where I had parked my car. Once there I grabbed my umbrella from the back seat and opened it up. I made my way back to the gravesite, and as I approached I could see Billy grab another beer as the rain soaked him.

"Hey, man, get underneath this umbrella" I said as I reached Billy.

"I'm OK, man. Ya want another beer?" Billy asked.

"Yeah, I do."

Billy handed me the ice-cold beer he was holding and then bent down and pulled another one from the soaked brown paper bag.

"So why are we born if shit like this can happen. Seems like no reason to live then, right?" Billy blurted out as he stared at the gravestone while the rain poured down from the dark, grey sky.

"I've thought about that, Billy, and I had an interesting thought. What if God brought Will into this world for just one reason."

"One reason. What would be the one reason?" Billy asked.

"What if it was to be there to save my life that night we were out on the lake," I replied.

"THAT'S IT!? TO BE BORN TO SAVE YOUR SORRY ASS?" Billy shouted out.

"Well, yeah, maybe I am a sorry ass, but what if one of the kids I have ends up discovering a cure for cancer or something else great like that. Then Will's and your actions that night would have had a tremendous impact not only on my life but the lives of millions of people in the world. Do you see what I'm getting at?"

"Yeah, well your kid better do something like that, Double G, cuz otherwise it's just a waste." With that said, Billy knelt down in the soaked grass right in front of Will's gravestone.

"Don't ya wish you were there to save Will from that bastard?" Billy asked.

"Yeah, man, of course I do," I replied as my eyes started to well up with tears.

"You got dealt a really shitty hand, Will," Billy said as he began to cry openly. "I love you, Will, and I'm never gonna forget you, man."

The rain intensified, and the wind picked up as well. Just then a clap of thunder rumbled in the distance.

Billy guzzled down his beer and then turned to me and asked for another.

"You sure you want to stay, man, it's getting really nasty out here?"

"Leave if you want to," Billy replied. "I'm saying good-bye to my friend, and I'm not leaving til the fuckin' beer is gone."

"I get it, man," I said as I handed Billy another beer and stood over him with my umbrella, trying to shelter him as best I could.

Billy and I stayed at Will's gravesite for another hour or so in mostly silence. As we did, the rain soaked us and the thunder and lightning roared and danced above our heads - just like the night we were on Will's dad's boat some fourteen years ago.

40 OH WHAT WEBS WE WEAVE PART 2

After months of having after-work rendezvous, spending times at hotels and in vehicles having all different types of wonderful sex, the shit finally hit the fan. One night, I planned to go out with Shannon for drinks after work, so I called Elizabeth and told her I was going out for drinks with Matt McGovern, one of the sporting goods store's assistant managers and a buddy of mine. What I wasn't anticipating at all was Matt, who didn't even work that night, calling my apartment wanting to talk with me.

After having drinks with Shannon that evening, I arrived home late and went into the bedroom and began to undress. Elizabeth, who I thought was asleep, began talking.

"So you went out with Matt McGovern tonight, eh?"

"Yeah, why do you ask?" I asked sheepishly.

"Well he called here around eight o'clock and wanted to talk to you." Oh shit! I thought.

"When I mentioned you had told me you were going out with him he seemed surprised. So, YOU SON OF A BITCH!" Elizabeth yelled. "I suspect you went out with someone else and I suspect it was a woman. YOU FUCKING SON OF A BITCH!"

With that Elizabeth leaped from the bed and stormed into the living room to sleep on the couch. I decided not to try to defend myself since I had been caught squarely in my lie. The next morning things were really tense between Elizabeth and me, but fortunately she didn't ask me who I had been with the previous evening. I realized that morning it wasn't fair to put Elizabeth through this and that I couldn't go on living like this either. So I decided in order to save my relationship with Elizabeth, one that I had invested so much time in, I needed to end my relationship with Shannon.

Unfortunately, this was easier said than done, for Shannon was a free spirit who was hard to resist. After all, she was fun, attractive, and the sex between us was awesome. The next time I saw Shannon I told her Elizabeth was on to us, but she told me she didn't care. That evening she paid for the hotel room and gave me the best sex I ever had.

I managed to cut back on the number of rendezvous we had, but I didn't completely stop them. It had almost become a game. I chose my spots better with the sole purpose of completely hiding this relationship from Elizabeth. Several months passed when one morning Elizabeth confronted me.

"I know that you are still spending time with whatever bimbo you have been spending time with over these past few months," she began.

"Dammit, I'm a good woman, and I'm good for you, Gregory."

I knew she was quite serious as she very rarely called me Gregory.

"But if you are more interested in this other woman, so be it. The only thing I ask of you is to make a decision, me or her. I cannot go on knowing that I'm sharing you with her." With that said, Elizabeth began to cry.

"OK," was the only response I could come up with.

Elizabeth got up and left the table, and there I was all by myself. When I really thought about it, I realized I was risking the best relationship I had ever had in my life because I couldn't control my libido. It wasn't like Elizabeth and I didn't have sex. We did, and it was great, too. The more I thought about it, I came to realize that by bedding Shannon, I was completing something I had started many years ago and had always hoped I could finish. I decided then and there my relationship with Shannon had to end.

About a week later, a group of store employees planned to go out after work, and I had decided to go along too. I had not seen Shannon all week, but that evening she was at work and I knew she would be going out to the bar as well. Once we all got to the bar the beers began to flow, and I knew if I wasn't careful there was a good chance of ending up sucking face with Shannon. I didn't want that to happen this time.

The joint we went to that night was right next to Wrigley Field, and since parking is hard to come by there, we all had to park pretty far away. During the evening one of the other department managers, a girl named Virginia, mentioned she had parked really far away. Now I had been attracted to Virginia since the first time I had saw her. She was about six feet tall, very athletic, and had a very cute, Irish-looking face. Although I was attracted to her, I had no intention of ever acting on it. However, this evening I thought that she might be able to help me avoid leaving the bar with Shannon.

My plan was to offer to walk Virginia back to her car and then get a lift from her back to mine. I would be on my way home before Shannon even realized I wasn't coming back to the bar. This, I hoped, would plant the idea in Shannon's mind that I was serious about ending our relationship.

When Virginia announced around midnight that she was calling it a night, I quickly piped up that I thought she should be escorted to her car since it was parked so far away. I didn't look at Shannon fearing the look she was probably shooting me could prove fatal and instead helped Virginia on with her coat and walked her to the door. My plan was working perfectly.

Virginia and I walked back to her car, chit chatting along the way. Once we reached it, we both got in. We continued to talk, and that's when my plan backfired. Much to my surprise, Virginia confided in me that she had been attracted to me since she had been transferred to our store. She went on to tell me how disappointed she was when she found out that I was already engaged.

"It seems all the good ones are taken," Virginia lamented.

"Believe me, I'm not one of the good ones," I replied.

With that said, I reached over and pulled her cute, Irish face toward mine and kissed her gently. She kissed me back with a great deal of passion. We continued on for quite a while. Virginia eventually gave me a lift to my car, and I gave her a final kiss good-bye.

"Holy shit," I said out loud to myself as I drove home. "Here I was ready to make a stand and end a relationship and what do I do? I end up starting another one! I'm a real piece of work!"

I smiled to myself, partly out of embarrassment for having fucked up my plan but also partly out of pride as I realized how many chicks were digging me.

The next time I worked, both Shannon and Virginia were working. Boy, was I ever uncomfortable in this situation. Shannon didn't seem too upset that I had left the bar with Virginia, and I suspected that Virginia hadn't mentioned our little interlude to Shannon. But nonetheless, it was uncomfortable. Here I was, living with and engaged to one woman, in an affair with another that had gone on for a while, and now had an opportunity to begin a romantic relationship with a third. Fucking crazy, I thought to myself.

I finally decided that my original intention of ending my relationship with Shannon was a sound one. The thought of starting a relationship with Virginia was tempting since I was attracted to her and now knew she was attracted to me. But I couldn't stop thinking about how unfair I had been to Elizabeth all these months and how much I really did love her. Sneaking around, lying, and cheating didn't make me feel very good about my behavior or myself.

I decided to rededicate myself to the relationship I had with Elizabeth and go forward with all of our wedding plans. I also planned to tell Elizabeth about my relationship with Shannon. As soon as I came up with this plan of action, I felt at peace, as if a huge weight had been lifted from my shoulders. That night I had a heart-to-heart talk with Shannon in the parking lot of the sporting goods store. Shannon shed some tears when I told her I couldn't go on seeing her but then told me she understood and wished me well. A week later, she quit her part-time job at the store and was again out of my life.

My "confession" to Elizabeth about Shannon came out in dribs and drabs. Elizabeth, of course, had known for a while that something was going on, but she never pressed me for any details. Every so often I would "leak" a little bit of information, like a comment about a bar that Elizabeth and I had never been at together.

Elizabeth would say something like, "Oh, were you there when you were having that affair with that girl at work?"

So we left it at that, and I promised Elizabeth nothing like this would ever happen again.

41 GOOD-BYE DAD

My dad, a three-pack-a-day smoker for most of his life who also drank too much and didn't eat very well, had quit working about two years earlier and his health had been rapidly deteriorating. The years had finally caught up to him, and I sensed that the end was near.

In looking back and reflecting on my father's life, from my perspective, during the years I knew him, he didn't have much of a life at all. For years he worked, stopped at a tavern on the way home for a couple of beers, and then came home and ate dinner alone and drank some more beer. On the weekends he went out and bought some beer and then basically sat in our apartment while he drank, smoked, watched TV, and read the paper or a book.

After he quit working, this routine was pretty much his life every day. He was diagnosed with acute emphysema and walking any distance at all was now really beyond his capabilities. Every now and then, I dropped by to see him and maybe drank a few beers and watched some of a Cubs game with him.

It was hard to see him in such bad health and realize it had been his own doing. But my dad had had a rough life. His mother and father both died when he was still a young boy, and he ended up living with his older brother. From what I have been told, my dad was pretty much left to fend for himself, and I imagine that is probably why as an adult he lacked any type of self-discipline.

As a high school student, my dad was injured in a football game and was diagnosed with a condition in which any type of bump to the body could result in a painful and deep bruise. As he once told me, this condition ended his athletic career in high school.

When he finished high school, he began working for a weapons manufacturer during World War II and eventually met my mother there. Once again, bad luck struck him as an errant airplane propeller blade ripped through my dad's inner thigh and left him with a deep, gruesome scar, which appeared to be almost bone deep. I suppose with these types of events as your life's foundation. it would be easy to become a little cynical.

I think my mom was drawn to him because he was charming and since his parents had died when he was so young she likened him to her father who had been an orphan as well. However, as my mom discovered, my dad was as different from my grandfather as night is from day. My dad was a gambler and drinker with very little interest in his family life where as my mom's dad loved his family life above all.

I know now that there were times during their marriage when my mom contemplated leaving my dad but being a good Catholic woman I think her conscience wouldn't allow it. Now my dad was dying, and there wasn't much I or anyone else could do but to watch and wait. I prayed that when his end did come, it would be quick and painless and wouldn't put my mom through too much grief.

I remember a conversation I had with my dad around this time. I asked him what he thought happened to a person after they died.

"Nothing," he replied to my question.

"What do you mean nothing?" I asked hoping for a further explanation.

He then pointed with his index finger toward the ground and said, "I think you're put into the ground and that's the end of you."

I nodded my head indicating to him I now understood what he meant. I didn't feel like raising any other possible scenarios with him since I knew he wasn't religious, and after all I respected his opinion.

One night not long after our end-of-life conversation, I received a call from my mom. Dad had a real rough night sleeping and breathing. She had called an ambulance, and they brought him to Alexian Brothers Hospital in Elk Grove Village. He was admitted and placed in the intensive care unit. Mom said she didn't think he was in very good shape, and she thought it would be a good idea if I came to see him as soon as possible.

I drove to the hospital the next day and met my mom in the I.C.U. Mom explained dad had been going in and out of consciousness since he arrived. We reached his room and I walked in and saw he was awake. He had an oxygen tube inserted into his nose, which allowed him to breathe. His eyes were open, and when I said hello he said hello back.

I noticed that the tips of his fingers had begun to turn black and blue. Probably due to oxygen deprivation, I thought. His body was finally beginning to shut itself down. It had finally taken all of the abuse it could handle.

Dad raised his hands, and they shook like a leaf on a branch being blown by a strong wind. He began talking in mumbo jumbo sentences, something about a basketball game, and then my mom said, "It's Greg, Jack. Greg is here to see you."

To which my dad, seeming to grasp who was standing in front of him, said, "Greg, you're a good boy," and then proceeded to speak some more gibberish. My mom and I left a little later. I think without saying it we both realized it was just a matter of time now.

The next day, dad lost consciousness and had to be put on a ventilator. I went to the hospital that night and saw him again, but to me he had already died. His hands were now almost totally black and blue, and although his eyes were open there was no life in them, just a blank stare. The only thing keeping him from his hole in the ground was the ventilator mouthpiece, which was wedged into and taped to his mouth.

I left that night knowing my dad would never hear my voice again nor me his. As I drove home I began to cry as I thought back to my previous visit and realized that the last words my dad would ever say to me was that I was a good boy. In some strange way, I felt comforted by this thought.

I got home from work the following evening and was in the shower when the call came. Elizabeth answered the phone, and on the other end was my mom. She told Elizabeth that my dad had died a little bit earlier. After saying good-bye to my mother, Elizabeth hung up the phone and walked to the bathroom door. She opened up the bathroom door and announced, "It's about your dad."

"Yes?" I said poking my head out from behind the shower curtain.

"He died a little while ago, honey," Elizabeth meekly blurted.

"Oh," was all that I could utter.

"I told your mom that you would call her back," Elizabeth continued.

"Good."

"Are you OK?"

"Yeah, I'm OK."

Elizabeth closed the bathroom door, and as I pulled myself back into the shower the water began to splash over me and a great feeling of sadness began to well up inside of me. I began to sob like a child.

"My dad is dead," I whispered to myself as I placed my two arms against the wall in front of me for support. I stayed beneath the flowing water for several minutes, sobbing as I contemplated what I had just been told.

When I got out of the shower I called my mom, and she seemed all right. She was going to begin funeral arrangements the following day with my sister Maureen. I told her if I could help in any way to let me know, and she promised me she would. The next day, I informed my manager at work and my teachers at school I would be taking some time off due to my father's death.

It was the middle of February, a week before my birthday, and all I could think about was my dad's death. My mom and sister made the arrangements which included my dad being waked in Rogers Park. We met with Father Mike Morgan, the older brother of my buddy Jimmy Morgan, the day before the wake. He explained the short memorial service he was going to perform. At the end of our meeting, he asked if any of the family members wanted to say anything the next day. All were silent when I suddenly spoke up.

"I would like to say something tomorrow, Father Mike."

"OK," Father Mike replied. "After the service, it will be your turn."

The following day a handful of people came to pay their respects. An old friend of my dad's had come as well as an old friend of my mom's. Other than that, there was a handful of relatives and some of my friends including Billy and Jimmy Morgan. How sad I thought to myself, my dad really didn't have any friends after all.

Father Mike performed a short prayer service and then introduced me to the small group of people sitting there, telling them I had a few words to say about my father.

I stood up and said, "I want to begin by thanking, on behalf of my mom, brother, and sister everyone for coming here today. I feel that my father was a very hard man to understand. However, I want to share with you a short conversation I had with him when I was young that provided me a lot of insight into who he really was and how he felt about life."

"One day when my father and I were walking from his car to our apartment building, I noticed a bunch of ant hills protruding from a crack between two slabs of sidewalk cement. As we got closer, I could see the ants busily at work. I said something to my dad like, wow, look at those ants, I'm going to step on them and wipe them out. To my surprise my dad said, in a stern voice I was unaccustomed to hearing, 'Don't do that, just let them be!' His tone of voice surprised me, and so I asked him why he didn't want me to step on the ants. 'Well, I think the ants are maybe just like us. They go through their lives doing their jobs, raising their families, and really not bothering anyone. And tonight there may be a mamma ant and her babies waiting for papa ant to come home with some food for them. But if you have stepped on papa ant and killed him, then he'll never come home and the mamma and babies will be very sad.'"

"I see, I replied to my dad as I reveled in his explanation."

Done with my story I continued, as I began to choke back tears of sadness.

"I think this story is a good representation of who my dad really was, a loving, caring, sensitive man. Thanks again everyone for coming today."

As I walked from the podium, I saw my Aunt Louise, who had helped raise my father, sobbing. As I passed her, I heard her say, "Yes, that was Jack."

Father Mike announced there would be a luncheon at a nearby restaurant and everyone began to file out. The funeral director approached our family and asked if we wanted to go to the casket and pay our final respects before we left. We all walked over to the casket and did just that. As I stood over my dad, I silently told him I loved him, that I would miss him, and then I asked God to watch over him. I bent down and kissed his forehead.

*   *   *   *

My mom decided my father's remains would be cremated and about a week after the wake, she retrieved his ashes from the funeral home. My mom wanted to drive to the cemetery where my dad's mother had been buried over fifty years ago and bury his ashes near her grave. I told her I would make the trip with her.

We chose a Saturday in early spring to bury dad. We left for the far south suburbs of Chicago to first pick up my Aunt Louise and then drove to the cemetery where dad's mom was buried. We picked up my aunt around ten-thirty, and she guided us to the cemetery. Once there, we found our way to my grandmother's gravesite. We only knew the section of the graveyard she was buried in as the small tombstones in this section were so old that the markings were indistinguishable from the passing of time and seasons.

My aunt, who was in very poor health due to a lifelong nicotine addiction, sat in the car as my mother and I walked through the graveyard, me with my dad's ashes in a box tucked underneath my arm. We approached my grandmother's burial site and decided to bury dad in the shade of a nearby tree.

With a small shovel my mom had brought, I dug a small hole in the ground that would be my father's permanent resting place. Once the digging was done, I slowly opened the box of ashes and began to pour them into the hole. With my hands I spread dad's ashes out so I could cover them completely with the dirt. With every shovel full of dirt I placed on top of them, they gradually disappeared.

"He's finally back with his mother," my mom remarked solemnly when I was done.

I looked up at her and saw tears beginning to well up in her eyes, the only tears I had seen her shed during this whole ordeal. I got up from my knees and gave her a big hug. I turned around and while gazing at the freshly covered hole, said, "Good-bye, Dad."

I wrapped my arm around my mother and led her back to our car where my aunt was waiting.

"How did it go?" my aunt asked us once we were back into the car.

"Fine," my mother simply replied.

We left the cemetery and headed to a local restaurant for lunch. As we walked into the restaurant, I noticed my hands were covered with dirt from the cemetery. I excused myself and went to the washroom to clean them. As I was washing my hands and watching the dirt swirl down the drain, a great wave of sadness crashed down on me as I realized what I had just done. I just buried my father, I thought, as I choked back tears with all of my might.

I left the washroom and made my way back to the table, but I really don't recall much else of the afternoon. The whole day was more emotional than I had expected, kind of like reliving my father's passing all over again. My dad's passing coupled with Will's recent death brought me to a very dark, depressed state of mind. I state of mind I had never been to before.

But life, like a river, keeps flowing along. It would be only a short while before all of my time and thoughts were once again preoccupied with Elizabeth, work, and school. That spring I graduated from college with a degree in social science and secondary education. That summer, I interviewed for a number of high school teaching jobs and was eventually offered one at an inner-city, girls Catholic high school, which I accepted. Elizabeth and I began to plan our wedding, which we decided would take place the following April.

42 FINALLY, THE BIG DAY ARRIVED

The new year promised to be a big one for Elizabeth and me. April 21 was our wedding date. As the new year started I began to workout at the school I was working at by running up and down the deserted stairs and hallways at the end of the school day. I wanted to lose weight and be in really good shape for our big day.

As April approached, we finalized the details of the wedding. For our honeymoon I made reservations at a resort in Jamaica based upon the recommendations of several of our friends who had stayed there on their honeymoon. About three weeks prior to the wedding, my travel agent called and told me the resort had been overbooked. He said he could get us into the newest resort on the island for the same price we had booked the original resort. This news didn't really bother me since I had been told by my friends that no matter where you stayed in Jamaica, you're bound to have a good time and enjoy yourself.

However, when I told Elizabeth, she broke down in tears and told me she felt that our wedding had been ruined. I assured her as best I could the new resort would be fine and we really shouldn't worry about anything. She finally calmed down and said she would hope for the best.

We planned on a fairly big wedding with approximately two-hundred guests. I invited most of the people I worked with at the high school, but only a couple of them attended. Elizabeth invited a lot of people from her work, and all of our relatives and friends were coming.

My best man was my brother Jerry. As such he was responsible for throwing my bachelor party. He arranged everything and planned it for the Saturday before the wedding. Billy and some of my other buddies picked me up that evening and we drove over to the bar where it was going to be held. My brother rented a large, private room in the back of the bar, and once we got there we started drinking and shooting the shit. A couple of hours passed and then the "entertainment" arrived.

There were two women, a brunette and a blonde. As we would soon find out, the blonde was in "training" so she wouldn't be performing that night. The brunette, who was drop-dead gorgeous, was the one who was going to perform. As she was getting ready, she asked that I sit in a chair in front of everyone. She started to perform, and although I don't recall many of the particulars of her performance, from what I've been told she was pretty good.

I had anticipated that at some point she might ask me to remove my pants, so as a joke I had drawn a big, red bull's-eye on my boxers, right over my crotch area. When she pulled my pants off during her performance, my buddies got a big hoot out of my bull's-eye.

After her performance, she told me to grab my clothes and follow her back to the bathroom where she had changed. Once we were in the room, which was part bathroom, part locker room, she grabbed a chair, wedged it beneath the doorknob so it couldn't be opened, and told me to sit down.

"Hey, would you be interested in a line," I asked her as I moved over to the chair.

"Hell yes!" she replied.

I laid out a couple of chokers, and we each took a turn doing one.

I sat back down in the chair as she kneeled down on the floor in front of me and told me my brother had paid for some "additional services." Not wanting to disappoint my brother, I felt obligated to cooperate. After the "additional services" had been performed, the brunette got dressed back into her street clothes.

"Here, take this and call me when you get bored with the married life and want to have a little fun and party with me," the gorgeous brunette, now fully dressed, said as she handed me a card with her number on it.

"OK, sounds good," I replied.

But once the gorgeous brunette had left the room, I tore up the card and threw it away. After an engagement of seven-plus years, Elizabeth and I were ready to commit to each other forever. I really did love her with all my heart, and although I knew a marriage could be tough at times, I felt if we worked at it we could have a great life together.

As the week of our wedding finally arrived, the excitement for it grew for both of us. Elizabeth was going to stay at her mother's house in Glendale Heights, a suburb of Chicago, the night before. All of her bridesmaids were going to meet there and take a limo into Chicago the following morning. My groomsmen met me at my apartment, and we all left together for St. Ignatius Church.

It was April 21, and on the Patch of Green the sun shined brightly. The exact opposite from the day we came to bury Will, I thought. I made my way into the church with my groomsmen. They led me to the sacristy, the area in the back of the church where the priests put on their robes prior to mass. My brother had gotten married in the Chapel of St. Ignatius some seventeen years earlier, and although his marriage hadn't worked out, I still felt good that I was to be married in the same church we considered our home parish. I just prayed that my marriage would last longer than my brother's.

Father Mike came into the sacristy and told us that my bride had yet to arrive. The wedding was to begin at three and it was already five minutes after three. As the minutes went by, I began to get nervous, but my groomsmen reassured me that my bride had probably just been caught in traffic. Finally, after what seemed like a lifetime but was actually about five more minutes, word filtered back to us that it was time to take our positions at the front of the altar.

As Elizabeth walked slowly on her father's arm toward the altar, I gazed at her and thought that surely she was the most beautiful woman I had ever seen. Her hair had been done splendidly, and her face was radiant. When they reached us, I shook her father's hand as he placed her hand in mine. He whispered to me, "Take good care of her," and I responded, "I will."

The marriage mass began, and it felt as if I was in a dream. Was this really happening, I thought, as I gazed upon my beautiful bride? My sweet Elizabeth and I were the center of attention in a grand wedding ceremony. How exciting!

Halfway through the ceremony, we sat down to listen to Father Mike's homily, which turned out to be quite good. We had met with Father Mike on several occasions as part of the Pre-Cana program, which the Catholic church requires before anyone can be married in the church. During our meetings, Father Mike learned about us as a couple, and he mentioned some of the things we had talked about during our conversations with him.

One of the topics Father Mike talked about was imperfection. He illustrated his point by talking about the Navajo Indians and their skill at weaving blankets. The Navajos' tradition is to deliberately miss-stitch a section of every blanket because the Navajos felt a miss-stitch was a true representation of how nature and life are. The Navajo believe that within perfection there still existed imperfection just as within a perfect union such as marriage there was bound to be some imperfections. In the years since our wedding, I've often thought back to this story when trying to accept my wife and later my children's imperfections as well as my own.

The wedding mass ended, and afterwards all of our close family members and people in the wedding party stayed for pictures at the church. Then it was off to the banquet hall we had rented for our reception. Once we got there, Elizabeth and I stood in the receiving line welcoming our guests. After everyone had arrived, we made our way to our table and it was time for the best man, my brother Jerry, to make the traditional marriage toast before dinner began.

"Good evening, everyone, can I have your attention?" my brother began. "Well obviously today's beautiful wedding is going to bring an end to my brother's bachelor days. So I think it would be only appropriate at this time to have all of the ladies sitting in the crowd, who may still have a key to Greg's apartment, come up here and turn it in."

Elizabeth, who was already nervous about my brother's toast, looked directly at me and all I could do was shrug my shoulders as if to say hey, I don't know what's going on here, which was the truth as I really didn't have a clue as to what was about to transpire.

Just at that moment, randomly, women began to get out of their chairs and walk up to our table and drop off a key. Old women, young women, tall women, short women, and even a couple of pregnant women! Everyone broke out in laughter as the key parade continued. Finally, after approximately twenty keys had been placed on our table, my brother continued his toast.

"Thank you, ladies, for your cooperation. I do want to propose a toast now everyone," my brother announced as he held a glass up in the air. "I want us all to toast to Elizabeth and Greg. May you have much love and happiness together for the rest of your lives. Here's to you."

The rest of the evening was a blur full of food, drink, dancing, and friends. We were very glad we had the ceremony and reception videotaped so we could relive and enjoy our big day again because at the time, it went by so fast.

At the end of the evening, Elizabeth and I said our good-byes and left the reception. As we got into our limo, I mentioned to Elizabeth that the way we felt at that moment must be how rock stars feel after a concert performance. Hot, sweaty, ears ringing, and dead tired but yet very happy.

Our limo drove us to a hotel near O'Hare Airport where we would stay overnight and leave the following morning for O'Hare to catch our flight to Jamaica. When we got to the hotel, Elizabeth and I made love for the first time as man and wife. We both realized that a new period of our lives had just begun.

The next morning our hotel room phone rang at six-thirty. It was our wakeup call. I answered it, acknowledged the caller, hung up, and promptly fell back to sleep. Our plan was to have a limo pick us up at seven-thirty so that we could catch our nine o'clock flight to Jamaica. Luckily for us, the limo driver arrived on time and called our room at seven-forty and woke us up.

"If we hurry by showering together and getting dressed quickly we should be able to make it to the airport in time for our flight," I announced to Elizabeth after hanging up the phone.

We did just that and made it to the airport with time to spare.

Once we got on the plane, we relaxed for the three-and-a-half-hour flight to Montego Bay, Jamaica. We landed about mid-day in Mo's Bay and then found our shuttle bus, which would carry us on the hour-and-a-half trip to the sleepy village of Negril, located on the western tip of the island.

As we made our way out of the terminal and into the hot, bright sunshine, we were beseeched by a wide variety of peddlers. They were selling everything from small trinkets, pop, ganja, and cold Red Stripe beer. I opted for the latter and bought four cold bottles for the ride. As we pulled away from the airport, I looked at Elizabeth and asked her what she thought.

"Nice," she answered smiling at me as I smiled back at her.

The road from Montego Bay to Negril had only a single lane running in both directions, and it was full of potholes, pedestrians, and animals. One of the best-selling t-shirts on the island proudly announced, "I survived the road to Negril!" Fortunately for us, our shuttle bus had a good air conditioning unit so outside of the bumps the trip wasn't too bad.

We finally arrived at our hotel at about three in the afternoon. We checked in and were led to our hotel room. Our room was on the first floor, and when we opened our patio door the Caribbean Sea and the beach was about fifty feet away. As we would find out a bit later, the nude beach at the resort was just west of our room.

We settled in and decided to take a walk around the resort. In the middle of the resort was a large, open-air stage and dining pavilion. We ate all of our meals there unless we chose to dine at one of the three other restaurants the resort also offered. Just off this pavilion was the resort's main pool as well as a disco.

The grounds themselves were immaculately kept with beautiful flowers and vegetation everywhere. There were three "tree houses" located in strategic areas of the resort. Each tree house was an elevated, open-air bar/grill designed to be a place where you could go to get a quick bite to eat or something to drink instead of having to go all the way to the pavilion.

Our week there was full of fun, food, sex, and drink. During our stay, Elizabeth and I couldn't help but notice a very attractive, well-endowed, red-haired woman who appeared to be staying at the resort by herself. We seemed to run into her everywhere we went in the resort, and I would invariable make some kind of remark about her.

"Yeah, I bet you would like to see her on the nude beach," Elizabeth would respond.

One afternoon during our stay, Elizabeth and I walked down to the regular beach to hang out and catch some rays. There were a number of lounge chairs spread out all over the beachfront.

"Hey, how about we grab these two?" I suggested to Elizabeth as I pointed to a couple of chairs within close proximity to the bar.

"No, let's go a little further," Elizabeth answered as she picked out a couple of chairs a little further away and led me in their direction. As I sat down I noticed there was a lounge chair situated in front of our chairs at the water's edge. There was a beach towel hanging over the back of the chair so I knew someone was occupying it but I really couldn't see who it was.

After we got situated, I went to the bar and got us a couple of drinks and then we settled into our chairs. After about an hour, I saw the towel on the lounge chair in front of us move. In an instant the beautiful redhead got out of the chair and stood up, facing us with nothing on but her bikini bottom. She had been lying in the chair topless! There is a God, I thought to myself as I gently nudged Elizabeth and slyly pointed in the direction of the redhead.

As my eyes drank in her beauty, especially her round, full, bare breasts, a guy came up to her and began a conversation. I could hear them talking but I didn't understand a word. He sounded as if he was speaking Italian, and as I would later find out, she was a German. After a few moments, it became apparent what they were talking about. The guy motioned for his wife to come over and when she did he handed her a camera. The redhead, still topless, then posed with the Italian guy as his wife took the picture. I turned to Elizabeth and began laughing out loud.

"What are you laughing at?"

"Hey, I may have talked about her looks but at least I never asked you to take a picture of us together," I replied.

"That's because I wouldn't!" Elizabeth shot back.

The nude beach on the property had also been a hot topic of discussion between us the entire week. We had spoken with some of the other couples we had met there as to who, if any of us, were going to visit the nude beach. Everyone said they were too shy or embarrassed with the exception of one person, me! I told everyone since I had been going fully clothed to the outdoor bar on the nude beach all week, I felt that at some point I should visit the nude beach in the buff so I wouldn't look like a hypocrite or weirdo.

So, late in the week while Elizabeth took a nap, I stripped down to my sandals and walked out from my hotel room and made my way down to the nude beach. It wasn't very crowded, so I just picked out a lounge chair and sat down. I lay there about fifteen minutes and soon became very hot so I decided I would take a refreshing dip in the nude pool, which was just adjacent to the nude beach.

As I walked toward the pool, I could see there were some nude men and women already at the pool. I dove into the pool, and its cool refreshing water felt great. I swam around for a while trying not to stare at the nude women who were lounging around the pool. After a while, I finally decided to end my swim and head back to my room.

As I was getting out of the pool, I saw an outdoor showerhead at the other end and decided I would rinse off under it. Just as I started toward the shower, a gorgeous, nude woman appeared, just beating me to the showerhead. We made eye contact and smiled to one another as she began to rinse off her glistening, tan body. As I did I continued to stand several feet away taking in every inch of her nude loveliness. She finally finished and turned to walk away, and as she did I watched as some beads of water on her bronze butt seemed to sparkle like diamonds in the late afternoon sun.

Our glorious week in Jamaica was coming to an end but not before one final adventure. I had become friendly with a young Jamaican named Luke who worked around the resort. He asked me one day if I wanted to rent some motorcycles and take a trip up into the hills. Elizabeth and I thought about it and decided to make that our last day's activity.

We met Luke near our hotel's entrance and walked a short distance to a stand on the side of the road where we could rent motorcycles. I rented one for Elizabeth and myself and one for Luke. Once we got the bikes, Luke suggested we drive toward his hometown of Lucea. We had passed Lucea on the way to our hotel, and I didn't think it was that far away. So we headed out on the two-lane road with sunshine above us, the blue Caribbean Sea just off to our left, and the lush, blue-green foliage of the Jamaican Blue Mountains to our right.

Our first stop was at a corrugated tin shack, which sat atop a mound of ground, within spitting distance of the Caribbean Sea. Luke told us this was his uncle's home. We walked into the yard and saw several goats and chickens mulling about. A man emerged from the shack and greeted us with a warm smile. Luke introduced us to his Uncle Richard.

"Welcome, would ja like to come inside mon?" Richard asked us.

"Sure," I relied.

The home was very small, made of tin with some wood planking used for main beams. We walked through the home and came out the back door. The backyard looked directly out over the sea. It was a beautiful view so I decided it might be a nice place to smoke a spliff. I asked Luke if it would be OK to smoke there. He told me he didn't smoke but that his uncle did so if we wanted to, it would be no problem. We lit up the spliff and shared it with our host.

When we were done, Luke announced that our next stop would be an old Spanish fort, which was well off the beaten path. We hopped onto our bikes and took off. Luke's uncle, who had his own bike, joined us. After about a fifteen-minute ride, we pulled off the main road and went down what seemed to be an alley. For a brief moment, the thought crossed my mind that if something bad was going to happen to us this would be the place. But that thought quickly disappeared as Luke snaked his way through an opening in a concrete wall. We followed and found ourselves in the overgrown courtyard of an eighteenth-century Spanish fort.

We got off our motorcycles and walked around the courtyard. Luke led us up a staircase, which brought us to the second-floor level. Rusted, Spanish-made canons still stood guard at the mouth of the bay. I stood there contemplating what it must have been like in Jamaica two-hundred years ago, a time in which the Spanish battled the English for control of the island, while the poor original inhabitants, the Arawak Indians, were all but being obliterated from it.

We took some pictures of the garrison and then got back onto our bikes. Luke told us he was going to take us up into the hills next, and off we went. We drove for quite a while before turning off the main road and then followed a twisty, turning road, which brought us higher and higher up the side of a Jamaican Blue Mountain. As we made our way around a blind corner, I saw just ahead that our guide Luke had pulled over to the side of the road and was conversing with a small group of young Jamaican boys. As I pulled up, Luke walked toward me and asked if we wanted to go swimming.

"Where?" I asked.

Luke pointed down the hill from our position on the road, and as I looked I could see a small waterfall, which emptied into a pond.

"Is it safe?" I asked.

"Ya, mon," Luke answered. "Besides, mon, dem boys will be ja lifeguards mon."

As Luke said that, one of the boys picked up a bamboo pole, which had to be twenty feet long. He walked to the edge of the pond, which I was to swim in, and sunk the entire length of the pole down into the blue-green water.

"NO BOTTOM, MON," the boy yelled to us as he began laughing.

"Der's a little cave, mon, just under and beyond da waterfall," Luke continued. "You should jump into da pool and swim to it, mon. Da boys day help you, mon."

I turned toward Elizabeth and asked her if she wanted to swim.

"No way!" was her instant reply.

Although this scenario had all of the elements of a honeymoon tragedy, I decided to be adventurous and go for a swim. I stripped down to my underwear and moved toward the pond. The Jamaican boys were hot dogging it up by leaping off of some surrounding trees and earth mounds into the deep pool of water, which stood at the bottom of the approximately fifteen-foot waterfall. They motioned for me to join them, and I did by doing a belly flop into the pond.

The water was cold and I could feel a strong current running away from the waterfall's showering stream. One of the Jamaican boys, who was by my side in the water, motioned for me to follow him as he began to swim toward the falls. I watched as he swam into the shower and then disappeared. However, if I looked closely, I could see him slightly up, out of the water waving to me from behind the waterfall's stream.

I decided to go for it and began swimming against the current toward the cave behind the falls. I reached the shower and could hear the encouragement from the Jamaican boy who had showed me the way. Once I was past the shower, I reached for his hand and he pulled me toward his position on a little rock ledge, which was directly behind the cascading water. Once I was sitting on the ledge, I looked out through the shower and saw Elizabeth and Luke standing at the pond's edge. Elizabeth was pointing our camera in my direction.

"THIS IS PRETTY NEAT," I shouted to my Jamaican lifeguard as he acknowledged me with a wide smile.

Several minutes later, I dropped back into the water and swam back out toward the falling water. It was easier going in this direction as I was now flowing with the current. I made it to the pond's edge and lifted myself out of the water and then made my way back to Luke and Elizabeth near the edge of the road.

As I was putting my clothes back on, the Jamaican boys started to make their way toward us.

"Now, mon, you haf to pay da life guards," Luke said.

"How much?" I asked.

"Up to you, mon," Luke answered as he shrugged his shoulders.

Elizabeth reached into her pocket and gave me a bunch of Jamaican bills. I counted out about the Jamaican equivalent of ten U.S. dollars and handed it to the boy who had been with me in the water.

"You share," I said.

Then Luke, in a somewhat worried tone of voice said, "Let's go, mon!"

As Elizabeth and I were getting on our motorcycle, I could hear the Jamaican boys arguing as to how my tip money should be divided amongst them. Suddenly my attention was diverted as another Jamaican boy came out of the bush. He had one eye and was drooling from the mouth. In his hand, he had a clump of wild, psilocybin mushrooms, which I think he intended to try to sell to me. Luke quickly drove up and wedged his motorcycle between the mushroom boy and us and then told us, in no uncertain terms, to get going. I obeyed Luke by gunning the bike and heading up the road.

Several minutes later, we finally reached the top of the mountain and began a slow, winding descent down toward the sea. Elizabeth and I had already been out in the Jamaican sun for five or six hours by now so when we reached the main road, we told Luke we were tired and ready to make the long trip back to our hotel. He smiled at us and turned his bike in the direction of our hotel.

As we headed back, Elizabeth complained of the pain that her sunburn was causing her. I reassured her we would be back at our hotel soon, but at one point I decided to pull over with Luke at a roadside bar just to get us out of the sun for a while and to have a quick Red Stripe beer.

After our beer, we got back on the bike, and I told Elizabeth we wouldn't stop again until we were at the hotel. With that, I hit the gas and off we went. About an hour and a half later, we arrived, lobster red, at the gates of our hotel. We said our good-byes to Luke and went into the resort and made our way to our room. Elizabeth collapsed in our bed for a nap while I went to find something cold to drink.

We promised each other the following day, as we made our way back to Montego Bay and our flight home, which would bring us back to reality, that we would come back to Jamaica in five or ten years to celebrate our wedding anniversary.

Once we got home, it was back to the grind. I decided that once the school year came to an end, I was not going to return to the school I was teaching at. My decision was primarily based on my very low salary. Elizabeth, on the other hand, was set, as she had recently received a promotion with her employer and a very substantial salary increase.

43 BAD LUCK COMES CALLING

The school year finally ended, and once again I was in the job search mode. I spent the summer sending out resumes and filling out applications. I decided I would look for a teaching position for the following year in the suburbs of Chicago, so I targeted school districts primarily in the north and northwestern suburbs.

The summer was quickly passing, and with September looming, I did not have a job offer even though I had had a number of interviews. I was really depressed and didn't know what I would do if I couldn't get under contract with a school for the next year when, one Friday morning, I received a call.

"Hello, my name is Terry Adams," the voice on the end of the line stated. "Is this Greg?"

"Yes, it is."

"I am the principal of Marian Central High School and I am calling in regards to the social studies position you applied for."

As those words rolled off of his tongue, I thought, Marian Central, did I apply there!?

"Yes, I remember," I replied to Mr. Adams.

"Well, I'd like to have you come out to the school for an interview. When would be a good time for that?"

"Any day next week."

"Alright then, how about Monday at ten in the morning?"

"Ten Monday morning sounds good."

"Great, I'll see you then."

"Agh, Mr. Adams, could you give the school's address?"

"Sure, our address is 120 West Main, Woodstock, Illinois."

"Got it, thank you, I'll see you on Monday."

"Sounds good, good bye now."

"Good bye."

As I drove out to the school on Monday I realized that Woodstock, Illinois, was really, really far away from my apartment in the city. After driving away from the city for about forty-five minutes, I exited onto a rural road and drove north toward Wisconsin. The landscape surrounding this road consisted primarily of dairy and horse farms. I was now in McHenry County, which was still pretty rural although I would find out later it was considered the fastest growing county in Illinois at the time.

Some thirty minutes later, I arrived at the school, a long two-story structure located on the outskirts of Woodstock. As I pulled into the parking lot, I thought that this school was way too far away for me to ever teach at. However, since I had made the trip out here I might as well go through with the interview. I slowly, reluctantly got out of my truck knowing I would never work here but reminding myself that I needed the interview for experience.

I walked into the deserted school and into the main office. After introducing myself to the receptionist, I sat down to wait to meet the school's principal. After about ten minutes, Mr. Adams appeared from his office and greeted me. Mr. Adams was in his early to mid-fifties, medium build and balding. He had bright green eyes and a friendly face. He escorted me into his office and asked if I would mind if the assistant principal, Mr. Burns, joined us.

"No, not at all," I said, thinking the more the merrier.

The interview was long and exhausting, but I felt I had left a very good impression of myself. Mr. Adams told me he was going to make a decision by the end of the week. I said my good-byes, and as I climbed back into my truck and pulled out of the parking lot I thought I would never see the school again.

The very next day, I was sitting around our apartment when the phone rang. It was Mr. Adams. He told me he wanted to offer me a teaching position for the coming year. I almost fell out of my chair! I didn't think a decision would be reached so soon. Having received so many rejections, I was shocked that somebody actually wanted me. I told Mr. Adams I needed some time to think about his offer. I told him I would call him the next morning with my answer.

I hung up and quickly called Elizabeth at work.

"Hey, I just got a call from the principal at Marion Central and he offered me that teaching position," I proudly announced.

"Did you tell him yes?"

"I told him I'd consider his offer."

"Call him back," she said. "This could be the break that you need."

"Yeah maybe, but this commute is going to be hell," I responded.

"Well, maybe we can move out closer to Woodstock. Think of the experience you can get," Elizabeth persisted.

I knew in my heart she was right, but I didn't want to admit it. I eventually agreed with her, and after our conversation I called Mr. Adams back and told him I would accept his offer. I drove to Woodstock the next day and signed a contract for the upcoming school year.

The students I encountered at Marian were very different than the students I taught at my previous school. My students the previous year were mostly Hispanic or black and usually from a lower income household. At Marian, almost all of my students were white and from middle to upper-income families. This didn't make teaching any easier or harder, just different. Because I was from Chicago, my students at Marian looked at me as an outsider. Throughout my tenure there, I sometimes shared with my students tales of my ill-spent days as a youth roaming the streets of Chicago with my two best pals, Billy and Will. The students were usually enthralled to hear about my youthful escapades as they were growing up in a completely different social environment - one that was more protected and isolated.

During my first year at Marian, I taught a government class to seniors, a combined psychology/sociology class to juniors, and a world cultures class comprised of all grade levels. In addition, I was the head coach of the boys' sophomore basketball team during the winter and an assistant coach to the boys and girls track teams in the spring.

Classes began at eight o'clock so in order to be at school on time, I woke up at five forty-five and was on the road by six-thirty. If the weather was bad, I had to leave earlier. During my first year, I put about twenty-thousand miles on my truck in nine months! Since I was using textbooks that were new to me, I had to read and write lesson plans almost daily. By the middle of the school year, I was constantly reminding myself that next year would be a lot easier since I had done most of the ground work during my first year.

* * * *

I was shaken out of the post-Christmas doldrums when I received some wonderful news. One morning Elizabeth announced she was pregnant, and our hearts soared with anticipation of a baby. Since the commute from Chicago was already getting to me and now thinking about having a baby around, I decided I really wanted to cut down on my commute by moving closer to Woodstock.

Knowing that in the spring I would probably be offered another contract to teach at Marian, I began working on Elizabeth to persuade her to move a little closer. We went apartment shopping one weekend in the suburbs and found a nice, large, modern one in Mt. Prospect, a northwest suburb of Chicago about halfway between where we currently lived and Woodstock. We signed a lease for the apartment, and on May first we moved from Chicago to Mt. Prospect. It was hard to move out of the city having spent my entire life there but I knew it was the right thing to do given the current situation.

Shortly after moving, I had arthroscopic surgery on my right knee, which had been diagnosed with torn cartilage and was getting progressively worse and more painful as time went by. I scheduled my surgery for a Friday so I could take the weekend to recover.

Elizabeth accompanied me to the hospital, and I was admitted and prepped for the surgery. The actual surgery took less than an hour The worst part was coming out of the anesthesia. I finally came to in the recovery room feeling very weak and woozy and in the presence of a nurse and Elizabeth.

"Now it's time to practice walking with crutches," the nurse told me in a way-too-cheery voice.

In my sorry condition, getting up and trying to maneuver on crutches was the last thing I wanted to attempt.

"I feel kinda nauseous," I announced.

"Here, try drinking some of this. It should help your nausea," the nurse said as she offered me some ginger ale.

I took a sip, and she asked me to try to stand up again. I pulled myself up and immediately felt as if the room was spinning. I must have lurched forward because both Elizabeth and the nurse reached out to catch me. They guided me back to my seat and once seated, I began to vomit into a small bucket by my chair.

After the vomiting session, I felt somewhat better. The nursed asked me if I was up for trying it again, and I told her I was. This time I felt much better when I got to my feet, although I was still a little wobbly. I wondered why it wasn't the hospital's policy to have patients practice walking with crutches before their surgery rather than afterwards when they are physically and somewhat mentally debilitated. I practiced with the crutches for several minutes, and then it was time to go home.

I was wheeled downstairs to an exit, and Elizabeth brought the car around. With her help I crawled out of the wheelchair and plopped myself into the back seat. The ride home was an adventure as my stomach did flip-flops all the way. Once at our apartment complex, I utilized my newly developed crutch-walking skills to get myself upstairs to our apartment. Once inside, I sat myself down on our bed, exhausted.

This was the weekend of the infamous Clarence Thomas/Anita Hill Senate investigation, so at least I had some interesting television to watch. A bit later Elizabeth cooked up some cheeseburgers with grilled onions. As I devoured them in bed, I thought that surely they were the greatest burgers I had ever had and Elizabeth was the best cook in the land.

The following day, Elizabeth had an appointment with her doctor. She left early that morning, and I stayed in bed reading the paper and watching television. Around eleven o'clock I heard Elizabeth enter the front door of our apartment.

"Elizabeth," I called out but she didn't respond.

I listened closely and thought I heard sobbing coming from the hallway outside our bedroom door. I called out her name again and still no response. I heard our bathroom door shut and knew for sure that she was home.

I struggled to get up and out of bed and finally managed to get myself up on my crutches. I made it to our bedroom door but began to get dizzy and light headed so I decided to lie back down. Once back in bed I lay there boiling over with frustration.

"ELIZABETH!" I yelled out.

WHAT!? she answered through the bathroom door.

"Are you alright?" I asked.

"Just peachy," she answered.

I could tell now that she was definitely crying.

"Could you please come in here?" I asked.

"JUST LEAVE ME ALONE!" she shouted through the bathroom door.

"Elizabeth, please come here and tell me what's wrong," I begged.

I heard the bathroom door open and through the bedroom doorway could see Elizabeth walking down the hallway toward me. Her eyes were red and swollen from crying and she held a tissue in her right hand as she still had tears streaming from her eyes.

"What is it?" I asked gently as she made her way into our bedroom.

"It's gone," she blurted, her voice cracking with emotion.

"Gone?"

"The baby, it never developed. I'm not pregnant anymore. The sack is there but the embryo never developed. Now I need a D and C to clean everything out. I'm never going to get pregnant," she explained as she began to sob uncontrollably.

Elizabeth sat down at the edge of the bed, and I sat up and wrapped her in my arms. I don't think at any time in my life I had ever felt so helpless. I knew there was nothing I could do except offer her support, which I tried my best to do.

"We're young. We can try again," I meekly suggested.

"Not for six weeks after the D and C," she blurted.

"That's OK," I said. "We'll still be young in six weeks," I added trying to lighten up the situation.

We sat quietly for about ten minutes as Elizabeth sobbed on my shoulder. I sat there wishing there were something I could do, anything to change the bad news we had just received. Elizabeth's crying finally subsided, and she left my side to call her mom and let her in on the bad news.

I went along with Elizabeth the day she had the D and C procedure. To my surprise Elizabeth's mom also joined us at the hospital. She and I waited for about an hour or so and then we were allowed to see Elizabeth in the recovery room. As soon as the anesthesia wore off, Elizabeth was allowed to go home, seemingly no worse for the wear.

* * * *

The school year was coming to a close, and all in all my first year at Marian had been a success. My sophomore basketball team hadn't had much luck. I caught some parental grief for it, but otherwise I couldn't complain. I was offered a contract for the following year, which I accepted. As the school year came to an end, I looked forward to relaxing and not driving anywhere for a couple of months. I thought that maybe after a week or so I might get bored and then want to find a part-time job but that idea vanished on the Fourth of July.

Elizabeth and I had been invited to Brian Murphy's house for a Fourth of July cookout. It was a pretty small group of our friends, really just a handful of my good buddies whom I had known since grade school.

We drank and socialized, and after a while someone suggested we play a pick-up game of basketball, just like we used to do in the schoolyard. We walked out to the front of Brian's house where he had set-up his portable hoop on the curb of the cul-de-sac. We chose sides and began to play in the hot, July sun.

Bob Garcia, who was on the other team, got the ball at one point and started to drive toward the basket. I left the man I had been guarding and moved toward Bob. I anticipated his lay-up move, so I jumped with all my strength to be able to block his shot when he began to go toward the basket. But instead of continuing with his move, Bob stopped short and ducked his body below me. As a result, I did a partial summersault in the air and ended up coming down hard, perpendicular to the ground, with my arms extended and the palms of my hands hitting the asphalt first while my feet were still high above my body.

I don't remember hearing a snap or crack at the time, although later several of my friends said they had and thought it was my head hitting the surface of the street. I ended up sprawled out on the ground with a deep aching sensation in both of my elbows. I struggled to get up. Once I had, I thought I could continue to play. However, when the ball was passed to me, I couldn't move my arms to catch it as my arms were in too much pain to even lift them above my waist. I complained out loud that I couldn't go on so my well-intentioned friends suggested I go out back and take a dip in Brian's pool. Their theory was that maybe the cool pool water would alleviate my pain.

I took their suggestion to heart and made my way to Brian's backyard. I gingerly lowered myself into the pool and the cool water did feel good on my arms; however, the pain did not dissipate very much. After a while I wanted to get out but realized I was now a prisoner of the pool as I could not lift myself out. Elizabeth got a couple of the guys to help me out.

"My imitation of a beached whale," I announced through clenched teeth as I was yanked out of the pool and ended up flopping onto the pool deck.

"What you need is some pain medicine," my good old buddy Billy announced.

Billy led me to a table and chair by the pool where I was given a very potent, very cold, summertime concoction. I drank it down with gusto and a bit later my elbows began to feel better. As I sat there getting drunk and feeling better, I began to recount the infamous St. Patrick's Day story, which involved a friend of ours by the name of Cary O'Connor and a party that occurred that evening.

On this particular St. Patrick's Day, one of my friends had a party, and it was pretty well attended. A snowstorm hit Chicago early that evening, so there was about six inches of snow on the ground by the time people started arriving. The party was in high gear when Cary O'Connor arrived around midnight. As he was walking up to the apartment building, he slipped and fell really hard on the sidewalk but managed to get up and limp into the party. As he limped into the party, everyone greeted him. He told them about his fall and how much his leg hurt.

Now two factors were working against Cary. First, we all knew him to be a great joker, so we didn't know whether to buy his story of his fall or not. Secondly, most of us were so buzzed we really weren't all that concerned with his injury so Cary settled down with us and began to party.

Every so often he would shout out something like, "I'M IN SO MUCH FUCKING PAIN. SOMEBODY TAKE ME TO A HOSPITAL!"

Everyone would laugh and somebody would hand him another beer, and he'd shut up for a while. This went on all night. When I left the party at around four in the morning, Cary was still lying on the couch in the living room drinking a beer.

About a week later, I heard from one of my friends what had happened to Cary. He ended up passing out on the couch. When he came to in the morning, now somewhat sober, he was in so much pain he asked someone to call him a cab to take him to the hospital. The party's host called Cary a cab, which he took straight to a local hospital. His leg was x-rayed, and doctors determined that it was in fact broken!

"That's a great story, Double G!" Billy's wife, Holly, remarked.

Soon others were reminiscing about some of our other youthful misadventures. Finally after several hours, Elizabeth decided it was time to go. By this time I was figuratively and literally feeling no pain. As we drove home in the darkness, we could see on the horizon bits and pieces of firework shows, which various towns were putting on in honor of the Fourth.

"I think I'm going to throw up!" I announced to Elizabeth about halfway home.

"Oh wonderful," she said as she pulled the car over.

"I caaaan't opeeeen da door," I announced glumly as I realized it hurt too much to try to raise my arms and pull the car door latch open.

Elizabeth got out of the car and came around the other side to open my door. I hung my head out and did my business. Finished, I leaned back in and Elizabeth had to slam the door shut as I wasn't able to. We drove the rest of the way without incident. I somehow managed to make it up to our apartment and our bedroom to pass out. I began to snore loudly so Elizabeth decided to sleep on the couch in the living room.

At approximately three-thirty in the morning I woke up with excruciating pain in both elbows.

"ELIZABETH!" I screamed out.

"WHAAAAT?" She yelled back in a sleepy voice.

"I need to go to the emergency room," I announced.

"We'll go in the morning," Elizabeth answered.

"I NEED TO GO NOW. CALL ME A CAB, PLEASE!" I screamed in a voice that shook the walls of our apartment.

I was pulling a Cary O'Connor!

Realizing the seriousness in my voice, Elizabeth made her way into the bedroom.

"I'm sorry I yelled, but I'm in some serious pain. The booze has obviously worn off, and I need something for the pain. It's incredible," I said to her through the darkness of our room.

"OK," she said. "I'll take you, but first you need to get dressed."

"No way," I said. "I'll go to the hospital without a shirt on."

I couldn't imagine the pain I would have had to endure just to get a shirt over my head and arms.

"You mean you're going to go there in just your flip flops and gym shorts?" Elizabeth asked.

"That's right," I answered, wincing as I managed to get myself up off of the bed.

We made our way to the car, me grimacing in intense pain with every step. I gingerly got into the car, and we drove the short distance to the hospital. Once there we made our way to the emergency room. I explained what had happened to me and was told the first thing that had to be done was an x-ray of both of my elbows.

"Could I have something for the pain first?" I asked.

I was told I would have to first endure the x-rays before they would give me any pain medication. I nodded my tired head in understanding and was led down a long hallway and into an x-ray room.

The x-ray technician came in and began manipulating my arms to get them in the proper position to take the x-ray. Later on Elizabeth told me that as I was being x-rayed she could hear my screaming in the waiting area, which was quite a distance from the x-ray room. Once the x-ray torture session was over, I was led into an examining room to await the results.

A short, agonizing bit of time passed before a nurse appeared and announced she wanted to give me a shot in my butt for the pain. I was never so happy to get a shot in my life. Before the nurse could even leave the room I began to feel the narcotic effect of the shot as it worked its way over my body, like an ocean wave crashing upon the shore and running up and onto a sandy beach. As the excruciating pain began to subside, I smiled and thought, now that's more like it.

A little bit later an emergency room doctor paid me a visit and told me the results of the x-rays.

"It seems you have, on each arm, identical fractures at the elbow. What I would like to do is to place each arm in a half cast and have you come back this morning to see our orthopedic specialist."

Wonderful, I thought.

After having the half casts applied, Elizabeth and I got up to leave the hospital, me in my flip-flops, shorts and each arm wrapped in a half cast, which forced me to have my arms positioned out in front of my body. I look like a goddamn Beach Boy Frankenstein, I thought. As we were leaving the ER waiting area, I noticed the wide-eyed glances from several of the people sitting there. I chuckled out loud and thought, thank god for that pain shot.

Later the same morning, I went back to the hospital and was examined by a wise-cracking orthopedic specialist.

"Here's another piece of evidence on how dangerous it is to be a weekend warrior," he announced to an intern at his side as he began his exam of me. He tested my range of motion and asked about my pain.

"Well, there're basically two ways that we can go," he began. "One route would be to place your arms in casts for about six weeks and keep them totally immobilized. The downside is that the arms may become so atrophied that at the end of the six weeks, you'll have to go to physical therapy just to get the use of your arms back. The other approach would be to have you use your half casts whenever you are going out of the home but to try and keep them off when you are at home. Now with this approach, since you're not completely immobilizing your arms I think that your recovery would be much sooner. However, since we are not immobilizing the arms all of the time, you will experience much more pain. The good news there is that I can continue giving you some pain medication for a while."

In my mind it seemed a no-brainer, the second route was the one for me. Elizabeth and I left the hospital and on our way, stopped at a pharmacy to pick up some pain medication. For the next four or five days I remained pretty much helpless. Elizabeth had to do, or help me to do everything. From getting out of bed in the morning to brushing my teeth at night and everything in between, if you know what I mean!

My friends who had been there on the Fourth couldn't believe it when I told them of my injury. Our Sullivan friend, Rick Ochek was to have his annual Christmas in July party in a couple of weeks, so I promised everyone

I would be there. I arrived at Rick's party with both of my arms in a half cast. Rick, ever the planner, had bought me one of those beer-drinking hard hats that allows you to perch two beers on top of your hat and sip the beers through the two siphon tubes that run down into your mouth. After drinking a couple of beers and rehashing the Fourth of July incident with everyone, Elizabeth and I left the party.

I spent the next four weeks or so laying low and recuperating from my injuries. I didn't drive for about three weeks and didn't attempt to golf at all that summer. I became pretty adept at opening doors and drawers with my feet. Fortunately for me, our apartment complex had a pool just outside our door. I spent most days lounging around it and sometimes I would get in it and try to do some exercises to strengthen my arms.

The summer definitely hadn't turned out the way I planned, but I just had to make the best of it. Of course there were days when I got down and felt sorry for myself, but Elizabeth was always there to pick me up and right my skewed perspective.

At the beginning of August, I received a letter from Marian High School regarding the beginning of the school year and when the teachers were scheduled to report. I actually was kind of excited thinking about the upcoming school year. At least it wouldn't be as boring as my apartment had become during the summer.

By the time classes began in September, my arms were in pretty good shape. My left elbow had very little pain, and its flexibility was very good. My right arm, which I had been using more of since the accident, still caused me some discomfort and could not be straightened out completely. Two conditions that, unfortunately, I still have to this very day.

But the anticipation of a new school year was upon me, and as I thought about it, I felt that my second year of teaching in Woodstock should be easier and more enjoyable. I had done lesson outlines for each of my classes for an entire year the previous year and my commute would be shorter since I had moved a little closer to Woodstock.

But what I hadn't thought about but began to about mid-school year, was that if our goals of buying a house and starting a family in the next couple of years were to become a reality, I would eventually be forced to leave Marian as my salary there wasn't enough to support a family.

As the year progressed, I grew wearier of teaching. My basketball team had a terrible season again, and my classes, especially my senior-level government class, which was my last class of the day, was a nightmare full of smart asses and malcontents.

In May, I was offered a contract for the following year but respectfully turned it down. I explained to my principal I felt that for myself and my future family I needed to find a better paying position. He told me he fully understood and offered to write me a very glowing letter of recommendation, which he did.

I said my good-byes in June. I could actually feel that some of my students, who had anticipated having me for classes the next fall, were truly disappointed when they heard I wouldn't be returning. I pulled out of the Marian parking lot for the last time on a hot June afternoon. I will really miss some of the good people I had worked with here, I thought, but I was also glad I wouldn't have to make that long, daily commute anymore.

Another long, hot summer lie ahead, and I was determined to figure out my next step in life. I spent the next couple of weeks researching and formulating a plan for the immediate future. I would still try to get a better paying teaching position in the suburbs, but I also thought I needed an alternative plan. The area that attracted me was human resources, so I began to look around and see what kind of human resource training was available.

44 BACK TO THE DRAWING BOARD

I woke up early one morning that summer, and after Elizabeth went to work, I was left in the quiet of our apartment to contemplate my next career move. I decided first and foremost I needed to bring in some income so I looked up a temp agency in our local phone book and made arrangements to visit them.

Once there, I was told that a disaster recovery service in the area had some long-term positions available. I told my interviewer I would be very interested in taking the position. I was given directions on how to get there and drove over that afternoon. The general manager and his assistant interviewed me and hired me on the spot. My job entailed running a film-cleaning machine. I ran spools of eight-millimeter film through the machine in an attempt to clean and revitalize them as the film had either suffered water or smoke damage during a fire.

I also explored the possibility of returning to school. Even though I had applied to a number of school districts once the summer began, it didn't look as if I'd be putting my teaching certificate to use any time soon. I finally decided to attend Roosevelt University's paralegal program with an emphasis on employee benefits, an idea I had originally hatched when I was working for the Michigan Avenue law firm.

I thought this would allow me to get a good introduction to employee benefit plans, which would also lend itself in helping me find a position in the human resources field. I also liked the field of law and thought that side of it would be interesting as well.

The program was nine months in duration and cost four-thousand dollars. I sensed Elizabeth wasn't thrilled with the idea when I told her, but she bit her tongue and give me her support. My classes were held on Tuesdays and Thursdays from six-thirty to nine and on Saturdays from eight-thirty to one. So I would work until three-thirty at my temp job, come home and shower, and then drive to the L station near our apartment. I would park my truck and catch an L train for the thirty-minute ride to the loop, located in the heart of downtown Chicago.

It was a hectic schedule but one I felt I would benefit from in the long run. About four months into my school year, we found out Elizabeth was pregnant once again. The baby was due in August of the following year. We prayed that everything would work out fine this time.

Elizabeth's doctor gave us a due date of August twenty-ninth, which happened to be the day of the famed Arlington Million horse race held annually at Arlington Park just outside of Chicago. It had been our tradition for the past four or five years to get a bunch of our friends together and go to the track for the races that day. When Elizabeth first told me the due date, I realized instantly it was the day of the Million.

"Maybe we should name the baby Arlington in honor of the race," I jokingly said to Elizabeth. "Maybe the middle name but not the first," she replied with a chuckle.

As the months rolled by, Elizabeth got bigger and bigger. We were both getting very excited at the prospects of becoming parents; however, I had a very practical problem that had to be addressed, namely finding a permanent, full-time job.

Fall became winter and winter became spring and as my tenure at Roosevelt University was about to end, summer began. A classmate who was an assistant vice president at First Chicago Bank, mentioned that the branch she worked at was looking for some full-time, temporary employees to do top-heavy testing on bank clients' retirement plans - a skill I had learned at Roosevelt!

I got an interview with one of the branch's vice presidents and the man I would directly report to. The interview went well. When we started talking compensation, I almost fell out of my chair when they announced they thought twenty dollars an hour would be a fair wage. Elizabeth and I went from a situation of financial struggles to relative prosperity overnight. It was really nice, even if it was only temporary. I couldn't have fallen into a better situation.

It was also at this time, while attending a barbeque at Billy's house, that Billy and Holly asked me to be the godfather to Melissa, their beautiful daughter who had been born several months earlier.

"Of course I will," I told them as I lifted up my beer bottle and clanked it against Billy's.

"Honey, I'm da godfather now so don't mess with me or you'll know what will happen," I said as I pointed a finger at Elizabeth.

She promptly responded by flipping me the bird.

"Who better to be beautiful Melissa's godfather than a former seminarian. Right, Billy!?"

"You got it, Double G."

"Oh paleeeeeze!" was Elizabeth's editorial comment.

45 ROTISSERIE BASEBALL

So I became the godfather, as I started a new temporary job, all the while preparing for our own child to arrive. If that wasn't enough to keep me busy, I also had my Rotisserie Baseball league to concentrate on.

That year we held our annual drafting of players at Mike Murphy's place. Every year the draft consisted of drinking, bull shitting about everything under the sun, and selecting the major league baseball players whose real stats would determine our individual team's success over the course of the baseball season. We each paid a hundred-dollar entry fee and throughout the year put more money into the pot every time we made a trade or picked up a player. The top four teams at the end of the baseball season would divide up the pot accordingly: first place seventy percent, second place fifteen percent, third place ten percent, and fourth place five percent. This usually meant the only person to really win any money was the first place guy, but at least the other three guys could brag that they got something back. The remaining guys were shit out of luck.

After the initial draft, we met once a month with each league member taking a turn hosting a monthly meeting. When my turn rolled around, I planned the meeting for a Saturday night when Elizabeth was out visiting her mom and therefore not at the apartment. After everyone arrived, I broke out some munchies and we drank some beers and talked about the league and everything else that was on our minds. This went on for several hours.

Later in the evening after the official meeting ended, some of the guys started to leave. Billy, Brian Murphy, Sean O'Reilly, and I were the last four guys in my apartment. All of a sudden Billy started a rant about how he felt Sean had been cheating us by colluding with Rich, who was a guy Brian Murphy worked with.

"The trades you're making don't make sense. I think you and Rich are colluding in order to let Rich win the league. He'll probably end up splitting the winner's share with you," Billy announced angrily.

"What the hell are you talking about?" Sean argued. "There's no way in hell I would ever do that."

"Dude, you're fuckin' trading good players for shit players to that guy," Billy responded. "You're either a dumb fuck or a cheater."

"I'M NEITHER!" Sean shouted back at Billy.

Suddenly, Billy jumped out of the easy chair he was in and lunged toward Sean. Billy threw a left hook that caught Sean square on his jaw and knocked him out of his chair. Brian and I jumped up instantly and grabbed a hold of Billy.

"YOU HAVE A PROBLEM, MAN!" Sean yelled at Billy as he got up and wiped away the tears that were welling up in his eyes.

With that said, Sean walked to the front door of my apartment and let himself out. Brian and I let go of Billy, glanced at each other, and shook our heads.

"Dude, what the fuck was that all about?" I asked Billy.

"The guy's a fuckin' cheat," Billy replied. "I've been tracking all of his trades this year, and either he is a complete idiot or he is in collusion with the other dude. And I think it's collusion."

"That still doesn't give you the right to punch him," Brian said.

"Yeah, man, we're not kids. We're grown men. We can't have guys afraid to come to meetings because someone is going to punch their lights out," I added.

"FUCK HIM. HE'S A CHEAT!" Billy reiterated as he sat down in the easy chair.

"Billy, this is serious shit," I said. "I feel obligated, and I'm sure Brian agrees, that we now need to bring this incident to the attention of the entire league and see what we want to do."

"Absolutely!" Brian chimed in.

"Hey, you guys do what you have to do. As commissioner I'm not going to let a guy get away with cheating," Billy answered.

"Dude, let's say he is cheating. Is punching him in the face the best way to deal with it?" I asked Billy as I stared directly at him.

"You have your ways, and I have mine," Billy said as he began to stand up. "Well, I'm out of here, gents," he then announced. Billy then walked to the apartment door and let himself out.

"What the fuck!" Brian said looking at me in disbelief.

"I don't know, man," I shot back as I shook my head. "All I know is when the other guys hear about this they're gonna say kick Billy's ass out of the league!"

"I know, and I feel the same way," Brian replied. "There is no place for violence in a Rotisserie baseball league. This is supposed to be fun. And this fucking guy is taking it way too seriously."

My mind began to race at the thought of my best friend being kicked out of the league he started.

"Maybe I can talk to Billy and get him to apologize to Sean at the next meeting and promise all of us that he'll never to do it again," I said knowing that if we kicked Billy out of the league, it would crush him.

"You think the guys would let him stay in the league if he apologized?" I quickly added.

"I don't know, but it would be worth a try," Brian answered.

Just at that moment my apartment's door buzzer rang.

"Who the fuck is that?" I asked out loud as I made my way over to the apartment's intercom system.

"Who is it?" I asked into the wall-mounted speaker.

"It's Billy."

I pressed my security door's buzzer to let Billy in, and as I did Brian let out a laugh and said, "What's he gonna do now, punch one of us?"

"Right!" I shot back smiling at Brian and walking over to the apartment's front door. I opened it and saw Billy walking up the stairwell.

"I forgot something," Billy announced as he arrived on my landing.

Billy walked into the apartment, went over to the easy chair he had been sitting in, and reaching underneath it pulled out a very small tape recorder, which was still recording.

"What the fuck, dude! You're fucking recording our meetings?" I asked.

"You never know who you can trust," Billy replied as he shrugged his shoulders and then proceeded to make his way to my apartment door, opened it, and let himself out.

"Can you fucking believe this guy?" Brian asked.

"Holy shit, this is crazy," I answered. "To secretly bring a tape recorder in here and tape us... I don't know what to make of it."

"Is he so paranoid that he needs to know what we're saying when he's in the john taking a leak?" Brian said as he let out a belly laugh.

"It appears that way, doesn't it?" I replied.

For about the next ten minutes Brian and I discussed what to do next. We agreed that all of the other members should be made aware of what had happened, including the hidden tape recorder. We also agreed we should suggest to all the members that everyone, besides Billy, arrive early to next month's meeting to discuss Billy's fate. With that decided, Brian took off and I was left alone in the silence of my apartment to reflect on the bizarre events of the evening.

* * * *

I reached out to Billy about a week later and told him I thought if he would agree to apologize to Sean and promise to never do something like that again and to never bring a tape recorder to our meetings most of the members would vote to let him stay in the league. Billy said he would think about it.

The month passed by quickly and then it was time to meet at Brian Murphy's place for our next league meeting. Everyone but Billy arrived about a half hour early to discuss Billy's actions at the last meeting and what, if anything, should be done about it. We went back and forth between reasons he should be kicked out of the league and reasons why he should not. I was hoping that if I could get Billy to apologize, the other members would allow him to remain in the league so that was the position I advocated during the discussion

252

After all, Billy was my best friend and the original founder of the league so I thought he deserved a second chance. Also by persuading the other guys to decide to allow him to stay in the league, I felt I would be going a long way in repaying my outstanding debt to Billy since I knew being the commissioner of our league was one of the things he really loved in life.

"You know we all have bad days," I said. "And remember if it wasn't for Billy, we really wouldn't have a league since he was the guy who originally organized it. Now was what he did wrong? Absolutely! Is kicking him out of the league for this one-time offense justified? I'm not so sure."

"Hey, man, I just come here to have some fun, drink some beers, and talk a little baseball. I don't want to have to worry about some paranoid motherfucker going off on me because he thinks I'm cheating," Rich, Brian's work buddy, stated emphatically.

"Hey, I know where you're coming from, but I've known Billy for an awful long time and I think this was just a one-time event," I said trying to help Billy's cause. "Sean, you're the one who got punched. If Billy were to apologize to you today and promise to not do anything like that again, would you be cool with him staying in the league?"

"You know, I know Billy's had a rough time of it during his life and I know deep down he's not a bad guy. So if he can apologize, I can find it in my heart to forgive and move on," Sean answered.

"Alright, guys, you just heard it from the guy he punched. He's willing to let him stay if he shows remorse and apologizes. What do you guys say?" I asked as I began to look around the room staring at each member individually. With each set of eyes I met, I either heard an "OK" murmured or saw a head nod yes.

"Alright then," I said. "Let's do this. When Billy gets here, Brian and I will take him into the den and tell him that everyone is expecting an apology from him. Then when he is ready to apologize, we'll bring him in, get it done, and continue with the meeting. Sound good?" I asked.

"Yep."

"Sure."

"Sounds good," the various members replied.

I anxiously glanced out the window as we all waited for Billy to arrive. After about twenty minutes, I caught a glimpse of him walking down the street carrying a bright red pocket folder under his arm, the one he always brought to these meetings. The folder contained a detailed list of all of the league's transactions for the year as well as week-to-week standings for all teams. If Billy were to be kicked out today, his organizational skills would be sorely missed.

The doorbell rang and Brian went to the door to let Billy in. They exchanged pleasantries and then Billy made his way into the living room. He gave a general hello to everyone present and then looked at me. I chose this opportunity to approach him.

"Hey, man, how ya doing?" I asked.

"OK, I guess," Billy responded.

"Hey, before the meeting starts can Brian and I talk to you in the other room?"

"Sure."

Billy and I walked into Brian's den and were immediately joined by Brian who had seen us walk out of the living room.

"I know you have had some time to think about everything since we last talked. I think if you make an apology to Sean today, we can all move on, OK?" I said to Billy.

"There's only one problem," Billy blurted out.

"What's that?" I asked.

"I'm not fuckin' apologizing!"

"Listen. man, we all talked about this situation before you got here and everyone has agreed if you can just apologize and say it won't happen again, we can forget about it and have some fun, what da ya say?"

"I still think Sean is cheating so I'm not sorry I punched him, and I'm not going to apologize," Billy said matter-of-factly.

"Alright then let me tell you what will happen if you don't. We have discussed this, and if you can't find it in yourself to apologize then we all have agreed you cannot remain in the league. Now you don't want that to happen, do you, Billy?" I asked hoping he would see the desperation in my eyes.

"I know I don't want that to happen to you," I added quickly.

"So you fuckin' guys are going to kick out the guy who started this league over this one incident?" Billy asked incredulously.

"We don't consider this a minor incident," Brian blurted out. "We can't have guys afraid to come to meetings, bottom line."

The three of us stood there in silence for a moment. I was thinking real hard for the right thing to say to Billy, the one thing that would turn the light on in his head and maybe help him see the error of his ways. But I drew a blank.

"All right give me a minute. Let me go in the other room and talk to the other guys," I said, not really knowing why.

I left Billy and Brian in the den and walked into the living room. As I entered, I was greeted by many anxious faces.

"All right we talked to him, and he has decided he is not going to apologize," I announced.

"Then he's out!" Mike Murphy exclaimed.

"That's what we agreed to before he got here," Bob Garcia said as he stared straight at me.

I'm not sure if I was hoping the guys would suddenly have a change of heart since Billy was here or if I was just trying to put off the inevitable.

"Alright then, then I'll go tell him that's our final decision."

I headed back to the den, dreading what was going to happen next. Upon entering the den, I looked directly at Billy.

"Billy, I don't want to see you kicked out of this league, but it's gonna happen if you don't apologize. Are you willing to reconsider and apologize to Sean today?"

I was really hoping Billy would see that his tenure in the league was now hanging by a thread. I hadn't hoped for anything so badly since I had held Billy in my arms and hoped that he wouldn't die from being hit by the train.

"No, I'm not gonna fuckin' do it," was Billy's terse reply.

"Well then," I began slowly. "I'm sorry to inform you but you should now consider yourself no longer a part of this league," I said, not really sure where the words came from.

Billy stared me straight in the eyes and then shot a glance toward Brian.

"You're kicking out the guy who started this league, unfuckin' believable! If Will was here, he'd see it my way!"

Billy's remark stunned and hurt me, like a slap to the face on a cold, Chicago winter's day. I wasn't so sure if Will were here he'd see it Billy's way but thought that if Will were here he might be able to talk Billy into seeing it our way. Will was always better than me at everything. What did it matter, I thought? Will would never be here again. He was gone, gone for good, and Billy was about to be gone as well.

Billy proceeded to pick up his bright red pocket folder, which he had placed on Brian's desk, and then made his way toward the living room as Brian and I followed him. Billy didn't utter a word to anyone as he crossed the living room floor, heading toward the front door of the house. Once there, he opened the door and let himself out.

"Holy shit, what just happened?" Rich asked as Brian and I walked back into the living room.

"He wasn't gonna apologize so Double G told him he was out," Brian explained.

"I'm surprised he didn't punch you," Rich responded.

"He's like, I can't believe you're tossing out the guy who started the league," Brian continued.

"So we're supposed to let him punch guys and because he started the league not do anything about it?" Brian's brother Mike asked.

"Well, now we need someone to step up and be the league commissioner," I said in an attempt to change the subject.

My announcement was met with catcalls and guffaws.

We spent the next forty-five minutes figuring out who would take over as commish. It was finally determined the best person was Brian Murphy. With that bit of business out of the way, we continued with some other league business.

When that was done, we sat around bull shitting and talking about how crazy it was that Billy couldn't bring himself to apologize even when he knew that if he didn't, we were going to toss him out of the league.

I finally left the meeting and drove home, and as I did I replayed the entire conversation I had with Billy that day. I still found myself searching for that one right thing I could have said to Billy that would have turned the light on in his head and maybe helped him to see the error of his ways. When I arrived home I still had nothing.

At the end of the baseball season, I had the unenviable task of having to go to Billy's house to collect the entry fee money he had collected from everyone at the beginning of the year. To say he was cold and distant when I arrived that evening is putting it mildly. Instead of inviting me in, he had me wait on his front porch stoop while he went back inside his house to grab the cash.

When he came back out, he handed it to me without a word.

"Hey, Billy, I just want you to know I'm sorry that things turned out the way they did."

"Yeah, me too."

With that, Billy turned around, walked inside his house, and shut the door.

Sadly, after the Rotisserie Baseball incident, my relationship with Billy was never the same. I would still talk to him occasionally by phone, but he rarely made it to any of the old gang's social gatherings. He had become a stranger to me.

46 ME A DAD

As the days of the summer rolled on, Elizabeth grew bigger and more uncomfortable. August arrived in Chicago as it often does with very hot and humid weather. Elizabeth's summer routine was to come home from work, change into something a little more comfortable, and then plop herself down on our bed in the comfort of our air-conditioned bedroom.

Each evening she would religiously quaff down a huge, thick, rich, chocolate milkshake, which we later believed contributed to the high birth weight of the baby. We had gone to Lamaze classes to help us prepare for the birth experience, and now it was just a matter of waiting until the due date and hoping everything went well.

The due date was a Sunday, and as I mentioned earlier, it happened to coincide with the Arlington Million horse race, which Elizabeth and I attended every year. As things worked out, in addition to the Million, I also had a seven a.m. golf tee time that morning. As we went to bed that Saturday night, I asked Elizabeth how she felt.

"No different," she said. "Plan on going, I don't think the baby will be arriving tomorrow."

So I was ready to head out to the links during the early morning hours and then maybe, if Elizabeth was up for it, head out to the racetrack in the afternoon.

The following morning came, and it broke dark and dreary. I slowly got up out of bed to take a shower and to go play golf. Once out of the shower, I saw that Elizabeth was awake so I asked her how she was feeling.

"I think my water broke last night when I went to the bathroom," she announced.

"Oh, shit," I said, surprised at how calm she was. "Then don't we need to get you to the hospital?"

"No, why don't you go golfing and then come straight home and see how I am."

"No way, I'm not going anywhere!"

"Don't be silly," she continued. "Even if I was to go into labor, it could be hours before the baby comes."

As it turned out Elizabeth's statement was quite prophetic, but I couldn't see leaving her for five hours to go golfing knowing that at any moment she could go into active labor and need to be rushed to the hospital.

"I'll tell you what," I began, "I'll skip golf but I will run out to the track and make a couple of early-bird wagers on the Million and then when I come home, we'll see how you are doing. If you are feeling up to it, maybe we will go out to the track later this afternoon."

"That's fine," she answered.

I gathered up my racing form and left for the track. I made the fifteen-minute drive to the track to make my wagers, not really thinking about the horses but rather about the distinct possibility that I would become a father on this day. It was early, about eight-fifteen in the morning and only a handful of broken-down horseplayers were milling about the quiet, off-track betting parlor.

I quickly parked my truck and made my way inside. After placing my bets, I walked briskly back to my truck under grey, overcast skies and drove straight back to our apartment. The whole trip took about thirty-five minutes. As soon as I walked into our apartment, I knew my decision to not go golfing had been a wise one as I saw that Elizabeth was now in pain from some early contractions. Her labor had begun shortly after I had left for my short jaunt to the track. Attending the races that afternoon was now definitely out.

"We need to go to the hospital," Elizabeth said through clenched teeth as I entered the apartment.

Immediately my heart fluttered and began to race. This is it, I thought, the big day, I'm gonna be a father. I silently asked God to help us through it.

We gathered up everything we needed and made our way to Elizabeth's car. The hospital was only about fifteen minutes away, and as we drove I tried to get Elizabeth to work on some breathing techniques we had learned in Lamaze class; however, she didn't want any part of it.

"JUST GET ME THERE!" she shouted at me through her pain.

We arrived at the hospital around nine-thirty that morning and were admitted quickly. The hospital was very progressive and provided us not with a typical hospital room but rather a birthing suite. The birthing suite was kind of like a hotel suite with a birthing bed. In addition to the bed, there was a small couch, chair, coffee table, and last but not least, a large, colored, big screen television. It was the kind of setting where not only could you birth a baby, but also host a small cocktail party at the same time.

As we soon found out, the television became our best friend. A short time after our arrival in the birthing suite, the doctor examined Elizabeth. The doctor announced that Elizabeth was only dilated to about four centimeters with the dilation goal being between eight or ten before the baby was born. So we had a while to wait hence the invaluable TV in the room.

As we waited, we watched a full line-up of Sunday morning and afternoon TV. We watched an entire baseball game (Cubbies), an Indy car race, and our beloved Arlington Million (no winners). By mid-afternoon

Elizabeth, was dilated to about six or seven so the doctor told her to begin pushing with each contraction.

We worked on our breathing together, but as the pain intensified, our breathing together seemed to fall apart. Elizabeth complained that the pain was becoming unbearable so the doctor suggested an epidural. Elizabeth, who was trying to put on a brave front, initially rejected the suggestion but after another hour of intense contractions and pain, she asked for an epidural. The epidural seemed to relieve her pain on only one side of her body so after a while the doctor administered another so that her pain was reduced on both sides.

When we first arrived at the hospital, Elizabeth asked me to call her mom to let her know it looked like today was probably going to be the day. I did just that, and much to my surprise, her mother appeared on the scene about an hour later. I wasn't especially pleased to see her arrive, as I had imagined Elizabeth and I would be alone for the whole experience. But rather than cause a scene, I greeted her warmly and kept my mouth shut during the whole ordeal.

As early evening arrived, stories of twenty-four hour deliveries were bantered about the room. If that turned out to be the case, our baby wouldn't arrive until about ten tomorrow morning! Oh please, God, don't let that happen to my poor wife, I thought.

As the hours dragged on, the pushing, pain, and tension grew. Finally at about ten o'clock, after some thirteen hours of labor, the doctor told us that she would allow another hour of pushing, but after that we should opt for plan B, Caesarian section. The look on Elizabeth's face when she heard this news was one of disappointment rather than fear.

"I'm sorry," she said to me as the doctor left the room, her eyes welling with tears.

"It's not your fault. That baby is just stubborn," I said trying to make light of the situation.

"Just like his daddy," Elizabeth said through her tears.

An hour passed and no progress. A bit later, several nurses came into the suite to take Elizabeth to prepare her for the surgery.

"Everything is going to be fine," I said as I bent down and kissed her.

The nurses wheeled Elizabeth out of the suite and the remaining nurse led me from the suite to a waiting room where I was given a pair of surgical scrubs and told to put them on, have a seat, and relax. Deep down I knew I was only capable of completing two of the nurse's instructions.

I fumbled with my new outfit and sat down as some obnoxious infomercial blared from a television in the room. I looked up at the clock on the wall, eleven forty-five, it read. We had been at the hospital for over fourteen hours. I just wanted to get this over with at this point, but a feeling of extreme helplessness came over me as I thought about the whole situation.

I was worried that the long labor might have a negative effect on the baby, but I was also very concerned with the operation. I prayed silently to God to protect Elizabeth and the baby. I sat there and waited and waited for what seemed like a lifetime. Finally a door opened and a nurse, dressed in full surgical attire, appeared.

"Mr. Garrity?" she asked.

"Yes."

"We've got your wife prepped, so you can come into the operating room now."

The nurse led me down a short hallway and then into a very cold room. I saw Elizabeth lying on a table surrounded by doctors and nurses. The nurse positioned me at Elizabeth's head. I bent down and kissed her on the forehead and whispered to her everything was going to be all right. A nurse handed me a small tray and instructed me to help Elizabeth should she become nauseous. I probably looked rather ridiculous standing there with a puke tray in one hand and my camera in the other.

As far as I could tell they began the operation by making an incision into Elizabeth's lower abdomen area.

"Can you feel anything?" the doctor with the scalpel asked Elizabeth.

"No," she responded.

I felt better knowing she wasn't experiencing any pain.

"OK, Elizabeth, you're going to feel a lot of pressure on your abdomen and rib cage. We need to push the baby up out of the birth canal. OK?"

"OK."

"One, two, three!"

With that said the doctor gave a great push to Elizabeth's abdomen.

"Ooohhh!" Elizabeth moaned as she began to vomit into the tray I was holding near her face.

The doctor began to pull the baby out of Elizabeth and the first sight I caught of the baby was a very large right shoulder, which had a streak of blood on it. As the baby was pulled out further I began to take some pictures, all the while holding the puke tray to Elizabeth's mouth.

"Look at the shoulders on this kid!" the doctor who had a hold of the baby remarked.

I had noticed the large shoulders but more importantly, I had just caught a glimpse of the baby's scrotum.

"It's a boy!" I whispered to Elizabeth whose face was green from the whole experience.

"Birth time twelve thirty-one a.m., birth weight ten pounds two ounces. He's a keeper!" the doctor joked.

Congratulations were passed all around the operating room as the baby began to work out his lungs. A nurse told me to accompany the baby up to the nursery while they finished operating on Elizabeth.

I kissed Elizabeth gently and told her I would see her in a little bit. I then helped the nurse push my newborn son out of the operating room and down the hall toward the waiting area. As we approached the waiting area, I saw Elizabeth's mom walking toward us.

"Grandma, come and see your new grandson!" I announced.

She walked up and cooed at the baby.

"How's Elizabeth?"

"She's a real trooper. They're closing her up now, and she'll be in her room in a little while. Meanwhile we need to get this little fella to the nursery."

"I'll walk down there with you."

So I, the proud daddy, and Elizabeth's mom, the proud grandma, walked together down to the nursery with my newborn son.

Once we arrived at the nursery, the nurse took the baby into it, and Elizabeth's mom and I stood at the observatory window, just amazed by the wonder of it all. After a while, another nurse came and told me I could go see Elizabeth in the post-op recovery room.

I was led to the room and there, behind a curtain, I found my beautiful wife. She was really worn out, and I was concerned with the way she was shaking. She told me she felt all right but was very cold, her body trembling as we spoke. I told her the baby was fine and in a little while she would be in her room holding him in her arms. A nurse came in to check on Elizabeth so I asked why Elizabeth was shaking so badly.

"It's her body's natural reaction to all of the trauma," she said matter-of-factly. "She's going to be fine," she continued in a reassuring voice.

It was now time for me to let them wheel Elizabeth up to her room so I made my way back upstairs and met up with grandma again.

"They're bringing Elizabeth upstairs," I said.

"Good."

About fifteen minutes later, a nurse came and told us which room Elizabeth was in. We made our way down to the room and upon entering, found Elizabeth lying in bed with the baby next to her.

"He's big, isn't he?" I said as we entered.

Elizabeth's mom rushed up to her side and gave her a big kiss, and asked her how she was. We all sat down and visited for a while, exhausted yet very excited. Finally grandma announced she was going to leave. Elizabeth insisted I walk her to her car as she was concerned for her safety since it was two in the morning by then.

Still dressed in my surgical scrubs, I escorted grandma to her car and said goodbye. As I walked back to the hospital in the heat of that summer night, I replayed the day's events in my mind, and concluded that it had been one of the hardest, most exciting days of my life, a day that had left me numb. I couldn't begin to imagine what it had been like for Elizabeth.

When I got back to Elizabeth's room, I sat down next to her bed.

"One of the nurses told me in the morning we would have to fill out a form indicating the baby's name, so… what are we going to call this little bugger?"

"William," Elizabeth replied without hesitation.

"William!?"

Now Elizabeth and I had discussed names for the baby for months, but William had never been mentioned by either one of us.

"I know you were devastated when Will was killed and you also felt very bad that you had never been able to repay him for saving your life. So let's honor his memory by naming our first born after him."

"You are unbelievable!" I said as I bent down to kiss Elizabeth, tears welling up in my eyes.

"William Arlington Garrity," Elizabeth announced.

"Wait a minute, how can his middle name be Arlington? He wasn't actually born on the day of the Arlington Million."

"Who cares? This little guy put me through hell. We're going to have his middle name be Arlington so we can always remind him that because he was so big it took him two days to be born."

I laughed out loud and nodded my head in agreement.

"William Arlington Garrity - has a nice ring to it," I said staring at the little bundle Elizabeth held close to her.

A little while later, as I began to doze off in my chair, Elizabeth suggested I go home and get some sleep. I said OK and rose to kiss Elizabeth and little Will goodbye. I drove home in the pre-dawn silence and thought about my plans for the day.

I needed to call work and tell them the news, call my mom, buy a newspaper as a keepsake for the baby, and buy some flowers for Elizabeth.

"Sounds good," I said out loud.

Once home, I cracked open a beer and chopped the end off of one of the Ashton cigars I had bought for the occasion. I sat down in my easy chair and as I took a sip of my celebratory beer and a puff on my celebratory stogie, I reflected on the very special feeling I was having at that moment.

"I'm very proud to be a father," I said out loud.

A little while later, I hit the rack some eighteen hours after leaving the apartment for our adventure into childbirth. All in all, it was a wonderful experience and the beginning of a new chapter in our lives.

* * * *

Due to the C-section, Elizabeth had to stay in the hospital three days. On the day they were to come home, I drove excitedly to the hospital. Once there, we had to wait what seemed like forever to sign last-minute paperwork before Elizabeth could be released. Once we had that out of the way, I loaded my family into the car for the short ride home. Elizabeth, still very sore, complained loudly every time I passed over a bump or rough spot in the road but she managed to survive the ride. I successfully got both of them upstairs to our spacious apartment.

As a couple the next two or three years became some of the most adventuresome of our lives. We were rookies at this parenting thing, and we definitely made our share of mistakes. This situation, coupled with the fact I was once again looking for a permanent job and we were also looking to buy our first house, made our lives really interesting.

Not long after Will was born, I received a job offer from a large accounting firm located downtown in the Prudential Plaza building. Although I didn't fancy the commute to Chicago, I accepted the position as I needed a steady, reliable source of income now that I was a family man.

47 SECOND TIME AROUND

In the three years since little Will had been born, I had only seen Billy a handful of times. One of those times was when I called and asked him if I could borrow his power washer. Elizabeth and I had bought an older home in a suburb of Chicago and its siding was in need of a wash.

Billy said yes, so I made arrangements to drive to his house one Saturday and pick it up. At Billy's house, he brought me to his garage and held his index finger up to his lips, giving me the "don't talk" sign. He turned on a portable radio and turned up the volume to its maximum level.

"I think my house and garage are bugged," Billy whispered as he leaned in toward me.

"Really!?"

Pointing out the opened garage door Billy continued.

"You see those roofers, two houses over?"

"Yeah I see them," I replied as I looked at a roofing crew busy placing new shingles on a house across the street.

"I think they're either fuckin' FBI or CIA!"

"And why would they be spying on you?" I asked.

"Not sure, but they obviously suspect me of something."

I didn't stay long at Billy's house, and on the drive home wondered what the hell had happened to make my best friend so paranoid. I also wondered what I could do to help him.

I found out much later, through the proverbial neighborhood grapevine, that not too long after I had picked up the power washer, Billy's wife Holly informed him, in no uncertain terms, that if he didn't seek help for his bizarre thoughts, she would leave him. Billy subsequently sought help and was diagnosed as a paranoid, schizophrenic. He was prescribed medications that helped control his delusional thoughts and behavior as long as he took them.

I got home that afternoon and power washed our house. That evening as we sat down to dinner Elizabeth, shared some exciting news with me and little Will.

"I'm pregnant again!" she announced.

"Awesome, Will, you are going to have a little brother or sister!" I said as both Will and I showered Elizabeth with kisses.

So we all prepared ourselves for the arrival of our second child. Since Elizabeth was in her mid-thirties, her doctor advised us early on in the pregnancy to have an amniocentesis so that they might detect any birth defects and give us the option of aborting the pregnancy. Elizabeth and I thought long and hard about it and decided not to have one since even if something was wrong, we wouldn't be able to bring ourselves to abort the pregnancy. So with some concern, coupled with great excitement, we looked forward to the big day. In just a short while Will would welcome home a baby brother or sister.

When Will was born Elizabeth took off thirteen weeks of work because of a special arrangement she had worked out with her company. This time the deal wasn't going to be as sweet. Elizabeth planned to stay at home only six weeks with the baby. After that, we were going to take the baby to our neighbor who lived across the street.

Our neighbor Abby was already taking care of Will full time and was willing to take in one more child. Elizabeth was nervous about this arrangement, but given our situation it was really our only option. I reassured Elizabeth it was only natural for her to feel this way but to remember that Abby was doing a great job watching Will and she would do the same with our next child as well.

In preparation for this baby we attended two classes. The first was a V-BAC class. V-BAC stands for vaginal birth after C-section. Our hospital's position on birthing was to always try the natural method of delivery before opting for a C-section, even if the previous birth was a C-section as Will's had been. We attended the class, and I hoped Elizabeth would be able to deliver this baby naturally so she and I could share that experience.

The other class we attended was a class for siblings. This class was designed to introduce Will to the idea of having a sibling and more specifically a baby around the house. It covered subjects like how big babies are, how to hold a baby, what sounds and smells a baby might make, etc. It was sweet how interested Will was in the class and how proud he was when he got his class certificate.

All systems were go when the due date of April 13 approached. Unfortunately for Elizabeth it came and went. Then finally, just after I woke up on the morning of April 29, Elizabeth announced, "Today is the day!"

As Elizabeth got dressed, I got Will up and dressed. After a quick breakfast, I called Abby and asked her if I could bring Will over early, as I needed to get Elizabeth to the hospital. Abby said of course and reassured me he could stay with her as long as needed. As I brought Will across the street I tried as best I could to explain to a three-year-old what was likely to occur that day. I kissed him good-bye, and as I walked back across the street I wondered if he really understood what was going on.

By this time, Elizabeth was really in some discomfort so we quickly loaded up the car and drove the short distance to the hospital, arriving about eight-thirty that morning. We were admitted right away and brought up to a birthing suite. A nurse asked Elizabeth for a urine specimen, and

Elizabeth hobbled as best she could into the washroom. While inside she let out a rather loud moan to which the nurse jokingly said, "Don't have that baby in there!"

Shortly after that, the doctor came by to check on Elizabeth.

"You're already dilated to six centimeters," the doctor announced. "There's a very good chance the baby will be born sometime this morning."

Wouldn't that be great, I thought. However, flashbacks of Will's birth came flooding into my mind, which helped temper my enthusiasm.

As the minutes turned into hours, things progressed rather nicely. By eleven-thirty Elizabeth was almost fully dilated and the pushing began. By noon the baby's head was visible, and I prayed this baby was small enough to be born naturally.

"Alright, Elizabeth, it's time to deliver this baby," the doctor announced.

"I CAN'T, I CAN'T!"

"ELIZABETH, YOU'VE GOT TO PUSH TO HAVE THIS BABY. NOW PUSH!" her female doctor shot back.

As she did the baby's head, which appeared severely misshapen to me, came out.

"You're doing great. Now one more really good push, Elizabeth," the doctor said encouragingly.

Another push and the baby, along with all of the afterbirth came rushing out. It was the most incredible event I had ever witnessed!

This baby was a bit smaller than Will had been. I couldn't really get a good enough look to determine the sex, but as they rushed the baby to a table to clean it up I heard the doctor announce, "It's a boy!"

"It's a boy, honey, are you OK?" I said as I quickly turned to Elizabeth. "I'm fine."

"I hope you're not disappointed."

"As long as it's healthy, I don't care what sex it is," Elizabeth replied.

I kissed her gently on her forehead and walked over to the area where they were washing up the baby. They had already cleaned him up and placed him in a soft blanket. The nurse handed him to me, and I walked him over to Elizabeth.

I held him close to Elizabeth as the doctor and nurses worked on cleaning Elizabeth up. This birth, when compared with the daylong ordeal of little Will's birth, went really smoothly. We were only at the hospital for about four hours before the baby was delivered. Thank God!

I stayed with Elizabeth and the baby a while and then left the hospital to do a few things. I went out and bought a *Chicago Tribune* for the baby just as I had done when Will was born. I thought someday each of them would find it interesting to peruse the pages of the newspaper on the day they were born to see what was going on in the world that day. As I left the store, I thought about my next stop. I had to pick up Will at Abby's house and try to explain the events of this morning to him. Elizabeth and I had agreed that afterwards, it would be a good idea if I drove Will to a toy store and had Will "buy" his new brother a gift and have his new brother "buy" him one as well.

I had called Abby from the hospital earlier and let her in on the good news. She promised not to say anything to Will. I arrived at Abby's and picked up Will, and we walked across the street to our house. Once inside, I sat my little three-year-old down on the living room couch.

"Will, I've got a big surprise for you."

"Is it a toy?" he chirped with his eyes aglow and a big smile on his face.

"A toy!" I laughed. "No Will it's not a toy but it's even better."

Then in an attempt to block the rising tide of disappointment on Will's face, I quickly blurted out, "You've got a baby brother now, Will. His name is John Daniel Garrity, but we're going to call him Jack. OK?"

"Alright," Will said and then added with arms spread wide, "Where is he?"

"He's still at the hospital with momma. So I thought what we would do is to go buy a little present for Jack and go to the hospital to visit him and ma. How does that sound?"

"OK," was Will's unenthusiastic response.

A bit later at the toy store, Will perked up when I told him he could also have a toy since Jack had asked me to buy his big brother something. Will searched the shelves for the perfect present for himself, after having spent all of two minutes finding the perfect teddy bear for Jack, his newborn brother. Oh well, what else could I expect from a three-year-old. Finally Will made his toy choice, a police station/bank robbery plastic site complete with a collapsing wall and figurines. He was now ready to meet his little brother.

We drove over to the hospital, and I think I was more excited to see Will's reaction to meeting his little brother than Will was in actually meeting Jack. Once we got to the hospital, Will's big concern was whether or not he could bring his new toy up to the hospital room. I was tired and wasn't going to argue, so we made our way up to the nursery. Will, me, a blue teddy bear, and a police station/robbery set.

As we entered the room, Elizabeth was sitting up cuddling little Jack. Will walked in very shyly and appeared afraid to get near the bed. We assured him that everything was all right, and slowly he made his way to Elizabeth and the baby.

"Will, meet your little brother Jack!" Elizabeth announced.

"Hi, Jack," Will replied in his cute, little toddler voice.

Several minutes later, after the novelty of his new brother had worn off, Will asked if he could open his new toy. I said no, but Elizabeth, in her infinite motherly wisdom, told him it was OK. Elizabeth then quietly suggested to me that I be a little lenient on Will since he had been such a good boy that day.

Will and I stayed with Elizabeth and Jack several more hours. Both grandmas came by while we were there and visited for a while. Finally it was time for me to get Will home and to bed. We both kissed Elizabeth goodbye and said our goodbyes to little Jack as well.

On the way home, Will asked if I could assemble his new toy completely when we got home. I didn't really feel like it, the events of the day having finally caught up to me, but I didn't want him to feel I wasn't giving him attention due to Jack's arrival. So once we got home, Will and I sat down and assembled the toy, stickers and all. Then I announced it was time for bed.

Once Will was in bed, I had two more duties to fulfill before I could retire for the night. My first was to smoke a celebratory cigar in honor of the birth of my son John Daniel Garrity. The second was to write a short note to Jack to be given to him at some point in the future. Here is what I wrote that evening:

4-29-97
Dear Jack,

Early this afternoon I witnessed your natural birth and to me it has to be one of the most remarkable events in life that a person can witness. I was almost brought to tears as I saw my second born come into this world. Minutes after your birth I was allowed to cradle you in my arms and when you looked up into my eyes I saw myself, my father and all the other men that I am descended from. You represent the future of our family. I will love you with my whole heart forever and will try to do my best to be a positive role model and raise you in such a way that you may reach your full potential.

I realize that as the "second child" you are bound to be shortchanged when it comes to attention, but please believe me that you will never be shortchanged when it comes to love. I love you, Jack, as I do your brother and believe it or not Will loves you too, although tonight at the hospital he didn't really show it. May good health and good fortune follow you all the days of your life.
Love,
Your Dad

* * * *

Elizabeth and baby Jack (we decided to call him Jack instead of John since that is what my father had been called) came home two days later, and all was right with the world, although I was still a little concerned with the shape of Jack's head. One side of it was misshapen, but I had been reassured by every doctor and nurse and everybody else that this condition was a result of the natural birth and only temporary. So I prayed for little Jacky's head and gave our new little addition all the love that I could.

Elizabeth stayed home with Jack for six weeks, and then it was time for her to return to work. Elizabeth and I wished she could be home longer but it just wasn't possible. It was really hard for her to go back to work but absolutely necessary if we wanted to meet our financial obligations. For the foreseeable future, we would be bringing both Will and Jack to Abby's house while we worked during the day.

48 A MAJOR DILEMMA

The daycare arrangement with Abby went well for about a year. Then one early June morning in 1999, I received a call at work from Elizabeth.

"Both of the boys had a meltdown just now," she announced through tears. "I was dropping them off and neither of them wanted to go inside Abby's. So I decided to stay home and be with them today. I CAN'T TAKE THIS ANYMORE!" Elizabeth shouted into the phone.

"Try to calm down. Everything is gonna be alright," I said, trying my damnedest to console her but having no luck. A little while later, I hung up the phone, wishing things could be different.

Ten minutes later, Elizabeth called me back and informed me that Abby had called and told Elizabeth she wanted to come over to our house and speak with her.

"What does she want to talk about?"

"She wants out of daycare," Elizabeth blurted. "I know it. It's in my gut."

"Well, let's not jump to conclusions."

As I finished my sentence, I heard our doorbell ring in the background.

"She's here," Elizabeth announced.

"OK, please call me later?"

"I will," Elizabeth promised and then hung up the phone.

I went back to work and anxiously awaited Elizabeth's call back. About thirty minutes later Elizabeth called and told me her instincts had been correct.

"She wants out of daycare and has given us her two week notice," Elizabeth informed me.

"Two weeks," I repeated softly. "That doesn't give us much time to find a replacement."

"No, it doesn't," Elizabeth answered.

We talked a little bit more and then said our good byes, Elizabeth weeping as I hung up the phone. My head was swirling with thoughts of our newfound dilemma as I tried to continue with my hectic work day. What the hell are we going to do with Will and Jack, our four and one-year-old, I asked myself silently.

I got up from my desk and walked into the lunch room area of our office and saw a co-worker named Chris standing there. Chris and I were on friendly terms so I decided to share Elizabeth's call with him. Chris responded to my plight by casually mentioning the arrangement that his sister and brother-in-law had.

"My brother-in-law works full time during the day and my sister works part time at a local retail store at night. You and your wife could do the same arrangement, but since you told me your wife makes more money than you I imagine you would be the one home with the kids."

"Hmmm," I said out loud as I pondered his suggestion. "That type of arrangement might be doable."

"And I know you could get a better part-time job than my sister has," Chris added.

After lunch I called Elizabeth, told her of my conversation with Chris, and asked her what she thought of the idea.

"It doesn't sound bad, but we need to discuss it a lot more. Oh and by the way, I've already made two appointments for us to check out two daycare centers."

"That's good," I answered. "We need to explore our options. Let's talk more about it tonight."

That evening after dinner we looked long and hard at our finances and talked about our situation. We figured we could just about meet our basic expenses on Elizabeth's salary. If I could work part time and bring home a couple hundred a week and if we could trim our non-essential spending a bit, we could probably get along for the next four years. By then Jack, our youngest, would be in first grade and in school full time, which meant I could go back to work full time.

After much discussion, we concluded that this idea was doable. However, Elizabeth still insisted we visit both daycare facilities, and she provided two very good reasons why. First, she said that seeing them would probably further persuade her into thinking that I should be at home taking care of the kids. Second, should our arrangement need to be changed in the future, we would have already checked out a couple of local facilities and know where we wanted to place the boys.

I went into work the following morning and spoke with my manager and told him of our two appointments at the daycare centers and then mentioned the possibility of me staying at home with the kids.

"I hope you like one of the daycare facilities," he said as I left his office.

We checked out the first daycare center that Friday afternoon. When we arrived, it was naptime. The facility was dark and there were little people stretched out on mats everywhere. Kinda depressing, I thought, as the elderly director led us through the darkened facility.

That weekend we discussed our situation further and pretty much concluded that I would quit my job to stay at home with the boys, in effect becoming a Mr. Mom. We kept our appointment at the second daycare facility that following Monday morning, and liked what we saw. However, at three-hundred dollars a week, we still thought it was worth trying to have me stay home with the kids and make it work out financially.

I got to work the following morning and went to see my manager. I explained everything Elizabeth and I had been thinking and talking about, and he said that he understood. Later that day, I gave him my formal letter of resignation, effective in two weeks.

That evening, Elizabeth and I sat down with Will and told him of our decision. I emphasized to him that everything would not be fun and games, and told him I planned to keep a well-thought-out structure to their day. I was going to work with him and his brother on developing certain skills such as reading, shoelace tying, and butt wiping. I could tell by the big hug and kiss Will gave me that he was happy with our decision.

I went to bed that night knowing that in two short weeks our lives would change drastically. As I lay there, I prayed to God for help so all of us could adjust to this change and thrive under it. I also thought about my own childhood a bit and even though I had more interaction with my father than either of my siblings, my father and I had very few interactions when I was at the ages my two sons were at now. So I wanted things to be different between me and my boys.

Finally, I thought about how strange life can be. How the passage of time whether it be twenty, ten, five, or even a couple of years can bring you to a whole new set of circumstances that will lead you in a life direction you never before could have imagined for yourself. How long ago and far away the days of drinking in the schoolyard and partying down at the beach now seemed to me. How insignificant the events of my young adulthood now appeared, compared to the important task I was about to undertake. I believed in my mind that the most worthwhile and fulfilling years of my life were just about to begin and hoped that I would be able to meet the challenges that lie ahead.

49 LATE NIGHT PHONE CALLS

Our lives are unpredictable, and just when all seems to be well something can arise that will bring you back down to earth and make you realize just how fragile life and your own existence are.

As a rule, I hate late-night phone calls. When my phone rings any time past nine o'clock in the evening, I usually fear the worst. As I walk to pick up the receiver, I always wonder what specter of bad news might await me on the other end. This time was no different as I got off the couch to answer my ringing telephone at a little after ten o'clock one evening.

"Hello," I said hesitantly.

"Greg?" asked the voice on the other end of the line.

"Yeah, Jimmy," I said having vaguely recognized the voice of my friend Jimmy Morgan.

"Do you have channel two news on?" he asked.

"No," I said, "why?"

"It's Billy," Jimmy replied. "He was just on the news, his picture. He, Holly, and their daughter are missing!"

"You're kidding me, right?" I asked hoping whole-heartedly he was.

"No, man," Jimmy answered in his most serious voice. "I wouldn't joke about something like this."

"Hold on, I want to switch phones and go into the living room and watch the TV," I said as I did just that. Having switched phones, I pushed the other phones on button and asked, "You there?"

"Yes," Jimmy replied. "I guess Billy's missing and so are his wife and kid."

"I hope he didn't do something," I responded, already suspecting the worse. As my words trailed off, I heard the familiar beep in my ear that signaled to me I had another incoming call.

"Hold on, Jimmy," I said as I hit my flash key and said, "Hello."

"Did you hear about Billy Smith?" the female voice on the other end asked.

"Who is this?" I asked having not immediately recognized the voice.

"It's Debbie Murphy. Were you watching the news?" she asked.

"No, I wasn't," I answered. "But Jimmy Morgan just called. In fact, he's on the other line."

"It's wild!" Debbie continued. "They all vanished. Billy didn't go to work the past two days and no one has seen Holly or their daughter."

"Man, I hope they're all right. Listen I have to go I've got Jimmy waiting, OK? I'll talk to you and Brian later."

273

"All right," Debbie replied just before hanging up.

I hit my flash key once again and asked, "Jimmy, you still there?"

"Yeah, I'm still here," Jimmy replied.

"It was Debbie Murphy. They saw the same thing that you did," I explained.

"Yeah, I can't believe it!" Jimmy said.

"Neither can I," I answered.

In disbelief and shock, we continued our conversation and then finished by promising to talk the following day. As I was hanging up, Elizabeth walked into the room and asked me what was up.

"It's Billy. They're all missing, Billy, Holly, and Melissa," I explained as I looked her in the eyes. Elizabeth's jaw dropped in astonishment.

"I hope he hasn't hurt them," she blurted out.

"I know," I said.

We stayed up a while longer channel surfing, trying to find out more but had no luck. Finally, I suggested that we turn in. Elizabeth agreed, and as we lay there in bed we talked briefly about Billy and Holly and the good times that we had shared with them. Elizabeth mentioned a conversation she had with Holly in which Holly confided to Elizabeth the deep love she had for Billy. I talked about what a wild and fun guy he could be sometimes, especially when we went down to the Indy 500.

I also reminded Elizabeth of how when I had first moved out on my own, I had a problem with my newly opened checking account and had been bouncing checks to everyone. Elizabeth and I could not figure out what was wrong. One night Billy stopped by my apartment to visit, and I mentioned the problem to him. He offered to look at my paperwork and after about twenty minutes discovered the problem. My bank had printed one account number on my deposit tickets and another account number on my checks, so of course I was going to bounce checks. I could not thank Billy enough that night for discovering the error.

Then I began to talk about the darker side of Billy. How he had punched one of our mutual friends at a Rotisserie Baseball meeting one night. The same meeting Billy had left my apartment only to return because he said he had forgotten something - that something turned out to be a tape recorder he had hidden under one of my chairs. At the time, he told Brian Murphy and me he didn't think he could trust anyone in our league. It was shortly after that meeting we voted to expel him from our league because he couldn't find it in himself to apologize for his poor behavior. At that point, most of us lost touch with Billy.

As I lay there in bed, I said a silent pray, hoping all would turn out well, but deep down I think I knew it wouldn't. Elizabeth and I tried to go to sleep, but we tossed and turned thinking about the situation. We both had a fitful night of sleep.

Morning came early, as our phone rang at five forty-five. Elizabeth answered it. Our friend Sean O'Reilly was on the other end. He had just heard on the radio that Billy Smith and the rest of his family were missing and that the police were still searching for them.

"I had to make sure I wasn't hearing things," Sean said to Elizabeth.

"You're not," Elizabeth replied. "We heard about it last night from Jimmy Morgan and Debbie Murphy. It was on the ten o'clock news."

As Elizabeth hung up the phone, I got out of bed and began my daily morning routine. I turned on my radio to see if I could hear the news report firsthand. The whole thing seemed so unreal, so dreamlike. I needed to hear it reported firsthand to make it seem real to me, and unfortunately, I didn't have to wait long.

"Chicagoan Billy Smith, his wife Holly, and their four-year-old daughter Melissa have been reported missing. The Chicago Police Department is asking anyone who may have any information about their whereabouts to contact the department," the reporter announced.

It's real all right, I thought.

As I got Will and Jack up for breakfast, I couldn't get the turn of events out of my thoughts. I must have replayed the radio newscast at least a dozen times in my mind. Always slowly repeating the line, "have been reported missing."

As I was putting the boys' breakfast of waffles on the table, my home phone rang.

"Hello this is Greg," I said into the receiver.

"Greg, it's Jimmy, what's going on?"

"Hey, Sean O'Reilly called me early this morning. He heard a radio report about Billy. They're asking for the public's help in locating them," I said.

"Well, that's good," Jimmy replied. We talked a little bit more and ended our conversation pondering the whereabouts of Billy and his family.

About an hour later, Jimmy called back. He had spoken briefly with a mutual friend of ours who had spoken with Billy's brother. He found out two days earlier Billy had made a phone call to his brother and told him that something terrible had happened to Holly. When his brother asked him to elaborate on what had happened to Holly, Billy hung up the phone. That was the last anyone had heard from him.

"Oh, Jesus, it sure doesn't sound good," I said to Jimmy.

"No, it doesn't," Jimmy replied.

"Elizabeth and I were talking about how much Holly loved him and how she was willing to accept him knowing the way he was and the problems that he was experiencing."

"Yeah," Jimmy said. "I was thinking how most women wouldn't have put up with his shit."

"Yeah, ironic how the love that made her stay with him may have very well led to her demise," I speculated.

"Oh boy," was Jimmy's reply. We hung up several minutes later, promising each other we would call should we hear anything new.

A bit later, Elizabeth called from work and told me one of her co-workers had gotten a call from her mother who was at home watching the news. The police were now reporting the same thing I had heard from Jimmy. The police announced they had received substantiated reports that Billy had told others he had done something terrible to Holly and that they were going to conduct a second search of their house. They also said that Billy was now a suspect in the disappearance of his wife and child and should be considered a dangerous individual. As Elizabeth relayed this to me, my stomach began to churn and for a moment the likelihood of vomiting became a very real, distinct possibility.

At noon my phone rang, and it was Jimmy Morgan again.

"I just saw the noon news," he announced. He paused a moment, and as he did I braced myself for whatever he was about to announce. "They found a body at Billy's house but haven't yet confirmed if it's Holly's."

"Oh no!" I said as I grabbed the edge of my kitchen counter to steady myself.

"You know," Jimmy continued, "you always see this kind of shit on TV and say to yourself, what type of person could do something like that?"

"Yeah, I know," I responded as a feeling of numbness washed over me like a Lake Michigan wave on a hot summer's day.

"Well, now we know," Jimmy said. "It's people just like us, just like Billy."

I said good-bye to Jimmy and went back to my chores but found it very difficult to concentrate on anything. I kept thinking about the past and all of the time I had spent with Billy. Those elementary school days taking him down to the office for his beatings at the hands of Mother Superior. The nights spent partying with him at the beach and schoolyard, our trip to Memphis, and of course the night he had his encounter with the L train. And finally that summer night so long ago, when he and Will had saved me from drowning in Lake Michigan. It all seemed so distant from the grim reality of today.

Later that afternoon, just as I was about to start dinner, Elizabeth called from work.

"I'm heading home now."

"That's good."

Then suddenly Elizabeth blurted, "It's Holly!"

"What, they've identified the body!?"

"Yes," was Elizabeth's reply. "One of my coworkers told me. She had been in the break room where we have a TV."

"Have they found Billy yet?"

"No, they have no idea where he is."

"It's all over the news now, huh?"

"Yes, it is."

I told Elizabeth I loved her and couldn't wait to see her, meaning every word of it.

I went out the front door of our house to retrieve our garbage cans from the curb as it was pick-up day. I felt a cold, hard rain on my face and thought to myself that the heavens were crying for Holly and her baby tonight. As I made my way back to the comfort of my warm home, I thought that the day was surely destined to be a day I would never forget.

That evening we ate dinner, gave the boys baths, read to them at bed time, and then collapsed in front of the TV. As Elizabeth and I watched TV, we talked about what had happened. When it was ten o'clock, we watched the news with the discovery of Holly's body the lead story. The reporter stated the reason police did not find her body when they initially searched the house a day ago was because it had been hidden in the safe room Billy had built in their basement and the police were not aware of it until today. The whereabouts of Billy and Melissa were still unknown, but police considered him the prime suspect in Holly's death and warned the public not to confront him but to instead call the police.

When the news ended, we turned off the TV and headed to bed, dazed from what we had just watched. Once in bed I tossed and turned for quite a while before drifting off to an uneasy slumber.

I later awoke to the phone on the nightstand ringing. I reached out in the darkness and picked up the receiver, momentarily fumbling it.

"Hello," I groggily said into the receiver.

"Greg, it's me."

The voice on the other end of the line rocked me to my very core, as if I had been struck by a bolt of lightning. I was no longer asleep but wide-awake now.

"Billy, where are you?" I asked.

Elizabeth, having heard me, popped straight up into a sitting position on the bed.

"If I tell you, you have to promise not to tell anyone, OK?" Billy asked.

"Alright."

"I'm in a cheap motel up in Wisconsin. About a three-hour drive from Chicago."

"Ask him about Melissa!" Elizabeth whispered to me.

"Is Melissa with you?" I gingerly asked.

"Yeah, she's asleep."

"Listen," he continued. "I want to turn myself in to the police, but I'm afraid if I try to do it by myself the cops are going to kill me. So I have a huge favor to ask."

"OK, what's that?"

"Could you drive up here and help me turn myself in?" Billy asked, the tone of his voice almost childlike. Like when a child asks an adult for something that they know they really don't deserve.

I cupped my hand over the receiver and turned to Elizabeth.

"He wants me to drive to where he's at and help him turn himself in," I whispered.

"You're not going to meet him!" Elizabeth whispered back to me in anger.

Uncovering the receiver, I said, "Billy hold on one sec OK?"

"OK."

I placed my hand over the receiver again and turned to Elizabeth.

"A long, long time ago Billy saved my life and I have owed him ever since. I also made a promise to Billy once that I'd always be there for him. I wasn't there to help Will when he needed me, but I can be there for Billy. Besides, Elizabeth, he wants to turn himself in. I need to go there to make sure Melissa is OK and that they don't hurt Billy."

"I'm so scared, Greg," Elizabeth said.

I took my hand off of the receiver.

"Billy?"

"I'm here.".

"OK, I'll drive up and help you turn yourself in," I announced as I began to get out of bed. "Hold on one second I want to get something to write with."

I put the phone down for a moment, walked over to the wall, and turned our bedroom light on. "Argh!" Elizabeth shrieked as she pulled the covers up over her head.

I made my way to the dresser and found a pen and a small piece of paper. I walked back to my bed, sat down, and picked the phone up.

"OK, Billy, where are you at exactly?"

Billy gave me the name of the motel and the name of the small Wisconsin town it was located in. He told me that he was in room 109.

"Alright," I said. "What friggin time is it anyway?" I asked. Billy and Elizabeth both blurted out that it was four-fifteen in the morning.

"All right, it'll take me about twenty minutes to get my shit together so I should reach you around eight this morning, OK?" I asked.

"Sounds good," Billy said.

"And once I'm there, we'll call the police and have you turn yourself in right?" I asked wanting to make sure Billy meant what he had initially said at the beginning of our conversation.

"That's the plan, Double G," Billy said adding, "I really appreciate you coming."

We said goodbye, and I hung up the phone.

"I'm so scared. I don't want you to go. What if he tries to kill you?" Elizabeth blurted out.

"You didn't hear his voice, Elizabeth. Billy's scared. That's why he called me to help him out. He knew I wouldn't tell him no."

"You know where he is. Why don't you just call the police and tell them where he's at?"

"He's like a caged animal, Elizabeth. The last thing he needs is a surprise assault from the cops. Remember Melissa is in that room, too. You don't want anything happening to her, do ya?" I asked.

As our eyes met I could see Elizabeth's worry and the fact that she was about to cry.

"Hey," I said as I gave her a big hug. "I'll be careful. I'm just going to meet him and then we're going to call the police and have them come pick him up, that's all."

"Please be careful," Elizabeth said through tears.

"I will, I promise."

I got out of bed and got dressed, made a cup of coffee, and kissed Elizabeth goodbye. I made my way through the darkness and climbed into my mini-van. I pulled out of our driveway and onto the street and headed north. I only lived several blocks from an on ramp to I90. I90 would take me to I294 North, which would take me up into cheesehead land, as us Chicago Bear fans affectionately referred to Wisconsin.

As there was virtually no traffic at this early-morning hour, about thirty minutes after leaving my house I crossed the border from Illinois into Wisconsin. I headed further north and kept replaying all the events of the last couple of days in my head. I always ended up at the same place, not believing I was driving to meet Billy so he could turn himself into the police because he had killed his wife.

The sun eventually rose over the eastern horizon, and I could see it would be a clear, bright day. That didn't do anything to improve my mood. About two hours or so later, I was exiting the highway and entering the small town in which the motel that Billy was holed up in was located.

I pulled into the parking lot of the motel and immediately saw Billy's car. I noticed that the rear license plate was missing, something I imagined Billy had done to conceal his whereabouts. I parked the mini-van and took a deep breath, telling myself everything would be OK as Billy was still the same kid I had grown up with. However, I only half believed myself.

I approached room 109 and knocked on the door.

"Who is it?" Billy asked.

"It's Greg, man," I answered.

Billy opened the door and I walked into the room. As I did I could see that Melissa was sleeping on the bed.

"Thanks for coming, man," Billy said.

Struggling for something to say I clumsily blurted out, "How are you doing?"

"Not so fuckin' good," Billy answered as he sat down on the bed. "I did something terrible to Holly… and now I gotta pay for it Greg."

"Well I'm here to help you do the right thing and to make sure Melissa is OK," I answered.

"Yeah, I was going to call my brother, but he's always been a prick to me. And, man, you've always been like a fuckin' brother to me. I knew I could count on you," Billy explained as he managed to flash me a weak smile.

Melissa began to stir and then turned over, opened her eyes, and looked straight at me. I said hello and she instinctively moved toward her dad and hugged him.

"Melissa, do you remember Mr. Garrity? He's one of my oldest and best friends," Billy explained to her.

Melissa shook her head no and then, looking at her dad said, "Daddy, I'm hungry."

"Alright let's get you a box of cereal then," Billy said as he picked Melissa up and plopped her in a chair next to a small, round, beat-up table that was positioned in one corner of the motel room. He made his way across the room and plucked an individual-sized cereal box from a suitcase that was lying on a dresser. He opened up the box and spread the contents on a napkin in front of Melissa.

"Sorry no milk today, but I'll get you a cup of water," he told Melissa as he made his way into the bathroom with one of the motel's glasses. He came out of the bathroom and placed the filled glass of water in front of Melissa.

"Now eat your cereal and drink some water," he said as he kissed her on the top of her head.

As Melissa began to eat the cereal, Billy motioned for me to walk toward the door with him. Once we were at the door, he whispered, "When she's done, I'll step outside for a moment with her. While we're outside you can call the police and tell them where we're at. Make sure to tell them I'm here. OK?"

"OK."

Melissa finished her cereal and asked if she could watch TV.

"Not this minute," Billy said. "I want to take you outside for a short walk to get some exercise OK?"

"Do I have to?" Melissa protested. Then she added, "When are we going to go home and see Mommy? I miss her, Daddy."

Billy shot me a quick glance, and I could see the terror in his eyes.

"In just a little while we'll be going home, honey," he answered. "Now put your shoes on and let's take a walk."

Melissa did as she was told. As Billy and Melissa walked toward the door, Melissa looked at me and asked, "Is he coming?"

"No, honey, Mr. Garrity has to make a phone call so we need to let him be by himself for a couple of minutes. Come on now let's go stretch our legs."

With that said, Melissa and Billy walked out of the room.

I walked over to the phone, picked up the receiver, and dialed 911. The phone rang twice before I heard, "Hello, 911 emergency dispatch. How may I assist you?"

"Hello, my name is Greg Garrity and I am a very close friend of Billy Smith. Billy Smith is wanted in Illinois as a suspect in the murder of his wife Holly."

"How can I assist you, sir?" the dispatcher interrupted.

"Billy Smith is wanted by the Chicago Police Department, and I'm with him right now in Princeton," I tried to explain.

"Just one moment, sir," the dispatcher said.

As I held the receiver to my ear waiting for the dispatcher to come back on the line, I felt as if I was about to explode.

"Hello, sir," the dispatcher said.

"Yes, I'm here," I answered.

"You said that you are with Billy Smith right now in Princeton?"

"Yes, that's correct. He wants to turn himself in."

"Sir, are you in danger?" the dispatcher asked.

"No, I...," as I began to answer, the door of the room swung open and Melissa came running in.

"Beat ya!" she exclaimed as Billy came walking in after her.

"Sir, are you in danger?" the dispatcher asked again.

"No, I'm not," I answered in a whisper. "I need you to send a squad car to the Half Moon Motel to pick us up so he can be sent back to Chicago."

"So you and Billy Smith are at the Half Moon Motel in Princeton. Is that correct, sir?" the dispatcher asked.

"Daddy, can I watch some TV?" Melissa asked her father.

"As soon as Mr. Garrity is off the phone, honey," Billy said as he stared at me.

"That's correct. Can you send over a squad to pick us up?" I asked in a very low whisper.

"I'm sending over a squad now," the dispatcher announced. "What room is Mr. Smith in, sir?"

"109."

"109?"

"Correct."

"All right, sir, please do not leave your location. Officers will be there very shortly."

"We won't," I answered and then hung up the phone.

"He's off!" Melissa announced.

Billy walked over to the TV and turned it on. Then, looking at me he asked, "Everything a go?"

"Yes, everything's a go."

"Can you put on Cartoon Network, Daddy?" Melissa asked.

"Give me a second, baby," Billy answered as he began to click through the channels.

I made my way toward the windows of the dingy motel room and drew back one of the shades and peered out. About two minutes after I had begun looking out, I saw a police squad car pull into the parking lot. Instead of pulling up to our room the squad car parked across the parking lot, not in a parking spot but horizontal to our room.

"I think this is Cartoon Network, honey," Billy announced.

"YEAH, CARTOON NETWORK!" Melissa shouted in genuine, childhood glee.

Just then, a second squad car and a state trooper vehicle pulled into the motel's parking lot. They parked end to end with the first squad. Their line of defense, I thought. The cops then got out of their cars and gathered on the far side of their impromptu line.

"What's up, Greg?" Billy asked noting that I was staring out the window.

"We have visitors," I answered.

Billy walked over to the widow and looked out. As he did, I shot a glance toward Melissa and could see she was engrossed in Cartoon Network.

Billy and I watched as the police huddled for several minutes and then dispersed, separating themselves, each cop taking a unique position behind one of the three squad cars.

"BILLY SMITH, THIS IS THE PRINCETON POLICE DEPARTMENT. WE KNOW THAT YOU ARE IN ROOM 109. YOU NEED TO COME OUT WITH YOUR HANDS UP IN THE AIR WHERE WE CAN SEE THEM," the police announced over a squad car's loudspeaker.

Hands, I thought. Don't they know he only has one arm?

"Who's that, Daddy?" Melissa asked with a quizzical look as the police's announcement shook her out of her Cartoon Network trance.

"Not sure, honey," Billy answered. "I have to go out and see. I need you to wait here, OK?"

"Will you be right back?" Melissa asked innocently.

"Of course, honey," Billy said as he made his way over to Melissa and bent over to give her a big hug and kiss.

"I love you, Melissa," Billy said as he kissed her for a second time.

"I love you, Daddy," she said as she went back to watching the T.V.

Billy walked over to me and whispered, "It's time."

"Are we going to leave her alone?" I whispered back to Billy thinking he would want me to join him as he walked outside into the not so friendly long arms of the law.

"Stay with her, please," he said. "I'll go out and turn myself in and then you guys can come out. I don't want her to see me get arrested."

"OK," I said.

"Thanks again for being here, Double G. I think that debt you owed me has finally been settled," Billy said as he extended his arm toward me and we shook hands.

Billy then walked over to the beat-up chair and picked up his coat. He put it on and quietly walked to the door. He opened it and made his way out, quickly closing it behind him.

"PUT YOUR HANDS UP IN THE AIR AND WALK TO THE MIDDLE OF THE LOT," the voice on the loudspeaker bellowed. I pulled back the shade slightly and peering out could see Billy doing what he had been told. I glanced toward the police cars and could now see all the police had their guns drawn and pointed at Billy.

"STOP RIGHT THERE," the anonymous voice announced. "NOW DROP TO THE GROUND AND LAY ON YOUR BELLY."

My eyes returned to Billy who was now standing in the middle of the lot with his arm still up in the air.

"Get down on the ground, Billy," I whispered out loud as I thought for just an instance he might be hesitating.

At that very moment, Billy brought his arm down and quickly reached into his jacket. He pulled out what appeared to be a handgun and pointed it at the police line.

"NO!" I shouted as I took two giant steps toward the door of the motel room.

As I swung the door wide open I was met with the bang, bang, bang sound of gunfire. As I stared out the doorway Billy crumbled to the ground, sixty feet in front of me.

"DADDY, I'M SCARED!" Melissa yelled from the bed. I spun around and made eye contact with this little girl who appeared to be shaking uncontrollable in fright. I quickly slammed the door shut and ran over to where Melissa was sitting. I reached down and scooped her up off of the bed and hugged her as she began to weep uncontrollably.

"It's OK, Melissa," I said to her knowing in my heart it never would be. As I stood there hugging Melissa, the sound of gunfire and the image of Billy crumbling to the ground was being replayed in my mind's eye. The boom of the cop's loudspeaker shook me out of my state of shock.

"WHOEVER ELSE IS IN ROOM 109 YOU NEED TO COME OUT WITH YOUR HANDS UP NOW," it announced.

"Melissa, honey, we need to go outside and talk to the police, OK?"

She was still crying too much to even realize that I was speaking to her. I walked over to the door and swung it open. I could see Billy lying in the middle of the parking lot all alone, a pool of blood forming by his side. The police, realizing someone else was in the room had not moved from their defensive line position. I walked forward three steps from the motel room's door and yelled out, "I HAVE A CHILD HERE, I DON'T WANT HER TO SEE WHAT JUST HAPPENED, SO I'M GOING TO CARRY HER TO YOU."

"PUT THE CHILD DOWN AND GET ON THE GROUND," the voice on the loudspeaker demanded. Melissa tried to turn her head to see what was going on so I hugged her closer and turned in such a manner so she could not see her father's bloodied body lying on the asphalt. I then began to walk slowly toward the police line.

"I HAVE NO WEAPONS," I shouted out.

I crossed the parking lot and made my way to within ten feet of a squad car when I heard approaching footsteps and suddenly felt a hand on my shoulder and the end of a gun barrel touching the back of my skull.

"ONE MOVE AND YOU'RE A DEAD MAN," the cop behind me shouted. Another officer rushed up and pulled Melissa out of my arms.

"NOW GET ON THE GROUND!" the cop growled as he pushed me forward. I fell to my knees hard and then lay down on my belly. I felt the cop frisking me for weapons, and then he grabbed both arms and pulled them behind me. I felt the familiar sting of handcuffs as he snapped them on my wrists and made them tight.

"GET UP," he shouted.

As I stood up, I saw I was now surrounded by police. In the distance I could hear the siren of another emergency vehicle approaching. I could also hear that little Melissa was still crying.

"Please don't let the little girl see her father," I begged to no one in particular.

"SHUT UP," said the cop who had placed the cuffs on me. "I'LL BRING THIS ONE DOWN TO THE STATION," he shouted to his commander.

With that he led me to the first squad car in the line of three and opened the rear door. He pushed me down into the back seat hard, which caused me to let out a painful groan as I felt the cuffs dig into my wrists. He slammed the car door shut and walked back to the other officers. He returned several minutes later.

We pulled out of the parking lot, and as we did I turned my head one last time toward the motel. I could see a bunch of cops huddled up around

Billy's body like a football team huddling up before the next play.

"Where's the little girl?" I asked.

"She's being driven to the station by a female officer," the cop answered.

We rode in silence the rest of the way to the station. Once in the parking lot of the station, the cop got out of the squad car and opened up my door. I scooted out of the back seat and got to my feet. The cop grabbed my left arm and led me into the police station.

We made our way past a large reception desk and into a narrow hallway. The cop opened up a door to a small room and led me in. Within the room was a small table and three chairs, two on one side and one chair on the other. The cop told me to sit down on the lone chair, which I did.

"I'll be right back," the cop announced. He left me alone in the silence of the sparse room. I closed my eyes and replayed the seen from the parking lot in my mind's eye. Trying to determine what Melissa might have seen. I was fairly sure she had not seen her father's crumpled body lying in the middle of the parking lot. I had been careful to carry her in such a way as to prevent that from happening. However, I also knew I could never be sure.

The door to the room opened and the young cop who had brought me here walked in accompanied by an older cop, who had thinning, close-cropped gray hair and piercing blue eyes.

"Take off the cuffs," the older cop barked to the younger cop. The younger cop did as he was told as the older cop took a seat across from me.

I rubbed my chaffed wrists as the younger cop remained standing next to me.

"What's your name?" the older cop asked as he took a pack of cigarettes from his shirt pocket.

"Greg Garrity."

"Smoke?" the older cop asked as he held the pack out to me.

"No thanks."

"Mind if I do?" he asked.

"No, that's fine," I responded, wondering what would have happened if I had said that I did.

The older cop pulled a lighter out of his pants pocket and lit his cigarette.

"Where do you live, Mr. Garrity?" the older cop asked exhaling a cloud of smoke as he did.

"I live in Elk Grove Village, Illinois."

"What's your relationship to Mr. Smith, Mr. Garrity?" the older cop asked.

"He's a childhood friend," I said, quickly realizing my grammatical mistake.

"Why were you in Mr. Smith's motel room, Mr. Garrity?" the older cop asked as he took another deep drag of his smoke and stared into my eyes.

"Billy called me in the middle of the night. He asked me to meet him so he could turn himself in. He told me he was afraid that you, ah the police, would kill him," I explained.

"Interesting," the older cop remarked. "Why didn't you call the police when he called you?"

"I thought he meant it. I thought he wanted to turn himself in. He knew what he had done to his wife was wrong. I know that may sound farfetched given the fact he pulled a gun on your officers, but that's what he told me last night," I blurted out.

"No, Mr. Garrity, that doesn't sound farfetched," the older cop replied. "Do you know what I think, Mr. Garrity?" he asked.

"No, sir, I don't," I replied.

"I think Mr. Smith lured you to his motel room not to help him turn himself in but to make sure his daughter wasn't hurt," the older cop explained. "Do you know what type of gun Billy Smith pulled on my officers, Mr. Garrity?" the older cop asked as his blue eyes once again met mine.

"No, sir, I didn't even know Billy owned a gun let alone knew he had one in that motel room," I answered.

"It was a toy gun, Mr. Garrity," the older cop announced. "Your friend committed suicide by pulling that toy gun out when he did. We think that was his plan all along," the older cop said as he took another long drag of his smoke. He then exhaled another great cloud of grey smoke from his lungs as I sat there, in silence, pondering what he had just said.

When our teacher had had enough of his poor behavior I had been the one kid in our elementary school who could be counted on to bring Billy down to the principal's office for his punishment. This time Billy had turned the tables. He wasn't going to let me bring him to the authorities to be punished for his actions. No, this time he was going to turn the tables and not let that happen. Billy had made the decision that for once, he was going to decide his own fate.

"Where's his daughter," I asked.

"She's in protective custody," the older cop said. "We are making arrangements to have her transported back to Illinois."

"And me," I asked.

"Mr. Garrity, I'm going to give you a pen and a pad of paper and I need you to write down everything that has happened to you from the time you picked up the phone last night to the point my officers put the cuffs on you, OK?"

"OK."

"Once I have that in my hands we will release you," the older cop said as he stood up.

"Oh, one last thing, Mr. Garrity," the older cop said as he walked towards the door and upon reaching it turned back toward me.

"What's that, sir?" I asked.

"I think your friend called the right guy last night," with that the older cop, with the piercing blue eyes, walked out of the room.

The young cop gave me a pen and a pad of paper, and I spent the next hour putting down on paper the events of the last five hours. When I was done, the young cop took the pad and pen and left me in the solitude of the small room. I waited in the room several hours replaying what had happened, hoping it was a dream but knowing it was my real nightmare.

The young cop finally came back in and announced I was now free to leave. I asked him if I could use a phone and if he could give me a lift back to the motel so I could get my van. He showed me into another room with a phone and I sat down and called Elizabeth.

She began crying as I told her what had happened, more out of pity for Melissa than empathy for Billy. I promised her I would be careful on my ride home. When I was finished talking to Elizabeth, the young cop gave me a lift back to the motel's parking lot.

There were still cops there as well as a news media truck now. I got out of the squad and thanked the cop for the ride. As I walked toward my van I looked toward where Billy had met his fate. His body was gone, but his bloodstain remained. I shook my head and thought what a long way we were from the Patch of Green, where our friendship had begun. I opened my van door, got in and started the engine. I made my way out of the parking lot and drove in silence for the next three hours.

*　*　*　*

The police, with the help of Billy's doctor, hypothesized that Billy must have stopped taking his meds about two or three weeks prior to Holly's murder - the meds that helped to keep Billy's paranoia and delusions in check. Though the police were never sure what the underlying cause for the violence was, the details of the incident were later released.

Billy had killed Holly in their kitchen one morning by striking her once over the head with a cast iron frying pan. He then carried her body down to the safe room that he had built in their basement. He fled to Wisconsin with Melissa and after several days there decided to call me and ask for help. The one person he knew couldn't turn down his request.

50 BACK AT THE BEACH

As I write this, I'm sitting on a beach chair at Albion Beach, in the heart of the Patch of Green. Playing in the sand nearby me are my three children. Some twenty-five years ago, I and my two best friends sat at this same beach, contemplating how we could turn a dull, hot summer day into something a little more exciting. Our solution ended up causing me to owe each of them a great debt, which I would try to repay over the course of our lives.

I'm still not sure if I have ever repaid them in full but do know that my opportunity for trying to has come to an end. I will go on living my life now without them and this causes me great sadness, which is only somewhat tempered by all of the warm memories I have of them from our years together. I think of Billy and Will often, and when I do I thank them silently for saving my life that fateful summer night for if it hadn't been for their heroic efforts, I wouldn't be alive today.

"HEY, DAD, CAN WE GO IN THE WATER?" my son Will yells out to me.

"Sure. Jack and Melissa, how about going in the water?" I ask my son and the newest member of our family.

When Billy's daughter was brought back to Illinois, her only living next of kin were Billy's bachelor-for-life brother, who didn't want to be responsible for her, and his elderly, alcoholic mother who was too sick and feeble to take care of her. Their solution was to place Melissa up for adoption, a fate that disturbed me greatly.

After careful consideration, Elizabeth and I decided we would try to adopt Melissa, knowing full well she would need much love and reassurance in the coming years. We were successful, and our little sweetheart has been living with us for the past year. Nightmares and withdrawn periods of behavior have come with the territory, but we have always responded with love and kindness and believe, that in the end, Melissa will develop into a fine, young woman.

"YES! I DO!" Melissa shouts back.

"ME TOO!" yells Jack.

"OK then, time to get wet," I announce.

It's funny how life is. When you are living it, the events that make up your life seem haphazard and coincidental. But later on, when you look back at the years gone by, you gain perspective and can see how all of the events are related and how the dots connect.

Some people, like Will, never get a chance during their life to reach their full potential while others, like Billy, have lives influenced by circumstances that are sometimes beyond their control. Unfortunately, these circumstances can often lead to misery and death.

On the other hand, some people, like me, live average lives spent just trying to survive and on occasion helping others get along with their lives. I'm happy now to have had such a life and to still be living it.

At this point in my life the only thing I know for certain is that you never want to turn on an electric fan and point it at a smoldering couch fire in an attempt to put it out. That just doesn't work!

"COME ON, DAD!" the kids shout to me in unison.

"LET'S DO IT, KIDS!" I shout back.

And off we go together, racing into the chilly waters of Lake Michigan, just off the shores of the Patch of Green.

ABOUT THE AUTHOR

I began writing this novel in 1993 as I commuted from my home, which was in a northwest suburb of Chicago, to my job located on Michigan Avenue in downtown Chicago. As I rode the rails I wrote down all of the stories I could remember from my youth and early adulthood growing up in the Patch of Green.

I eventually had six or seven notebooks worth of material and it was at that point I decided to write a fictional, semiautobiographical novel weaving this material into a story while also adding a healthy dose of writer's embellishments. Life of course got in the way, but once my sons had grown up I found the time to complete the manuscript and what you have just read is the result.

I want to thank you for taking the time to read the story and hope that you have enjoyed it.

If I have learned anything from my fifty-eight years of living on this wonderful planet of ours, as a member of the human species, it's this:

LOVE IS THE ANSWER!!!

Cheers,

Greg Kaup